3 9082 13537 2150
W9-AMV-682

LEGENDARY

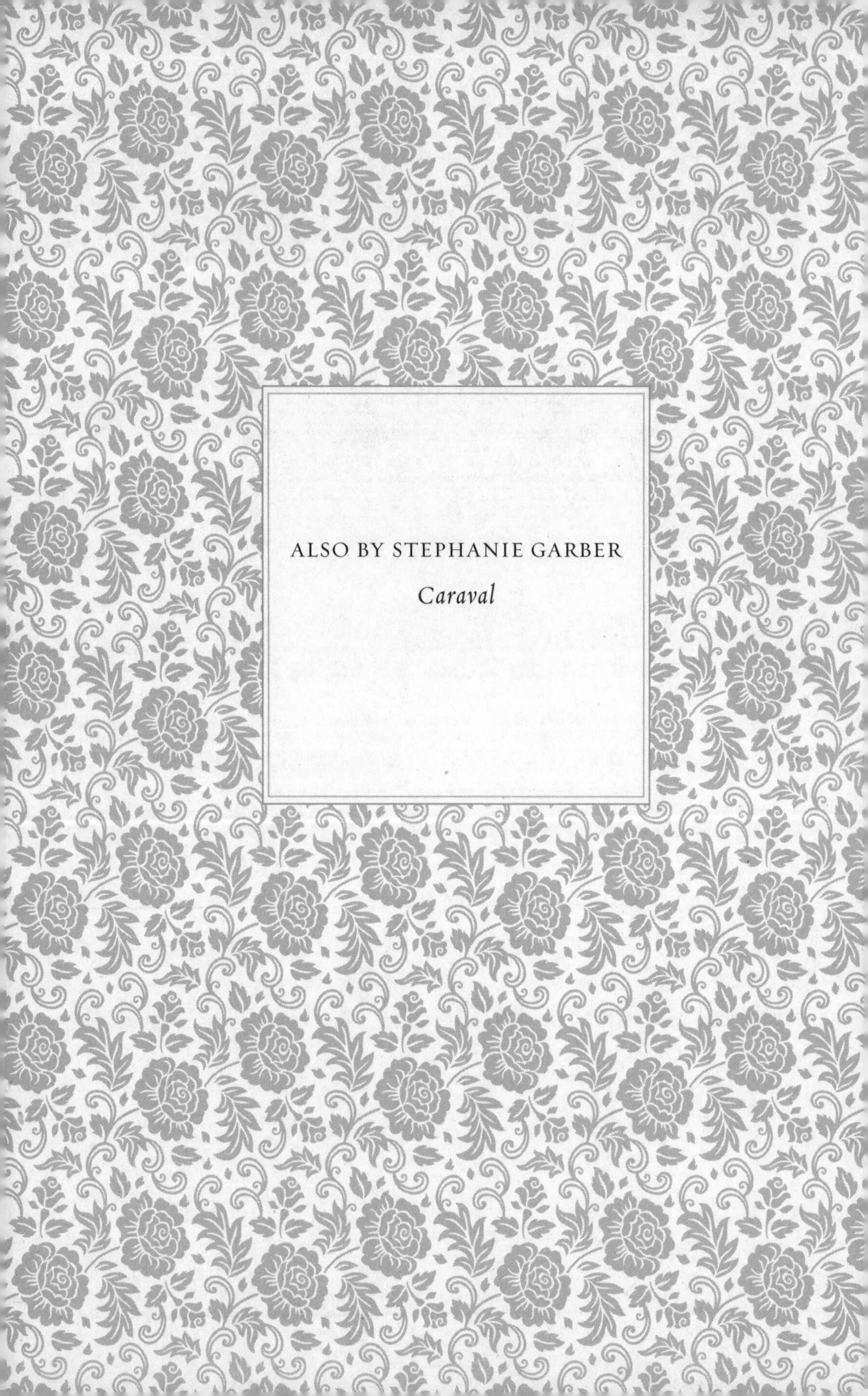

ALSO BY STEPHANIE GARBER

Caraval

LEGENDARY

A Caraval Novel

STEPHANIE GARBER

FLATIRON
BOOKS
NEW YORK

www.flatironbooks.com

Map by Rhys Davies

Library of Congress Cataloging-in-Publication Data

Names: Garber, Stephanie, author.
Title: Legendary : a Caraval novel / Stephanie Garber.
Description: First edition. | New York : Flatiron Books, 2018. | Summary: Having made a deal with a criminal to save her sister Scarlett from a disastrous arranged marriage, Tella must win Caraval and uncover Legend's identity, or risk losing everything, including her life.
Identifiers: LCCN 2018001435| ISBN 9781250095312 (hardcover) | ISBN 9781250192226 (international, sold outside the U.S., subject to rights availability) | ISBN 9781250095336 (ebook)
Subjects: | CYAC: Sisters—Fiction. | Performing arts—Fiction. | Games—Fiction. | Criminals—Fiction. | Fantasy.
Classification: LCC PZ7.1.G368 Le 2018 | DDC [Fic]—dc23
LC record available at https://lccn.loc.gov/2018001435

Our books may be purchased in bulk for promotional, educational, or business use. Please contact your local bookseller or the Macmillan Corporate and Premium Sales Department at 1-800-221-7945, extension 5442, or by email at MacmillanSpecialMarkets@macmillan.com.

First Edition: May 2018

First International Edition: May 2018

10 9 8 7 6 5 4 3 2 1

To Matthew, for the soapstone

To Allison, for telling me Dashiell was the wrong name

And to both of you, for being amazing siblings

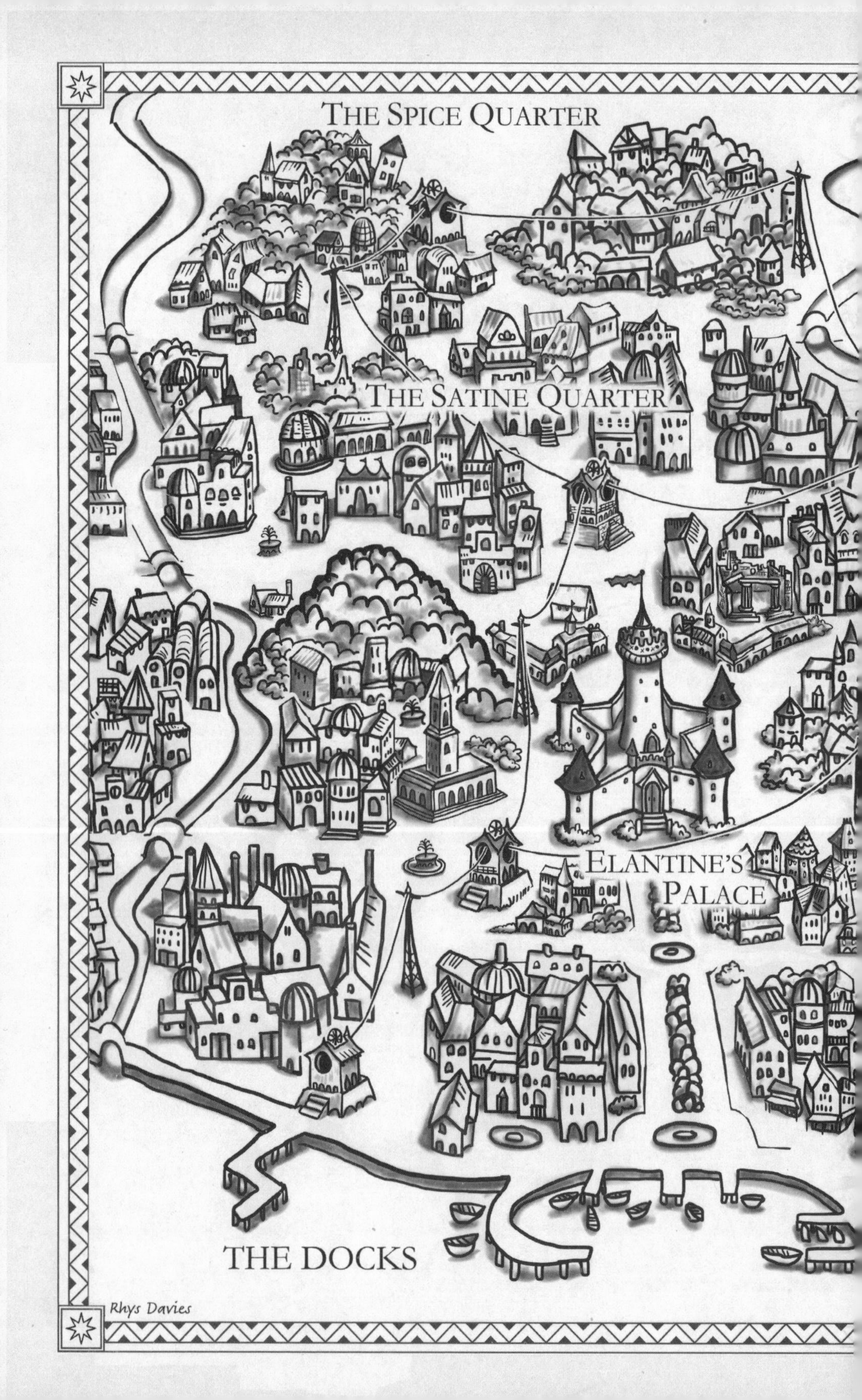
THE SPICE QUARTER
THE SATINE QUARTER
ELANTINE'S PALACE
THE DOCKS
Rhys Davies

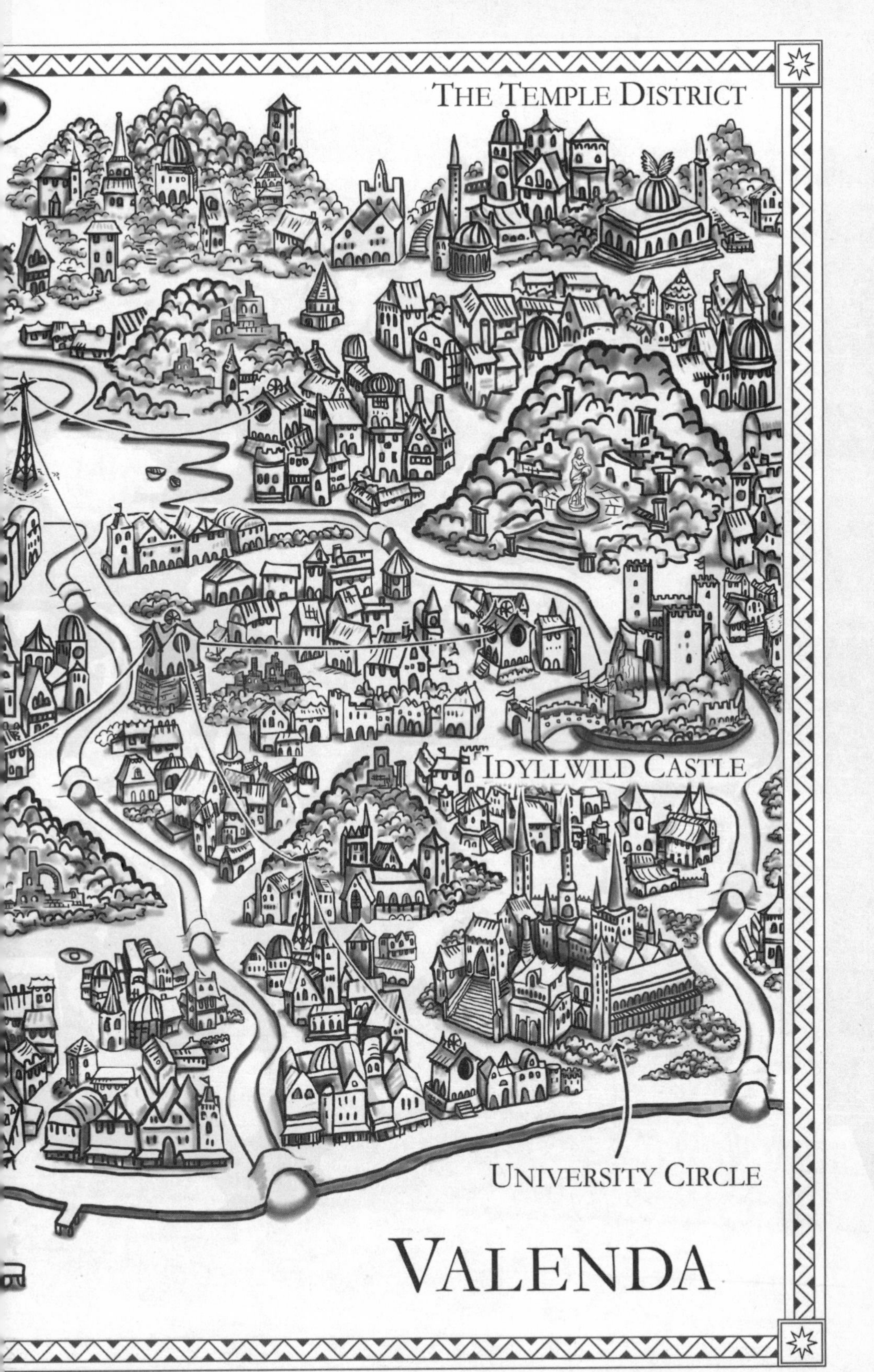
THE TEMPLE DISTRICT
IDYLLWILD CASTLE
UNIVERSITY CIRCLE
VALENDA

LEGENDARY

SEVEN YEARS AGO

While some rooms on the estate had monsters hiding beneath the beds, Tella swore her mother's suite concealed enchantment. Hints of emerald light dusted the air as if fairies came to play whenever her mother left. The room smelled of flowers plucked from secret gardens, and even when there wasn't a breeze, the sheer curtains billowed around the magnificent canopy bed. Above, a citrine chandelier greeted Tella with the musical sounds of kissing glass, making it easy for her to imagine the suite was a bewitched portal to another world.

Tella's tiny feet made no sound as she tiptoed across thick ivory carpets to her mother's dresser. Quickly, she stole a look over her shoulder and then snatched her mother's jewelry box. Slick and heavy in Tella's hands, the box was made of mother-of-pearl and covered in spiderwebbed gold filigree; Tella liked to pretend it was also charmed, for even when her fingers were dirty, they fortunately never left prints.

Tella's mother didn't mind if her daughters played with her dresses or tried on her fancy slippers, but she'd asked them not to touch this box, which only made it more irresistible to Tella.

Scarlett could spend her afternoons daydreaming about traveling shows like Caraval, but Tella liked to have *real* adventures.

Today she pretended a wicked queen was holding a young elfin prince captive, and to save him, she needed to steal her mother's opal ring, Tella's favorite piece of jewelry. The milky stone was raw and rough, shaped like a starburst, with sharp tips that sometimes pricked her fingers. But when Tella held the opal up toward the light, the stone sparked, covering the room in embers of luminescent cherry, gold, and lavender that hinted at magic curses and rebel pixie dust.

Sadly, the brassy band was too large for Tella's finger, though every time she opened the box, she still slipped it on in case she'd grown. But this day, right as Tella slid on the ring, she noticed something else.

The chandelier above her stilled as if it, too, had been caught by surprise.

Tella knew every item in her mother's jewelry case by heart: a carefully folded velvet ribbon edged in gold, bloodred scarlet earrings, a tarnished silver bottle that her mother claimed held angel tears, an ivory locket that wouldn't open, a jet wristlet that looked as if it belonged on the arm of a witch rather than her mother's elegant wrist.

The only item Tella never touched was the dirty-gray sachet, which smelled of moldy leaves and charnel-sweet death. *It keeps the goblins away*, her mother once teased. It kept Tella away as well.

But today, the ugly little purse flickered, drawing Tella toward it. One moment it looked like a bundle of rot and smelled of decay. A blink later, in its place rested a gleaming deck of cards, tied with a delicate satin ribbon. Then, in a flash, it was back to the nasty pouch before it transfigured into the cards again.

Abandoning her play mission, Tella quickly grabbed the silky cord and lifted the deck from the box. Instantly they stopped shifting.

The cards were so very, very pretty. Such a dark hue of nightshade they were almost black, with tiny hints of gold flecks that sparkled in the light, and swirly strands of deep red-violet embossing that made Tella think of damp flowers, witches' blood, and *magic*.

These were nothing like the flimsy black-and-white cards her father's guards had taught her to play betting games with. Tella sat down on the carpet. Her nimble fingers tingled as she untied the ribbon and flipped over the first card.

The young woman pictured reminded Tella of a captive princess. Her lovely white dress was shredded, and her tear-shaped eyes were as pretty as polished sea glass, but so sad they hurt to look at. Most likely because her head was caged in a rounded globe of pearls.

The words *The Maiden Death* were written at the bottom of the card.

Tella shuddered. She did not like the name, and she was not fond of cages, even pearly ones. Suddenly she had the feeling that her mother would not want her seeing these cards, but that didn't stop Tella from turning over another.

The name at the bottom of this one was *The Prince of Hearts.*

It showed a young man with a face made of angles, and lips as sharp as two knife blades. One hand near his pointed chin clasped the hilt of a dagger, and red tears fell from his eyes, matching the blood staining the corner of his narrow mouth.

Tella flinched as the prince's image flickered, there and gone, the same way the foul sachet had wavered earlier.

She should have stopped then. These cards were definitely not toys. Yet a part of her felt as if she was meant to find them. They were more real than the evil queen or the elfin prince of her imagination, and Tella dared to think that perhaps they would lead her on a genuine adventure.

The next card felt especially warm against her fingers as Tella turned it over.

The Aracle.

She did not know what the strange name meant, and unlike the other cards, this one did not appear to be violent. The edges were covered in ornate swirls of molten gold, and the center was silver like a mirror—no, it *was* a mirror. The shining middle reflected Tella's honey-blond curls and her round hazel eyes. But when Tella looked closer, the image was wrong. Tella's pink lips were trembling, and fat tears were running down her cheeks.

Tella never cried. Not even when her father used harsh words, or Felipe ignored her in favor of her older sister.

"I wondered if I'd find you in here, my little love." Her mother's soft soprano filled the room as she swept inside. "What adventures are you having today?"

As her mother bent toward the carpet where Tella sat, her hair fell around her clever face in elegant rivers. Her mother's locks were the same dark brown as Scarlett's, but Tella shared her mother's olive skin, which gleamed as if she'd been kissed by the stars. Though just then Tella watched her mother turn moonstone pale as her eyes latched on to the upturned images of the Maiden Death and the Prince of Hearts.

"Where did you find these?" Her mother's sweet voice remained, but her hands swiftly snatched the cards, giving Tella the impression she'd done something very wrong. And while Tella often did things she wasn't supposed to, usually her mother didn't mind. She'd gently correct her daughter, or occasionally tell her how to get away with her little crimes. It was her father who was easily angered. Her mother was the soft breath of air that blew out his sparks before they could ignite into flames. But now her mother looked as if she wanted to start a fire and use the cards for kindling.

"I found them in your jewelry box," Tella said. "I'm sorry. I didn't know they were bad."

"It's all right." Her mother ran a hand over Tella's curls. "I didn't mean to frighten you. But even I don't like to touch these cards."

"Then why do you have them?"

Her mother concealed the cards inside the skirts of her gown before setting the box on a high shelf by the bed, beyond Tella's reach.

Tella feared the conversation was over—as it undoubtedly would have been with her father. But her mother didn't ignore questions from her daughters. Once the box was tucked safely away, her mother folded herself onto the carpet beside Tella.

"I wish I'd never found these cards," she whispered, "but I will tell you about them if you swear to never touch this deck, or another deck like this, again."

"I thought you told Scarlett and I never to swear."

"This is different." A corner of her mother's smile returned, as though Tella was being let in on a very special secret. It was always this way: when her mother chose to focus her glittering attention on Tella alone, she made Tella feel as if she were a star and the world revolved around only her. "What have I always told you about the future?"

"Every person has the power to write her own," Tella said.

"That's right," her mother said. "Your future can be whatever you wish. We all have the power to choose our own destiny. But, my sweet, if you play with those cards, you give the Fates pictured inside them the opportunity to shift your path. People use Decks of Destiny, similar to the one you just touched, to predict the future, and once a future is foretold, that future becomes a living thing, and it will fight very hard to bring itself about. This is why I need you to never touch those cards again. Do you understand?"

Tella nodded, though she didn't truly understand; she was still at that tender age when the future seemed too far away to be real. It also did not escape her notice that her mother never said where the cards came from. And that made Tella's fingers clench a little tighter around the one still in her hand.

In her haste to pick up the deck, Tella's mother hadn't noticed the third card Tella had turned over. The one still in her possession. The Aracle. Tella carefully hid it beneath her crisscrossed legs as she said, "I swear to never touch a deck like this again."

ISLA DE
LOS SUEÑOS

I

Tella was no longer floating.

She was on the damp ground, feeling far, far away from the bright, sparkly thing she'd been the evening before. Back when Legend's private isle had radiated amber-tipped light, which breathed enchantment and wonder, along with a hint of deception. A delectable combination. And Tella had reveled in it. During the party to celebrate the end of Caraval, she had danced until her slippers were stained with grass and sipped flutes of bubbly wine until she'd practically floated.

But now she was facedown on the cold, hard forest floor.

Not daring to open her eyes, she groaned and brushed bits of nature from her hair, wishing some of the other remnants from last night could be as easily swept away. Everything reeked of stale liquor, pine needles, and mistakes. Her skin itched and crawled, and the only thing worse than the spinning in her head was the twisted soreness in her back and neck. Why had she thought falling asleep outside was a brilliant idea?

"Argh." Someone grunted the not-quite-satisfied sound of a person on the verge of waking up.

Tella opened her eyes, peered to the side, and then closed her lids immediately. *Dirty saints.*

She was not alone.

Amid the towering trees and the untamed greens of the forest floor, Tella had flashed open her eyes just long enough to glimpse a dark head of hair, bronzed skin, a scarred wrist, and a boy's hand covered with a black rose tattoo. *Dante.*

It all rushed back in a surge of blurry memories. The feeling of Dante's experienced hands wrapped around her hips. His kisses on her neck, her jaw, then her mouth as their lips became intimately acquainted.

What in all the hells had she been thinking?

Of course, Tella knew exactly what her thoughts had been during the Caraval performers' party the night before. The world had tasted like magic and starshine, like granted wishes and dreams come true, yet beneath it all, death still coated Tella's tongue. No matter how much champagne she drank, or how warm the air grew from dancing, Tella still shivered from the chilling recollection of how it had felt to die.

Her jump from Legend's balcony had not been an act of despair; it had been a leap of faith. But for just one night she hadn't wanted to think about it, or why it mattered. She wanted to celebrate her success, to forget everything else. And Dante had looked like the perfect way to do both. He was attractive, he could be charming, and it had been too long since she had been properly kissed. And, saints, did Dante know how to kiss.

With another groan, he stretched beside her. His large hand landed on her lower back, warm and firm, and far more tempting than it should have been.

Tella told herself she needed to escape before he woke. But even asleep, Dante was so good with his hands. He idly ran his fingers up her spine to her neck, lazily digging into her hair just enough to make her back arch.

His fingers stilled.

Dante's breathing grew suddenly quiet in a way that told Tella he was now awake as well.

Swallowing a curse, she hastily pushed up from the ground, away from his stilled, skilled fingers. She didn't care if he saw her sneaking off; it would be far less uncomfortable than exchanging any forced pleasantries before one of them became bold enough to make an excuse for why he or she needed to rush away. Tella had kissed enough young men to know that anything said by a boy right before or directly after she kissed him could not be believed at all. And she really needed to leave.

Tella's memories might have been blurry, yet somehow she couldn't manage to forget the letter she'd received before things became interesting with Dante. A stranger, face hidden underneath the cloak of night, had slid the note into her pocket and disappeared before she could follow. She wanted to reread the message right away, but considering what she owed the *friend* who'd sent it, she did not think that would be very wise. She needed to return to her room.

Damp earth and spiked tree needles snuck between her toes as she began to slink away. She must have lost her slippers somewhere, but she didn't want to waste time searching for them. The forest was tinged with indolent honey light and punctuated by heavy snores and murmurs that made Tella think she and Dante weren't the only ones who'd passed out under the stars. She didn't care if any of them saw her sneaking away from the pretty boy, but she didn't want anyone telling her sister.

Dante had been more than a little nasty to Scarlett during Caraval. He worked for Legend, so it had only been an act—but although Caraval was over, it was still somewhat difficult to weed out the bits of fact from fiction. And Tella didn't want her sister further hurt because Tella had chosen to have some fun with a boy who'd been so cruel to Scarlett during the game.

Thankfully the world remained asleep as Tella reached the edge of the forest, and then, Legend's turreted house.

Even now, with Caraval officially ended, and all the candles and lanterns inside unlit, the mansion still breathed wisps of beguiling ember-glow light, reminding Tella of tricks yet to be played.

Until yesterday, this estate had contained the entire world of Caraval. Its grand wooden doors had led visitors to elegant balconies draped with lush red curtains, which surrounded a city made of canals, streets that had minds of their owns, and uncanny shops full of magical pleasures. But in the brief time since the game had ended, the turreted house had shrunk in size and the ephemeral wonderland hidden within its walls had disappeared, leaving behind only the parts that would normally belong inside of a grand house.

Tella trotted up the closest staircase. Her room was on the second floor. With a rounded robin's-egg-blue door, it was easy to find. It was also impossible to miss Scarlett and Julian, standing next to it, holding on to each other as if they'd forgotten how to say the word *good-bye*.

Tella was glad her sister had finally lost herself in some happiness. Scarlett deserved every joy in the Empire, and Tella hoped it would last. She'd heard Julian didn't have a reputation for stringing girls along, he never carried on relationships after Caraval, and he'd not even been scripted to stay with Scarlett after bringing her to Legend's isle. But he lied for a living, which made it difficult for Tella to trust him. Yet, as the pair stood there with their arms wrapped around each other, and their heads leaning closer together, they looked like two halves of the same heart.

Their eyes stayed locked as Tella crept around them toward her room.

"Is that a yes?" Julian murmured.

"I need to talk to my sister," Scarlett said.

Tella halted in front of the door. She swore the letter in her pocket grew suddenly heavy, as if impatient to be read again. But if Julian had just asked Scarlett what Tella had hoped, then Tella needed to be a part of this conversation.

"What is it you want to talk to me about?" Tella interrupted.

Scarlett pulled back from Julian, but his hands remained wrapped around her waist, weaving through the blushing ribbons of her dress, clearly not ready to let her go. "I asked your sister if you'll both go with us to Valenda for Empress Elantine's seventy-fifth birthday celebration. There will be another Caraval and I have two tickets." Julian winked.

Tella tossed her sister a grin. This was exactly what she'd hoped for. Although a part of her still couldn't believe the rumors she'd heard over the past week were true. Caraval only occurred once a year, and she'd never known of two games being played so close together. But Tella supposed even Legend made exceptions for the empress.

Tella continued to look at her sister hopefully. "I'm surprised this is even a question!"

"I thought you didn't like Elantine's Day because it always overshadowed your birthday."

Tella wobbled her head as she weighed her answer. Her true reasons for wanting to go had little to do with Elantine's Day, although her sister was correct. For as long as Elantine had been empress of the Meridian Empire, her birthday had been a holiday, Elantine's Day, which was ushered in with a full week of parties and dances, bended rules, and broken laws. On the girls' home isle of Trisda, this holiday was only celebrated for one day, on the thirty-sixth day of the Growing Season, but it still overshadowed Tella's birthday, which had the misfortune of occurring the day afterward.

"It will be worth it to visit Valenda," Tella said. "When do we leave?"

"Three days," Julian answered.

Scarlett puckered her mouth. "Tella, we need to discuss this first."

"I thought you've always wanted to go to the capital, to see all its ancient ruins and the carriages that float through the sky, and this will be the party of the century! What's there to talk about?"

"The count."

Julian's brown skin went gray.

Tella's face might have done the same.

"The count lives in Valenda, and we can't let him see you," Scarlett said.

Scarlett was the overly cautious sister, but Tella couldn't blame her for this reservation.

Count Nicolas d'Arcy was Scarlett's former fiancé whom Scarlett's father had arranged for her to marry. Before Caraval, Scarlett had only written him letters, but she'd believed herself in love with him. She'd also thought the count would keep both her and Tella safe—until Scarlett met him during Caraval and learned what a despicable human being he was.

Scarlett was right to worry about the count. If Scarlett's former fiancé discovered Tella was alive, he could send word to their father—who believed Tella was dead—and it would shatter everything.

But things would also fall apart if Tella didn't go with Legend and his performers to the Empire's capital city of Valenda. She might not have had the chance to reread the letter from her friend, but she knew what he wanted, and she would never get it for him if she was separated from Legend and his performers.

During Caraval, Tella hadn't been entirely certain who worked for Legend. But all of his performers would be on the boat to Valenda—Legend might even be on the boat as well, giving her the opportunity she needed to finally get the one thing her friend required.

"The count is so concerned with himself he probably wouldn't recognize me even if I walked up to him and gave him a slap in the face," Tella said. "We only met for a moment, and I was not looking my best."

"Tella—"

"I know, I know, you want me to be serious," Tella cut in. "I'm not trying to mock you. I'm fully aware of the danger, but I don't think we need to be afraid of it. We could just as easily perish in a shipwreck, but if we let that fear stop us, we'll never leave this isle again."

Scarlett grimaced and turned to Julian. "Would you mind giving my sister and me a moment alone?"

Julian answered against Scarlett's ear, too low for Tella to hear. Whatever he said made Scarlett blush. Then he left and Scarlett's mouth flattened into a line as she and Tella enclosed themselves in Tella's room.

Inside, unmentionables were everywhere. Stockings peeked out from the drawers of a dresser topped off with bonnets, while a variety of capes, gowns, and petticoats formed a path to her bed, which was covered in a teetering pile of furs that she'd won in a card game.

Tella knew Scarlett thought she was lazy. But Tella had a theory: Neat rooms were easy to rifle through and search undetected because it was simple to put carefully placed things exactly where they'd been. But messes, on the other hand, were difficult to re-create. With one sweeping gaze, Tella could see no one had been brave enough to lay a finger on her personal disaster. Everything appeared untouched, even though there now seemed to be an additional bed, which Tella imagined must have magically appeared, or more likely had been carried upstairs for her sister.

Tella didn't know how long they'd be allowed to stay on the isle. She was relieved they weren't being kicked out right away, although if they'd been evicted, maybe Scarlett would have been more eager to travel to Valenda. But Tella didn't actually want her sister to be forced into anything; she hoped Scarlett would make the choice for herself. Though Tella could understand her sister's reluctance. Tella had died during the last game. But that had been her decision, it was for a good reason, and she wasn't planning on dying again. It had been as horrid for Tella as it had been for Scarlett. And there were still so many things Tella wanted—*and needed*—to do.

"Scar, I know you think I wasn't being serious out there, but I think we need to start being happy rather than serious. I'm not saying we need to participate in Caraval, but I think we should at least go to Valenda with Julian and the others. What's the point of all this glorious freedom if we don't enjoy it? Our father wins if we keep living as if we're still trapped beneath his heavy fists."

"You're right."

Tella must have misheard. "Did you say I'm right?"

Scarlett nodded. "I'm done with being scared all the time." She still sounded nervous, but her chin now lifted with something like determination. "I'd rather not play the game again, but I want to go with Julian to Valenda. I don't want to trap myself here like our father trapped us on Trisda."

Tella felt a surge of pride. Back on Trisda, Scarlett held on to her fear, as if it would keep her safe, but Tella could see her sister fighting to let it go. She really had changed during Caraval.

"You were right last night, when you encouraged me to give Julian another chance. I'm glad I went to the party, and I know I'll regret it if we don't go with him. But," Scarlett added, "if we go to Valenda, you have to promise you'll be careful. I can't lose you again."

"Don't worry. I swear it." Tella solemnly took her sister's hands and squeezed. "I enjoy my freedom way too much to let it go. And, while we're in the capital, I'll be sure to wear impossibly bright dresses so I'll always be impossible to lose."

Scarlett's mouth tilted toward a smile. Tella could see her sister trying to battle it, but then it transformed into a melodious laugh. Happiness made Scarlett even prettier.

Tella giggled with her until their smiles matched, as if worries were things made for other people. Yet Tella could not forget the letter in her pocket, reminding her of a debt to be paid and a mother who still needed to be saved.

It had been seven years since Tella and Scarlett's mother, Paloma, had disappeared.

There was a period of time that started about a year after her mother left, when Tella preferred the idea of Paloma being dead. If she was still alive, Tella reasoned, she'd made the choice never to return to her daughters, which meant she couldn't have really loved them. But if Paloma was dead, then maybe she'd intended to return, but had never been given the chance; if she was dead, it was possible she'd still loved Scarlett and Tella.

So for years Tella clung to the hope that her mother had met death, because no matter how hard Tella tried, she could not stop loving her mother, and it hurt too much to imagine that her mother didn't love her back.

Tella pulled out the letter she'd received from her friend. Scarlett had left to tell Julian they'd go with him to Valenda. But Tella didn't know how long she'd be gone, so she read swiftly.

Dearest Donatella,

Congratulations on escaping your father and surviving Caraval. I am pleased our plan worked, although I had no doubts you would survive the game.

I am sure your mother will be quite proud, and I believe you should be able to see her soon. But first you must keep up your end of our bargain. I hope you haven't forgotten what you owe me in exchange for all that I've shared with you.

I plan on collecting my payment very soon.

Truly yours,

A friend

The aching in Tella's head returned, and this time it had nothing to do with the drinks she'd consumed the night before. She couldn't shake the sense something was missing from the letter. She swore there'd been more to it when she'd read it at the party.

Tella held the message to the butterscotch light streaming through her window. No hidden lines of script appeared. No words shifted before her eyes. Unlike Legend, her friend didn't lace his letters with magic tricks, but she often hoped he would. Maybe then she'd be able to confirm his identity.

She'd first contacted him more than a year ago, to help her and her sister escape from their father. But Tella still had no idea who her friend was. For a while she had wondered if her correspondent was actually Legend. But her friend and Legend could not be the same person—the payment her friend referred to made Tella certain of that.

She still needed to acquire this payment. But now that she and Scarlett were going to Valenda with Legend's players, Tella felt more confident she would. She had to.

Her pulse danced faster as she hid her friend's letter and opened her smallest trunk—the one she'd not allowed the players to rifle through during Caraval. She had filled it with money pilfered from her father. But that was not the only treasure it concealed. The interior was lined with an unappealing burnt-orange and lime-green brocade that most people would never look at closely enough to notice the slit along the edge of it, which allowed her to hide the catalyst for this entire situation: *The Aracle*.

Tella's fingers tingled as they always did when she pulled out the wicked little card. After her mother disappeared, her father had gone mad with rage. He'd not been a violent man before, but when his wife left him, he'd changed almost instantly. He'd thrown her clothes in the gutter, turned her bed into firewood, and burned everything else into ash. The only items that had escaped were the scarlet earrings Paloma had given to Scarlett, the raw-fire opal ring that Tella had stolen, and the uncanny card in Tella's hand. If she'd not taken this card and the ring right before her mother left, Tella would have had nothing to remember her mother by.

The opal ring had shifted color shortly after her mother's disappearance, turning fiery red and purple. The edges of the Aracle card were still made of molten gold, but the image in its shimmering center had changed as well, countless times. Tella hadn't known what it was when she'd first stolen it from her mother's Deck of Destiny. Even days later, when she'd looked in the mirror and seen fat tears streaming down her cheeks—re-creating the image the Aracle had first revealed—Tella didn't piece it together. It wasn't until more time went by that she noticed that when the Aracle revealed an image, it always came to pass.

At first the images were inconsequential: a maid trying on Tella's favorite gown; her father cheating at cards. Then the visions of the future grew more upsetting, until one day, immediately after Scarlett's engagement to the count, Tella saw a most disturbing image.

Scarlett was dressed in a snow-white wedding gown, studded with rubies and petals and whisper-thin lace. It should have been beautiful. But in the Aracle's vision, it was stained with mud and blood and tears as Scarlett sobbed violently into her hands.

The horrid image remained for months, as if the card were asking Tella to prevent her sister's arranged marriage and change the future—not that Tella needed prodding. She'd already been forming a plan for her and her sister to run away from their controlling father, one that involved Legend and Caraval. Tella knew if anything would tempt her risk-averse sister to take a chance at another life, it would be Caraval. But Legend wouldn't respond to any of Tella's letters, just as he'd never responded to Scarlett's.

The image on the Aracle incited Tella to search for more information about Legend. There were wild rumors Legend had killed someone during a game years before, and Tella hoped finding out more about that would convince him to pay attention to her.

To fuel her search, Tella collected on every favor she was owed until she'd been told to write to an establishment called Elantine's Most Wanted. It was supposedly a business in the Meridian Empire's capital city of Valenda. No one ever told her exactly what sort of business it was in. But after Tella asked for information about Legend, the shop responded with a message that said:

We've found a man who's agreed to help you, but be warned, he often requires payments that involve more than money.

When Tella wrote back to ask for this man's name, the man himself simply replied:

> *It's best if you don't know.*
> *—A friend*

Tella always took this response to mean her *friend* was a criminal, but he'd been a faithful and clever correspondent. The information he'd provided about Legend was not what she'd expected, but using it, Tella had written to Legend again and pleaded for his help.

She succeeded this time. Legend replied to Tella, and as soon as he agreed to help her and her sister escape their father, the Aracle changed from Scarlett in a wrecked wedding gown to Scarlett at a lavish ball, in a gown made of rubies that drew the eye of every suitor she walked by. *This* was the future Tella wanted for her sister, full of glamour, celebrations, and choices.

Unfortunately, a day later the vision was replaced by another glimpse of the future that had not changed since.

Tella didn't know if the enchanted card would show the same awful picture today; after everything that had happened during Caraval, she hoped that perhaps it had changed.

But the image hadn't shifted.

All the air and hope fled Tella's lungs.

The card still showed her mother. She looked like a battered version of the Lady Prisoner, depicted in Decks of Destiny, covered in blood, and caged behind the harsh iron bars of a dim prison cell.

This was the future that had prompted Tella to make another request of her friend and ask him if he could also help find her mother. Tella's previous searches for Paloma had led nowhere, but her friend, who was not bound to a backwater island like Tella, clearly had better ideas and methods of how to search.

She had memorized his reply by heart.

Dearest Donatella,

I'm looking into the request regarding your mother and I already have a strong lead. I believe the reason you couldn't find her before is because Paloma was not her real name. However, I will not be able to reunite you with her until you pay me back for the information I sent you about Caraval Master Legend.

In case you forgot, I need Legend's true

name. The others I've tasked to do this have all failed. But since you'll be spending time on his private isle, I'm sure you will succeed. Once you have the name, we can discuss my payment for finding your mother.

Yours,

A friend

This news about Paloma's name was the only information Tella had learned about her mother since she'd left seven years ago. It gave Tella genuine hope. She had no idea why her friend wanted Legend's name, whether it was for personal use, or if it was information another client had tried to purchase. But Tella didn't care; she would do whatever it took to uncover Legend's name. If Tella could do this, she believed she would finally see her mother again. Her friend had not let her down before.

"Good lord!"

Tella looked up to see her sister's large eyes go wide as she reentered the room. "Where did you get all those coins?" Scarlett pointed at Tella's open trunk.

But at the word *coins*, Tella's thoughts were suddenly elsewhere. Her friend had wrapped a strange coin inside the last letter he'd sent. That's what she was missing! It must have slipped out of her pocket when she'd been tumbling around the forest floor with Dante.

Tella needed to get back to the forest and find it. She concealed the Aracle inside her pocket as she shot toward the door.

"Where are you going?" Scarlett called. "Don't tell me you stole all that money!"

"Don't worry," Tella replied. "I took it all from our father, and he thinks I'm dead."

Before Scarlett could respond, Tella raced from the room.

She moved so fast she was already outside of the turreted house, on a street lined with hatbox-shaped shops, when she realized she was still barefoot. A mistake she felt quickly.

"God's teeth!" Tella yelped. She was only halfway to the forest and it was the third time she'd stubbed her toe. This time she swore a rock jumped up from the cobbled street and attacked her exposed feet on purpose. "I swear, if another one of you bites my toes I will drown you in the ocean where the mermaids can use you to wipe their—"

Tella heard a low, deep, and unnervingly familiar chuckle.

She told herself not to turn around. Not to give in to her curiosity. But being told no—even from herself—only made Tella want to do the opposite.

Carefully she snuck a look over her shoulder, and instantly regretted it.

Dante strutted down the other side of the quiet street with amused eyes fixed on her.

Tella averted her gaze, hoping if she ignored him he'd stay on his side of the road and pretend he hadn't just seen her yelling at a rock.

Instead he crossed the street, intentionally striding toward her with those impossibly long legs of his, broad mouth smiling as if he had a secret.

Tella told herself her stomach only tumbled because she hadn't eaten that morning. Dante might have slept on a forest floor, but not even a blade of grass clung to his polished boots. Dressed in inky shades of black, without so much as a loose cravat, he looked like a dark, wingless angel who'd been tossed from the heavens and landed on his feet.

Tella had a sudden flash of the way he'd approached her at the party last night, and her insides did another flip. He'd responded with disinterest that bordered on ignoring her when she'd first said hello. But then she'd caught him watching her from the across the party—just glimpses, here and there—until, out of nowhere, he'd appeared at her side and kissed her until her knees gave out.

"Please don't stop such an interesting speech on my account," he said, returning her to the present moment. "I'm sure I've heard far more colorful curses."

"Did you just insult my use of profanity?"

"I thought I asked for more dirty words." His voice pitched so low Tella swore it curled the ribbons trailing down the back of her dress.

But this was Dante. He talked like this to all the girls, flashing his devastating smile and saying wicked and beguiling things until he got them to unbutton their blouses or lift their skirts. Then he pretended they didn't exist. She'd heard the stories during Caraval. So Tella should have been safe to assume that after last night this boy would never speak to her again, which was what she wanted.

Tella enjoyed the kissing, and maybe once upon another time she might have been tempted by the idea of more. But the problem with more was it could also bring more feelings, like love. Tella wanted nothing to do with love; she'd learned long ago it was not in her destiny. She gave herself the freedom to kiss as many boys as she liked, but never more than once.

"What do you want?" Tella asked.

Dante's eyes widened enough to betray surprise at her sharp tone, yet his voice remained pleasant as he said, "You dropped this in the forest last night." He held out one large palm, showing her a thick brassy coin embossed with a disjointed image that resembled half of a face.

He had her coin! Tella could have leaped out of her skin to grab it, but she doubted acting too eager would be wise.

"Thank you for picking it up," she answered coolly. "It's not valuable, but I like to carry it as a good-luck charm."

She reached for it.

Dante pulled his hand back, and tossed the brassy disc into the air before catching it. "Interesting choice for a charm." Suddenly he looked more serious, thick brows drawing closer together over coal-dark eyes, as he flipped the coin over and over, letting it dance between his tattooed fingers. "I've seen some odd things during Caraval, but I've never known someone to carry one of these for luck."

"I suppose I like to be original."

"Or you have no idea what it is." His rich voice sounded more entertained than before.

"And what do you think it is?"

Dante tossed the coin once more. "It's said these were forged by the Fates. People used to call them 'luckless coins.'"

"No wonder it's never worked well." Tella managed a laugh, but something gnawed—foolishness, perhaps—at not having recognized the object.

Tella had been obsessed with the Fates ever since finding her mother's Deck of Destiny. There'd been thirty-two of them, comprising a court of sixteen immortals, eight places, and eight objects. Every Fate was known for one particular power, but that wasn't the only reason they'd come to rule most of the world centuries ago. It was also said they couldn't be killed by mortals, and that they were faster and stronger, too.

Centuries ago, before they'd vanished, the Fates pictured in Decks of Destiny had ruled over most of the earth like gods—cruel ones. Tella read everything she could about them, so she'd heard of luckless coins, but she felt ridiculous admitting it now.

"People called them luckless because finding one was always a bad omen," Dante said. "The coins were rumored to have the magic ability to track a person's whereabouts. The Fates would slip them into the pockets of their human servants, their lovers, or anyone else they wished to follow, keep close, or control. I've never held one before today, but I've heard if you spin a luckless coin, you can see which Fate it belonged to."

Dante set the coin atop the edge of a nearby bench.

An unpleasant thrill danced up Tella's spine. Although he seemed to know a lot of obscure history, she couldn't tell if Dante put faith in the power of the Fates, but she believed in them.

The Maiden Death was said to predict the loss of a loved one or family member. And within days of flipping it over, and seeing the maiden with her head caged in pearls, Tella's mother had vanished. She knew it was childish to believe that turning the card had caused this disappearance. But not all childish beliefs were wrong. Her mother had warned her, the Fates had a way of twisting futures. And Tella had seen the Aracle, time and time again, predict futures that came to pass.

Tella held her breath as Dante gave the object a sharp twist.

Whir, whir, whir.

The coin twirled until the etchings on either side began to take a solid shape, merging together as if by magic to form a brutally familiar picture. A dashing young man with a bloody smile, and the sort of havoc-wreaking grin that made Tella picture teeth biting into hearts and lips pressed against punctured veins.

Though it was small, Tella could clearly see the image. The cruel young man held one hand near his pointed chin, clasping the hilt of a dagger, while red tears fell from his eyes, matching the blood staining the corner of his mouth.

The Prince of Hearts.

A symbol of unrequited love and irrevocable mistakes that never ceased to fill Tella with both dread and morbid bewitchment.

Scarlett had spent half her childhood obsessed with Legend and Caraval. But Tella had been fascinated by the Prince of Hearts ever since he'd predicted her loveless future when she'd pulled him from her mother's Deck of Destiny.

The myths claimed the Prince of Hearts's kisses had been worth dying for, and Tella had often wondered how such a deadly kiss would feel. But as she'd grown, and kissed enough boys to realize that no kiss could be worth dying for, Tella started to suspect the stories were merely fables to illustrate the dangers of falling in love.

For it was also said the Prince of Hearts was not capable of love because his heart had stopped beating long ago. Only one person could make it beat again: his one true love. They said his kiss had been fatal to all but her—his only weakness—and as he'd sought her, he'd left a trail of corpses.

A fresh chill licked the back of Tella's neck, and she slapped her palm atop the coin.

"I take it you're not a fan of the prince?" asked Dante.

"The coin looked as if it was about to topple off, and then I'd have to chase it."

The corner of Dante's mouth edged up; he couldn't have looked less convinced.

It also didn't escape Tella's notice that he'd just spoken of the Prince of Hearts as if he and the other Fates were still walking around the Empire, and not vanished for more than a century.

"I don't know why you're really carrying that coin," Dante said, "but be careful. Nothing good has ever come from anything a Fate has touched." His eyes lifted skyward, as if the Fates were watching from above, spying as they spoke.

Then, before Tella could respond, Dante was confidently walking away, leaving Tella with a coin that burned her palm, and the uncanny sensation that perhaps there was more to the pretty boy than she'd originally suspected.

Tella found herself thinking of unrequited love and kisses worth dying for as she spun the Prince of Hearts luckless coin on the same bench Dante had. Why had her friend given her a relic from such an ancient myth? She hoped it wasn't because he didn't trust her and wanted to keep track of her.

Maybe the rare coin was a gift from her friend to remind Tella of just how skilled he was at acquiring things that were difficult for most people to find—a reminder that he was the only one who knew how to locate her mother.

A shop bell rang. Just a tiny, pixie-light sound, but Tella snatched her coin up and looked down the street, to where a young man swaggered out of a shop. She followed the deep red lines of his morning coat up to the young man's vibrant eyes, greener than freshly cut emeralds—

And a bath of crimson clouded Tella's vision.

She knew this young man. He'd shed his eye patch since Caraval, but he still had the same ink-black hair, overstated aristocratic clothes, and impossibly vain expression as Count Nicolas d'Arcy—Scarlett's former fiancé.

Tella's hands clamped into fists, nails digging crescents into her palms. She had only officially met Count Nicolas d'Arcy once, but she spied on him on several occasions during Caraval. She'd seen him chase after her sister, and heard that once he'd caught her, he'd been willing to do unspeakable things to keep her. Scarlett had managed to escape. But Tella could have strangled him, or poisoned him, or mangled his pretty face, if Legend had not promised in one of his letters that he'd remove her sister from the game if Tella strayed from her role and interfered in any way.

So Tella had been forced to do nothing.

But the game was over now; Tella could do as she pleased.

The count was currently several shops away, too busy gazing at his reflection in a window to notice Tella. The wise thing would have been to sneak onto a different street so that he wouldn't discover she was still alive.

But Tella meant it when she'd said she doubted the count would recognize her if she walked up to him and slapped him in the face. For what he'd done to her sister during Caraval, he deserved more than a slap, but Tella didn't have any poison in her pockets.

She stalked closer. Maybe she'd throw in a well-aimed kick, and—

One hand clamped over Tella's mouth, while another banded

around her waist. She kicked, but it didn't stop her assailant from dragging her back into a splinter-thin alley.

"Takeyourhandsoffme!"

Tella pitched forward as the arms around her dropped away.

"It's all right." The voice was low with a lilting accent. "I'm not going to hurt you, but don't run."

Tella spun around.

Julian's dark hair was still mussed from Scarlett's fingers, but his eyes were no longer the warm liquid amber they'd been when he'd gazed at her sister earlier. They were tight around the corners, hard.

"Julian? What in all the hells are you doing?"

"I'm trying to stop you from making a mistake you'll regret." His gaze shot down the narrow redbrick alley, back toward the street with the loathsome Count Nicolas d'Arcy.

"No," Tella said, "I'm pretty sure if I make this mistake, I'll be very happy. I'm surprised you don't want to bloody him as well, for what he allowed my father to do to you." She nodded toward the jagged scar that went from Julian's jaw to the corner of his eye. Caraval players could come back to life if they died during the game, but their scars remained. Tella had heard that during Caraval Scarlett's fiancé had just stood there, doing nothing to stop Tella's father as he'd sliced Julian's face.

"Trust me," Julian gritted out, "I've wanted to bloody up Armando more than once, but—"

"Armando?" Tella interrupted. Not the count. Not Nicolas. Not d'Arcy, or that filthy piece of garbage Count Nicolas d'Arcy. Julian had called him Armando. "Why did you just call him Armando?"

"From the look on your face, I think you've already guessed. Armando was never engaged to your sister. He works for Legend, just like I do."

Tella swayed on her bare feet as Caraval's familiar mantra rushed back: *Remember, it's only a game. We want you to be swept away, but beware of being swept too far away. . . .*

That villain.

Tella had thought herself immune, since she'd been writing letters to Legend as he planned the game. But apparently she'd been wrong. Legend had fooled her, exactly like he'd fooled everyone else. It had never occurred to Tella that an actor might have been playing the role of her sister's fiancé.

Legend truly did deserve the name he'd given himself. Tella wondered if Legend's games ever ended, or if his world was an endless maze of fantasy and reality that left those caught inside it forever suspended somewhere in between the two.

Across from her, Julian pulled at the back of his neck, looking more nervous than apologetic. Julian was impulsive. Tella doubted he'd thought through the consequences of telling her the truth. He'd probably just reacted when he'd spied her about to go after Armando.

"My sister has no idea, does she?"

"No," Julian said. "And for now I want to keep it that way."

"Are you asking me to lie to her?"

"It's not as if you haven't done it before."

Tella bristled. "I did that for her own good."

"This is for her own good, too." Julian crossed his lean arms and lounged back against the alley wall.

In that moment Tella wasn't sure she liked him at all. She hated the claim he'd just made. Saying something was for someone else's own good was almost always another way of justifying something wrong. Of course since she'd said it first, she couldn't properly berate Julian the way she wanted.

"We're going to Valenda in a few days," Julian went on. "What do you think your sister will do if she discovers that she never met her real fiancé during Caraval?"

"She'd look for him," Tella admitted. It would be easy to do since he lived in Valenda. Tella had never understood it, but Scarlett had really wanted to marry this man whom she'd never even seen a portrait of. She'd imagined him with hearts in her eyes, always reading the best things into his bland, unromantic letters.

Scarlett would probably claim it was curiosity, but knowing her sister, deep down she'd probably feel as if she needed to give him a chance, which could be disastrous. Tella once again saw the image of Scarlett sobbing in a bloodied wedding dress. The Aracle showed that she'd erased that future, but there was still a chance it could come about.

"Scarlett won't like it when she finds out you've lied to her," Tella said.

"I think of it as fighting for her." Julian rubbed the dark stubble covering his chin. He looked and sounded like a boy a little too eager to jump into a street brawl, yet Tella sensed genuine mettle beneath his words. She still felt a little uncertain as to how long Julian's affections toward her sister would last, but in that moment Tella imagined Julian would cross any and every moral line to keep Scarlett's heart. Oddly, it made her trust him more.

It might have made Tella's life easier to refuse him; then Scarlett wouldn't worry about Tella being spotted by the count while they were in Valenda, because the *real* count had never seen her face. But, despite how much simpler it could make things, Tella couldn't take the risk of telling her sister the truth. A union between Scarlett and the count would end in heartbreak and devastation. The Aracle had shown this, and the card never lied to Tella.

"All right," she said. "I agree not to say anything to Scarlett about Armando."

A half nod, as if Julian knew Tella would comply with the deception.

"Despite my actions during Caraval, I don't enjoy deceiving my sister."

"But it's hard to stop once you start."

"Is that how it is with you? You spend so much time lying you can't tell the truth?" The words came out sharper than Tella intended, but to his credit Julian didn't bite back.

"Caraval might all feel like a lie to you, but it's my life—my truth. This last game was as real for me as it was for your sister. While she was fighting for you, I was fighting for her." His voice roughened. "I might have lied to your sister about who I was, but my feelings for her were genuine. I need more time with her before she learns anything else that might make her doubt me."

"What happens if Scarlett sees Armando is still on the island?"

"Legend is sending him to Valenda early, along with a few other performers."

How very convenient.

"Since I'm doing this for you, I want a favor," Tella added with a bit of inspiration.

Julian rocked his head back and forth, appearing to consider it. "What sort of favor?"

"I want to know Legend's real name. Who is Legend, *really*?"

Julian laughed before she even finished. "Don't tell me you're in love with him too."

"I know better than to fall in love with Legend."

"Good. And no," Julian said, no longer laughing. "That's not even close to a fair trade, and, even if it were, I can't tell you Legend's name."

Tella folded her arms across her chest. She hadn't really expected him to answer. The few performers she'd been able to question had given her similar responses. There'd been lots of chuckles and smirks, and some had just ignored her altogether. She imagined it was because most of them had no clue as to who Legend really was, but Julian's response was different enough to make her hope she'd finally found someone better informed.

"If you can't tell me Legend's name," Tella said, "point me in the direction of someone who can, or we don't have a deal."

All remaining traces of Julian's humor vanished. "Legend's identity is his most guarded secret. No one on this isle will reveal it to you."

"Then I suppose I'll just have to expose the truth about Armando to Scarlett." Tella turned to leave the alley.

"Wait—" Julian grabbed her wrist.

Tella resisted the urge to smile. He was desperate.

"If you promise not to tell Scarlett about Armando, I'll share the name of a performer who might answer some questions."

"Might?"

"He's been with Caraval since the beginning, and he knows things. But he doesn't give away information for free."

"I wouldn't believe him if he did. Tell me his name and we have a deal."

"It's Nigel," Julian answered quietly. "He's Legend's fortune-teller."

Tella had never met Nigel, but she knew who he was. The young man was unmistakable. Every inch of Nigel, including his face, was covered in bright, lifelike tattoos that he used to predict the future. Of course, Nigel's role sounded different on Julian's lips, as if he wasn't truly there for those playing Caraval, but to pass on information to the master of Caraval.

"Be careful," Julian added, as if Tella needed another warning. "Fortune-tellers aren't like you and me. They see the world as it could be, and sometimes they try to bring about what they want, rather than what should be."

5

The air was full of salt and secrets. Tella took a deep breath, hoping the evening was also threaded with the magic that haunted Legend's ship, *La Esmeralda.*

Everything about it breathed enchantment. Even its swollen sails appeared charmed. They blazed red in the day and silver at night, like a magician's cloak, hinting at mysteries concealed beneath, which Tella planned to uncover that night.

Drunken laughter floated above her as Tella delved deeper into the ship's underbelly in search of Nigel the Fortune-teller. Her first evening on the vessel she'd made the mistake of sleeping, not realizing until the following day that Legend's performers had switched their waking hours to prepare for the next Caraval. They slumbered in the day and woke after sunset.

All Tella had learned her first day aboard *La Esmeralda* was that Nigel was on the ship, but she had yet to actually see him. The creaking halls beneath decks were like the bridges of Caraval, leading different places at different hours and making it difficult to know who stayed in which room. Tella wondered if Legend had designed it that way, or if it was just the unpredictable nature of magic.

She imagined Legend in his top hat, laughing at the question and at the idea that magic had more control than he did. For many, Legend was the definition of magic.

When she had first arrived on Isla de los Sueños, Tella suspected everyone could be Legend. Julian had so many secrets that she'd questioned if Legend's identity was one of them, up until he'd briefly died. Caspar, with his sparkling eyes and rich laugh, had played the role of Legend in the last game, and at times he'd been so convincing Tella wondered if he was actually acting. At first sight, Dante, who was almost too beautiful to be real, looked like the Legend she'd always imagined. Tella could picture Dante's wide shoulders filling out a black tailcoat while a velvet top hat shadowed his head. But the more Tella thought about Legend, the more she wondered if he even ever wore a top hat. If maybe the symbol was another thing to throw people off. Perhaps Legend was more magic than man and Tella had never met him in the flesh at all.

The boat rocked and an actual laugh pierced the quiet.

Tella froze.

The laughter ceased but the air in the thin corridor shifted. What had smelled of salt and wood and damp turned thick and velvet-sweet. The scent of roses.

Tella's skin prickled; gooseflesh rose on her bare arms.

At her feet a puddle of petals formed a seductive trail of red.

Tella might not have known Legend's true name, but she knew he favored red and roses and games.

Was this his way of toying with her? Did he know what she was up to?

The bumps on her arms crawled up to her neck and into her scalp as her newest pair of slippers crushed the tender petals. If Legend knew what she was after, Tella couldn't imagine he would guide her in the correct direction, and yet the trail of petals was too tempting to avoid. They led to a door that glowed copper around the edges.

She turned the knob.

And her world transformed into a garden, a paradise made of blossoming flowers and bewitching romance. The walls were formed of moonlight. The ceiling was made of roses that dripped down toward the table in the center of the room, covered with plates of cakes and candlelight and sparkling honey wine.

But none of it was for Tella.

It was all for Scarlett. Tella had stumbled into her sister's love story and it was so romantic it was painful to watch.

Scarlett stood across the chamber. Her full ruby gown bloomed brighter than any flowers, and her glowing skin rivaled the moon as she gazed up at Julian.

They touched nothing except each other. While Scarlett pressed her lips to Julian's, his arms wrapped around her as if he'd found the one thing he never wanted to let go of.

This was why love was so dangerous. Love turned the world into a garden, so beguiling it was easy to forget that rose petals were as ephemeral as feelings, eventually they would wilt and die, leaving nothing but the thorns.

Tella turned and left the doorway before she could think another cruel thought. Scarlett deserved this happiness. And maybe it would last. Perhaps Julian would prove himself worthy of Scarlett and keep his promises. It did look as if he were trying.

And, unlike Tella, Scarlett wasn't the one who'd been doomed to unrequited love by the Prince of Hearts.

The hallway shifted again as soon as Tella closed the door. The path of petals before her vanished and a new trail formed out of ginger smoke and incense—the scents that always lingered around Nigel.

Again, Tella sensed that Legend was toying with her as the smoking curls of incense widened into the shape of hands and waved her toward an open door.

Tella's skin heated as she stepped inside. Waxy yellow candles lined the edge of the room, and in the middle of it all was Nigel, lounging atop a bed covered in a velvet quilt the deep shade of plum wine. His lips, surrounded with tattoos of barbed blue wire, stretched wide, not quite a smile, more like the opening of a trap.

"I wondered when you'd pay me a visit, Miss Dragna." He motioned for Tella to take a seat against the mountain of tasseled pillows positioned at the foot of his temporary dais. Just like during Caraval, Nigel only wore a stretch of brown cloth, leaving all his vibrant tattoos exposed.

Tella's eyes fell to the circus scenes depicted on his thick legs, transfixed by the vision of a woman with feathers for hair, dancing with a wolf in a top hat. Not wanting Nigel to interpret the meaning, she quickly lifted her eyes, only for them to land on his arm and the image of a broken black heart.

"What is it I can do for you?" asked Nigel.

"I don't want my future told. I want information about Legend."

The tattooed stars around Nigel's eyes glittered like wet ink, eager and intrigued. "How much are you willing to pay for this?"

Tella pulled a purse of coins from her pocket.

Nigel shook his head. Of course he would not accept her money. Coins were not the preferred method of payment in the world of Caraval.

"Traditionally we perform once a year, giving us months to recover," said Nigel. "This time Legend has given us less than a week."

"I'm not giving you any days of my life."

"I do not desire your life. I want your rest."

"How much?" Tella asked cautiously. She had gone days without sleeping before. Giving up a few nights of rest didn't seem too great of a sacrifice. But that was how these bargains always appeared. On the surface, Legend's performers made them sound like insignificant inconveniences, but they were never that straightforward.

"I will take from you in proportion to what I give you," Nigel said. "The more questions I answer, the more rest I will receive. If I give you no answers of value, you will lose nothing."

"And when will you take my sleep?"

"As soon as you leave this room."

Tella attempted to see every angle of the deal. It was the evening of the twenty-fourth and they were scheduled to arrive in Valenda the morning of the twenty-ninth. There were four days of travel left. Depending on how much sleep he stole, she'd be exhausted by the time they reached Valenda. But if he gave her concrete information about Legend, it would be worth it.

"All right. But I will only give you my sleep as long as we are on this boat. You cannot take anything from me while we're in Valenda."

"I can work with that." Nigel retrieved a brush along with a tiny pot full of burning orange liquid from the stand beside his bed. "I'll need your wrist to complete the transaction."

Tella hesitated. "You're not going to paint anything permanent on it, are you?"

"Whatever I draw will disappear as soon as you pay me in full."

Tella stretched out her arm. Nigel moved with practiced skill; his cold brush swirled and twirled along Tella's skin, as if he often used body parts as a canvas.

When he finished, a pair of eyes, exactly like hers, peered back at Tella. Round and hazel-bright. For a moment she swore they pleaded with her not to make this choice. But losing a little sleep felt like a small sacrifice if it would give her the information she needed to fulfill the debt to her friend and finally end the last seven years of torment that had begun the day her mother had left.

"Now," said Nigel, "what is it you wish to know?"

"I want Legend's true name. The one he was called before he became Legend."

Nigel ran a finger over his barbed-wire lips, drawing a drop of blood—or was the blood tattooed on the tip of his finger?

"Even if I wanted to, I could not tell you Legend's name," said Nigel. "None of his players can reveal this secret. The same witch who banished the Fates from earth centuries ago gave Legend his powers. His magic is ancient—older than he is—and it binds us all to secrecy."

Though no one was certain why the Fates had vanished and left the humans to rule themselves, there were mumblings they'd been vanquished by a powerful witch. But Tella had never heard anyone say this was the same witch who had given Legend his powers.

"That still doesn't tell me anything about Legend's true identity."

"I'm not finished," Nigel said. "I was going to tell you: Legend's magic prevents his true name from being spoken or revealed, but it can be won."

Spider legs danced over Tella's skin, and one of the painted eyes on her wrist began to close. It fell swiftly, in a way that made her feel as if she was running out of currency, but also very close to the answer she needed.

"How do I win the name?" she asked quickly.

"You must participate in the next Caraval. If you win the game, you will come face-to-face with Legend."

Tella swore one of the stars tattooed around Nigel's eyes fell as he finished. It was probably all the ginger smoke and pungent incense addling her brain, giving her visions of living tattoos.

She should have left then. The eyelids on her wrist were more than halfway closed now, and she had the answer she needed—if she won Caraval, she'd finally have Legend's name. But something about Nigel's last words left her with more questions.

"Is what you just said a prophecy, or are you telling me that the prize for the next Caraval is the real Legend?"

"It's a little of both." The tattoos of barbed wire piercing Nigel's lips turned to thorns, and black roses bloomed between them. "Legend is not the prize, but if you win Caraval, the first face you see will be Legend's. He plans to personally give the next winner of Caraval their reward. But, be warned, winning the game will come at a cost you will later regret."

Tella's skin frosted over as the painted eyes on her wrists closed shut, and her mother's familiar warning flashed back: *Once a future is foretold, that future becomes a living thing and it will fight very hard to bring itself about.*

Then it hit her. A wave of fatigue so intense it knocked her down against the cushioned bed. Her head spun and the bones in her legs turned to dust.

"What's happening?" she panted, her breathing abruptly labored as she fought to sit up. Was there more smoke in the room, or was it her vision blurring?

"I probably should have clarified," Nigel said. "The spell on your wrist does not take your ability to sleep, it makes you fall asleep so that you can transfer the rest you receive to me."

"No!" Tella swayed as she pushed up from the bed, vision narrowing until all she could see where glimpses of scoffing tattoos and snickering candlelight. "I don't want to sleep all the way to Valenda."

"I'm afraid it's too late. Next time, do not agree to bargains so easily."

There were shipwrecks more graceful than Tella. As she stumbled away from Nigel's quarters her legs refused to walk a straight line. Her hips continued to bump into walls. Her head knocked against more than one hanging lantern. The journey to her room was so perilous she lost her slippers, yet again. But she was almost there.

The door wobbled before her eyes, one final obstacle to conquer.

Tella focused all her strength to pull it open. And—

Either she'd entered the wrong room, or she'd already begun to dream.

Dante had wings. And, holy mother of saints, they were beautiful—soulless jet-black with midnight-blue veins, the color of lost wishes and fallen stardust. He was turned toward his nightstand washing his face, or maybe he was kissing his reflection in the mirror.

Tella wasn't entirely sure what the arrogant boy was doing. All her blurring eyes could see was that his shirt and coat were gone and a massive pair of inky wings stretched across the ridges of his back.

"You could be an angel of death with those things."

Dante tossed a look over his shoulder. Damp hair the color of black fox fur clung to his forehead. "I've been called many things, but I don't know if anyone has ever said I'm an angel."

"Does that mean you've been called death?" Tella slumped in the doorway, legs finally giving out. She hit the floor with a graceless thud.

A laugh, delicate and light and very female, came from the other side of the room. "I think she swooned at the sight of you."

And *now* she was going to throw up. There was another girl in the room. Tella got a noxious glimpse of a jade-green dress and shining brunette hair before Dante's body stepped into her line of her vision.

He slowly shook his head. "What did—"

Dante's gaze landed on the closed pair of eyes painted on her wrist.

He made a jagged sound that could have been a chuckle. But Tella wasn't sure. Her hearing was nearly as muddled as her head. Her eyes gave up and closed.

"I'm surprised he got to you." Dante's words were very close now, and low.

"I was bored," Tella mumbled. "It seemed like an interesting way to pass the time."

"If that's true you should have just come to me." Dante was definitely laughing now.

. . .

The next several days were a blur of unfortunate hallucinations. Nigel took all of Tella's dreams, but he left her with the nightmares. There were terrifyingly realistic images of her father forever taking off his purple gloves, as well as visions of shadows and shades of dark that did not exist in the mortal world. Cold, damp hands stroked her hair and others ripped out her heart, while bloodless lips drank the marrow from her bones.

Before experiencing death during Caraval, Tella would have said the dreams felt like dying over and over again. But nothing felt like death, except for Death. She should have known better than to think Death wouldn't haunt her after she'd escaped. Tella was amazing; of course Death would want to keep her.

But although she'd dreamed of Death's demons, when Tella came to consciousness, she was greeted by a goddess.

Scarlett stood next to her bed holding a tray of treasure, one laden with cream biscuits, eggs fried in butter, nutmeg custards, thick brown-sugared bacon, and a mug of spicy drinking chocolate.

Tella stole the fattest cream biscuit. She felt groggy, despite sleeping for days, but eating helped. "Have I told you how much I love you?"

"I thought you would be hungry after what happened."

"Scar, I'm sorry, I—"

"There's nothing to apologize for. I understand how easy it is to be tricked by Legend's performers. And everyone on board this ship thinks Nigel took too much from you." Scarlett eyed Tella, as if hoping she'd confess exactly why she'd gone to the fortune-teller.

Although Tella wanted to justify her actions, she sensed this was not the time to bring up the deal she'd made with her friend. Scarlett would be horrified to learn her sister had been writing to a stranger she'd met through Elantine's Most Wanted, which was a shady establishment at best.

Tella had been telling Julian the truth when she'd said she didn't enjoy lying to her sister. Unfortunately, that didn't always prevent her from doing so. Tella kept secrets from Scarlett to protect her from worrying. Their mother's disappearance meant Scarlett stopped being a carefree girl at an early age and became more of a caretaker for Tella. It wasn't fair, and Tella hated adding to the burdens her sister already carried.

But Tella wondered if Scarlett had already found out what she'd done.

Scarlett kept nervously smoothing out wrinkles in her skirt, which seemed to grow more rumpled with every touch. During Caraval, Legend had given Scarlett a magic dress that shifted in appearance—and right now it looked as anxious as Scarlett. Her sleeves had been made of pink lace but now they were turning gray.

Tella took a fortifying sip of chocolate and forced herself to sit up straighter in the bed. "Scar, if you're not upset about the deal I made with Nigel, what's bothering you?"

Scarlett's mouth tilted down. "I wanted to talk to you about Dante."

Damn it all. It wasn't what she'd expected, but it wasn't good, either. Tella had forgotten about passing out in Dante's room. He must have carried Tella back here and Scarlett must have seen him, half-naked and holding Tella close to his chest.

"Scar, I don't know what you're thinking, but I swear there is nothing going on between Dante and me. You know how I feel about boys who are prettier than me."

"So, nothing happened between the two of you after Caraval ended?" Scarlett crossed the small cabin and picked up a pair of silver slippers, the same ones Tella had left in the forest. "He dropped these off last night along with an interesting note."

Tella's stomach turned as she plucked the thin sheaf of paper poking out from one of the shoes.

> *I've been meaning to return these since that night we spent in the forest.*
>
> *—D*

He really was a blackguard. Tella crumpled the note in her fist. Dante must have written it to torment Scarlett for rejecting him during Caraval.

"All right," Tella said. "I confess, Dante and I did kiss the night of the party. But it was terrible, one of the worst kisses I've ever had, definitely not something I would wish to repeat! And I'm so sorry if doing that hurt you, I know he was terrible to you during Caraval."

Scarlett pursed her lips.

Tella had probably taken the lie a little too far. One look at Dante and any girl could tell he knew what to do with his lips.

"I don't care that you kissed him," Scarlett said. "If I'd met him before Julian, I might have ended up kissing him too."

A highly disturbing image popped into Tella's head, and she understood her sister's unease even more acutely. The idea of Scarlett and Dante together made Tella want to threaten him to stay far away from her sister, not that Tella thought it was even a possibility. But if just the notion worried Tella—who was all for Scarlett enjoying herself—she could only imagine how troubled her overprotective sister felt.

"I don't want to control you," Scarlett continued. "We've both experienced enough of that. I just don't want you hurt. Caraval begins tomorrow at midnight, but as I learned during the last game, Legend puts his game pieces in place far in advance." Scarlett shot another uneasy look at the slippers Dante had returned.

"You don't have to worry, Scar." And for once Tella spoke the absolute truth. "I trust Dante even less than I trust most people, and I know better than to let myself get swept away by Caraval."

"I thought you said you weren't going to play."

"Maybe I've changed my mind."

"Tella, I wish you wouldn't." Scarlett smoothed her now completely gray skirts, this time leaving sweaty streaks. "What happened with Nigel reminded me of the more regretful things I experienced. I don't want that for you."

"Then play with me." Tella's words flew out impulsively, but even after giving them a second thought, it felt like a brilliant idea. Tella had watched Caraval from behind the scenes, but her sister had actually played and won. As a team they would be unbeatable. "If we're together, you can make sure I don't get tricked by performers like Nigel again. And I can ensure you'll have fun. We'll take care of each other."

Scarlett's dress immediately perked up, as if it were all for the idea. Its drab gray lace turned raspberry red and spread from her sleeves to her bodice, like attractive armor. Unfortunately, Scarlett still appeared wary. She'd gone from endlessly smoothing her skirts to anxiously wrapping her piece of silver hair around her finger, a streak she'd earned after losing a day of her life in the last Caraval.

Tella considered telling Scarlett the real reason she needed to play and win, but she doubted mentioning their mother would help her cause. Scarlett didn't talk about their mother. Ever. Whenever Tella had tried to talk about Paloma, Scarlett either changed the subject or ignored her completely. Tella used to think it was too difficult for Scarlett, but now Tella thought Scarlett's hurt had turned to hatred for the way their mother had left them.

Tella understood the feeling; she preferred never to talk about their father, and she avoided thinking of him as well.

But their mother wasn't monstrous like their father.

"Crimson"—several knocks rattled the door to their small cabin—"are you in there?"

Scarlett's expression immediately changed at the sound of Julian's voice; worry lines softened to smile lines.

"We've reached Valenda," Julian added. "I came to see if I could carry you and your sister's trunks to the deck."

"If he wants to haul my luggage, please let him in," Tella said.

Scarlett didn't need to be told twice.

The moment she opened the door Julian grinned like a pirate who'd just found his treasure. Tella swore his eyes genuinely smoldered as he looked her sister over.

Scarlett beamed back. So did the lace on her dress, deepening into a fiery shade of red as her skirt went from full to fitted.

Tella slurped her chocolate, loudly, interrupting the couple before their longing looks could shift into lustful kisses. "Julian, please help me out," Tella said. "I'm trying to get Scarlett to partner with me during Caraval."

Julian sobered instantly. His gaze flickered to Tella, suddenly sharp. It was as brief as a flash of lightning, but unmistakably clear. He did not want Scarlett to play the game. And Tella knew exactly why. She should have thought of it herself.

If Scarlett played, she'd learn the truth about Armando—that he'd performed the role of her fiancé in the last Caraval—and both Julian and Tella's lies would be exposed. It would be far worse for Julian than it would be for Tella, but it would be the most painful of all for Scarlett.

"On second thought," Tella said lightly, attempting to correct her mistake, "maybe I should play alone. You'll probably slow me down."

"Too bad. I want to play now." Scarlett's large hazel eyes returned to Julian, glittering in a way they never had back on Trisda. "I just remembered how fun the game could be."

Tella smiled in agreement, but it felt so forced it was hard to hold on to.

Nigel had warned her that if she won the game it would come at a cost she'd later regret. Scarlett had tried to warn her about the game as well. But until this moment Tella hadn't felt the force of either warning. It was one thing to be told about the risks of Caraval, but it was another to see them playing out. Even though the last game was over, her sister hadn't fully escaped.

Tella didn't want to end up like that, and she didn't want to drag Scarlett through anything that might bring her more pain. But if Tella didn't play and win the game, she might never see her mother again.

THE MERIDIAN EMPIRE'S CAPITAL CITY, VALENDA

7

According to the myths, Valenda had once been the ancient city of Alcara, home of the Fates pictured inside every Deck of Destiny. They'd built the city with their magic. Magic so ancient and undiluted, even centuries after the Fates had vanished, remnants of their glowing enchantments remained, turning the hills of Valenda so bright that at night it could illuminate half the Meridian Empire.

Tella didn't know if this entire myth was true, but she believed it as she took her first glimpse of Valenda's twilight port.

A violet sunset cast everything in deep purple shadows and yet the world before her still glittered, from the tips of its primeval ruins, formed of crumbling columns and massive archways, to the concord waters lapping *La Esmeralda*. The rickety piers on her home isle of Trisda looked like brittle bones compared to the thick, living wharfs that stretched before her now, flanked with clippers and schooners waving billowing mermaid-green flags. Some were captained by women sailors, boldly dressed in slick leather skirts and boots that went up to their thighs.

Tella already loved it here.

Her imagination stretched as she craned her neck to look up.

She'd heard there were sky carriages that flew above the hilly city like birds, but it was different to view them in person. They moved through the darkening lavender sky with the grace of painted clouds, bobbing up and down in pops of orchid, topaz, magenta, lilac, corn silk, mint, and other shades Tella had yet to see. They didn't actually fly so much as dangle from thick cords that crisscrossed Valenda's various districts.

"Come on," Scarlett urged, clutching Julian's hand as they started down the crowded dock. "A special group of sky coaches will take us directly to the palace. We don't want to miss them."

Their ship had arrived late, so everyone was moving at a heightened pace. There were lots of *Careful theres* and *Watch yourselfs*. Tella's short legs hurried to keep up as she clutched the tiny trunk in her hands, which held the Aracle along with most of her fortune.

"Pardon me." A wisp of a boy dressed like a courier appeared at the end of the pier. "Are you Miss Donatella Dragna?"

"Yes," Tella answered.

The courier beckoned her toward a group of barrels at the edge of another dock.

Tella wasn't about to follow. She never fully believed her nana's stories about how dangerous the streets of Valenda could be for a girl. But she did know how easily a person could disappear on a dock. All it would take was for someone to drag her onto a ship and shove her belowdecks while heads were turned the other way.

"I need to catch up to my sister," Tella said.

"Please, miss, don't run off. I won't get paid if you leave." The young courier showed her an envelope sealed with a circle of golden wax that formed an intricate combination of daggers and shattered swords. Tella recognized it instantly. *Her friend.*

How did he already know she was in Valenda?

As if answering her question, the luckless coin in Tella's pocket pulsed like a heartbeat. He must have been using it to track her, further proof he was skilled at finding people.

Tella called toward Scarlett and Julian, telling them that she'd catch up later, and slipped onto the other dock with the courier.

Once hidden behind a cluster of heavy barrels, the messenger quickly passed Tella the communiqué and then darted away before Tella could break the seal.

Inside the envelope were two squares. First was a simple sheet covered in familiar writing.

Welcome to Valenda, Donatella—

My apologies for failing to greet you in person, but don't worry, I won't remain a stranger. I'm sure you're as eager to find your mother as I am to learn Legend's name.

Knowing you, I imagine you'll be participating in Caraval, but just in case, I've included an invitation to the first night's festivities.

Bring the coin I gave you to the ball before midnight. Keep it in your palm, and I'll be sure to find you. Don't be late—I will not linger.

Until then,

—A friend

Tella pulled out the other card, revealing a pearlescent page covered in ornate royal-blue ink.

Legend has chosen you to play a game
that may change your destiny.

In honor of Empress Elantine's 75th birthday,

Caraval will visit the streets of Valenda
for six magical nights.

Your journey will begin at the Fated Ball
inside Idyllwild Castle.

The game officially begins at midnight,
on the 30th day of the Growing Season,
and ends at dawn on Elantine's Day.

The thirtieth was the following day.

Far too soon for Tella to meet her friend.

Nigel had said the only way for her to uncover Legend's name was to win Caraval. She needed another week to play—and win—the game. Surely her friend would give her one more week.

But what if he said no and refused to reunite her with her mother?

An unruly wave rocked the dock, but even after it stabilized Tella remained unsteady, as if fate had blinked and the future of her world had reshaped.

Quickly, she set the small trunk in her hands down on the dock. Behind the barrels, she was concealed from view. No one saw her open the trunk, though even if an entire boatload of people had been watching, it might not have stopped her. Tella needed to check the Aracle.

Her fingers usually tingled upon contact, but when she touched the paper rectangle they went numb; *everything* went numb as Tella saw a new image. Her mother was no longer trapped behind prison bars—she was blue-lipped, pale, and dead.

Tella gripped the card so tight it should have crumpled in her hand. But the magical little thing seemed to be indestructible. She sagged against the damp barrels.

Something new must have happened to alter her mother's future. Tella had slept the past four days. The shift shouldn't have been a result of her actions, unless it had something to do with the conversation she'd had with Nigel.

Julian had warned Tella that fortune-tellers like Nigel toyed with the future. Maybe he had sensed something in Tella's destiny that put Legend at risk. Or perhaps Legend wanted to toy with Tella for trying to uncover his most closely guarded secret, and whatever Legend now planned had shifted her mother's fate.

The thought should have frightened her. Legend was not a good person to have as an enemy. But for some twisted reason the idea only made Tella want to play his game more. Now, she just needed to convince her friend to give her another week so she could win Caraval, uncover Legend's name, and save her mother's life.

By the time Tella reached the carriage house, night had covered the city with its cloak. Outside the evening was chilled, but inside the carriage house the air was balmy, hazy with amber lantern light.

Tella walked past stall after stall of colorful coaches, all attached to thick cords that led to every part of the city. The line dedicated to the palace was at the very end. But Scarlett was nowhere in sight. She'd told her sister that she'd catch up later, yet Tella was still surprised Scarlett hadn't waited for her.

The carriage hanging before Tella bobbed as a burly coachman opened an ivory door and directed her into a snug compartment covered in buttery cushions laced with thick royal-blue trim that matched the curtains lining the oval windows.

The only other passenger was a golden-haired young man Tella didn't recognize.

Legend's performers had taken two ships to Valenda, and Tella imagined there were performers working for Legend whom she'd never met. But she suspected this young man was not one of them.

He was only a few years older than her, yet he looked as if he'd spent centuries practicing disinterest. Even his rumpled velvet tailcoat appeared bored as he lounged against the plush leather seats.

Intentionally looking away from Tella, he bit into an intensely white apple. "You can't ride in here."

"Pardon me?"

"You heard me clearly. You need to get out." His drawl was as lazy as his cavalier posture, making Tella think that either he was completely careless, or this young man was so used to people hanging on his words, he didn't even try to sound commanding.

Spoiled nobleman.

Tella had never met an aristocrat she liked. They'd often come to her father for illegal favors, offering him money, but never respect; they all seemed to think their trickle of royal blood made them superior to everyone else.

"If you don't wish to ride with me, you can get out," she said.

The young noble responded with a mild tilt of his golden head, followed by a slow curl of narrow lips as if he'd bitten into a mealy part of his apple.

Just leave the coach, warned a voice in her head. *He's more dangerous than he looks.* But Tella wasn't about to be bullied by a young man too lazy to brush the hair from his bloodshot eyes. She hated it when people used their wealth or title as an excuse to treat others poorly; it reminded her too much of her father. And the carriage was already ascending, flying higher into the night sky with every one of Tella's rapid heartbeats.

"You must be one of Legend's performers." The young man might have laughed, but it sounded too cruel for Tella to be sure. He leaned across the intimate space, filling the carriage with the sharp scent of apples and irritation. "I wonder if you could help me with something I've been curious about," he continued. "I've heard Legend's performers never truly die. So maybe I'll push you out to see if the rumors are true?"

Tella didn't know if the young man's threat was serious, but it was too tempting to hold back from saying, "Not if I shove you out first."

This earned her a flash of dimples that might have been charming, yet somehow they managed to look unkind, like a winking gemstone in the hilt of a double-edged sword. Tella couldn't decide if his features were too sharp to be attractive, or if he was just the sort of handsome that hurt to look at, the devastating type of lovely that would slit your throat while you were busy staring into its cold quicksilver eyes.

"Careful, pet. You might be one of the empress's guests, but many in her court are not as forgiving as I am. And I'm not forgiving at all."

Crunch. Sharp teeth took another bite of his white apple before he let it slip from his fingers and drop onto her slippers.

Tella kicked the apple back in his direction, and pretended she wasn't concerned in the least that he'd act on his threat. She even went so far as to turn her head away from him and toward the window while their carriage continued to skate above the city. It must have worked; from the corner of her gaze she saw the young man close his eyes as they passed over Valenda's renowned districts.

Some districts were more infamous than others, like the Spice Quarter, where rumors claimed deliciously illicit items could be found, or the Temple District, where various religions were practiced—supposedly there was even a Church of Legend.

It was too dark to distinctly see anything, but Tella continued to look until the carriage began its descent toward the palace and she could finally make out more than dim starry-eyed lights sparkling up at the sky.

All she could think was, *The storybooks lied.*

Tella had never cared much for castles or palaces. Scarlett was the sister who'd fantasized about being whisked away by a rich nobleman or a young king to a secluded stone fortress. To Scarlett, castles were bastions of safety offering protection. Tella saw them as fancy prisons, perfect for watching, controlling, and punishing. They were larger versions of her father's suffocating estate on Trisda, no better than a cage.

But as her coach continued its slow, downward drop, Tella wondered if she'd been too hasty with her judgments.

She'd always pictured castles to be things of gray stone and mold and musty corridors, but Elantine's bejeweled palace set fire to the night like treasure snatched from a dragon's lair.

She thought she heard the young nobleman snort, probably at some dazzled expression she'd made. But Tella didn't care. In fact, she pitied him if he couldn't appreciate the beauty.

Elantine's palace sat atop Valenda's highest hill. In the center of it, her famed golden tower burned beacon-bright in shades of copper and blazing coral. Regal and straight, until near the top where the structure arched like a crown, it was a mirror image of Tower Lost from Decks of Destiny. Tella held her breath. It was the tallest building she'd ever seen, and somehow it looked alive. It ruled like an ageless monarch, presiding over five arching jeweled wings, which stretched out from the tower like the points of a star. And Tella would get to live inside of this star for a week.

No longer feeling as exhausted, she practically bounced in her seat as the coach finally landed.

Across from her the lazing nobleman ignored her as she slipped out the door into the cavernous carriage house.

Tella wondered if she was the last to arrive. The only sound she heard was the heavy cranking of the notched wheels that moved the carriage lines. She didn't see any of Legend's performers or her sister. But in between the lines of rocking coaches there were a number of armor-clad, expressionless guards.

One guard shadowed Tella's every move, the clink of his armor following her, as she left the carriages and entered the empress's luscious grounds. Legend's performers might have been Elantine's guests, but as Tella passed timeworn stone gardens and elaborate topiaries, she had a sudden impression that the empress didn't trust her visitors. It made Tella wonder why she'd invited them to stay in the palace and perform for her birthday.

Tella had heard that when she was younger Empress Elantine had had a wild streak. She'd snuck into the forbidding Spice Quarter and pretended to be a commoner so she could have all sorts of scandalous adventures and romantic trysts. Unfortunately, for most of Tella's life, the empress had been known to be far less daring. Perhaps inviting Legend's performers here was her way of being reckless once again. But Tella doubted it; someone who ruled as long as Elantine didn't do so with thoughtless abandon.

Somehow the inside of the palace was even more magnificent than its jewel-bright exterior. Everything was impossibly large, as if the Fates had built it merely to show off their might, and then simply left it behind when they'd disappeared. Glittering lapis floors reflected Tella's entrance as she passed blue quartz columns larger than oak trees and crystalline oil lamps as tall as people.

Up and down the massive marble staircase, servants flitted about like flurries of snowflakes, but again Tella saw no signs of her sister or any other performers.

"Welcome." A woman dressed in a proud shade of blue stepped in front of Tella. "I'm head matron of the sapphire wing."

"Donatella Dragna. I'm here with Legend's performers, and I fear I'm a little late."

"I'd actually say you're very late," the matron told her, but she spoke with a smile, which gave Tella a bit of relief as the woman looked down at the list in her hands, softly humming. Until slowly the pleasant sound faded and stopped.

Her smile disappeared next. "Could you repeat your name once more?"

"It's Donatella Dragna."

"I see a Scarlett Dragna."

"That's my sister."

The woman looked up, eyes briefly darting to the guard who'd escorted Tella in. "Your sister might be a welcome guest, but I'm afraid I don't have you written down. Are you certain you were invited?"

8

No. Tella hadn't been invited to the palace, but if Scarlett was on the list, Tella should have been too. Legend was playing with her. He must have removed her from the guest list after Tella's conversation with Nigel.

She took a deep breath, refusing to be nervous, but she imagined every servant in the wing could hear the pounding of her heart. It would be so easy for the guard who'd escorted her there to toss her out into the night. No one would even notice right away, given how often Tella intentionally disappeared, and that she'd already been separated from Scarlett along with everyone else she knew in Valenda.

"My sister," Tella said, "she's staying here. I could share her room."

"That would be unacceptable," the matron answered, more stiffly than before.

"I don't see why it matters," Tella said. "If anything my sister would prefer it."

"And who is your sister? Is she a royal monarch with a fifth of the world at her fingertips?"

Tella bit back from saying something that would only have her tossed out faster. "What about one of the other wings?" she asked sweetly. "There must be one empty room in such a large palace."

"Even if there were rooms, you are not on the guest list, so you cannot stay."

At her words the guard stalked closer, armor echoing across the exquisite foyer.

It took everything Tella had to keep from raising her voice. Instead she forced her lips to tremble and her eyes to turn watery. "Please, I have nowhere else to go," she begged, hoping the woman had a heart somewhere beneath her starched dress. "Just find my sister and let me stay with her."

The matron's lips pinched, appraising Donatella in all her pathetic splendor. "I can't let you stay here, but perhaps there's a free cot or nest in the servants' quarters."

The guard shadowing her snickered.

Tella's heart sank even further. *A nest in the servants' quarters?*

"Excuse me." The low voice rumbled directly behind her, a rough brush against the back of Tella's neck.

Her stomach dipped and tied a knot.

Only one person's voice did that to Tella.

Casually Dante came up to her side. A silhouette of sharp raven-wing black, from his perfect dark suit to the ink tattooing his hands. The only light came from the shimmer in his amused eyes. "Having a problem with your room?"

"Not at all." Tella willed her cheeks not to flush with embarrassment, hoping he'd not overheard the conversation. "There's just a tiny mix-up, but it's been resolved."

"What a relief. I thought I heard her say she was putting you in the servants' quarters."

"That's only if there's room," the matron said.

Tella could have turned mortified-green and sunk into the lapis floor, but to her shock Dante, who usually enjoyed laughing at her, didn't so much as tilt the corner of his mouth in diversion. Instead he turned the full force of his brutal gaze on the matron. "Do you know who this young lady is?"

"I beg your pardon," said the matron, "who are you?"

"I oversee all of Legend's performers." Dante's voice was full of more arrogance than usual. The type of tone that made it impossible for Tella to discern if he was speaking the truth or making up a lie. "You do not want to put her in the servants' quarters."

"Why is that?" asked the matron.

"She's engaged to the heir to the throne of the Meridian Empire."

The woman's brows drew together warily. Tella's might have done the same, but she instantly covered her surprise with the sort of haughty expression she imagined a royal heir's fiancée might wear.

Of course, Tella didn't even know who the current heir was.

Elantine had no children, and her heirs were killed off faster than the news could travel to Tella's former home on Trisda. But Tella didn't care who her fake fiancé was, as long as it kept her from sleeping in a nest.

Unfortunately, the matron still looked skeptical. "I didn't know His Highness had a new fiancée."

"It's a secret," Dante responded flawlessly. "I believe he's planning on announcing the engagement at his next party. So I'd recommend not saying anything. I'm sure you've heard what his temper is like."

The woman went stiff. Then her eyes darted from Dante to Tella. Clearly she didn't trust either of them, but her fear of the heir's temper must have outweighed her good judgment.

"I'll check again to see if there's another room available," she said. "We're full for the celebration, but perhaps someone we expected hasn't arrived."

The moment she left, Dante turned back to Tella, leaning close so that no eavesdropping servants could hear. "Don't rush to thank me."

Tella supposed she did owe him a bit of gratitude. Yet the exchange coated her with the thick sensation that Dante was doing her the opposite of a favor. "I can't figure out if you've just saved me or landed me in an even more unfortunate situation."

"I found you a room, didn't I?"

"You've also given me a bad-tempered fiancé."

One corner of his full mouth lifted. "Would you rather have pretended to be my fiancée? I considered saying that, but I didn't think that would be the best choice since—what was it you said to your sister?" He tapped a finger against his smooth chin. "Ah yes, when we kissed it was terrible, one of the worst, definitely not something you would wish to repeat."

Tella felt the color drain from her face. God's blood! Dante was absolutely shameless. "You were spying!"

"I didn't need to. You were loud."

Tella should have said she hadn't meant it—*he had to have known she hadn't meant it*—but the last thing she wanted was to boost Dante's pride. "So this is revenge?"

He leaned even closer. Tella couldn't discern if the humor had left his gaze or if it had just shifted into something deeper and darker and a little more dangerous. His warm fingers intentionally skimmed the length of her collarbone. Her breathing hitched. Yet she didn't pull away, even as his eyes became nearly level with hers, coming so close she could feel the sweep of his lashes.

"Let's just say we're even now." His lips moved to the corner of her mouth.

Then, right before making contact, he pulled away. "I wouldn't wish to repeat something so unpleasant for you."

Without another word, Dante strutted off, his wide shoulders shaking, as if he were laughing.

Tella burned. After what Dante had just done, they were far from even.

The matron returned several rapid heartbeats later, with a smile tighter than fresh stitches. "It seems we have an available suite in Elantine's golden tower."

Tella swallowed a gasp. Maybe Dante had done her a favor after all.

Next to the city's numerous ruins, Elantine's golden tower was the oldest structure in the Empire. Rumored to have walls made of pure gold and all sorts of secret passages for monarchs to sneak out of, many believed it wasn't just a replica of Tower Lost from the Decks of Destiny but that it was the actual tower, with dormant magic hidden inside it.

"Guests are not normally allowed in the tower," the matron said as she led Tella from the sapphire wing into a glass courtyard, where fancifully dressed clusters of people meandered under opalescent arches and crystal trees with silver leaves. Unfamiliar with palace culture, having grown up on an unrespected conquered isle, Tella wondered if they were part of Elantine's court, or if these were some other guests that the matron had mentioned.

"You're not to have any visitors," the matron continued. "Not even your fiancé is welcome inside your room."

Tella might have said she'd never dream of letting a boy enter her room, but it was probably best not to pile too many lies on top of each other or they might all come tumbling down.

At the end of the courtyard there was only one set of doors to the golden tower, so grandiose and heavy it took three sentries to pull each one open.

Tella didn't realize the guard from the carriage house still followed her until he was stopped as Tella and the matron were both let through. Either word of Tella's *engagement* had traveled swiftly through the palace, or this head matron was as important as she thought herself. Tella hoped for the latter, knowing as soon as the real heir discovered her ruse, she'd certainly be exposed and kicked out of the palace—or worse. Until then she'd decided to enjoy the charade.

Contrary to the stories, the inside of the tower wasn't golden; it was old. Even the air smelled archaic, full of forgotten stories and bygone words. On the lower level there were aged stone pillars formed of chipped columns, and decorative capitals carved to look like two-faced women, all lit by crackling black torches that smelled of incense and spells.

From there, the matron shepherded her up floor after creaking floor, each one as old as the first. The door they finally stopped in front of looked so aged, one touch and Tella imagined it might fall off the hinges.

No wonder guests never stayed in here.

"A guard will be posted outside your door at all times." The matron rang the bell around her neck, summoning a sentry in striking white metal armor. "I'd hate to see anything happen to you as the heir's fiancée!"

"For some reason, I don't believe that's true," Tella said.

The matron's smile returned, spreading slowly, like a stain. "At least you're sharper than you look. But if you really are engaged to the heir, then it's not Her Majesty's guards you should fear."

"I actually don't believe in fearing anything." Tella shut the door, leaving the woman in the hall before she could say another pointed word, or Tella could blurt out more things she shouldn't.

It wasn't smart to upset servants. Of course, it also wasn't wise to lie about being a royal heir's fiancée. She'd have to pay Dante back for that one.

Though, to his credit, he had garnered her a fantastic suite. The tower might have been a relic, but her rooms were marvelous.

Moonlight flooded in through the windows, casting everything in a dreamy glow. Someone had already set a tray of good-night sweets atop one of the sitting room's dainty glass tables. Tella plucked a star-shaped cookie as she wandered past two white stone fireplaces into a lavish bedroom covered in carpets of glory blue. They matched the heavy curtains hanging from the inviting canopy bed. Tella wanted to collapse atop it and sleep all her troubles away.

But she needed to write Scarlett first and let her know she was—

Two voices tripped out of the corner.

Tella's eyes cut to a cracked door in the crook of the room, which likely led to the bathing room.

She heard the whispers again. Servants, who must have been unaware Tella was there. One voice was light and chirping, the other warm and soft, making her think of a petite bird talking to a plump bunny rabbit.

"I honestly feel sorry for her," said the bunny girl.

"You're saying you wouldn't want to be engaged to the heir?" chirped the birdy one. "Have you seen him?"

"I don't care what he looks like. He's a murderer. Everyone knows there were seventeen people between him and Empress Elantine's throne. Then one by one all the other heirs died in horrific ways."

"But that doesn't mean the current one killed them all."

"I don't know," murmured the bunny. "I heard he's not even part of the noble bloodline, but he's murdered so many people the real heir won't step forward."

"You're ridiculous, Barley!" The bird girl squawked out a laugh. "You shouldn't believe every rumor you hear."

"What about the rumor that he killed his last fiancée?"

Both maids went abruptly quiet.

In the tense silence Tella thought she heard Death's rasping laugh. It grated like rusty metal sawing into bone. The same exact sound had greeted her as she'd plunged from that awful balcony during Caraval. A gruesome welcome to a hideous kingdom. Now it served as a chilling reminder that she'd once been Death's, and he wanted her back.

Tella was going to kill Dante. Slowly. With her hands.

Or maybe Tella would use her gloves to kill him—she'd tie the sheaths of satin around his throat—then she would use her naked hands to finish off the job. Not only had the brooding bastard given her a fake fiancé with a bad temper, he'd chosen a murderous one. Tella might have been able to appreciate how well constructed his petty vengeance was if she'd not been the subject of it.

Tella continued to think of different ways to harm or embarrass Dante as she stumbled out of bed the next morning. She could find him that night at the ball, when Caraval began, and accidentally spill wine all over him. Of course, since Dante was so fond of black, that might be a waste of wine, and most likely just make her appear clumsy.

Maybe she could make him jealous instead, by looking stunning, and arriving on the arm of some handsome boy. But Tella doubted she had enough time to find a handsome young man to go with her to the ball, and making Dante jealous really should have been her furthest concern.

Tella needed to focus on meeting her friend before midnight and convincing him to give her an extra week to play Caraval and uncover Legend's name.

Then she'd see her mother again.

It'd been so long Tella could no longer recall the sound of

Paloma's voice, but she knew it was both sweet and strong, and sometimes Tella missed it so much she wanted nothing more than to hear it again.

"Miss Dragna." A sentry knocked heavily on her door. "A package has arrived."

"Give me one minute." Tella searched for her trunks, needing to dress, but apparently they'd either been lost or they weren't allowed inside of the tower. All she possessed was the ugly little trunk she'd carried with her off the boat, and she'd not put any fresh clothes inside it.

Tella opened the door once she'd finished slipping on her gown from the day before.

The guard's entire face was hidden behind a pearly white box as tall as a wedding cake, topped with an oversize velvet bow as thick as frosting.

"Who sent this?" Tella asked.

"There's a note." The guard set the box atop a tufted chaise the color of harbor light.

The instant he left, Tella removed a sheer vellum envelope. Her skin didn't prickle with magic, but something felt *not right.* Though the entire package was as white as chaste kisses and pure intentions, the sitting room felt darker since the gift had entered. The sun's shine no longer poured through the windows, leaving dimness that turned all the elegant furniture to wary shades of green.

Tella cautiously opened the envelope. The letter was covered in heavy black script.

MY DEAREST FIANCÉE,

WHAT A SURPRISE IT WAS TO HEAR OF YOUR ARRIVAL—AND I'D FEARED I'D HAVE NO ONE TO DANCE WITH AT THE FATED BALL TONIGHT. I HOPE YOU DON'T MIND THAT I'VE CHOSEN A GOWN FOR YOU TO WEAR. I WANT TO BE SURE I CAN SPOT YOU IMMEDIATELY. I'D RATHER NOT HAVE TO HUNT YOU DOWN BEFORE WE OFFICIALLY ANNOUNCE OUR ENGAGEMENT.

UNTIL THEN,

There was no signature, but Tella knew who the letter was from. *Elantine's heir.* It seemed he had spies in the palace.

Nothing good could come from this.

With clammy fingers, Tella tore the lid from the box, half expecting to a find a funeral frock or some other monstrous creation. But to her astonishment the gown didn't resemble anything remotely threatening. It looked like a fantasy a garden had cried.

The skirt was indulgent and full, formed of massive twirls of skyfall-blue peonies. Real peonies. They brimmed with sweet, clean fragrance, each one of them unique, from the subtle shifts in hue to the size of the blooms. Some were still tucked into tight periwinkle buds, not quite ready for the world, while others had exploded into bursts of lively petals. Tella pictured herself leaving a trail of blue flower petals as she danced.

The bodice appeared even more ethereal, such a pale shade of blue it was practically sheer, covered in the front by intricate sapphire beadwork that grew into ropes of necklaces, which hung across an otherwise bare back.

She shouldn't have considered wearing it.

But it was magnificent and regal. Tella imagined what Dante's face would look like when she showed up to the ball looking like the heir's true fiancée.

This would be the perfect revenge.

Tella reread the note that accompanied the dress. Knowing it was from the heir made it feel like a threat. But nothing about it was actually menacing. He sounded more curious than anything—perhaps he was impressed by the audacity of her claim and merely wanted to meet her. It still felt like a risk to wear the gown, but as Tella liked to tell her sister, there was more to life than staying safe.

Though Tella wondered if she wasn't taking a few too many risks that night.

Right after hanging up the dress, another guard knocked and delivered a letter from her sister.

Dearest Tella,

I was so relieved to hear you made it safely to the palace, and more than a little surprised to learn they placed you in the golden tower—I can't wait to hear how that happened!

I hope you don't mind, I've agreed to spend the afternoon with Julian. But I still plan on going with you to the Fated Ball for the start of Caraval. I'll meet you at the stone garden outside the carriage house an hour before midnight.

Love,

Scarlett

It was wrong that this letter concerned her more than the missive from the heir. But Tella had nearly forgotten asking Scarlett to play the game with her. She'd done it before learning she'd need to meet her friend at the ball.

Tella deflated against the bed. This would complicate things.

Unless Tella confessed all of her secrets to Scarlett.

It was a terrifying thought. Scarlett wouldn't be pleased to learn she'd been deceived by Armando during Caraval, or that Tella had been searching for their mother. And Tella couldn't even guess what her sister would think about Tella's new fake fiancé. But Scarlett was the most loyal person Tella knew: She would be upset, but it wouldn't prevent Scarlett from helping Tella win the game.

And Tella needed to win the game.

10

Night and his mistress the moon were both out to play when Tella reached the starlit stone garden where she was supposed to meet Scarlett before beginning their grand adventure.

The Fated Ball at Idyllwild Castle marked the official beginning of Caraval. But that night there'd be celebrations all over the city. At each one, the first sets of clues would be distributed so that people from across Valenda could play.

Even the air buzzed with anticipation and excitement. Tella could feel it licking her skin, as if it wanted to drink in her frenzied emotions as well.

Tella wasn't usually anxious. She liked the thrill that came with taking risks. She loved the feeling of doing something bold enough to make her future hold its breath while she closed her eyes and reveled in the sensation that she'd made a choice with the power to alter the course of her life. It was the closest she ever came to holding real power.

But, Tella also knew not every gamble paid off.

She'd spent all day thinking about it as she explored the palace grounds in a failed search for rumored secret passages. She felt mostly certain tonight would go as planned. Scarlett would understand when Tella confessed all of her secrets. Tella's friend would then give her a week to play the game and uncover Legend's name, so she could erase the terrible future that the Aracle had showed, and finally find out who her mother really was and why she'd left so many years ago.

Tella had succeeded at far more complicated plots and yet she could not shake the growing premonition that all her plans were about to unravel.

She ran her fingers over the luckless coin concealed in her pocket. Her friend said that he would be sure to find her as long as she had the coin, and Tella wondered if he was already at Idyllwild Castle searching for her.

Perhaps the heir was looking for her as well.

Tella released a nervous laugh. She was definitely in over her head, but at least she'd soon have her sister with her.

In the distance a bell sang out, marking the time as a quarter past eleven. Less than one hour left until Caraval officially began. Tella was running out of time.

Her friend had wanted her at the party before midnight.

But Scarlett was nowhere in sight.

A few skyfall-blue petals rained from Tella's flowering gown as she shot an uneasy look around the garden, hoping for a glimpse of one of her sister's cherry dresses. But Tella's only companions were the immobile statues.

The legends claimed that at one point during the Fates' indomitable rule, the statues in Elantine's stone garden had been real people. Mostly outdoor servants, going about their palace duties, pruning shrubs, picking flowers, and sweeping paths, when, for no fault of their own, they'd been turned to stone.

It was said the Undead Queen had done it. Apparently she didn't believe the current sculptures looked lifelike enough, so she asked another Fate to transform a group of servants into statues.

Tella looked into the wide stone eyes of a young maid, imagining that her panic now mirrored Tella's own.

It wasn't like Scarlett to be tardy.

Unless her sister wasn't coming, or something had happened to her.

Nervously Tella went to the edge of the garden, craning her head toward the hedge-lined path back to the palace. She might have started down it to try to find her sister, but another person was already on it.

Dante.

Tella's already anxious stomach did another flip.

He'd traded in the black clothes he seemed to favor for nevermore gray. But his tall boots and the silk cravat around his neck were both deep shades of blue-black smoke, matching the curls of ink on his ungloved fingers. He looked like a freshly woken storm, or a beautiful nightmare come to life so he could personally haunt her.

Tella considered darting behind one of the statues. He was supposed to spot her from far away at the ball. He was supposed to be dazzled by her extravagant gown, and jealous when he spied her flirting with another man. He was not supposed to see her nervously standing in a garden by herself.

She hoped he'd walk right by the statues without noticing her. But Dante's gaze had already found her. It took hold of Tella like a pair of hands wrapping around her waist and holding her in place as he approached. His shadowed eyes took their time trailing from her unbound hair to the ribbon tied around her throat, where they darkened and rested a full second before dropping.

Tella didn't usually blush, but she felt a rush of color find her cheeks.

Dante looked up and gave her a fallen star's smile. "You should always wear flowers."

A few of the shyer blossoms on her gown finally bloomed, and Tella met Dante's eyes with one of her most dazzling smiles. "I'm not wearing these for you. The dress was a gift from my fiancé."

Dante's eyebrows arched, but it wasn't with the jealousy she'd hoped for. He eyed the gown as if it were something filthy, and then he looked at Tella as if she'd gone completely mad. "You need to be more careful with what you say."

"Why's that? Are you jealous and afraid someone other than a matron might actually believe me? Or are you suddenly nervous because Elantine's heir—the fiancé *you* gave me—is a murderous fiend who might kill me for claiming we're engaged?"

Before Dante could answer, Tella swept past him, toward the path to the palace and hopefully her sister. It was now half past eleven and growing closer to midnight. She needed—

"Donatella." Dante snatched her wrist before she could take a second step. "Just tell me you're not going to the Fated Ball at Idyllwild Castle."

"That would be a lie."

Dante's fingers tensed around her wrist. "There are other parties. You shouldn't be going to that one."

"Why not?" Tella pulled away. "I enjoy drinking and dancing, and even you acknowledged that I look rather spectacular." She did a half twirl, letting the petals of her skirt brush against his polished boots.

Dante gave her a look so withering the flowers that had just swept his trousers retreated back into buds. "Idyllwild Castle belongs to Elantine's heir. Do you know what will happen to you there if he discovers you're claiming to be his fiancée?"

"No, but it might be interesting to find out." She flashed an impish smile.

A line of frustrated red started up Dante's neck. "Elantine's heir is unhinged; he hasn't just killed the other heirs—he's murdered anyone who he's believed might get in his way to the throne. If he suspects for a second you're one of those people, he will end you, too."

Tella resisted the urge to flinch or cower. A part of her recognized that wearing the dress and risking the heir's attention might have been a poor idea, but it rattled Dante, so Tella refused to think of it as a mistake.

"Isn't everything you just described what you wanted to happen when you told your lie?"

Silence followed and a fresh chill ripped through the garden, making Tella suddenly aware of how cold the night had grown. Unseasonably cold, as if the weather were taking Dante's side and warning Tella to go back inside Elantine's palace.

"You looked pathetic," Dante finally said. "I wanted to help, but I was also upset with you for what you'd said on the boat, so I picked the worst person I could imagine without thinking it through." He didn't tell her he was sorry, but his thick brows creased and his eyes tipped into something that looked like genuine regret. People tossed around the word *sorry* far too easily, as if it were worth even less than the promise of a copper. Tella rarely believed it, but she found she believed this. Probably because it was the sort of thing she would have done.

"Now this is an interesting pairing." Armando strode into the garden tapping a fashionable silver walking stick against several of the more frightened-looking statues.

"What do you want?" Dante asked.

"I was going to ask you a similar question." The elegant accent Armando had used to play the count during Caraval was replaced by a raspier voice as he angled his perfectly groomed head from Tella to Dante, and said, "I thought you were interested in the prudish sister."

Tella's hand worked on instinct, pulling back and slapping Armando across his face. "You don't get to talk about my sister, ever."

Armando lifted a gloved hand to his purpling jaw. "I wish you'd given me that warning an hour ago. Your sister slaps even harder than you do."

Alarm flooded Tella. "You talked to her."

"It seems she didn't fully understand the concept that Caraval is only a game. Pretty, but not terribly bright."

"Watch it," Dante warned. "I'll do more than slap you."

Armando's sharp emerald eyes lit up with amusement. "You must really like this one, or does Legend have you working her the way Julian worked her sister?"

Tella could have smacked him again, but Armando was already gliding backward.

"A word of advice before tonight's party: Don't repeat the mistakes your sister made in the last game. And you might not want to wait around for her, either." Armando continued to the exit as he said, "She wasn't pleased to find out I wasn't her real fiancé. When I left her and poor Julian, their conversation was heated; I don't imagine it will simmer until after the ball."

"Filthy, wretched—" Tella loosed a string of inelegant curses at his disappearing back. She knew nothing could really be believed during Caraval, but she was convinced that even when he wasn't acting, Armando was as vile as the roles he played. "I'm going to pray that angels come down and cut out his tongue."

Dante's gaze traveled skyward, and Tella swore more than one star blinked out of existence as he said, "I'm sure many would thank you for that."

Tella still fumed. "Why does Legend even keep him around?"

"Every good story needs a villain."

"But the best villains are the ones you secretly like, and my nana always said Legend was the villain in Caraval."

Dante's lips twisted into something like a smirk. "Of course she did."

"Are you saying she was lying?"

"Everyone either wants Legend, or wants to be Legend. The only way to keep innocent young girls from running off to find him is to tell them he's a monster. But that doesn't mean it's all a lie." Dante's lips widened into a taunting smile and his dark eyes shimmered as they returned to Tella.

The scoundrel was teasing her. Or perhaps he was Legend and couldn't resist talking about how others were so obsessed with him. Dante was definitely handsome and arrogant enough to be Legend, but Tella imagined the master of Caraval had more important things to do on the first night of the game than torment her.

Another bell rang in the distance. Midnight would approach in fifteen minutes. If Tella didn't leave at this moment she would be late to meet her friend.

It felt wrong not to run back to Scarlett; Tella could only imagine how upset her sister must have been to learn how deeply Armando, and everyone else, had deceived her during Caraval. Tella hadn't wanted her to find out this way. But Tella's friend was already at the ball, and in his letter he'd said he would not wait past midnight.

Tella did not enjoy the idea of abandoning her sister. But Scarlett would forgive her, and the same could not be said for her friend if Tella arrived late.

"As delightful as this rendezvous has been," she told Dante, "I'm tardy for a party, and I imagine you have a job to do."

Before he could attempt to stop her, she loped toward the garden's exit. More stars winked out as Tella made her way to the glowing carriage house, where a servant helped her inside of a topaz coach still smelling of its last rider's perfume.

Dante slid in right behind her.

"Will you please stop following me?"

"Maybe Armando was being honest, for once, and it's my job to follow you." Dante stretched out in the seat across from her, his long legs practically filling all the empty space between them.

"You know what I think?" Tella said. "You want an excuse to spend the evening with me."

Dante's mouth formed a wry smile as he slowly ran a wide thumb over his lower lip. "I hate to break your heart, but I think of girls the way I imagine you think of ball gowns; it's never a good idea to wear the same one more than once."

If Tella could have shoved him out of the carriage and replaced him with the spoiled nobleman from the other day, she would have. Instead she gave him her sweetest smile.

"What a coincidence, that's the same way I see young men."

Dante held her gaze for a moment and then he laughed, the same deliciously low sound that always made her stomach tumble.

Attempting to ignore him, Tella turned toward the window as the box lifted into the lightless night.

She didn't know where the stars had gone, but somewhere in between the garden and the carriage they'd vanished, turning the sky into an ocean of dark. Sooty and black and—

The night shimmered.

In between one moment and the next the world exploded with silver.

Tella shot her gaze toward the carriage window just in time to see the lost stars return. Glowing brighter than before, they danced into new constellations. She counted more than a dozen, all forming the same bewitching image—a sun with a starburst inside and a glittering teardrop inside of the star. The symbol of Caraval.

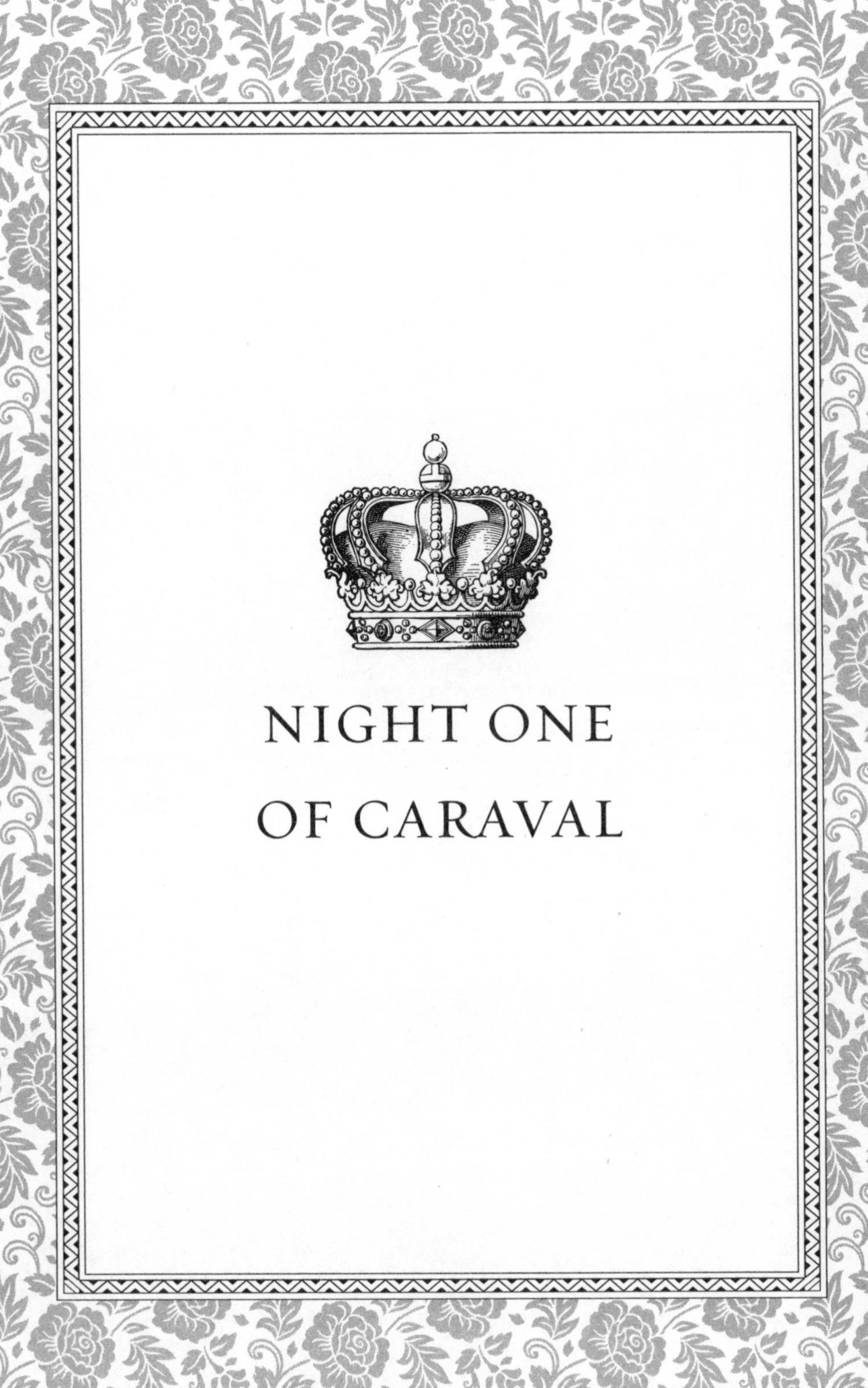

NIGHT ONE
OF CARAVAL

11

Tella once heard that during another performance Legend had changed the color of the sky. But she'd not thought he was powerful enough to wrangle the stars.

According to myths, the stars weren't merely distant lights, they were beings older than the Fates, as terrible and powerful as they were mesmerizing and magical. And somehow Legend had manipulated them all.

"I'm surprised Legend doesn't do this to the sky every night," Tella said.

"He probably would if he could." Dante's tone was matter-of-fact, but Tella thought she glimpsed something deepen in his eyes as he looked out of the carriage window. "Magic can be fueled by time, blood, and emotions. Because of the hopes and dreams of those attending Caraval, Legend's power is at its peak during the game. The constellations should re-form every night. Tonight the symbols rest above the different parties and balls marking the start of Caraval, but tomorrow there will be only one constellation, to guide the participants toward the district where the next set of clues is hidden."

Tella might not have officially played the game before, but she knew the basics of how it worked. The first rule to remember was that Caraval was only a game. It took place at night, and at the beginning of the game everyone was given the same clue to start them on a journey, which would lead them toward other clues and eventually the prize. Scarlett had needed to find five clues during the last Caraval, and Tella imagined something similar would be true for this game.

But first she needed to locate her friend.

The carriage made a rocky landing, or perhaps it was Tella's heart as she heard the last of twelve bells ringing in the midnight hour.

She slipped the luckless coin from her pocket to her hand, praying it would let her friend know she'd arrived to Idyllwild Castle just in time.

Holding the coin tight, she scanned the grounds for her friend, but she didn't know anything about his appearance. All she saw were crackling torches circling a raised castle that looked trapped somewhere between a ruin and a fantasy. The crumbling white sandstone gleamed beneath Legend's temporary constellations, showing off ancient battlements, crumbling parapet walks, and fanciful towers lined in vines of black-tipped red roses.

The gleaming fortress could have been borrowed from a young girl's dream, yet Tella noticed the moat surrounding it contained waters so dark they didn't reflect any of Legend's stars. She wondered if it was because the fanciful exterior of the castle was merely a magical glamour, or if the stars were one of Legend's illusions and Tella had been tricked by them.

Only minutes into the game, and already Tella was questioning what was real and what wasn't.

She peered back toward the water, looking for her friend again, or for a boat to reach the castle, but it seemed there was only one path to the fortress—a highly arched, narrow bridge of interlocking diamond-shaped stones.

"Searching for your fiancé?" Dante asked.

"Careful," Tella warned, "you sound jealous."

"I'm hoping you'll come to your senses," Dante said. "This is your last chance to turn around. Our host doesn't like to make it easy for people to come or go."

"Then it's a good thing I enjoy a challenge."

"It seems we finally agree on something." Dante tucked Tella's arm into the solid crook of his elbow, as if silently accepting a dare.

"I thought you didn't like wearing the same girl to a party twice." Tella boldly met his eyes.

Dante's coal-dark gaze shined with something wicked as he leaned down, warm lips brushing her hair and making other traitorous parts of her jealous as he said, "I do whatever my job requires."

Cocky son of a witch.

Tella should have pulled away, but up close the bridge was even narrower than it appeared from afar and without any rails—exactly like the balcony she'd leaped from during Caraval. The fall that had killed her.

Her fingers dug deeper into Dante's arm. She hoped he'd think of it as part of the little games they played. That he wouldn't detect any lingering terror as she asked him a question, in need of a distraction before her legs ceased working, or her lungs stopped breathing. "So what does Legend want with me now?"

"I can't tell you."

"But you can say that he tasked you to follow me?"

"I didn't say that, only that he might have. Maybe you were right in the carriage, and I want to spend the evening with you. Maybe I think you were lying to your sister about our kisses in the forest, and I plan to prove it."

Dante gave her a smile so dissolute and devastating, Tella swore it made the bridge a little weak. But she couldn't let it make her weak. Too much was at stake tonight, and she'd already kissed him once.

"Even if I chose to believe you, I'd have to remind you that I have a fiancé and I'm not inclined to cheat."

Dante's glorious smile vanished the instant she said "fiancé."

Tella grinned and patted him on his arm, about to finally pull away when they reached the top of the bridge.

Holy saints. Her breath caught, trapped like a bird inside of her throat. The bridge had narrowed and she swore they were higher up than she had ever been in her life, with no rails or net or anything but merciless waters to capture her if she slipped and fell. She fought to take another step, but everything she saw made her faint, lightheaded, dizzy.

And was it just her, or did the torches around Idyllwild Castle now reek of sulfur, as if Death himself had decided to stoke their flames, another reminder he was always watching, waiting to take her back?

"Don't think about it," Dante warned.

"I'm not going to jump," Tella said.

"That's not what I was saying." His lips moved to her ear. "I've died more times than I can remember. Every time, I used to fear I wouldn't come back, until I learned that it's the fear that feeds him. It's the same way hopes and dreams give Legend so much power during Caraval."

"I'm not afraid of death." But even as she said the words, Tella looked down and, to her horror, found her arm clinging much tighter to Dante's.

He pet her arm once, mocking and indulgent.

But Tella wasn't about to let him win whatever competition they were playing.

"I'm just not fond of cages," she said, "and this places looks like one giant dungeon."

He laughed, quietly. Different from the rich sound he'd made in the carriage. Tella wasn't sure why, but she sensed she'd find out the reason for his subtle amusement as soon as they entered the party.

Tella thought she knew what to expect inside of Idyllwild Castle.

She'd been to Caraval before; finding Tella had been the entire purpose of the last game. But while that sounded exciting, in truth Tella had been forced to spend most of her time sitting like a trapped princess in a tower, waiting to be found. She'd snuck out on occasion. But slipping into the back doors of Caraval's gaming rooms and spying on her sister from the shadows was not nearly the same as being one of the real players and entering Legend's decadent world with the intent of getting swept away.

Tella had no intentions of being swept away now. It was past midnight, and she needed to find her friend before he left. But, with every step she took inside the castle, Tella had to fight the urge to forget why she was there and just enjoy the game.

The air tasted like wonder. Like candied butterfly wings caught in sugared spiderwebs, and drunken peaches coated in luck.

Again, she wondered if Elantine's heir wasn't so bad. Perhaps only the rumors about him were terrible, started by people jealous of his position. His ball looked like a celebration she would have put together. Though Tella had no idea if that actually said something about her or her host.

She continued to grip her luckless coin, hoping her friend was still at the party. But even as Tella searched for him, she couldn't help noticing every surface of the celebration was a riot of indulgent activity.

From the grand ballroom's arched entrance it looked as if another Fate had come to life in bursts of furry and feathered colors. The Menagerie—a card that represented the start of a new story or adventure.

Women and men with bodies covered in feathers and heads crowned with tiny curved horns dangled from the ceiling, twirling and spinning around thick sheets of gold or magenta silk that hung like massive party ribbons. Below them, performers in costumes made of fur, more feathers, and paint slathered over skin prowled and crawled as if they were wild chimeras escaped from another world. Tella saw performers dressed to look like tigers with dragon wings, horses with forked tails, snakes with lion manes, and wolves with ram horns, who growled and nipped and sometimes licked at the heels of guests. There were a few low balconies where shirtless men with wings as large as angels' and fallen stars pushed grinning couples back and forth on giant swings hanging from canopies of thorns and flowers.

Tella heard Dante snort by her side.

She might have spent a little too long eyeing the beautiful men who looked like fallen stars and angels, futilely hoping one might be the friend she sought. The rest of her just wanted to take it all in. She'd dreamed of parties like this. She knew she didn't have time to waste. But her eyes strained to see every glistening inch as her fingers longed to touch, and her mouth strained to take a bite, not just of the food, but of the party itself. Of the dragon wings, and the careless laughs, the way people tossed their heads and cast around glances that ranged between shy and ravenous. It all looked so innocent and wicked at once, and Tella longed to experience every tempting piece of it.

At the top of the ballroom stairs she tilted her head to look up at Dante, who could have been her shadow with all the sharp points of his inky tattoos peeking out from his shadow-dark suit. "Why aren't you dressed like a leopard with butterfly wings, or a unicorn?"

A sliver of a grin. "Not even Legend could make me dress like a unicorn."

"But unicorns are magical, and then all the ladies would want to pet you."

This time Dante's snort sounded more like a laugh he was trying to hold back.

Tella couldn't help smiling; she might not have liked him, but she enjoyed that he found her funny. She also appreciated that he seemed uninterested in all the ladies who looked his way and appeared as if they really would be willing to pet him, even though he wasn't dressed like a unicorn.

"Greetings!" Jovan, one of Legend's friendliest performers, dropped in front of Tella and Dante like a marionette. Thick ribbons were attached to her dark brown arms and legs, keeping her feet just off the ground as they happily kicked, ringing the silver bells on her shoes.

Jovan was the first face people saw when they entered Caraval, but she really did so much more than welcome players into the game. She was often a walking clue card disguised as a friendly face, pointing guests in the direction they needed to go. Her amiable disposition was an invaluable skill, also used to reassure those in danger of going mad that it was really only a game.

Unlike most of the other performers, Jovan was not costumed like a chimera. She was dressed like Jester Mad—another Fate from the Deck of Destiny.

A patchwork mask concealed half of Jovan's face with bright rainbow colors that matched the right side of her cape. The garment's other side was entirely black, exactly like the hood that cloaked the left half of her face. A mercurial Fate, Jester Mad symbolized *happiness destined not to last.*

"Welcome, welcome to Caraval, the grandest show by land or by sea. Inside you may come face-to-face with a Fate, or steal bits of destiny—"

"It's all right," Tella cut in. She genuinely liked Jovan. During the last game she'd helped Tella sneak out from her tower room more than once. But Tella didn't need to hear Jovan's speech right now. As enticing as Caraval was, there was little point in playing the game if Tella's bargain with her friend fell through; he was her only solid link to her mother, and saving her was more important than anything. "I've already heard it. You can skip it and hand us the first clue."

"Maybe you just think you've heard it." Jovan jingled the bells on her shoes. "This greeting is a little different from last time." She cleared her throat before reciting the rest from memory.

"As fantastical as Caraval might feel, the next five nights are very real.

Elantine has invited us here to save the Empire from her greatest fear.

For centuries the Fates were locked away, but now they wish to come out and play.

If they regain their magic the world will never be the same, but you can help stop them by winning the game.

To do this you must be clever and follow the clues to find the dark object that can destroy them forever.

Once you have it, Legend will give you a prize so rare I'm not allowed to utter it here."

Jovan kicked her feet when she finished, ringing the bells on her shoes once more as the ribbons on her arms and legs lifted her up, up, up into the frosted fog covering the ceiling. As she ascended, a red card with charred edges dropped from above like a singed chimera feather.

Tella picked it up; the exact same words Jovan just spoke covered the tiny page. "That's it? When Scarlett played, I thought she signed a contract in blood."

"Every performance is different. When your sister played, we had to work at making everything seem more dangerous than it was, because it was only a game."

Tella snorted. "If you're trying to tell me it's real this time, it's not going to work. I've already heard the whole speech about not being swept too far away."

"But have you heard it tonight?" Dante's voice dropped as he brushed closer, fingers grazing the petals on her dress.

Tella's eyes fell to the singed welcome card in her hands. As Dante had said, it didn't contain any warnings about being swept too far away. In fact it mentioned the opposite: *As fantastical as Caraval might feel, the next five nights are very real.*

Tella didn't believe it for a heartbeat, and yet she couldn't resist looking up at Dante and asking, "If the game is real, does that mean everything between us is real?"

"You'll have to be more specific than that." He plucked a petal from her skirt, rubbing it between his fingers as he started down the stairs without her.

In other words, *no.*

Nothing between them was real, because Caraval wasn't real. People loved Caraval because it was a fantasy come to life; no matter how twisted the game became at the end of it all, it was still only a game. Tella could not let herself be swept away by it.

At the bottom of the steps Tella squeezed her coin once again and scanned the crowd for anyone who might look a bit like a criminal, hoping to find her friend. Though a part of her had begun to fear he'd already left. It was well past midnight now and his last letter had warned that he wouldn't wait.

But Tella wasn't ready to give up. Her searching gaze wove past actors on stilts, covered in cream and chestnut fur, and men decorated to look like swans with fangs, rowing upside-down polka-dot umbrellas through the flower-covered streams that led toward the center of the ballroom.

"I don't think you want to go that way."

Tella turned and nearly smacked into Dante's chest. He was right behind her once more, standing taller than any boy had the right to. She had to strain her neck to watch his line of vision travel past a woman wrestling with a wolfman and a young gentleman playing fetch with a handsome half-tiger, until finally Dante's vision landed on the massive silver cage in the center of the ballroom.

Tella stiffened.

She had glimpsed the cage's thick iron bars upon entering, but she'd not realized all the dancers on the ballroom's dance floor were inside it. From afar they looked more like captive animals. Her shoulders shuddered. No wonder Dante had been laughing earlier.

"You really weren't joking about hating cages?" Dante asked.

"Who enjoys cages?" Though from where Tella stood, it appeared half of the ball did.

"They're fools," she went on. "This is Caraval—Legend might trap all of them in there and tell them they can't get the first clue unless one person agrees to stay inside forever."

This earned her another deep laugh. "Is that what you think Legend does?"

"He tried to keep me trapped up in a balcony during the last game."

"But you snuck out. If Legend had really wanted to hold you captive, he wouldn't have let that happen."

"Perhaps I'm just an excellent sneak."

"Or maybe you only think you are." Dante's fingers skimmed the nape of Tella's neck, just a gentle touch, but Tella had a vivid flashback to the way his hands had felt right before she'd left him in the forest that morning.

He'd let her go. He'd pretended not to care or notice, yet he'd found her shortly after. He'd teased her about the cursing, and been kind enough to return her coin with just a little more teasing.

"You know," Tella mused, "if I didn't hate you, I might actually enjoy your company."

All hints of Dante's smile vanished. "We should leave."

"What—"

He grabbed Tella's hand, swifter and tighter than any of the times he'd taken hold of her before. It all seemed to happen at once, giving Tella only a moment to realize that his eyes were no longer on her. They were narrowed on something—*or someone*—standing behind her.

"Trying to run off with my fiancée?"

The superior drawl skimmed the back of Tella's shoulders, as cool and polished as a freshly sharpened sword.

Elantine's heir.

Now *this* is an interesting surprise." Genuine amusement lit a pair of silver-blue eyes, as dazzling as crashing waves, shadowed by untamed hair so gold it could have been turned into coins.

"It's you." All the air escaped Tella's lungs.

The boy from the sky carriage—the same indolent young nobleman who'd threatened to toss her from a coach and dropped a half-eaten apple onto her slippers—flashed a delinquent smile. "You can call me Jacks."

In a move far more gentlemanly than anything she'd seen him do the other night, he took her free hand to brush a kiss across her knuckles. His narrow lips were soft and cold, bringing a fresh chill that tripped all the way up Tella's arm as he spoke low words against her hand. "I didn't actually think you'd be brave enough to wear the dress."

"I hate to see a good gown go to waste," she said, flippant, as if his presence had not completely unhinged her. Elantine's heir wasn't supposed to find her so quickly. He wasn't *really* supposed to find her at all. And he wasn't supposed to be the reckless boy from the carriage—that didn't fit with the image she'd had.

The heir—*Jacks*—had sounded ruthless and far from lazy. Yet this young man with his bloodshot eyes and untamed hair appeared to be the epitome of careless. The bone-white breeches clinging to his lean legs were clean, but his scuffed sable boots looked as if they were meant for a stable rather than a party. He didn't even bother with a tailcoat. His bronze cravat was tied all wrong, crooked against the throat of a pale shirt that could have done with quite a bit of ironing.

Tella wondered if the wicked rumors about him were wrong, or if Jacks chose to cultivate an idle image on purpose. His golden hair fell over one eye, yet he looked down on Tella with all the confidence of an emperor as he said, "Shall we dance?"

Dante cleared his throat and tugged Tella closer.

Jacks's mouth twisted, his smile far more feral than friendly. "Surely you're not trying to keep me from my fiancée at my own party."

Dante's grip tightened. "Actually—"

"Don't mind him, he's just jealous," Tella cut in, before Dante could do something unfortunately noble, like confess the charade was all his doing. Not that Tella understood why she was protecting the person partly responsible for this predicament. Or that Dante even needed protecting. Perhaps she just wanted to prove that she didn't need him taking care of her.

Tella removed herself from his grip.

Dante clenched his jaw so tight she heard his teeth grate together. But Tella didn't spare him another look. She could manage this on her own.

She held out her hand.

Jacks ran one slender finger over his savage smile, leaving her hand untaken.

Then he took her by the hips. Cool, sinuous, and solid, his arm snaked around her, reeling her scandalously close to his side.

She swore Dante actually growled this time, as Jacks drew her away and into the sweaty crowd of revelers.

The heads of several guests had turned to look at Dante after he and Tella first entered the party. But now Tella swore every set of eyes followed the reckless young heir now clutching her waist. He kept her extremely close as he guided her past fountains dripping sinful liquors, and partygoers flirting with performers costumed like cotton-tailed foxes and half-human leopards.

"I'm surprised you haven't tried to run," he said.

"Why would I do that?"

"Because," he spoke into her hair, each word as slow and languorous as the lazy strokes of his fingers against the bottom of her rib cage, "I don't think I made a very good impression during our first encounter, and by now I'm guessing you've heard the rumors that I'm a soulless madman who will do anything to get the crown."

"You're saying they're not true?"

"If they were true, you'd already be dead." His lips remained pressed against her hair. To anyone they passed it probably looked as if he was truly enamored, on the verge of inappropriate, almost as if he were trying to start more rumors. Tella didn't know what she'd expected would happen if the heir found her, but it was definitely not this.

"If I'm a murderer," he murmured, "do you really think I would have let you live after hearing you'd claimed to be my fiancée to get into the palace?"

"If all of this is your way of saying you don't plan any retribution for a little fib, then we should part ways. I'm actually here to meet someone else."

Tella felt Jacks's cold mouth move downward, frowning, against her hair.

"I'm disappointed, Donatella. I thought I was your *friend*. But not only were you late, now you're trying to escape me." His idle tone turned sharp and something terrible twisted inside of Tella's gut. "Is this because you don't have my payment?" Jacks looked down on her with a smile so disturbing it could have made an angel weep.

Unholy saints from hell.

Tella fought to breathe as all her plans and hopes began to crumble.

Jacks couldn't be her friend. She couldn't have been writing letters to the heir to the Meridian throne for more than a year.

She stumbled but Jacks's arm tightened, keeping her from falling and holding her much too close as they continued through the revelers. This had to be a mistake. Tella's friend was supposed to be a lowly criminal who dealt in secrets, not the unpredictable and murderous heir to the throne, who, from the pitch of his voice, did not sound inclined to forgive her for her failure.

Tella tried to pull away.

Jacks held tight, his nimble fingers stronger than they looked. "Why do you keep disappointing me?" His hands clung to her as if she really were his fiancée while he guided her closer to the colossal cage in the center of the ballroom. The irony was not lost on Tella. She'd contacted him to help her escape the prison her father had turned her life into, and now Jacks was ushering her toward a new set of bars.

Frightened blue petals rained down from her skirts. Tella's pounding heart told her she needed to run away as soon as possible. But if she fled, she had no idea who else to turn to to help her find and save her mother. Tella was starting to feel desperate. The pounding of her heart drowned out all the soaring party music. All she could hear was blood rushing through her ears.

But there was still hope.

Jacks might have been heir to the throne, destined to inherit more wealth and power than Tella was capable of imagining. But for all the privilege and connections that brought, it seemed as if certain things—like Legend's true name—weren't within his grasp, or he would have never helped Tella in the first place. All she needed to do was convince him that she was still useful.

Tella exhaled deeply and grabbed one of his hands. She leveraged his surprise to tow him behind a triple-tiered fountain spilling falls of crimson liquid that smelled like wine. From the outside it probably looked as if they couldn't wait to put their hands all over each other. Inside, Tella felt as if she were walking along a fraying tightrope.

"I'm sorry," she said as soon as they were alone. Her gaze went everywhere except for him. As much as she wished to say it was part of an act, this was one of those moments she was truly afraid. "I didn't mean to panic after finding out who you were. I'm so grateful for all you've done; the last thing I wanted was to disappoint you."

She swallowed and looked up at him with wide, pleading eyes. If he was capable of sympathy, it didn't show. There were ice storms warmer than the way he watched her.

"I've been looking for you since the moment I arrived," Tella rushed on. "I don't have Legend's name, but I can get it by the end of this week—"

Drunken words tumbled around them, cutting off Tella as another couple drifted toward the fountain they were next to.

Inside a heartbeat Tella's back was pressed against the uncomfortable ridges of a nearby pillar and Jacks was pressed to her—a show for the unwanted company.

Tella shut her eyes.

Jacks's mouth dropped to her neck, cool lips hovering over her skin as he murmured, "I've heard promises like yours before, but they are always lies."

"I swear I'm telling the truth," she whispered.

"I'm not sure I believe you, and I no longer just want Legend's name." Another graze of his breath as Jacks's cold mouth traveled higher, ghosting over her jaw without actually touching her skin.

Tella opened her eyes and sucked in a sharp breath.

His gaze was ravenous. She knew they were only playing a role for the couple drifting by, yet Tella imagined Jacks's mouth widening enough to bite her, the same way he'd sunk his teeth into that white apple the other night.

Then as quickly as he had pressed her back against the pillar, he was pulling away. The couple that had happened upon them had already stumbled off to somewhere else.

Jacks's eyes stayed on her, narrowed in a way that could have just as easily been displeasure or amusement at her growing discomfort.

"I like you, Donatella, so I'll give you one more chance. But, since you failed to bring me the information I asked for, I'll need to alter the conditions of our agreement. If you succeed with both tasks, then, and only then, will I consider reuniting you with your mother."

"So you know where she is?"

Jacks's nostrils flared. "You dare to question me when you're the only one who's failed to keep her promises? If you'd brought me Legend's name, you'd be looking at her now. Instead I'll give you until the end of this song to make your choice."

The music all but stopped—save for one clear cello note that might expire any second.

"Tell me what you want," Tella said.

A faint twitch at the corner of Jacks's mouth. "I now need two things from you instead of one. I've worked very hard to become Elantine's heir, but the rumor I'm engaged to you has put my position in jeopardy. It's already spread across the court. If it's exposed as a lie, given my reputation, people will expect me to kill you. If I don't, I'll be seen as weak, and then I'll be the one who's killed."

"What are you proposing?"

"According to every whisper in the palace, a proposal has already happened."

"Are you asking me to marry you?"

He laughed. "No." But for a moment, Tella swore Jacks cocked his head as if considering her. "I don't wish to wed you. I only need you to pretend you're my fiancée until the end of Caraval. Once the game is over, we can say our engagement was part of it and dissolve it with no harm done."

It should have been an easy yes. Tella had faked an engagement before. Yet something about this bargain struck her as off. It felt like making a deal with one of Legend's performers. There was no way it could be as simple as Jacks made it sound. There had to be something else he wasn't sharing.

"What else do you want?" she asked.

"I need to make sure you can follow through with this request first. If you can convince everyone at this ball that we're deeply and truly in love, then I'll tell you the second thing I want." Jacks stole Tella's hand, his soft leather gloves pressing firmly against her bare skin.

"Time to see how good of an actress you are." He flashed his dimples, all carefree, boyish charm. But Tella could not forget how quickly he could turn from careless to cruel as he drew her away from their hidden alcove toward the looming cage where everyone was dancing.

More fragile blue petals fell from her gown.

Tella took a steeling breath. She didn't know what she would do if she failed, and she wasn't quite sure what she'd have to do to succeed in convincing the entire ball they were in love.

The thick bars of the cage smelled of metal and royal ambition. The air was almost too thick to breathe, sweltering with warm bodies, perfume, and whispered seductions. Jacks's fingers tensed as they entered. Briefly Tella imagined he didn't like cages either, but it was far more likely he was trying to keep her from running off.

There were even more dancers clustered inside the cage than she'd realized. Overlooked ladies and the occasional couple rested on the raised satin cushions strewn about the edges, while colorful skirts and suits twirled atop the marbled green dance floor as if they were flowers being tossed by the breeze.

Tella spied a few familiar faces.

First she saw Caspar, who'd played the role of Legend in the last game, as well as the role of her fiancé. Dressed in a tawny suit that make him look foxlike, he appeared to be whispering secrets to another handsome young man, who probably had no idea Caspar was a performer. Just beyond, lounging on a cushion, Nigel frightened off nobles and made them blush all at once as he traced the barbed-wire tattoos inked around his lips.

Then there was Armando. An attentive courtier in a scarlet gown pawed at his white coat with her red fingernails. But rather than enjoy her attention, Armando's gaze fixed on Tella. The cage grew warmer as his emerald eyes followed her. This wasn't the mocking way he'd looked at her earlier. His interest clung to her as if she were the night's first act of entertainment.

And he wasn't the only one staring.

No longer was everyone only looking at Jacks. Tella swore their intrigued gazes and painted eyes had all jumped to her. Tella liked attention, but she wasn't sure she enjoyed this level of scrutiny. It made the stifling cage feel suddenly small. The light inside had turned from whiskey colored and celebratory to unnerving shades of brassy plum. She especially felt the women, judging her freshly mussed curls and her nearly backless gown as they whispered to one another words that Tella didn't need to hear to imagine. Few things were quite so brutal as critical ladies.

A trio of girls around her age, all dripping jealousy, actually tried to trip her as she passed.

"Relax," Jacks murmured. "We're not going to convince anyone we're engaged if your eyes keep darting around as though you can't wait to escape."

"We're inside of a cage." Tella tilted her head toward the dense bars above, where iron chandeliers crawled with blue and white vines that swayed back and forth as if they, too, wished to flee.

"Don't look at the cage. Keep those pretty eyes on me." Jacks took Tella's chin in his fingers, cold, even through the gloves. Around them, hissed words and torrid conversations mingled with softer sounds of flowing liquor, hushed laughter, and animal rumbles. But when Jacks's lips parted a second time, Tella only heard the melodic sound of his voice as he whispered, "I know it's not just the cage that's scaring you, darling."

"You're giving yourself far too much credit."

"Am I?" He dropped his hand from her chin to her neck, soft leather resting against her pulse. He stroked slowly, just a delicate brush of his gloves, which unfortunately made her cowardly heart beat faster.

"Relax," he repeated. "The only thing you should think about is that you're more desirable than anyone else in this room. Every person here wishes they were you."

"You're definitely giving yourself too much credit now."

His laughter was surprisingly disarming. "Then tell yourself everyone wishes they were me, dancing with you." With a grin he must have stolen from the devil, Jacks looped an arm around Tella's hips and swept her onto the dance floor.

For someone who'd made it sound as if he was concerned about his reputation, it surprised Tella how much he acted as if he couldn't care less about what everyone else thought. Another dance was currently under way and he cut directly through all the other couples. He was completely disrespectful, yet far more skilled than anyone she'd ever danced with.

Jacks's every movement was carelessly graceful, matching the musical cadence of his words as he murmured in her ear, "The key to a charade like this is to forget it's an act. Invite the lie to play until you become so comfortable with it that it feels like the truth. Don't tell yourself we're pretending to be engaged, tell yourself that I love you. That I want you more than anyone." He reeled her closer and ran a hand up the back of her neck, toying with the ribbon around her throat. "If you can convince yourself it's true, you can convince anyone."

He spun her around the floor again as thick berry-red ribbons twirled down from the top of the cage. Each one dripped feather-clad acrobats who tossed out handfuls of stardust and cut-glass glitter, covering the world in imitation magic as Tella and Jacks continued to whirl and twirl until everything spiraled into gold-dust and haze, flower petals, and fingers weaving through hair. And for a moment Tella dipped her imagination into the treacherous fantasy that Jacks had described.

She remembered the first time they met. She'd thought him insolent and indolent yet distractingly handsome. If he'd not been such a beast she might have wondered if he tasted like the apple he kept biting, or something else a little more dangerous. Then, for the sake of their charade, she imagined he'd felt the same attraction, and that from the moment Jacks saw her in that carriage, he knew he wanted Tella more than he'd ever desired any other person in his life.

This dance wasn't about keeping his murderous reputation so he could win the throne; this was about winning her.

It was why he'd given her such a gorgeous gown.

Why he danced with her now.

Tella pretended love was a place she wanted to visit, and tested out a flirtatious smile.

Jacks dazzled her with an uneven grin.

"I knew you could do this." He brought his mouth to her ear and kissed the tip of it tenderly, as soft as the brush of a whisper. Her chest fluttered as his mouth dropped lower, and he kissed her again with a little more pressure, lips lingering at the delicate corner of her jaw and her neck. Tella's fingers curled into his back.

The music around them surged, violins dancing with harps and cellos in a decadent and debauched rhapsody, threatening to transport her to another time and place.

Every person inside the cage was still watching them spin with rapt interest. The ballroom teemed with eager eyes and sneering mouths as Jacks's lips continued to dance over Tella's throat the way their steps waltzed over the floor.

"Maybe we should give them something to really gossip about." His knuckles brushed her collarbone, drawing her attention back to him. "Unless I still frighten you."

Tella gave him a wild smile, even as her heart leaped against her rib cage. She needed him to know that she could do this. "You never frightened me."

"Care to prove that?" Jacks's bright eyes fell to her mouth.

A dare.

The blood in Tella's veins surged hotter.

Tella didn't usually think before kissing a young man. One moment she just found his mouth on top of hers, or hers on top of his, followed by tongues seeking entry as hands fumbled around her body. But she didn't suppose kissing Jacks would be like that. She had a feeling his skilled hands knew exactly what to do, where to touch her, how hard to press. And his lips—they were being playful now but she didn't know if they would be gentle with her mouth or a little rough, and her pulse raced at the thought of either possibility.

Jacks cupped her cheek and twirled her in another circle. "Help me convince them," he whispered.

Tella didn't know why she hesitated.

It's just one kiss.

And she was suddenly very curious. He would be the emperor one day, and he wanted to kiss Tella while all of the most important people of the Empire watched.

She slid her hand up to his neck. His skin felt colder, shivering beneath her fingers. Clearly Jacks was not as serene as he appeared.

"It seems as if you're the one who's nervous now," Tella teased.

"I'm just wondering if you'll think differently of me after this." Then his mouth was crashing against hers. He tasted like exquisite nightmares and stolen dreams, like the wings of fallen angels and bottles of fresh moonlight. Tella might have moaned against his lips as his tongue slipped between hers and explored.

Every solid inch of him pressed against every soft, curving piece of her. His fingers knotted and tugged at her curls. Her hands roamed under the hem of his shirt, discovering the firm muscles of his lower back. It was the way people kissed behind locked doors and darkened alleys, not a kiss for lit dance floors where everyone in the Empire could see. Yet Jacks didn't seem to care.

His fingers found the ribbon around her neck and slid beneath it, crushing her lips even closer to his. He wasn't tasting her, he was devouring her, as if he'd just found something he'd thought he had lost. Then his hands were sliding underneath the ropes of jewels crossing her bare back; he must have torn off his gloves because his fingers were icy and bold against her heated skin, clutching and claiming and making her wonder if this wasn't a charade after all.

She whimpered.

He groaned.

It was the sort of kiss she could have lived in. The sort of kiss worth dying for.

God's teeth.

A kiss worth dying for. Only one person in the history of the Empire had ever kissed like—

Jacks bit her, sharp teeth digging into her lip hard enough to draw warm blood.

Tella pulled away abruptly, shoving her hand against his chest. There was no heartbeat.

Blood and saints. What had she done?

In front of her Jacks seemed to glow. His skin had been pale but now it appeared otherworldly in its radiance.

The ribbon once tied around her neck dangled from his slender fingers like some sort of prize, and a drop of the blood he'd spilled when he'd bitten her now rested at the edge of his narrow mouth.

Tella was going to be ill.

"What did you just do to me?" she breathed.

Jacks's chest heaved almost as much as hers, and his eyes had gone feverish around the edges, but his voice was lazy once again, almost dispassionate as he said, "Don't cause a scene right here, my love."

"I think it's too late for that." She wanted to call him by his name, *the Prince of Hearts*, but she wasn't quite ready to utter the words out loud.

His dimples reappeared, cunning this time, as if he knew exactly what she was thinking.

She waited.

Waited for Jacks to tell her she was wrong. Waited for his assurance that his kiss would not kill her. Waited for him to tell her she should know better than to put too much faith in old stories. Waited for him to tease her for being so gullible and believing that he was a long-lost Fate who'd returned. Waited for him to tell her that he was not the Prince of Hearts.

Instead, he licked the blood at the corner of his mouth. "You should have brought me Legend's name."

14

For a moment Tella's entire world stopped breathing. Every person near the dance floor had ceased moving, their rapt faces frozen in exaggerated states of shock at Tella and Jacks's display. For a heartbeat Tella could only hear the cut-glass glitter tinkling softly as it continued to fall to the floor.

The Prince of Hearts—the Fate famous for his fatal kisses, who had haunted both her dreams and nightmares, and cursed her to unrequited love after drawing his card from her mother's Deck of Destiny—was not merely a myth. He was real, and he was standing right in front of Tella. His pale skin glowed so unnaturally, if the entire ballroom hadn't been frozen, she imagined they'd have all seen him for what he truly was.

He wasn't entirely human, or human at all. He was something magical, something other, something wrong. A Fate.

And she had kissed him.

"I didn't expect you to look so surprised. The coin I sent was a rather obvious hint." Jacks reached for her and carefully smoothed out one of her curls, his hands much gentler than they'd been moments ago. She wanted to rage, to scream, to slap his reddened mouth, but it seemed he'd put her, along with the entire ballroom, under a spell.

"What have you done to everyone?" she breathed.

"Stopped their hearts. It's like pausing time. It won't last long, unlike what I've done to yours." His jaw twitched as his cold gaze traveled toward her chest.

Tella took a shallow breath, because apparently that was all she was capable of. When they'd danced her heart had pounded, her veins had heated, her blood had raced. But now she could feel her heart struggling, beating too slowly, a weak echo of what it should have been. "Am I going to die?"

"Not yet."

Tella's knees buckled.

Jacks gleamed brighter. "This is going to be so much fun, I almost hate to tell you there's still a way to save yourself."

"How?"

"Bring me the second thing I want."

"What is that?" Tella gritted out.

Jacks's long fingers finished smoothing her hair, and his eyes met her gaze once more. She'd called his eyes silver-blue before, but now they shined just silver, twinkling with growing pleasure as her terror multiplied. "I want Legend the man, not just his identity. I want you to win the game and then give him to me."

Before Tella could react, the moment shattered and the ballroom flooded with sound once again. She swore she'd never witnessed so many intentionally loud whispers, covered up with artificial smiles, as partygoers pretended not to be scandalized by Jacks and Tella's display. Though one person did not appear to be hiding how he felt. *Dante.*

Tella's already mangled insides twisted further.

Dante stood casually with one elbow propped against a thick metal bar near the mouth of the cage, but the rigid set of his jaw, the hooded sweep of his gaze, and the derisive line of his lips told Tella that he was far from calm. He looked furious.

His reaction shouldn't have angered her. And her kiss shouldn't have angered him, given that Dante was partly responsible for this mess. Unless he was only acting, which made more sense. Pretending to care about her was probably one of the roles he'd been given for Caraval.

Jacks's gaze followed Tella's and sharpened.

"I think he still believes you're his." Jacks's pale skin gleamed brighter as he stroked a thumb under his chin, looking as if he were coming up with a truly terrible idea.

"This doesn't involve him. Dante is one of Legend's performers," Tella hissed. "He's just playing a role. He doesn't even *like* me."

"That's not how it looks from here." Jacks pressed his cold lips to her forehead, a mockery of a kiss, as he said, "I don't give second chances, but I'm giving one to you. I wasn't lying when I said that I want this charade to be convincing. If anyone discovers this engagement is a lie, or uncovers the truth about me or our arrangement, the consequences will be unfortunate. Take your tattooed friend over there." Jacks turned his eyes toward Dante again. "You said he's one of Legend's performers, so I can't kill him this week. But if he discovers the truth, I could easily end his life once the game is over."

"No!" Tella objected, right as Jacks raised his voice above hers to announce, "Since it seems I've momentarily stolen everyone's attention, now would probably be a good time to share some excellent news."

As if the partygoers were puppets or part of an orchestrated dance, each of their coiffed heads angled his way.

"Many of you know my former fiancée, Alessandra, died late last year. Her death was a great loss to the Empire, one I thought I'd never recover from. But as you can see, I've found someone else, someone who I hope you will all adore as much as I do. Meet my new fiancée, Donatella."

The room filled with applause and fresh clouds of stardust as the performers above tossed sparkling paper stars onto the scrambling people below.

To Tella's eyes it all looked like ash.

Her own smile had never felt so wrong as she forced her lips to curve for the crowd.

"I hate you," she whispered.

"Have I been unfair?" Jacks murmured. "I gave you what you asked for, now I want what I'm owed."

"Oh, look!" someone cried. "The falling stars! They're the first clue."

The ballroom erupted into even more chaos. Some of the falling stars were clues, but it seemed others were full of nothing save for dazzling dust, which filled the cage with fantastic shimmering clouds when touched by the partygoers.

Caraval's games had truly begun. As everyone around her reached for falling stars, Tella thought of all the times she and Scarlett had dreamed about Caraval, about Legend. Now Tella had to win the game or she would never dream again. And she doubted her sister would either. Tella had promised Scarlett she'd be careful, but already Tella had failed her.

The edge of Jacks's poisonous mouth twitched. "You should take one of the clues, my love."

"Don't call me—"

"Careful, darling." Quick as a snake, he pressed two firm fingers to Tella's bruised lips. "You don't want to destroy the beautiful deception we've just created. Now," he said sweetly, "give my fingers a kiss for everyone still watching."

Tella bit them instead. They tasted like frost and wishes gone wrong.

She expected him to pull away, for his sharp face to fill with color and his words to turn ugly and angry. But Jacks just left his cold fingers in her mouth, pressing them against her teeth and her tongue. Her stomach filled with lead, as something purely evil shimmered in his unearthly eyes.

"I'll let you get away with this for now, but this is my last mercy." He brushed his fingers over the spot where he'd bitten her lip, before pulling them from her mouth. "If you do not win Caraval and bring me Legend before Elantine's Day, you'll learn just how deadly my kisses really are."

Up until that accursed night, Tella had loved glitter. As a little girl she'd often stolen tiny bottles of it from shops, imagining one might contain real dust from the stars, full of magic able to grant her wishes, or turn dirt into diamonds. But none of the bottles had been enchanted, and the glitter from the ball wasn't real stardust, either, just pulverized glass. By the time the bells cried out three in the morning and she climbed into the sky coach with Jacks, it didn't even sparkle; it clung like a parasite to her arms and the parts of her gown where flowers had once been.

You should have brought me Legend's name.

Jacks hadn't said a word to her since they'd exited his wretched castle. He lounged across from her, a lazy nobleman once again, unknotting his bronze cravat as if he'd just finished a series of tedious tasks: *attending a ball, dancing, cursing Tella with his murderous lips.*

"I take it you're afraid of me now," he drawled.

"You're mistaking fear with disgust. You're a loathsome monster." And she had trusted him. "You tricked me."

"Would you have preferred me to make the kiss kill you right away?"

"Yes."

The bow of Jacks's mouth dipped down, though not a trace of sadness touched his eyes. He probably wasn't capable of it, just as he was said to be incapable of love.

. . . his heart had stopped beating long ago. Only one person could make it beat again: his one true love. They said his kiss had been fatal to all but her—his only weakness.

Oh, how Tella wished she was his weakness. She'd have loved to destroy him.

Tella often imagined she knew what people thought when they saw her. One look at her honey-blond curls, her girlish smile, and her pretty dresses, coupled with the fact that she liked to enjoy herself, and people dismissed her as a silly girl. Tella might have been many things, but she was far from silly or worthless or whatever labels people liked to affix because a person was young and female. Tella liked to think that was where much of her strength came from.

She was bold. She was brave. She was cunning. And she was going to come out of this triumphant—no matter the cost.

"If you'd brought me Legend's name," Jacks said, "this would have turned out differently."

"If that's true, why do you now want more than just his name?"

"Why settle for only a name when you can win the game and give me Legend?" Jacks's tone was dismissive, as careless as his idle posture. But Tella believed there had to be much more to his demand. She wanted to press him further, but she doubted he'd tell her exactly what he wanted with Legend. And there were other questions Tella needed answers to more.

She leaned back in her seat, mimicking Jacks's cavalier pose. "How do I know any of this is real? How do I know you're not merely playing a part in Legend's game?"

"You want proof that I'm a Fate and my kiss will truly kill you?" Amusement lit Jacks's eyes; it seemed he was capable of emotion after all, because the idea of demonstrating how deadly he was appeared to excite him a bit too much.

"I'll pass on that," Tella said. She didn't actually believe Jacks was part of Legend's game. His kiss had not been worth dying for, although if Tella had never actually died, she might have argued otherwise. Kisses were meant to be temporal, brief but exquisite moments of pleasure. But Tella could have kissed Jacks into eternity. It wasn't just the way his lips had moved over hers, it was the desire behind them, the wanting, the way Jacks had made Tella feel as if she were the one person on earth he'd spent his entire existence searching for. In that moment she'd managed to forget she'd been left by her mother and repeatedly suffered at the hands of her father, because Jacks had made her feel as if he'd hold on to her forever. It might have been the most convincing lie she'd ever been told.

Then she'd seen him glowing, and Tella had known. She still didn't understand how no one else at the ball had seemed to notice it. Even now, some of the glow had worn off, but Jacks still looked utterly inhuman, viciously beautiful. Capable of killing with only one press of his lips.

It was still surreal to believe he was a Fate. She wondered how long he'd been back on earth, and if the other Fates had returned as well. But she didn't know how many more minutes he'd humor her, and she still needed answers to other questions.

"I want my mother's real name," she said, "and proof you know where she is and that you'll bring me to her after all of this is done. That's the only way I'll believe this is all real."

Jacks twisted one of his teardrop cuff links—or was it supposed to represent a drop of blood? "I think you know this is real, but I'll humor you."

The coach dipped as Jacks reached into his pocket and pulled out a crisp rectangular card.

Even in the carriage's dim lighting the print on it was unmistakable. Such a dark hue of nightshade it was almost black, with tiny hints of gold flecks that sparkled in the light and swirly strands of deep red-violet embossing that still made Tella think of damp flowers, witch's blood, and magic.

Bumps rose all over Tella's arms.

It was one of the cards from her mother's Deck of Destiny. Tella had seen other decks over the years, but all of them had been inferior to the glowing, almost magical images on the deck of cards her mother had possessed.

Tella warred with the desire to reach for it and leap out of the carriage before it could predict another ill future.

But when Jacks turned the card around it did not reveal a Fate. It showed an alarmingly lifelike picture of her mother, Paloma, with dark locks of hair cascading over shoulders that looked thinner than Tella remembered. Paloma stood with her palms outward, as though pressed hard against a window, almost as if she were trapped inside of the card.

"This is where your mother has been for the past seven years," Jacks said.

Tella pried her eyes away from the card to see if the Fate was toying with her, but the amused glimmer that lit his eyes moments ago was gone. His face had turned as cold as the blood now chilling Tella's insides.

"I don't believe you," she said.

"Which part? That it's your mother, or that she's been trapped inside this card?"

Jacks set the card atop Tella's clenched fists. It did not tingle like the Aracle, it throbbed, painfully slow, a dying heartbeat. Tella knew it was dying because it matched her own slowly beating heart.

It couldn't be real. It shouldn't be real. But Tella found herself believing it was real as the card's weak heartbeat continued to thud against her fist. "How is this possible?"

"It's easier than you would think," Jacks said, "and I can tell you from experience it's torturous."

A slice of moonlight fell into the carriage, illuminating Jacks's face. His expression was impassive, but for a moment he looked so pale, Tella swore she saw the skeleton beneath his skin. She'd definitely been wrong to think him incapable of emotion. Perhaps he was unable to love, and maybe his other feelings weren't that of a human being, but the terror that had just pulsed from him was so powerful she'd felt it.

"You were trapped inside of a card," Tella breathed.

Jacks tilted his head away from the moonlight so that his features were shadowed in dark, making it impossible to read his face as he said, "Where do you think all the Fates went when we disappeared so long ago?"

Tella's stomach plummeted as the coach began its descent. She'd heard rumors the Fates had been banished by a witch. Others said they'd turned on one another. There was even one story that claimed the stars had transformed them back into humans. But she'd never heard that the Fates were all trapped inside of cards.

"But that's a tale for another time," Jacks said. "All you need to worry about is winning the game so you can bring me Legend."

Jacks's gaze fell to the crumpled star in Tella's hand—the first clue, which she'd not even looked at. "Open it."

When Tella didn't move, Jacks took it from her hand, unfolded it, and read aloud:

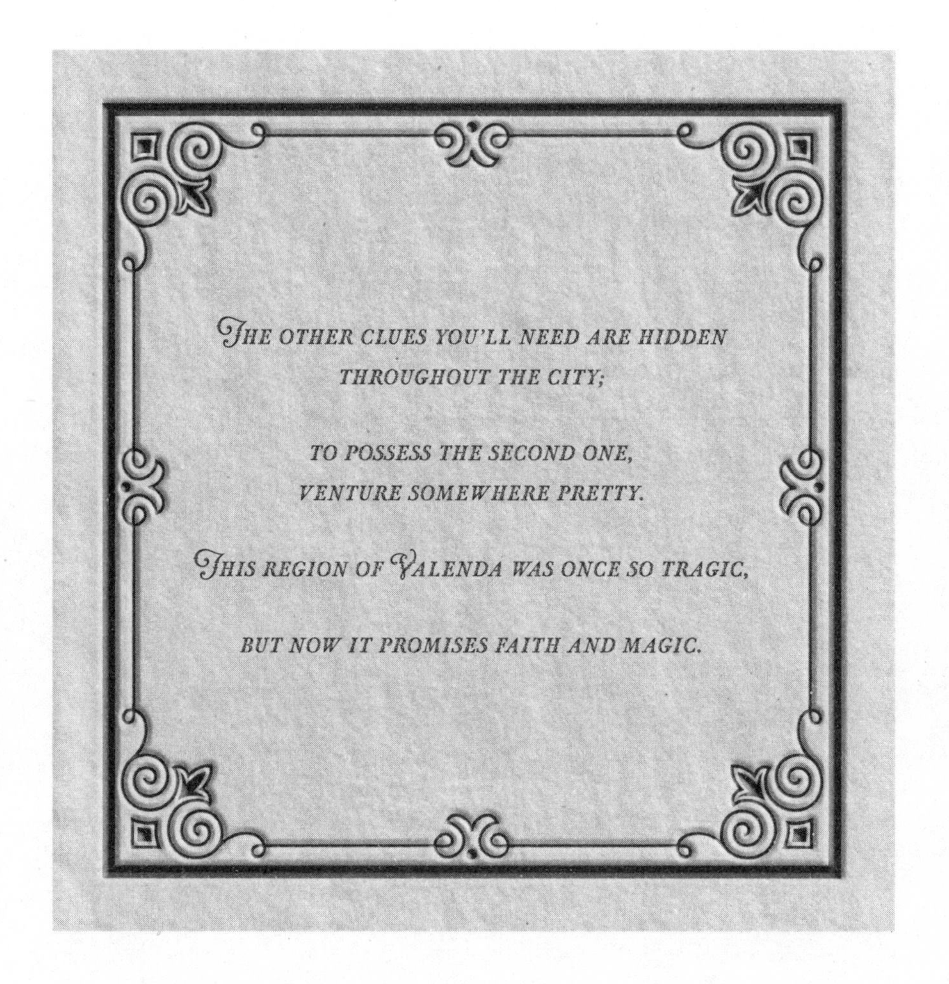

THE OTHER CLUES YOU'LL NEED ARE HIDDEN THROUGHOUT THE CITY;

TO POSSESS THE SECOND ONE, VENTURE SOMEWHERE PRETTY.

THIS REGION OF VALENDA WAS ONCE SO TRAGIC,

BUT NOW IT PROMISES FAITH AND MAGIC.

He paused. "It sounds like the Temple District."

"Am I supposed to thank you for that insight?" Tella snarled.

"I'm attempting to save you time." His tone took on more of a bite. "I might have delayed the full power of my kiss, but you will still experience some of its effects. The game ends at dawn on Elantine's Day, giving you five more nights to find the remaining clues. I'm the only one who can free your mother. If you lose the game and fail to bring me Legend, she will remain trapped inside this card forever, and you will die—"

He cut off as the coach landed heavily on the ground.

Tella reached for the door.

"One more thing." Jacks nodded toward the card with her mother. "Keep her safe. If anything happens to this card, not even I will be able to save her. When you win the game, make sure you have the luckless coin I gave you and I'll find you before Legend arrives. Until then, my love, try not to die."

Jacks blew Tella a kiss as she stepped out into the biting night.

Death visited Tella while she slept. The tips of his claws stroked the back of her neck, while his shadow followed her into pristine dreams, poisoning all the colors until everything tasted of dust and withered to ash.

Soon you will be mine once more.

The rasp of Death's rotting voice woke Tella with a start. She shot up in bed, her tongue heavy, wet hair clinging to her scalp. Yet her heart didn't pound. If anything, it felt as though it worked a touch more slowly than it had the night before.

Beat . . . beat . . . beat.

Nothing.

Beat . . . beat . . . beat.

Nothing.

Beat . . . beat . . . beat.

Nothing.

Damn Jacks and his cursed lips.

Tella clutched her damp sheets with one hand and the card imprisoning her mother with the other. She'd bent its edges during her nightmarish sleep, wrinkling the corner right above her mother's dark head. Clearly it was not indestructible like the Aracle. Tella would have to be more protective of it.

"I'm so sorry," she whispered to her mother. She didn't want to part with the card, but it felt a little too risky to keep on her person.

Tella shuffled to the tiny chest where she stored the Aracle and slipped the card with her captive mother inside. Then she pulled out the Aracle.

So much had happened, Tella needed to see if the new deal she'd made had changed her mother's future yet.

The Aracle felt hotter than usual. But the future it showed had not shifted. The vision of her mother's empty eyes stared back at Tella, as dead as they'd been the last time.

But her mother wasn't dead yet. For now she was only trapped. Tella refused to be discouraged. She would win Caraval, and she would fix this. "No matter what it costs."

As soon as the words left Tella's lips the Aracle burned the tips of her fingers. *Magic.* Tella felt it, heating her entire hand as the Aracle's image flickered and shifted from Paloma lying dead, to Scarlett and Tella embracing their mother with the same abandon they had as little girls.

It looked so real, Tella could almost feel her mother's arms, strong and soft and warm. A soft sob bubbled up in Tella's throat.

Then, almost as quickly as it appeared, the image returned to her mother's corpse.

"No!" Tella screamed.

The vision shifted once more, returning to Scarlett and Tella reuniting with their mother.

"Miss Dragna!" A guard knocked heavily on her door. "Is everything all right in there?"

"Yes," Tella said distractedly as the card continued to shift. Tella had never seen it do anything like this before. It transformed from death to delight, as if showing Tella that what happened next was all up to her, and whether she managed to win this game for Jacks.

Tella put the Aracle back inside the trunk and, with renewed resolve, she pulled out the first clue.

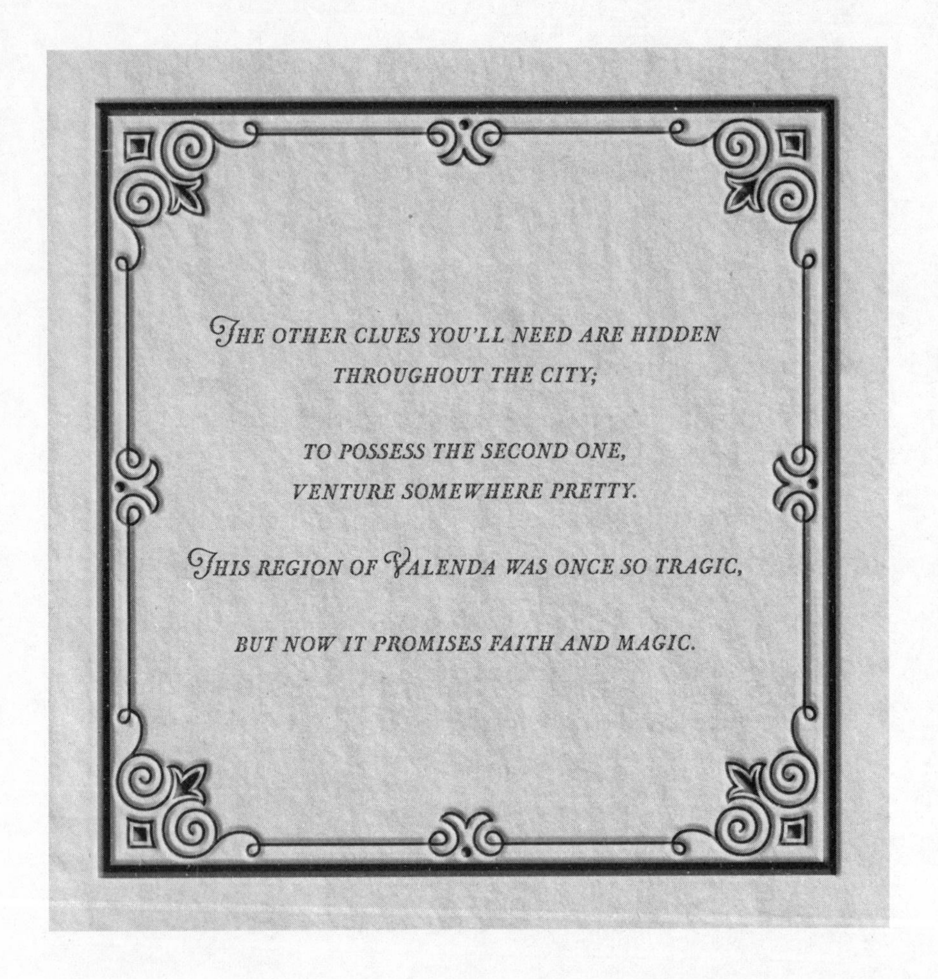

THE OTHER CLUES YOU'LL NEED ARE HIDDEN THROUGHOUT THE CITY;

TO POSSESS THE SECOND ONE, VENTURE SOMEWHERE PRETTY.

THIS REGION OF VALENDA WAS ONCE SO TRAGIC,

BUT NOW IT PROMISES FAITH AND MAGIC.

During the last Caraval, Scarlett had received one card with hints about all five clues at the start of the game, but it seemed this game would follow another pattern. According to this clue, and what Dante had said in the carriage, a different district of the city would hide a new clue each night. Tella would need to find them all to win, and then she would come face-to-face with Legend.

Unfortunately, since Caraval was only played at night, Tella could not begin to search until that evening. And it seemed Jacks already had plans for her during the day.

At the end of her bed rested a familiar box. It looked exactly like the one Jacks had sent the day before, only this time it was wrapped with a golden bow instead of a white one.

IF YOU'RE GOING TO BE ENGAGED TO THE NEXT EMPEROR, YOU'LL NEED TO DRESS LIKE IT.

Tucked inside with the message was a small card with a thorny purple border.

Minerva's Modern Wear

Clothing the progressive half of Valenda, since before the Elantine Dynasty— and we'll be dressing them after as well.

By appointment only.

On the back of the card someone had scrawled the words *Satine District,* along with a time, which had been crossed out and rewritten:

TWO HOURS
ARRIVE ~~ONE HOUR~~ BEFORE NOON.

THIS IS NOT A REQUEST.

The order was almost laughable, given how little Jacks seemed to care about his own appearance. But Tella imagined Jacks's directive to appear wasn't so much about appearance as it was about possession: he wanted to make it clear that she now belonged to him.

Demon was too appealing a word for him.

If this engagement had been real, this note alone would have convinced Tella to break it off. But that wasn't currently an option.

Inside the box, Tella found a pair of elbow-length nude gloves with blue-pearl buttons. She tossed them to the side and pulled out the matching dress beneath. She hated how lovely it was. How the neckline was off the shoulders—a style her father never let her wear. He'd have turned absolutely purple at the sight of this dress. Covered in sapphire-blue lace that clung to a nude shell, the gown was delicate and feminine and a little scandalous all at once.

Tella still wanted to ignore the appointment and throw the dress aside along with the gloves; she didn't like the idea of Jacks dressing her up like his doll. But her trunks still hadn't arrived. And Jacks had made it clear that to save her mother and her life Tella not only needed to win the game, she needed to be a convincing fiancée.

Beat . . . beat . . . beat.

Nothing.

Beat . . . beat . . . beat.

Nothing.

Beat . . . beat . . . beat.

Nothing.

Her heart wasn't slower than when she'd woken up, but it wasn't faster, either. She tried to eat a rushed breakfast and then hurry to the carriage house, but her everything was slightly sluggish.

It took more effort than it should have to keep alert as her coach landed. Perhaps that's why Tella found herself standing on a street teeming with bloated shadows, searching for Minerva's ModernWear.

Though Tella had yet to explore the city, she knew all about the different regions of Valenda, the illicit Spice Quarter, the brazen Temple District, the imperious University Circle, and the elegant Satine District. The last was where Tella was supposed to have been. One of the more glamorous parts of the city, the Satine District was said to be a labyrinth of glistening dress shops, hat shops, and sweet shops, all soaked in petal-fresh colors.

But, either Tella had her facts wrong or she was in the incorrect place. The shops around her were as dark as an unkindness of ravens, packed between alleys that smelled of unmentionable things, and full of patrons who were far from the genteel sort she'd expected. Clad in her delicate gown of sapphire-blue lace, Tella looked like a character who had wandered into the wrong story.

As she searched for Minerva's ModernWear, Tella observed lots of fantastically gaudy jackets, overly amorous couples leaning against lampposts, women smoking pungent cigars, and lots of exposed corsets in harsh hues—burnt oranges, overripe yellows, bruised blues, and ruddy reds.

Every other post had painted signs tacked to it. Some had the word *Wanted* printed above a picture. Others said *Missing Person*. A few surprisingly decorative ones announced the advent of Elantine's Day, though they appeared as out of place as she must have.

Tella resisted the urge to cross her arms over her chest and reveal her discomfort as she passed a series of poisonous shops.

Mandrake's Medicines—To Kill Nasty Colds, Maladies & More

Fausto's: For all your Fennel, Feverfew, and Foxglove Needs!

Hemlock & Hawthorn's Herbery

She was certainly not in the right district. This looked—and smelled—more liked Valenda's infamous Spice Quarter, where people traveled when they wished to purchase contacts for assassins, untraceable poisons, people—or just certain body parts. It was also a home for gambling pits, drug dens, and brothels. None of which were legal in Valenda, so they all existed belowground in primeval passages, accessible only through passwords and hidden doors from the exotic spice shops above.

"Not sure a pretty thing like you should be on these streets alone, even in daylight."

Tella took a nervous step back, though the woman who addressed her looked too old to cause any harm.

The crone had to be at least five times Tella's age, with wrinkled hands stained with ink, and gleaming white hair that nearly reached the ground she swept. Back and forth, the old woman wiped all the dirt and grime away from the front steps of Elantine's Most Wanted.

Tella loosed an uneven breath. The Spice Quarter might have been a stranger to her, but this ramshackle store called to her like an old friend. It was the same place where she'd sent all her letters to Jacks.

Tella had never actually been certain if it was a genuine business or merely an address people used to ferry illicit requests and letters. But clearly it was very real. She'd seen Wanted posters for criminals tacked throughout the quarter, and apparently they'd all come from here.

Tella drew nearer, to better look inside. Parchment posters flapped, flickering black-and-white images, with some of the most interesting criminals she had ever seen. Alluring and disturbing, she wondered if the portraits were bewitched, for they tempted her to climb the steps and come all the way inside, to take a closer peek, the same way her mother's Deck of Destiny had tempted her to play with it all those years ago.

Of course that had led her nowhere good.

"Are you lost?" asked the old woman. "This isn't a district where you want that to happen."

In the distance, bells began to chime. If Tella counted she imagined there'd be ten in total. She was definitely late for her appointment now. Maybe she could come back to explore the shop later.

"I'm searching for Minerva's ModernWear," she said.

The woman's gaze turned shrewd. "Not sure what you need in that place, but I think it's just down that road." She lifted her chin toward a sign down the block labeled *Wrong Way.*

"Watch yourself," the woman called. "Minerva's isn't—"

But Tella didn't catch the rest of the warning as she disappeared down the street. It didn't take long for her stomach to start sweating, and her heart to labor a little more with its beats. But she kept jogging, until she reached a sunlit sidewalk lined in shops as pretty as freshly wrapped packages. Minerva's ModernWear rested on the corner. Closed lilac drapes sheltered the windows and heavy plum awnings shaded the door like sleepy bows.

Scarlett would have hated it, given her distaste for the color purple.

Tella felt a stab of guilt then that she'd left the palace without checking in on her sister, especially after what Scarlett had learned about Armando last night. But Scarlett had also probably heard of Tella's engagement. The moment Scarlett spoke with Tella, she'd know for certain it was a hoax, and very likely try to do something heroic about it that would place her in all sorts of danger that Tella could not allow.

Scarlett was Tella's person—the one someone in the world whom Tella could always count on. Tella might not have believed in falling in love, but she had literally bet her life that Scarlett loved her. Tella would destroy the world before she allowed anything to happen to her sister.

"Pardon me." Tella struggled to catch her breath as she reached the front of Minerva's, where a barrel of a man with slicked-back hair and a plum suit the same hue as the shop guarded the door as if he were an extension of it. "My name's Donatella Dragna."

"A little early, aren't you?" said the man.

Tella was fairly certain he had it backward and that she was rather late. The first of many peculiar observations. The second was the unnecessary number of locks the man unlatched before opening the dark purple door and letting her inside.

Minerva's ModernWear was not an ordinary dress shop. In fact, as Tella entered, she wondered if it was a dress shop at all.

The foyer was decorated with sumptuous lilac lounges, amethyst carpets thicker than uncut grass, and violet vases filled with flowers the size of small trees that smelled of lavender and expensive tobacco. But for all the finery around her, Tella didn't detect any frocks or fashionable accessories.

"Aren't you a vision?"

Tella jumped as a plump seamstress came flitting out of a pair of double doors. Her orchid-colored hair was bobbed boldly at her chin, matching the measuring tapes wrapped around her neck like jewelry. "He told me you were spirited, but he didn't mention how pretty you were. No wonder you captured his attention."

Tella didn't want to smile, given that it wasn't her choice to be here or to be in this relationship with Jacks, but it was rather nice to be fawned over.

"You're earlier than I expected, so you may have to sit for a bit. Would you like any wine or cake while you wait?"

"I never say no to wine or cake."

"I'll have some sent straightaway." The seamstress ushered Tella into another plush purple hall lined in velvet wallpaper and closed doors as dark as black cherries, with equally dark whispers coming from behind them.

"How much poison can these cuff links hold?" muttered a man.

Behind the next door a woman crisply explained, "It's woven between the lace, just a gentle tug and you'll have a garrote."

A couple of doors down Tella heard someone giggling, followed by an accented voice saying, "The sleeves are this puffy so that you can hide a derringer inside. Feel that tiny cradle."

Hidden pistols. Poison. Garrotes.

Definitely not normal, though of course the same sentiment could have been applied to Tella's fiancé. *Fictional fiancé*, she corrected. Although for a charade of an engagement it seemed Jacks was going to a surprising amount of effort.

The seamstress stopped in front of a closed door at the end of the hall. "Why don't you go in and get situated, pet? I'll pop back with your items in a few."

The woman disappeared down the hall and Tella reached for the doorknob. She half expected to find chandeliers made of poison bottles dangling from an aubergine ceiling, mirrors lined with swords, and dressing hooks made of silver daggers.

She'd not expected to see him.

Tella's stomach dipped and her heart might have flipped, the same way it always did whenever she met Dante.

He didn't lounge or rest, he possessed.

In the corner of the suite, atop a raised platform, he sat back in an excessively large black leather chair as if he ruled the world from it. His generous shoulders and chest consumed his temporary throne rather than the other way around. His posture was straight but not rigid, as if he didn't know how to slouch, only how to take up space.

Arrogant scoundrel. Yet even as Tella thought the words, heat spread across her chest as she said, "What are you doing here?"

"Waiting for you."

"How did you know I would be here?"

A slow, superior raise of his brows.

Tella's world tilted once again. "You sent the letter?"

"Disappointed I'm not Jacks?"

She slammed the door shut. "Are you mad? Do you know what my fiancé will do if he discovers this?"

"He'll only find out if you tell him," Dante answered coolly. "And there's no need to pretend with me that you two are actually engaged."

Silent alarms filled the dressing chamber as Jacks's words rushed back to Tella:

Take your tattooed friend over there . . . he's one of Legend's performers, so I can't kill him this week. But if he discovers the truth, I could easily end his life once the game is over.

"Maybe I'm not pretending." Tella started to put on her sweetest smile, but she imagined Dante would know it was false, and she needed to convince him this was the truth. She twisted her mouth into the sort of smirk usually worn by overconfident young men. "When Jacks and I kissed, did it look as if I was acting?"

Dante's intense gaze remained frustratingly level, but Tella swore a muscle ticked near the corner of his jaw. "I'm not sure what you two are doing, but I don't believe you're getting married."

"Why?" Tella challenged. "Because you doubt the heir to the throne would want to marry me?"

A slow curl of his lips said more than any insult ever could. "Do you really want me to answer that?"

Red burst across Tella's cheeks. She was trying to keep Jacks from killing him, but Dante couldn't stop being cruel. "Did you just come here to mock me?"

"What have I said that's mocking? You leap to too many conclusions, Tella." He leaned closer as he said her name, drawing out the syllables, as if it were something he wanted to hold on to. "Maybe I was going to tell you that you're clever and funny and beautiful. I always thought you were too smart to marry a murderer."

"And I've always thought some risks are worth taking," Tella countered, ignoring the way Dante's use of the words *clever* and *funny* and *beautiful* continued to flutter about inside her. "Jacks is handsome and rich, and soon he's going to rule the entire Meridian Empire, which means I'll be the next empress. So, I suppose I should be thanking you for making our introduction possible."

Dante's eyes blazed, a brief spark of fire. He might not have liked what she'd said, but maybe Tella had finally convinced him.

"If you really think I did you a favor—" Dante cut off.

The line of his vision fell, the fire dying in his eyes. He pushed up from his chair, leaped from the platform, and captured Tella's wrist in one abrupt move. "What happened to your hand?"

Drip.

Drop.

Drip.

Each sound mirrored her slowing pulse. Dark, red, unforgiving blood fell from her nails, soaking every fingertip on her right hand. *Jacks.*

Coldness swept over Tella's skin and started sinking in like claws. That wretched, deceitful, remorseless, pain-enjoying prince of vile. It wasn't enough that he'd cursed her to unrequited love; he really was killing her. The slower heartbeats weren't merely in her mind.

White and black spots danced before Tella's eyes.

Three more fat beads of blood fell from her fingernails, leaving fresh stains on the amethyst carpet. But all Tella heard was Jacks's mocking voice warning her there would be side effects from kissing his cursed lips.

"I didn't realize I was still bleeding," Tella lied. "I caught my hand in a carriage door earlier. I should probably go and get it looked at."

Dante held her tighter. "I can take care of it." He yanked off his cravat; his movements were terse, but his hands were excruciatingly careful as he pressed the fabric to her fingers.

Tella's breathing hitched.

Dante shouldn't have been touching her so tenderly, or pulling her closer with every movement, and she shouldn't have been letting him. She should have pushed his giant hands away. Growled at him as he slowly wrapped the warm silk that had encircled his throat around her bleeding hand. Not only because of Jacks's threats, but because of who Dante worked for.

Tella really tried not to give much thought to what would happen when she handed Legend over to Jacks, but she doubted it would be a favorable outcome. Legend could be wicked, but the Prince of Hearts was evil. The sort who'd rip a girl's heart from her chest and sink his teeth into it as if it were an apple.

To protect herself, she needed to stay away from Dante. Even if for a brief moment she just wanted to close her eyes and collapse in his arms.

"Tell me what really happened last night after the heir took you away." His voice was soothing and commanding all at once, like the crackle of flames devouring wood. Fierce and fatal, yet somehow steady and reassuring. The type of voice a girl could have easily been consumed by.

"I really don't need your assistance." Tella yanked her hand away, freeing it from the silk and spattering her lacy gown with blood as she broke Dante's spell before it could be fully cast.

He looked as if he wanted to reach for her. If her unsteady legs so much as swayed his way, she imagined he'd capture her in his arms and hold her so close she'd willingly confess her every sin and secret.

But he didn't honestly care. He was just acting. Playing a role.

She forced herself to take a step back.

A vein throbbed in Dante's neck. "Why won't you let me help you?"

"Maybe I don't want your help!"

Another bead of blood dripped to the floor.

Stars joined the spots in front of Tella's eyes. And before she could take more than one step back, Dante was there, holding her wrist once more, and maybe he was holding her a little more together, as he finished the job he'd started. Tella wouldn't admit it to him, but she felt a little less light-headed as his wide, warm hands wrapped her bloody fingers inside his cravat.

"I'd let you go, but you just admitted you need help." His voice was softer than before. "Tell me what that murderer wants from you."

Why did he have to be so stubborn? Couldn't he just wrap up her fingers and leave her alone?

"Can't you just let this go and pretend you believe it?" she asked. "You're worried about me, but this endangers you, too. If Jacks finds out you know the truth, he'll hurt you in ways that not even Legend can fix." She said it like a threat, but rather than releasing her, Dante gave her a flash of teeth that looked a lot like a smile.

"I didn't think you cared about me," he said.

"I don't," Tella snapped.

It would have been more convincing if she'd pulled her hand away.

She didn't need his help to win the game, and she didn't trust him, but she unfortunately liked the feel of him. The bleeding had brought a chill that hadn't been there before, but Dante managed to erase it as he cradled her hand and leaned in closer, until Tella's back was against the door, and Dante's body was moving closer to hers.

There was still enough room for her to grab the handle, to escape if she wanted. And she told herself that's what she wanted. But her fingers were as stubborn as he was—they refused to reach for the exit.

"Tell me what he wants from you," Dante said roughly.

"He wants to marry me, that's it."

Dante shook his head.

"You know, it's starting to feel really insulting that you keep refusing to believe that."

"Maybe I just don't believe that's all that he wants." Dante's free hand found Tella's cheek and tilted her face toward his.

A flush went down her neck all the way to her toes as he slowly stroked her jaw.

"If you don't tell me, I will figure it out," Dante said.

And doom himself in the process—or reveal her plans to Legend and damn Tella as well as her mother.

Tella forced herself to remove his hand from her cheek. "I don't dislike you, Dante. In fact, if you weren't a mere actor, I would probably really like you. You're almost as good-looking as you think you are. But I want more than a pretty face. Jacks can give me that. He can give me everything I've ever desired." Tella pressed her lips together and briefly closed her eyes, as if imagining the kiss she'd shared with Jacks on the dance floor.

When she opened her eyes again, Dante's face was a bare inch away, and his eyes were as black as spilled ink.

Heat uncurled low in Tella's stomach.

"Either you don't want much, or you're lying," Dante said. "I might believe you'll actually go through with marrying him, but given what I know about you, I doubt someone like him can fulfill your every desire."

When he finished, his lips were so close, one careless move and her mouth would brush his. Tella raised her chin slowly, aware she was walking a treacherous line as she gave him a look made of pure heat. "Maybe there are things you don't know about Jacks."

Dante answered with a grin, but it wasn't kind or warm or soft like grins were supposed to be. It was calculated, the slow, teasing way someone curved his lips just before he turned over a winning hand of cards. "Are you saying that because he's the Prince of Hearts?"

Tella froze, and even the blood spilling from her fingertips stopped as everything inside her panicked, sharpening her senses further. If she wanted to persuade Dante that she had no idea what he was talking about, she'd need to recover quickly, but playing naive would only convince him she was in over her head. And maybe Tella was. She was cursed, her mother was trapped inside a card, and to save them both, Tella was now playing a game involving two infamous immortals—one of whom wasn't supposed to exist anymore.

Yet even before reaching Valenda, Dante had talked about the Prince of Hearts as if he was still alive. It seemed oddly coincidental, especially as she recalled the opening of Jovan's welcome speech:

Elantine has invited us here to save the Empire from her greatest fear.

For centuries the Fates were locked away, but now they wish to come out and play.

What if Jacks was one of the Fates who'd come out to—

No. Tella refused to finish the thought. Believing the game was real led straight to madness. The other obvious explanation was that Jacks was playing a role in the game. But the blood dripping from Tella's fingers and the heart dying in her chest felt like solid proof he was the real Prince of Hearts.

Dante had to be bluffing, gambling with lies just as he'd done with the matron at the palace when he'd first claimed Tella was engaged to Jacks.

"If Jacks really was the Prince of Hearts, I'd already be dead from his kiss."

"Maybe you're his one true love. Or he's allowed you to live because he has other plans." Dante's eyes quickly traveled toward the fitted lines of Tella's lacy sapphire gown, as if he somehow knew Jacks had sent it.

"Don't stare at me like that," Tella said. "You're the one who claimed I was engaged to him."

A final drop of blood fell to the floor, grimly punctuating her sentence.

Dante looked at it and his entire face shifted. His familiar arrogance fell away as he said, "You're right. This is my fault. I made a bad choice. But I swear, when I said you were engaged to the heir, I didn't know he was the Prince of Hearts."

"Then how did you figure it out?"

"When I saw you dance with him at the ball. The Fates aren't natural; they don't belong in this world, just like those of us who have died and come back to life." Dante swallowed thickly, and when he spoke again his voice was unusually quiet. "Everyone else at the ball might have been oblivious, but after he kissed you I saw him glowing—"

Bustling footsteps sounded in the hall outside.

Dante's mouth slammed into a line.

The footsteps grew louder and closer.

"You might want to pretend you don't know me," he said.

"Why?" Tella asked.

"I'm not exactly supposed to be here."

"I thought you arranged this!"

Dante's mouth kicked into a dry smile. "Did I actually say that?"

Bastard!

He pushed off the wall as Tella's mouth fell open. Though she should have known he hadn't actually arranged it. He'd just hijacked her note and crossed out the proper time.

Before she could curse him out loud, someone shoved against the other side of the door.

Tella tripped forward as the door crashed against her.

Dante caught her instantly, two solid arms snaking around her hips, right as the seamstress stepped inside the room.

The woman's eyes landed on their compromising position, before moving to the spatters of blood on Tella's dress and the floor. "I don't know what you're doing in here, young man, but you have half of a second to leave before I tell the heir about this. And I think we all know what will happen then."

"Be careful," Dante countered, "you're making His Deadly Highness sound predictable."

Dante's hands slipped away from Tella as he whispered in her ear, "I know you don't want to believe me, but Caraval is more than just a game this time. I'm not sure what the Prince of Hearts has promised you, but to the Fates, humans are nothing more than sources of labor or entertainment."

Tella's heart managed to kick out a few extra beats, returning to almost a normal rate as Dante left. If Jacks hadn't cursed her, she imagined it would have been pounding loud enough for everyone inside of Minerva's to hear.

Once Dante was gone the seamstress was all smiles again. She set some cake and wine atop a small table that Tella hadn't noticed. It was as if nothing had happened, though Tella wondered if the woman would be reporting everything that occurred to Jacks.

The seamstress spoke of Jacks constantly as she forced Tella to stand so she could fit her dresses. To Tella's dismay, none of them contained any hidden weapons. But Tella couldn't deny the garments were stunning. There were gowns that changed color in the sun, and capes sewn with thread made of stardust so they would always glitter at night.

But according to the seamstress, Tella hadn't even seen the best creations. The woman stepped back into the hall and returned a moment later behind a triple-tiered silver cart.

Someone gasped. Probably Tella.

She might have hated Jacks with the rage of a thousand cursed women, but she had to admit that when he wanted, he knew how to dazzle.

The cart was covered in the most sensational assortment of masks and crowns and capes, made of leather, precious metal, and gossamer-thin fabrics. Every item was fitted to exactly her size and worth a noble's fortune. Some were lined in feathers, others in jewels or polished pearls. All of it monstrously beautiful, like the treasures of a magical nightmare, which she supposed Jacks was.

The seamstress smiled proudly. "His Highness wanted you to have your choice of costumes for Elantine's Eve. But be careful, since everything has been made especially for you, the paint is still wet on a few of the masks."

Tella edged closer to the sparkling cart.

She'd never worn a costume for Elantine's Eve. On Trisda, Empress Elantine's birthday was only celebrated on one day, but in Valenda, Elantine's Eve was supposed to be even more fantastical than Elantine's Day. To celebrate, everyone dressed in costume and took on the role of whoever they dressed as.

Supposedly Valendan monarchs were descended from the Fates, and on the eves of their birthdays it was whispered that the Fates came back for one night, to judge whether a ruler was worthy to reign another year. Therefore, some believed that behind a few of the masks and costumes were the genuine Fates, returned from wherever they'd disappeared for one night of mischief, havoc, and wonder.

Tella imagined the timing of this tradition was why Legend had chosen the Fates to theme this particular Caraval. She could already imagine how Legend would toy with people by having his performers pretend to be the real Fates.

Tella took her time examining the cart. She spied the mask of the Prince of Hearts, but instead of crying painted-red tears, this one wept rubies. The Shattered Crown—which represented an impossible choice between two paths—was tipped in gleaming black opals, dark polished cousins to the ring on Tella's finger. But it was not nearly as glorious as the Unwed Bride's veil of tears, made of real diamonds. It seemed every greater and lesser Fate was there. Tella saw the Poisoner's elaborate cloak, Mistress Luck's feathered hat, Chaos's spiked gauntlets, the Lady Prisoner's porcelain mask with frowning lips made of crushed sapphires.

"Does the heir always go to so much trouble for his ladies?"

"Never," the seamstress answered. "In fact this is the first time he has ever had us design anything for someone other than himself."

Tella feigned a smile. Jacks probably used different tailors for every one of his cursed consorts.

"Choose whichever one you fancy the most and then I'll have you fitted for the costume to go with it."

Every piece glimmered brighter as Tella considered them a final time.

The Maiden Death was out of the question. Tella would not let her head be caged in pearls, and merely thinking about the Maiden Death returned Tella to that day when she'd first flipped over her terrible card and brought about her mother's departure.

The Assassin's skeleton mask was not very attractive. Her Handmaiden's masks were more interesting—she'd always liked the look of their lips sewn shut with crimson thread—but Tella didn't like that the Fates themselves were merely puppets of the Undead Queen. Wearing the Undead Queen's jeweled eye patch felt tempting—it was said she'd traded her eye for her terrible powers—but Tella wanted to make a bolder statement. She liked the Fallen Star, but given how flattering the golden costume was, she imagined half the girls and boys on the street would be dressed as Fallen Stars. And for once Tella wasn't sure she wanted to look pretty.

"What's this one?" Tella picked up a long black veil attached to an unlovely ring of metal covered in black candles. At first she'd thought it belonged to the Murdered King, but his crown was made of daggers, and it was grimly attractive. This was not lovely at all, and Tella doubted it would be easy to see through the veil, yet there was something fiercely arresting about it. For the life of her, she couldn't recognize which Fate it belonged to.

The seamstress paled. "That wasn't supposed to be on this cart." She tried to snatch it away.

Tella stepped back and gripped the crown tighter. "What is it? Tell me or I'll leave without any masks at all."

The seamstress's mouth pinched together. "It's not part of a traditional costume. It represents Elantine's missing child, the Lost Heir."

"Elantine had a child?"

"Of course not. It's just a nasty rumor people started because they'd rather not see your fiancé take the throne."

"Well, that sounds like the perfect costume."

"You're a fool, girl," said the woman. "Whoever put that on my cart did it as a warning to the heir—and to you."

"Don't worry, I'm only doing it as a joke," Tella said. "My fiancé is very fond of tricks. He'll have a great laugh when he sees me, and it will prove to whoever put it on your cart that I'm not scared."

The seamstress creased her mouth. "We don't have a dress to go with it."

"If Jacks hired you, I'm sure you can figure out something." Tella placed the waxy crown of candles atop her head and turned toward the mirrored wall. The gauzy black veil shrouded her features completely, shifting her into a living shadow. Absolutely perfect.

If there was one costume that declared that despite Jacks's kisses and curses he would never fully own her, it was the crown of the Lost

Heir. Maybe it was a foolish choice to be so defiant, but it was one of the few choices Jacks had given her.

The seamstress shook her head, again muttering something about Tella having no idea what sort of game she was playing.

But Tella knew exactly what type of game she was a part of: one that would destroy her and the people she cared about if she didn't win.

17

Tella rode back to the palace beneath the slow descent of a falling sun. It was late afternoon, that warm hour of the day where the cerulean sky was usually tinged with gold and butter and wisps of peach light. But to Tella's eyes all the colors above could have been called sepia at best. Everywhere she looked the sky was brownish, and dullish, and just wrongish enough to make her wonder if the afternoon was off or if it was her vision.

By the time she reached the palace she was half convinced another one of Jacks's side effects was watching the once bright world lose all its color. But perhaps the true side effect was paranoia. Unlike the dull outside, Tella's tower suite was as blissfully blue as before—from the periwinkle canopy above her bed to the tinted teal waters waiting for her in the bath.

But Tella didn't have time to wash up more than her hands. She barely had enough minutes to change from her stained lace gown into a new dress from the seamstress. Made of midnight-blue satin and thick black velvet stripes that slashed down a full skirt, the gown was darker than Tella's usual attire, but something about the combination made her feel fierce enough to battle Jacks and Legend and anyone in Valenda participating in Caraval.

With a fresh bounce to her step, which she hoped wouldn't leave, Tella marched out of her bedroom into the main suite, and swallowed a curse at the sight of her sister.

Scarlett sat in front of one of the unlit white fireplaces. Tella didn't know how Scarlett had found her way in, but she shouldn't have been surprised. If Scarlett Dragna had a magical ability, it would be the power to always find her sister. Tella didn't know if older sisters were always connected to their younger siblings this way, or if it was something special between the two of them. Tella would never admit it to Scarlett, but knowing her sister could track her down regardless of the obstacles was one of the few things that truly made Tella feel safe, though it wasn't always convenient or comfortable.

Tella was not proud of herself for avoiding Scarlett. She'd had a valid reason not to go to her last night, but she should have made time to check in on her that morning and to apologize for not telling the truth about Armando.

As Tella stepped deeper into the room, Scarlett's head remained down toward her hands, where she held the pair of nude gloves that Jacks had sent that morning.

"Did you know gloves are a symbolic gift?" Scarlett rubbed the soft sheaths between her fingers. "It's out of fashion now, but I once read that at the start of Elantine's reign giving a pair of gloves was a custom connected with asking for a girl's hand in marriage. I think it was supposed to be a young man's way of saying he'll take care of a girl by giving her gloves to protect her hands."

"I'd prefer something a little less symbolic and a little more practical, like blood."

Scarlett's head shot up from the gloves. "That's not very romantic."

But Tella swore a bolt of red shot up her sister's throat and color flooded her cheeks, as if the idea thrilled her more than it repulsed her. *Interesting.*

Tella had only said it to bring a bit of levity, but maybe she'd meant it a little, and since the statement seemed to have pulled Scarlett's thoughts in a brighter direction, Tella continued. "I read about it in one of your wedding books. It was an ancient marital custom. People would drink each other's blood to synchronize their heartbeats. So that even when they were parted they could sense if the other was safe or afraid by the pace of their hearts. That's what I would want, someone who would give me a piece of himself rather than scraps of fabric."

"So, did your fiancé give you a vial of blood before he proposed last night?"

A curse burned Tella's tongue. Her sister was supposed to be there to talk about Armando. But it seemed Scarlett was avoiding that subject, not that Tella could blame her. Though she wished she'd not focused on this topic instead. "How did you hear?"

"I might not have gone to the ball last night, but I didn't curl up and hide beneath the palace," Scarlett said. "Although even if I had, I imagine I'd have still caught the rumors about the heir's very public display of affection and whirlwind engagement to a girl named Donatella."

"Scar, I can explain, you don't have to worry."

"Do I appear worried?"

Scarlett might have looked a bit somber, but now that her head wasn't bowed Tella was surprised to see there were no anxious lines around her hazel eyes, her pink lips weren't pinched, her hands weren't wringing, and her voice was pleasantly light.

It was actually unnerving. Scarlett worried all the time, even when there was nothing to fret about, and right now there were definitely things that should concern her.

"So you really don't care that I'm engaged?" Tella plopped onto the tufted chaise across from Scarlett.

"Tella, I know you're only kidding, but this is veering into slightly uncomfortable territory for me. Can you just tell me what really happened?"

Blast it all. This was exactly what Tella feared.

Scarlett continued to give her sister a smile that was both strained and a little patronizing, as if Tella were a very young girl caught up in a make-believe fairy tale. Tella couldn't blame her. In some ways that was exactly how it felt to Tella. She was staying in a golden tower. A wicked prince had cursed her and imprisoned her mother, and if

Tella failed at her task, they'd both be doomed, and so would Scarlett, who'd be left without anyone.

Tella took a deep breath. She had convinced her sister of a sham engagement during Caraval, and she could do it again. She had to do it again if she wanted to keep her sister safe.

"I know it seems sudden and unbelievable," Tella said. "I still can't fathom it myself. The truth is we've been writing letters for over a year, but I had no idea he was the heir until last night. So when he proposed I couldn't say no—"

"Tella, stop." The color fled from Scarlett's cheeks. "I don't know what you're trying to do, but this really isn't humorous."

"It's not supposed to be. If you'd been there last night, you would have seen and understood."

"Last night was the start of Caraval," Scarlett argued. "Everything that went on in that ballroom was just a game. You know that."

"Scar, I know what Caraval is." And Tella knew how ludicrous she sounded. She could see now it had been a mistake to tell her sister about the letters—the story sounded too close to Scarlett's own history. But Tella had the Aracle, she could prove what she was saying, and maybe it was time her sister heard the full—or almost full—truth. "This is different, Scar. And it isn't just about me, it involves our mother—"

"No," Scarlett snapped, her voice so sharp it rattled the chandelier. "It's never different, no matter how much you want to believe it. I don't care what it involves. When I played, it seemed impossible for it to be just a game. Legend planted Julian in our lives before the game had even begun. Then I saw him die, and I saw you die. And even once it was all done, and I knew which parts were real and which parts were lies, I found out I was wrong, that I broke up with a fake fiancé because I had never met the real one." Scarlett's voice cracked. Tella swore she saw the words shatter on the carpet and spill across the palatial floor as her sister finally fell apart.

Tella had pushed her too far. She'd also not meant for this. She had not wanted Scarlett to be deceived so deeply, or fall in love, end up heartbroken, head-sick, and confused. Caraval was supposed to bring them both freedom from fear and confinement and miserable marriages.

"If it helps, I was tricked too." Tella shoved up from her seat and cautiously moved closer. Scarlett was taller than Tella, and yet somehow she looked small and unusually fragile as she hunched in front of the empty fireplace. "I swear I had no idea the count was played by an actor until after it was over. But I'm still very sorry."

"I know," Scarlett mumbled. "I'm not upset at you. I should have figured it out on my own. It wasn't as if no one told me that it all was only a game. I imagine it's too late to stop you from playing, but Tella, please, be cautious." Scarlett looked up abruptly. "I know Caraval can be magical and romantic and wonderful, but the spells it casts aren't easily shaken off, and half the time I don't even think people realize they have been bewitched."

"Scar, if you're right, and it's all just a game, then doesn't that mean there's nothing for you to worry about? Unless you don't really believe it's only a game?"

"It's not the game I'm worried about," Scarlett said. "I'm thinking about your heart, Tella. I don't know what's really going on with you and these engagement rumors, but I know that Caraval has a way of making people fall in love, and sometimes it's with people who might not be entirely real."

Tella wasn't fool enough to say out loud that it would never happen to her. She also believed that when girls voiced sentiments like that aloud they were usually wishing for the opposite to occur, daring the Fates to bring the one thing they claimed not to want.

But Tella wanted love about as much as she wished to contract a disease. There were no kisses worth dying for. No souls worth merging with. There were many beautiful young men in the world, but Tella believed that none of them could be trusted with something as fragile, or valuable, as a heart—especially when her heart had been doomed by the Prince of Hearts to be broken long ago. And even if that wasn't her destiny, she wasn't about to fall in love with someone who was only playing a role.

Of course she couldn't say any of this to Scarlett right now, not when Tella could see her sister's heart crumbling because of Julian.

The very thing he'd done to keep her was the very thing that had broken them apart. Tella should have tried harder to convince him to tell the truth. She knew it wasn't all her fault, but she could have helped prevent some of this.

"I don't believe it's as hopeless as it seems," Tella said. "I think Julian is so used to lying it's all he knows how to do. Before now I don't imagine he's ever had a reason to change. But I believe he loves you; it's clear to anyone who sees the way he looks at you. You're the starlight to his darkness, and if you feel the same about him, you should give him another chance."

"I want to think you're right," Scarlett said. "But Julian promised not to lie to me at the end of Caraval, and he couldn't even keep that vow for one day."

Tella had broken promises just as fast, but now was probably not a good time to bring that up. And she didn't want to make Scarlett's choices for her. She did believe that Julian loved her sister, but maybe his life was so entrenched in lies that he was incapable of change, and Scarlett deserved more than that. Tella just hoped whatever she did, Scarlett wouldn't start thinking about the count again.

She perched on the edge of the stony white fireplace, next to her sister. "So do you just plan on hiding in the palace all week?"

"I don't know." Scarlett's gaze grew distant as she peered out the window toward the rest of the palace and the city beyond. Her mouth twisted with a thought. Then she tilted her head, her eyes taking in all the elegant blue furniture before they lifted toward the ceiling, where a host of carved cherubs watched from above.

"Maybe I'll stay in here," Scarlett said. "This suite is large enough to build another suite in."

"Which reminds me," Tella asked, "How *did* you get in here?"

A piece of Scarlett's smile returned. "I might have thrown a vase in my room last night and accidently opened an entry to a hidden tunnel." She crossed over to the second fireplace and ran a hand along the edge of the mantel until something clicked. The scent of cobwebs and sooty secrets moved through the air and several bricks shifted all at once.

"That's brilliant!" Tella clapped.

Scarlett's face brightened. "If you want, I'll show them to you."

Tella was certainly curious. But from the closest window she could see the colors outside had changed. All the browns had shifted into promising shades of bronze. A final good-bye before the sun went down. Soon night would make her appearance; a new one of Legend's constellations would materialize in the sky. Caraval would start once more, and Tella didn't want to be late.

According to what Jacks had said the night before, and to what Tella suspected as well, the first clue she'd received, which spoke of a region that provided promises of both faith and magic, made her think the second clue would be found in the Temple District. Tella hadn't seen that part of the city yet, but she knew it was larger than the Spice Quarter and the Satine District put together. It could take all night to search.

"Maybe you can show me later," Tella said. "It's almost sunset, I should be leaving."

Tella hadn't even said the word *Caraval*, but just like that, Scarlett's grin faded.

Tella reached for Scarlett's hand. It was hard enough to leave her when Tella knew her sister was hurting; the last thing she wanted was for Scarlett to worry about Tella on top of it. "I know you don't trust my judgment right now. But, I know which parts are just a game—"

Scarlett cut in with a sigh. "It's not that I don't trust you. I don't trust Legend, or anyone who works for him, and I think you'd be wise to do the same. At least remember the stories Nana Anna told us—Legend likes to be the villain."

Tella grinned. "How could I forget? That was always my favorite part."

But it couldn't be true for this game. If Legend was really the villain, then there was only one possible person he could be—*Jacks.*

Tella didn't even want to consider it, though she could picture Jacks in a top hat and tailcoat, holding out a red rose while his lips curved into a wicked smile. And maybe if Tella's fingertips hadn't started bleeding in front of Dante that morning, she might have been tempted to think Jacks was really Legend, and all of this was just a cruel trick.

But Tella knew Jacks was the real Prince of Hearts. She knew it as deeply as she'd known that her sister would be able to wish her back to life if she died. Tella had felt Jacks's power since the moment they'd kissed. It was different from the magic of Caraval. Legend's power glittered like dreams come to life, while Jacks's magic was nightmarish. Even now she felt it, incrementally slowing her heartbeat.

Beat . . . beat.

Nothing.

Beat . . . beat.

Nothing.

Beat . . . beat . . .

Nothing.

A ticking clock inside her chest.

Tella didn't want to be cursed, and face the possibility of death. But she wanted to save her mother, she wanted to see her again in the flesh, to find out who she really was and why she'd left. And if Jacks was Legend or one of his actors, that would never happen.

Jacks could not be Legend. But if he was, then Legend was a greater villain than Tella had ever imagined.

NIGHT TWO OF CARAVAL

A crimson constellation of stars glittered above the Temple District.

From Tella's sky carriage it had looked like an enchanted cluster of roses in full bloom. Now that she was in the district, standing beneath the stars, the entire image was harder to take in. Instead of seeing a constellation of roses, the ruby lights looked like drops of spilled star-blood, shimmering unnatural light on the world below.

Even without the eerie rose-gold glow from above, the Temple District would have been an odd place. Wailing cries of worshippers, whispered prayers of sinners, ancient chants, and a number of strangely dressed people surrounded Tella as she trod a mosaic of timeworn streets lit by torches as tall as people.

Tella didn't know if this part of the city was always so popular or if the crowds were only because of everyone participating in Caraval and searching for the second clue.

She reached into her velvet pocket and reread the first clue under the burning red torchlight:

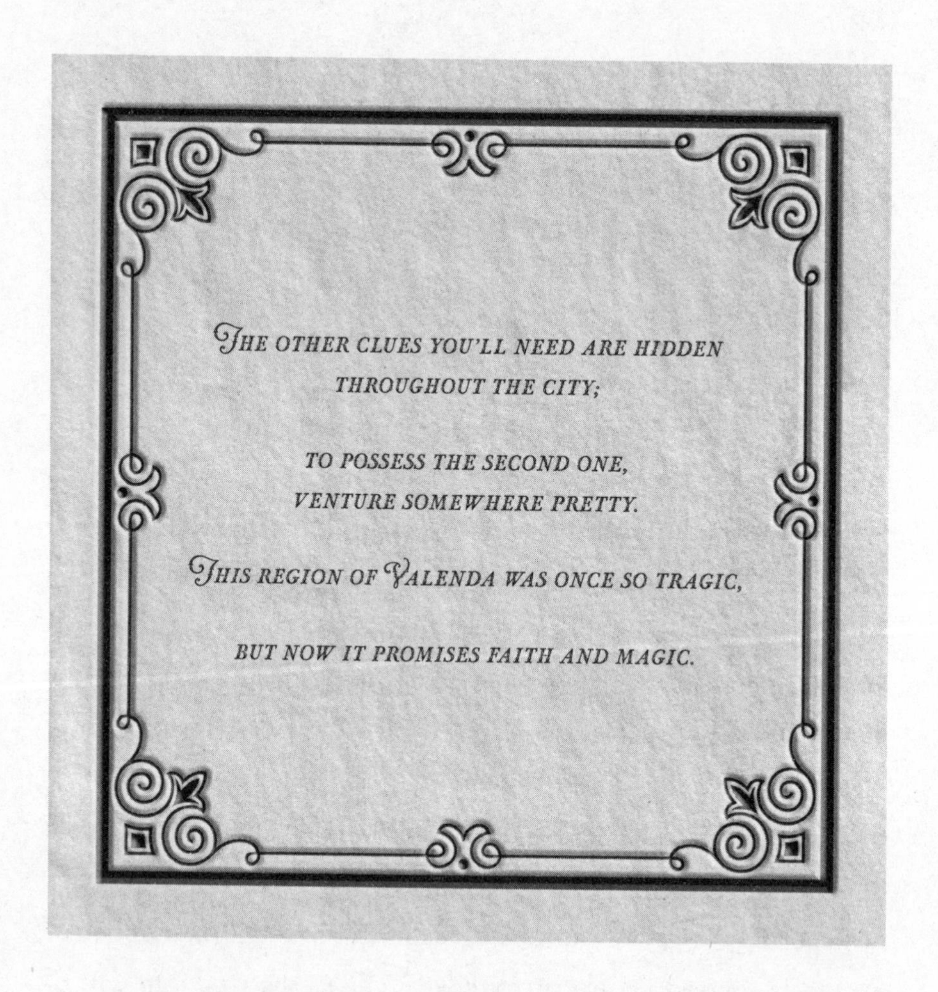

THE OTHER CLUES YOU'LL NEED ARE HIDDEN
THROUGHOUT THE CITY;

TO POSSESS THE SECOND ONE,
VENTURE SOMEWHERE PRETTY.

THIS REGION OF VALENDA WAS ONCE SO TRAGIC,

BUT NOW IT PROMISES FAITH AND MAGIC.

The description definitely fit the Temple District, where all manner of interesting religions and beliefs were practiced, but it could have applied to almost any of the worship houses.

Tella passed towering tabernacles, antique missions, and fresh young bathhouses where visitors could wash themselves in holy spirits—or at least those were the claims.

On Trisda, religion was unornamented and simple. People prayed to specific saints for what they wanted and asked priests for forgiveness by writing their sins on paper that the holy women and men would burn. But here, Tella wasn't sure if people were actually worshipping or performing.

She'd heard people could practice whatever faith they wanted as long as they remained within the district borders. But only a few of the religions looked as if they were true faiths in higher powers. Many of the spiritual practices Tella observed looked more like shows meant to thrill and tantalize tourists into willingly emptying their pockets.

Before arriving she'd been told there was even a Church of Legend, which seemed like the most obvious place to search for the next clue. Unfortunately, the Church of Legend was hidden from plain view. Finding it was supposed to be like a game. Tella might not have minded if she'd been at her full strength, but her legs were shakier than they should have been, and her breath was a little shallow.

As she searched street after street, Tella saw churches dedicated to each element. The fire worshippers were her favorite; they danced in front of their temple with sticks made of flames. Next door was a church formed of waterfalls, which flowed over statues of mermen and mermaids that people threw shells before as offerings. From there Tella passed a row of tabernacles dedicated to the various Fates.

These crumbling structures looked older than the rest. Some were merely ruins, remnants of the days when the Fates still ruled. Few people currently worshipped the Fates, though there was a large group gathered in front of Mistress Luck's Shrine, all of them dressed in elaborate green-feathered caps and voluminous capes.

But no matter how hard Tella searched, she saw no symbols of Caraval. No roses—other than those in the sky. No black hearts. No top hats. Although there were people in costume—or "religious garments," as she'd heard others call them. As Tella pushed her tired limbs to keep going, she spied horned helmets for those who honored ancient warrior gods, and necklaces made of bones for those who worshipped Death. She didn't know if she needed different attire for her destination, but it seemed whatever she didn't own could be bought from one of the carts on the street.

"Would you like a ghost hood?" someone called. "Keeps away the demons. Only three coppers."

"Or if you'd prefer to meet the demons, we have beads of depravity!" called his partner. "Only one copper."

"What makes you think I'm interested in demons?" Tella teased.

The vendor flashed a grin of missing teeth. "You're here. People claim they search these streets looking for saviors, but that's rarely what they find."

"Then I suppose it's good the man I'm looking for has never claimed to be a savior." Tella blew the vendor a kiss and delved farther into the crush of eager tourists, greedy traders, and enthusiastic Valendans participating in Caraval.

The people on the streets were thicker than maggots on death, except for on the stretch of ivory road in front of the Temple of the Stars.

Tella's legs slowed a little. She knew she couldn't stop, but it was distressingly tempting. This was by far the prettiest of the temples. A bastion of stones as white as goddess robes and innocent sacrifices. But Tella knew the temple's insides were far from pure or holy.

The stars supposedly walked on earth long before the Fates, so long ago that they were more legends than anything else. But people whispered with true belief that no matter how they looked up in the skies, the stars were not angelic creatures made of light and angel dust. Some said the stars were the ones who'd created the Fates, which many claimed made the stars the most vicious beings of all.

Yet, there were still those who willingly joined the congregation believing someday the stars would return and richly reward all those who followed them. Tella had heard the richest of people tithed things like their free will, their beauty, and their firstborn children for a chance to become members.

"If you want to enter you'll need the right clothes!" someone called from across the way. "We sell acolyte sheaths for only five coppers."

"You don't want to join that temple, not when I can offer you something better at a lower price!" another merchant cried. His voice was familiar.

Tella turned and promptly wished she hadn't.

Julian, dressed in alexandrite-green traders' robes, stood with his arms spread wide, drawing Tella's stunned attention to a series of altars with men tied to them, chilled smiles on their moon-white lips, and eyes on the ruby skies as if they were the most willing of sacrifices.

"Julian, what—what are you doing?" Tella stammered.

"My apologies, lovely miss, have we met before?" He studied her as if he'd never seen her.

Tella knew he was playing the role he'd been assigned for Caraval. But it was still disturbing to watch his gaze turn greedy, as if she were a lamb he wanted to shepherd down the wrong path.

"I don't remember you," he purred, "but you're pretty so I'll give you a deal. You can feel the same ecstasy as my tied-up friends for only four coppers!"

"Or you can atone for your sins for free." A woman in a dazzling white cowl drew Tella's attention away from this alarming version of Julian, and toward another unnerving site. She motioned to a series of cages and stocks, reeking of sweat and regret and unwashed bodies. These people didn't look quite so willing as Julian's sky-worshipping sacrifices. And Tella wasn't looking for redemption or atonement; she wanted to find Legend.

"You probably shouldn't stare, or they'll take it as a yes and shove you in one of those prisons as well."

Tella turned to see Dante, standing across from a Bleeding Throne fountain.

He leaned one jacketed elbow against a tarnished silver door, the color of disillusioned dreams and bad decisions. Or maybe he was the one who looked like a bad decision.

In Decks of Destiny, Fallen Stars were always pictured as deceptive gods or goddesses in twinkling golden capes and thin white sheaths. But as Tella looked at Dante, covered in ink-dark shades of black that blended in with the night, she imagined the pictures on the cards could have been mistaken. Gold shimmered no matter what, but few people could make darkness glitter the way he did.

"You need to quit following me," Tella said.

"Maybe I'm actually helping you." He straightened the fresh black cravat around his neck as his gaze latched on to the door behind him, landing on a Caraval symbol etched atop the doorknob's bulbous brass handle.

The entrance to the Church of Legend.

"I would have found it on my own," Tella huffed.

"Of course you would have." Dante continued to stand directly in front of the door, grinning a little too wide as Tella stepped closer.

"Weren't you the one who said you see girls the same way we see party dresses, only to be used once?"

"Clearly I view you a little differently." He reached for one of her errant curls and wound it around one tattooed finger, the black rose on the back of his hand spinning until it turned red beneath the ruby starlight. With every turn he drew her closer. He made it easy to ignore her achy legs and her dying heart. He twisted the hair around his finger in the same way she imagined he wanted to wrap her around his finger.

As if she would ever let him.

Arrogant. Overconfident. Vain. Impossible. She hated the way he refused to leave her alone, how he took her insults the same way other boys might take a compliment, and that his interest in her was clearly only part of his role. And yet she could never seem to push him away.

"If you're here to learn about Legend," he said, "I can tell you more than anyone inside there."

"Would you tell me who he is?" Tella asked.

"You know I can't do that."

"You could if you were Legend."

Dante's voice rumbled with a laugh. "If I was Legend I'd definitely never tell you."

"Because you don't trust me?"

"No," he answered slowly, gently tugging her even closer. "I'd hold on to my secret because I'd want to keep playing the game with you, and if I told you the truth it would spoil all the fun."

His eyes stayed locked with hers, as if there was something unspoken he was trying to say. If another boy had looked at her that way she might have felt momentarily special. People rarely looked each other in the eye for prolonged periods of time. There was almost something more intimate about it than touching. When Dante looked in Tella's eyes he wasn't watching the rest of the world. He wasn't looking out for himself. He was risking part of his person to focus solely on her.

Tella wondered if this was the true allure of Caraval, not the magic or the mystery, but the way Legend's players knew how to make people feel. During the last game, Julian had constantly pushed Scarlett outside of her comfort zone. Dante was doing the same thing to Tella, but instead of pushing, he was pulling her toward him, attempting to reel her into his intoxicating sphere by pretending he cared, and that he didn't merely want her, but a part of him needed her. She sensed it in the subtle way he held his breath as he waited for her answer. It was terrifying how such a small thing could hold so much power.

He was definitely good at his job. She knew he was only acting. That he didn't actually care or need her. And yet instead of walking past him into the Church of Legend she found herself wanting to play along with him for just a little longer. "So if you were Legend and we were partners, would you be helping me win or sabotaging my efforts?"

"Definitely helping." Dante began untwisting her hair, letting his warm fingers brush her neck, and then leaving them on her pulse as he whispered, "Even if I wasn't Legend I would want you to win."

He kept his eyes on hers as if there was something else he needed to say, and it scared Tella how much she wanted to hear it, even though she couldn't have believed it. She didn't really believe Dante was Legend either. As fun and clever as Tella was, so were countless other girls, and she imagined the master of Caraval had better things to do than follow any of them around. And yet, she couldn't completely dismiss the idea, because as much as it might hurt later on, and as foolish as it could make her in the end, a part of her wanted it to be true, wanted to believe that something inside of her burned bright enough to capture Legend's uncapturable attention.

Tella's sluggish heart skipped a beat at the thought. With Dante's warm fingers on her pulse she imagined he felt it. His eyes were shining brighter than his smile, but maybe it was because he could also feel her starting to give in to him, falling for the act he was inevitably putting on.

"I wish I could believe you." She said it like a joke as she leaned back, until his hand fell away from her neck.

She started to reach for the door.

Then his fingers were around her wrist, tugging her back to him. There was something almost desperate about the way he held on to her. "What if I told you the real reason for this game? Would you believe I wanted to help you then?"

"Dante, I never believe anything you say."

"But you remember my words well enough to repeat them."

Tella didn't respond, which he took as an invitation to continue. "Do you know how Legend gained his magic?"

"I thought it came from a wish, that one impossible wish we're all supposed to get if we want something enough." She said it skeptically. Although her sister had used a wish to bring Tella back to life in the last game, a part of Tella had always doubted Legend's epic magic came from something so simple. And maybe Tella liked the way Dante responded when she challenged him, the way his eyes shimmered and his fingers tightened around her wrist, as if he didn't plan on letting her go until he had the last word.

"Everyone does get a wish," Dante said, "but each wish needs magic to help it along. And Legend wanted especially powerful magic. So he sought out the witch who'd cursed the Fates."

"How did he find her?"

"In a land far away. If Legend wants something, he'll go beyond the ends of this earth for it." Dante's tone was intentionally untrustworthy, as if telling a mythical story to a child, and yet the hand around her wrist grew hotter with each word. He kept speaking in the same devil-may-care tone, but the weight of what he'd said felt heavier than anything else he'd told her that night.

"When the witch that Legend visited banished the Fates, she took half of their magic, so that even if the Fates returned, they would not have the same power as before. It was this magic that she used for Legend's wish. But she warned Legend that if the Fates ever managed to break her curse, they would kill to get their magic back. I think this was her way of ensuring the Fates never returned. The witch knew that in order to keep his powers forever, Legend would eventually have to destroy the Fates, or be destroyed."

Dante stood close enough to whisper as he finished. He didn't mention Jacks, but he didn't need to. Tella couldn't help adding what she already knew about the Fates to what Dante had just said. The pieces fit too well not to put them together.

She'd learned from Jacks that the Fates had all been imprisoned in a deck of cards. If there was any truth to what Dante said, half of the Fates' powers had been taken as well, which possibly explained why Jacks wanted Legend. Maybe Jacks had escaped from the cards but he wasn't at his full power, so he needed to take them back.

Jacks had made it sound as if the other Fates were still trapped. But Legend must have known that the Prince of Hearts was free. For Legend, that was probably enough to make him decide it was time to destroy all the Fates.

For centuries the Fates were locked away, but now they wish to come out and play.

If they regain their magic the world will never be the same, but you can help stop them by winning the game.

Tella shook her head. This was just what Scarlett had warned her would happen. She'd said Tella would be unable to tell the difference between the parts that were real and the parts that were merely a game.

Tella knew Jacks was real. But it was madness to start believing the game was real as well.

Tella slid her wrist from Dante's grip. "Thank you for that *interesting history.*"

"Wait, before you—"

Dante cut off.

Tella tensed, afraid she'd started bleeding again, but Dante's eyes weren't on her. She looked over her shoulder, to where his gaze had abruptly gone. She thought she saw Jovan. Only instead of being dressed like Jester Mad, as she had been last night, she was cloaked in a robe. It whipped around her ankles as she scurried away.

Dante turned back to Tella, quickly reached inside his jacket, and pulled out a pair of black elbow-length gloves. "If you won't accept my help, at least take these." He pressed on one of the pearl buttons lining the gloves.

Click.

Click.

Click.

Click.

Click.

Five knife-sharp razors shot out from the fingertips.

"You're giving me gloves with razor blades?"

Tella felt suddenly relieved Dante's fingers were no longer on her rapidly heating skin, as Scarlett's words rushed back: *"Gloves are a symbolic gift . . . connected with asking for a girl's hand in marriage . . . a young man's way of saying he'll take care of a girl, by giving her gloves to protect her hands."*

Tella's skin burned even hotter as the razors glinted in the torchlight. Ten tiny promises of protection. But Tella knew Dante wanted to marry her about as much Jacks did. He'd probably just stolen the gloves on his way out of Minerva's, from a girl who just happened to have the same size arms and fingers as Tella.

"What do you want in exchange for these?"

"Maybe I just want to make sure I see you again." Dante pressed the pearls once more to retract the blades before folding the gloves into her hands.

Then the impossible bastard was striding away.

He went in the same direction as the cloaked figure who looked like Jovan. Tella was half tempted to follow, but that was probably what Dante wanted—to distract her from entering the Church of Legend and finding the next clue.

Tella turned back to the door, but the symbol of Caraval was gone, vanished like magic, which felt like further confirmation she was in the right place.

Tella's religious experiences on Trisda might have been limited to desperate prayers and smuggling letters through the priest's small confessional, but as she entered the Church of Legend, she could instantly tell this was not an ordinary place of worship.

"Welcome." A dusky-skinned girl in a dainty top hat greeted Tella with a curtsy made of narrowed eyes and red ruffles. So many red ruffles. Tella knew Legend favored red, but this girl seemed desperate. Red ruffles wrapped around her platinum gown like a stripe on a cane of candy.

"Congratulations on finding our door, but now you must choose carefully if you wish to enter the church."

The girl waved a ruffled arm and several brassy candelabras sparked to life, illuminating more than a dozen sets of stairs. All covered in thick ruby carpets, they writhed in every direction, up and down and side to side, like escaped blood veins before they disappeared into the black beyond. Some stairs appeared to be more worn than the others, but all of them shimmered with the same dull oak lighting, hinting at shine that had long since dimmed.

"Only one of these will lead you to where you wish to go," said the girl.

"And where will the others take me?"

The girl's crimson smile dripped at the corners. "That's a mystery you must risk if you wish to join our congregation and serve the great Legend."

Tella didn't wish to join anything, she definitely had no plans to serve Legend, and she really didn't feel like climbing up or down any stairs, but she had heard that finding the church was supposed to be like a game.

Tella examined the ruby stairs again. Each possessed a different personality, like the playful golden-lined corkscrews to her right. Then there was the adventurously carved case that stretched straight ahead as if it were a bridge to a fantasyland. The rickety stairs to her left appeared untrustworthy, as did the twisting wrought-iron case without handrails that she wasn't about to attempt. Lastly, Tella's eyes fell on a luscious black marble case, polished to a mirror-shine and covered with a deep, untouched garnet-red carpet. They appeared to go down instead of up.

Tella tried to see where the other girl's eyes darted, curious as to which path she would choose. But her gaze remained narrowed on Tella.

"Decide?"

Tella's eyes returned to the lush marble case with the untouched garnet carpet. The girl's expression didn't shift, but she swore her shoulders stiffened. She didn't want Tella taking those steps, and Tella had a feeling it wasn't because this girl feared for her safety.

"Are you sure you wouldn't rather choose another set?" asked the girl.

"I think I'll like what I find at the end of these."

The girl laughed, but it sounded forced as Tella swept onto the immaculate black marble staircase and took her first step down.

The marble stairway didn't feel quite like Legend, but Tella sensed that it was trying. With each flight the air grew colder. Candles on the wall winked out, while mysterious black stains spotted the once immaculate carpet and the smooth banister, mimicking drops of dried blood. But Tella had seen enough real blood spatter to know how it usually fell and the color it turned once it dried. Not blood here, an illusion.

Just in case, Tella pulled out Dante's razor-tipped gloves. They smelled of him, like ink and secrets. But unlike Dante, they were cool to the touch as she slid them on, liking the gentle weight of the hidden blades at the tips of her fingers.

After a few more steps she stole a waxy candle from a sconce. Behind it, holes poked through the wall so bits of dry wind could make the lights flicker. At least they were clever here. Though Tella regretted wearing such a heavy gown as the stairs grew steeper. The wind holes in the walls disappeared next, covered up by thickly framed portraits—all of young men, with top hats.

At first she wondered if these were the church's members, but the faces were all too handsome, and a little too wicked. *Legend.*

Not real pictures of him. No one knew for certain what he looked like, but clearly members of the church had attempted to render him. Tella saw skin tones ranging from translucent white to dark shades of brown. Some faces were narrow and as sharp as curse words; others were almost cherubic in their curves or seraphic in their chiseled edges. A few faces were scarred, some grinned, while others glared. Tella's heartbeat stopped entirely as she spied a narrow face that reminded her of Jacks, with silver-blue eyes and golden hair. The final portrait winked, as if it were all a great joke.

Perhaps it was. Perhaps Legend was toying with her yet again, and the stairs went on forever and ever and ever. Tella's lethargic legs turned to liquid at the thought. Maybe there was no way to ever truly find Legend, and the church represented an endless search for a man who was unsearchable.

Or perhaps Tella was being overdramatic.

Brighter light lit the stairs below, making it clear there was an ending in sight. Tella shoved her torch in an empty sconce and quickened her pace.

A few steps later pitchy notes of music sounded—a squeaky violin, cimbalom, and a banjo. Tella wouldn't have said the music was pretty, but it was just the right combination of strange and enticing, matching the tavern she found at the bottom.

She'd expected more red, but everything was green instead,

glowing like ripening magic. Tella no longer felt fatigued as she breathed it all in, as if the air was as intoxicating as the drinks the tavern served.

Dark green kerosene lamps illuminated pale mint-green glass tables, while velvet green settees cushioned people sucking on glowing cubes of green sugar, or sipping vials of vivid lime liquid. Even the floor was covered in tiny emerald tiles, which reminded Tella of mermaid tails. This was nothing like the taverns back on Trisda, which only came in shades of dull and smelled of dashed dreams and cheap rum. It wasn't quite like the pubs of Caraval, either, but it was an interesting attempt.

With its quirky music and glowing green drinks, it bordered on the type of surreal that made Tella imagine it could have been a Fate pictured on the Decks of Destiny. *Tavern Emerald*, she would have called it. Where answers to dangerous questions could be found. There was the Blank Card in the deck, and Tella may have wondered if this saloon was perhaps that undepicted Fate. But for all its sparkle, once Tella looked closer she thought it seemed more like glitter pretending to be stardust.

It seemed even the steps she'd seen upon first entering weren't as dangerous as the ruffled girl wanted Tella to think, but merely a test as Tella had been warned. Between the tables, the bar, and the floating balconettes, Tella spied the ends of all the other staircases—every set led to the same place. Like Caraval it seemed this church was full of illusions, and clearly its members enjoyed them.

The patrons in the tavern seemed to have traveled from all over. As she wove deeper inside, Tella's ears picked up hints of different languages, while her eyes saw skin colors ranging from pale to dark. The fashion choices were varied as well, but almost everyone had one thing in common: top hats.

Tella had no idea if people wore them because they worshipped Legend or wanted to be him, but almost every person in the bar had one. Some hats were stout, some were straight, others curved or were purposely bent out of shape. A few had feathers, veils, or other bits of cheeky adornment. Tella even spied a top hat with horns coming out the sides, and one young woman had two miniature pink top hats that popped out of her head like ears.

Maybe this was the real reason why Dante had fled rather than followed her. Perhaps he was jealous of all of the people who so blatantly worshipped Legend. Not that Tella should have been thinking of Dante, or wondering what he would have said if he were there with her.

Tella looked past all the merriment, searching for where a clue might be hidden, until her eyes landed on a queue of people. They lined up in front of a pair of black velvet curtains rimmed in gaudy gold tassels. Again, it was a bit too garish, a touch too blatant to truly feel like Legend. It felt more like the way people perceived him, an image she believed he was happy to perpetuate. In the last Caraval, Caspar, the actor who had played the role of Legend, had put on a performance that had been dazzlingly over the top. But Tella did not imagine the real Legend was that way.

Although Tella had not uncovered Legend's true identity, she had received letters from him. The messages came without adornment; one had only contained a single sentence, and still she'd felt his magic pulsing through those simple words.

As beguiling as the Church of Legend was, Tella imagined it had Legend all wrong. Caraval might have been extreme in all of its splendor, but she didn't think he was.

Yet she found herself drawing closer to the tasseled curtains. The line in front of them buzzed with eager whispers, lots of hands tightening cravats, pinching cheeks to bring color, and straightening top hats. Though, unlike the rest of the tavern, it appeared not everyone wore a top hat, giving Tella the impression these people weren't members of the church, but players in search of the next clue.

Tella neared the front of the line, not wanting to wait at the end, nor thinking it wise to try to sneak in without waiting at all.

"Excuse me," she asked a girl who wore a feathery fascinator with a gauzy crimson veil over her eyes. "What is everyone waiting to see behind the curtain?"

"If you don't know, then maybe you don't belong here."

"Ignore her," said the lanky boy at her side. Dressed a little more casual than the rest, in a collarless shirt and a pair of loose gray striped trousers held up by two cherry-red suspenders. "My sister forgets we're just playing a game, and gets a little too competitive."

"It's all right," Tella said. "My sister, Scarlett, thinks I'm the same way."

The lanky boy's eyes stretched wide, and Tella swore the girl in the veiled hat inhaled sharply. "Did you say Scarlett, as in the Scarlett who won the last game?"

"Oh, my sister and I didn't play the last game," Tella said. But she made her voice shake enough to instill a sliver of doubt. It was a risk to her true identity, but Caraval wasn't won by playing it safe. And it seemed to be working already.

The lanky boy stepped back, looking more protectively at Tella as he made room for her to join them in the line. "I'm Fernando, this is my sister, Patricia, and this is our friend, Caspar."

Tella tried to hide her surprise as a familiar performer reached for her hand.

"It's a pleasure to meet you." Caspar treated Tella similar to the way Julian had, as if they'd never crossed paths before. It wasn't quite as unnerving as Julian's disturbing performance. But it still threw Tella off balance, making her feel as if perhaps Caspar really was a stranger after all.

Caspar had pretended to be her fiancé as well as Legend in the last performance, but he now used a musical accent that Tella had never heard from him. He'd also changed out of the posh clothes he'd favored during the last Caraval to a rugged ensemble similar to Fernando's attire.

"Caspar's the one who told us the man who started this church is on the other side of the curtain," Fernando said.

"This man is also an expert on the Fates," Caspar cut in smoothly.

"He knows about the object we need to find, the one capable of destroying them," Fernando added.

Patricia made a show of rolling her eyes. "You keep forgetting this is only a game. The object is just a symbolic item needed to win. Legend doesn't really want to destroy the Fates. They've already been banished. When you say it like that, you sound like an idiot."

Fernando's cheeks reddened.

Tella agreed with his sister's assessment but she didn't like the way the girl was making a point of embarrassing her brother.

In front of them, a couple stepped behind the tasseled curtain. Fernando and his sister were up next. But all of Fernando's giddiness was gone. He was now peering at the green tiles on the floor while Patricia gazed up at Caspar for approval, as if she'd just said something very clever. To his credit Caspar didn't encourage her.

But Tella decided to take things one step further. Siblings were supposed to support each other, not tear each other down.

"I think you're wrong." She directed each word toward Patricia, speaking quickly so that the girl couldn't interrupt with any sighs or rolling eyes. "Legend has never held two Caravals so closely together. Experts on the game are saying it's because this one is real. If you pay attention, you'll feel it. The magic in the air isn't merely Legend's—it's the Fates, trying to come back. But the only way they can do that is by taking Legend's power."

Caspar's brows arched up in surprise, his eyes piercing Tella with a look that made her feel as if she'd just spilled a secret she wasn't even supposed to know. "Where'd you hear all of this?"

"I heard something similar," Fernando chimed in. "But I was told that if Legend succeeds in destroying the Fates, he won't only keep his power, he'll take all of their powers as well."

Dante hadn't mentioned this part. Not that Tella had decided to believe his story. But it was difficult to ignore the way Caspar's face had turned bone-white.

"What if the Fates' powers have something to do with the mysterious final prize?" Patricia interjected, speaking with the sort of confidence that made it impossible to tell if the pressure of the group had changed her mind, or if she didn't want to be left out of the conversation. "Maybe Legend will give the winner one of the Fate's powers. I think I'd take the Undead Queen's. She never ages."

"None of the Fates are supposed to age," said Tella, Caspar, and Fernando in unison.

Now it was Patricia's turn to blush. "You didn't let me finish."

"Go ahead, then," Caspar said.

But apparently Patricia didn't know that the Undead Queen's true power was the ability to control anyone foolish enough to pledge service to her. Patricia stayed silent until Caspar turned to Fernando. He looked at the other young man with a smile so warm it made Tella wonder if she'd only imagined Caspar's skin turning pale.

"What about you?" Caspar asked. "Which Fate's power would you want?"

Fernando toyed with his suspenders as he appeared to think on it. "I'd probably pick Maiden Death."

Tella stiffened.

Patricia gaped at her brother. "You'd want to kill people?"

"Maiden Death doesn't kill anyone," Fernando said. "She's one of the good Fates. She senses when tragedy is about to happen and she warns people. I'd want to be able to do that."

If only Fernando was right. In Tella's experience, the Maiden Death sealed rather than thwarted Fate. Though perhaps things might have turned out differently if Tella had actually known what the Maiden Death represented when Tella had first pulled her from her mother's Deck of Destiny. Then maybe she could have done something to prevent her mother from leaving.

Caspar turned to Tella. "What about you, which power would you desire?"

Tella might have been fascinated with the Fates, but she wasn't sure she wanted any of their terrible gifts. The Fates weren't all bad; Mistress Luck brought people fame and good fortune, but given the capricious nature of luck, even that could turn sour. And while the Aracle gave Tella helpful glimpses of the future, it had also brought her grief after grief. The Assassin could move through space and time, but as tempting as that power was, Tella also imagined it could bring bits of madness. It would be even worse to have all the Fates' powers. She could see why someone like Legend would want them. With that much magic he could rule the world. But Tella doubted that Legend or the world would be better for it.

The curtains before them parted again, saving Tella from answering the question as Fernando and Patricia were beckoned inside.

Tella turned back to Caspar, but he'd already slipped away, most likely off in search of another pair to play with.

It was probably for the best. Caspar's reaction to Tella's story had made her question things better left unquestioned. Tella didn't know what she'd find on the other side of the black tasseled curtain, but if it involved the next clue, she assumed her head would be toyed with even more. Best to have it on straight before she stepped inside.

There were no clocks on the tavern walls, only mirrors and lanterns, bottles, and more attempted renderings of Legend. So Tella didn't know how long she waited, just that too much time seemed to slip past before the curtain finally parted once more and a familiar voice beckoned her inside.

Tella felt as if she'd slipped inside a bottle of poison. Like the rest of the tavern, everything on the other side of the tasseled curtain was green—from the glass-tiled floors to the long mirrored walls and the trio of clamshell chairs. Green as ripening hatred, raw jealousy, and Armando's emerald eyes.

Tella sucked in a sharp breath at the sight of him.

Even though he had never been truly engaged to her sister she would always think of him as the villain he played in the last game.

Tonight Armando's deep green eyes were lined in black, making them look like freshly set gemstones. His sleek suit was ivory, except for the crimson cravat tied around his throat, and the black top hat on his head. The hat sat at an angle, with a satin band of red wrapped around it, and something about it made Tella imagine it wasn't so much a tribute to Legend as a prop to make players wonder if Armando was perhaps the true master of the game.

Tella sat smoothly in the empty chair across from him, as if just the sight of Armando's immaculate white suit didn't make her want to push the pearl buttons on her gloves and shred his clothes to scraps. But if she did, he would not give her the next clue, and if anyone in this strange church possessed it, she imagined it was the devil across from her.

His mouth smiled, but the expression did not touch his eyes, as if they were just another part of his costume. Unlike most of Legend's other performers, Armando made no attempts at saying anything charming. It made it easy to dislike him, easy to believe he wasn't acting, and that he *was* the role he played. "How's your sister?"

Tella bristled. "I told you, don't ever mention her."

"Or what, you'll dig your claws into my cheek and scratch my face?" Armando's gaze dropped to her gloves. "If you feel a need for revenge, go ahead, but I still think I did your sister a favor. No one wants to be the only one who doesn't know a secret. And she'd have been far worse off if she'd discovered the truth after this week."

"You could have been less nasty about it."

"If you believe that, you still don't know how this game works. All of Legend's performers are given a role to play, a person that we are each meant to become during the game—that's what really moves Caraval forward, not rhyming clues. So, yes, Miss Dragna, I did have to be nasty about it." Armando's eyes turned hard and sharp with every word, as if each one made him more of a villain.

If Tella could have placed a wager on it she'd have bet that he relished the role. He'd played a monster in the last game as well, and from his lack of apology Tella guessed he'd enjoyed that, too. Was that why he always played the role, or was there something more to it?

As Tella considered the question, she heard her nana Anna's voice repeating part of a story she'd told many times. *The witch also warned that wishes come with costs, and the more he performed, the more he would transform into whatever roles he played. If he acted the part of a villain, he'd become one in truth.*

Tella had always remembered her nana saying Legend liked to play the villain, and that it had turned him into one. But that wasn't the exact truth. Legend became the roles he played, which meant he only became a villain if he took on the role of one—as Armando had done.

Tella hadn't considered it before. She hated Armando for what he'd put her sister through. To imagine him being Legend felt like giving him a compliment, and she didn't want to give Armando anything unless it caused a significant amount of pain.

"Even you have a role in this performance." Armando picked up a Deck of Destiny from the center of the table and began to shuffle. "You might think yours is unscripted, but I can tell you the minute you stepped inside here you thought about hurting me, you're probably still thinking about it right now. Legend is manipulating you, guiding you onto a path until the only remaining choice is the one he wants you to make."

"And why would he do that?" Tella asked.

"Answer that and you've really won the game." Armando sat his

Deck of Destiny in the center of the table and motioned for Tella to cut. The cards were gold with silver whorls, and much thicker than usual, as if made from real bits of metal—difficult to destroy, like the futures they predicted.

Tella stared but did not touch. She might have been obsessed with the cards after that day when she'd first found her mother's deck, and she might have allowed herself to look at the Aracle, but she'd never drawn cards from a Deck of Destiny to read her future. She'd kept that promise to her mother—and once had been detrimental enough.

"I think I'll pass on the reading. I didn't come here for cryptic words about the future."

"But you do want the next clue?"

"I thought you just said the clues are meaningless."

"No, I said the game isn't really about the clues, but they're still necessary to show people, like you, the correct path."

"Maybe I'll look up at the stars and follow Legend's constellations instead."

"The constellations help people play but they won't lead anyone to winning, and I suspect you want to win." Armando nudged the deck closer to Tella's side of the table, scratching the glassy surface.

"Why do you care so much about my future?"

"I couldn't care less, but Legend is very interested."

"I'm guessing you say that to everyone who sits here."

"True. But I actually mean it with you." When Armando grinned this time it lit up his entire face. His lips parted in a perfect smile, his eyes turned a dazzling green, and for a moment Tella imagined that if he were just a little kinder Armando would have been heartbreakingly handsome. "Either play with me, or feel free to try your luck at another temple."

As if on cue, bells rang twice, heralding two in the morning. Later than she'd realized. She'd have to move quickly to find another one of Legend's players in a different temple. But there was a chance they'd want to read her future, just like Armando.

She reached for the metal deck.

The cards were cold enough to feel through the tips of her gloves. Once she finished cutting them Armando spread them out in front of her. A fan of silver and gold. It should have shone, but after a moment the gold turned black and the silver whorls tarnished as if warning her that her future would turn darker as well.

"Choose four. One at a time."

"I know how this works." Ignoring the obvious ones directly in front of her, Tella reached for a buried card on the far left, scratching the table once again as she slid it out and turned it over, revealing an all-too-familiar bloody smile.

The Prince of Hearts.

The air in Tella's lungs went arctic. He was truly inescapable.

Armando chuckled, dry and mocking. "Unrequited love. It seems things with you and Dante won't work out after all."

It might have hurt if Tella harbored any delusions of the contrary. But she knew better than anyone else what the bloody prince represented. No matter what Tella claimed about love, the Prince of Hearts was the real reason she never let herself grow attached to any of the young men who showed interest. Tella knew how to capture a boy's attention, but it was doomed never to last. Fate had already decided no one she loved would ever love her back.

This time Tella flipped over the closest card, the one so obvious it probably expected her to look it over.

Or not.

The Maiden Death.

Again.

"I've always liked this card." Armando traced the pearls around the maiden's face with cold precision. "Death stole her from her family to make her his immortal consort. Yet she refused him, so he encased her head in a cage of pearls to keep anyone else from having her. Even then she still defied him, every night sneaking off to warn the loved ones of those he was about to take."

"I'm familiar with her history," Tella said.

"Then why don't you look more worried about losing someone you care for?"

"Because I've already lost her."

"Perhaps you're about to lose someone else," Armando rasped. For a young man who claimed not to care about her future, he seemed to enjoy how dark it was.

Pretending to ignore him, Tella flipped over another card. She didn't pay attention to where she took it from, imagining it would be the Aracle—following the same pattern she'd discovered as a child. But instead of a gold-lined mirror, the card before her revealed a sharp black crown tipped with gleaming black opals, and broken into five ragged pieces.

The Shattered Crown.

Suddenly Armando no longer looked entertained. His mouth opened and shut like a puppet who'd not been fed any words.

"Is this one not terrible enough for you?" Tella asked.

Although, truthfully, this card didn't bother Tella nearly as much as the others. The Shattered Crown represented an impossible choice between two equally difficult paths. But Tella didn't believe in impossible choices. In her experience one path was always clearly worse than another. Yet Tella still hesitated before flipping over a fourth card; the Shattered Crown was new, and while a masochistic part of Tella was curious as to what other surprises fate might have in store, she was tired of Fates toying with her future.

"I need to see another card," said Armando.

"Why?" Tella asked. "I've just shown you three dreadful ones, isn't that enough?"

"I thought you were familiar with fortune-telling. Every story has four parts—the beginning, the middle, the almost-ending, and the true ending. Your future is not complete until you flip over the fourth and reveal the true ending."

"I still don't understand why Legend cares about any of this."

"Maybe you need to ask yourself that question, not me?" Armando's eyes dropped to the upturned cards, which told a story of broken hearts, lost loved ones, and impossible choices. Tella didn't see how any of it connected to Caraval, unless, like Jacks, Legend also found pleasure in the pain of others.

She closed her eyes this time, hoping for a favorable Fate like Mistress Luck, or Her Majesty's Gown, which signified bold changes and extraordinary gifts.

The card's smooth metal surfaces didn't spark with magic like the Aracle she kept hidden away. But she did feel something as her fingers danced atop them. Most of the cards were cool to the touch, but a few were icier than others and some were warmer. Then there was one that burned with so much heat Tella was tempted to lift her hand. She flipped it over instead.

The metal glowed violet as a lovely woman in an ash-lavender gown stared at Tella from behind the bars of a giant silver birdcage.

The Lady Prisoner.

A knot formed inside of Tella's chest, and not just because this card reminded her of the vision that the Aracle had shown of her own mother. The Lady Prisoner held a double meaning: sometimes her picture promised love, but usually it meant sacrifice. In all the stories, she was said to be innocent of any crimes, but she let herself be caged in the place of someone she deeply loved.

Nigel's words returned to Tella then. *Be warned, winning the game will come at a cost you will later regret.*

Tella glared at Armando. "I've chosen my cards. Give me the next clue."

His mouth twisted into something unreadable.

"If you even try to tell me you can't—"

"Keep your claws in your gloves." Armando rose from his chair and crossed the small space to press his hand against one of the mirrors on the wall. It opened with a hiss, exposing a cool tunnel formed of earth and ancient spiderwebs.

Tella had heard there were secret passages hidden throughout all of Valenda. This must have been one of them.

"Follow this path until something urges you to stop, and there you'll find the next clue. But remember, Miss Dragna, Caraval isn't about the clues. Your sister didn't win because she solved simple riddles. She won because of what she was willing to sacrifice for those riddles, and for what she was willing to sacrifice in order to find you."

21

The world of the game and the world outside of it were beginning to blur into each other. Tella could feel the pieces of both fitting too neatly together.

The game was not real. Tella knew this. Everyone knew this. Yet, as she traveled through Armando's hidden tunnel toward the second clue, she found herself questioning if maybe the game was more real than she wanted it to be.

Tella had entered Caraval believing her bargain with Jacks was genuine, and if she won the game and brought him Legend, she would be able to save her mother. After the ball, she'd also come to believe that Jacks was the true Prince of Hearts, a Fate who'd somehow escaped. But this was where she'd stopped believing.

To even be tempted by the idea that any part of the game was real could lead her into a dangerous mental spiral. Legend was not out to destroy the Fates, and the Fates weren't out to destroy Legend.

But if Tella was right, and if it was all a game, would she really meet Legend if she won? Or would he be played by another actor?

Legend was always played by actors. Yet Tella had believed that it was different this time. Nigel had promised. *If you win Caraval, the first face you see will be Legend's.*

Tella had felt the world shift when he'd said the words, felt the power in them, the same fortune-telling magic she felt whenever she touched the Aracle. She would meet Legend if she won the game. But if the real Legend appeared at the end, did that mean the rest of the game was real? Did it mean that Fates other than Jacks were trying to return, and if they did, would Legend be destroyed?

Tella was so lost in her questions she barely noticed how long she walked or where Armando's serpentine tunnel led. Until she heard the voices echoing against the tunnel's ancient stone walls.

Tella picked up speed, following the sounds until they guided her to a cobweb-covered door. It was not the first door she'd seen, but it was the first time she'd stopped. She recognized the voices on the other side.

Scarlett and Julian's.

They were muffled by the dirty door, but unmistakable. Tella knew her sister's voice better than her own, and Julian's voice was something else altogether.

When Tella first met Julian back on Trisda, she hadn't been attracted to him the way her sister Scarlett was. But she had enjoyed the sound of his voice. Velvety and sonorous, Julian had a voice meant for casting spells. But tonight he'd have broken them instead. He sounded like salt without the sea. Rough, alone, and lost.

The scent of soot and cobwebs snaked up Tella's nose as she leaned closer to the door, imagining her sister's room inside the palace would be found just beyond it.

"Thank you for letting me in," Julian said. "I didn't think you wanted to see me again."

"I always want to see you," Scarlett said. "That's why this hurts so badly."

In the silence that followed, Tella pictured her sister on the other side of the door. It was now past three in the morning. Scarlett must have been standing in her nightgown, though knowing her, she'd probably grabbed a blanket to cover up. Tella could see her tugging it close, as her sensible head and her hurt at being lied to fought against her aching heart and her desire for Julian.

"My sister thinks I should give you another chance."

"I agree with your sister."

"Then give me a good reason to trust you again. I want to, but last time you lied to me after one day." Scarlett's shaking tone told Tella she was on the verge of tears.

Tella was intruding on a private moment. She needed to leave them alone, to start down the tunnel again.

"What about your sister—"

Tella stopped moving.

"—how many times has—"

"Don't bring Tella into this."

"I just want to know why this is different," Julian said. "Why can you forgive her for lying about Caraval and Armando and all the other things she's kept from you?"

"Because she's my sister." The fight returned to Scarlett's voice. "You should understand that. Isn't that the entire reason you lie so much for your brother, Legend?"

Tella's entire world froze.

Legend was Julian's brother.

How had Scarlett kept this a secret?

Because Tella had never asked.

Although it still felt like the sort of thing Scarlett should have shared. If it was true it would solve everything. Tella wouldn't need any more clues to win the game. She would only need to convince Scarlett to coax Legend's identity out of Julian.

But Julian was a liar and he worked for Legend. Tella wasn't sure anything he said could be trusted. This could also be part of the game. A trick. A distraction, to keep Tella from finding the clues that would lead her to the real Legend.

Unless it was one of the clues?

Armando had told her that if she followed the tunnel she'd find the next clue.

Tella listened carefully to whatever Julian might say next.

"Crimson," he pleaded, "please, I'm trying everything I can to keep you."

"Maybe that's our problem," Scarlett said. "I don't want you trying to 'keep me.' I want to know who you really are."

Whatever Julian responded was too low for Tella to clearly make out. And then she heard him leave.

Tella probably should have waited longer before opening the door and bursting into Scarlett's room, but once she entered it would be no secret she'd been eavesdropping.

Tella turned the knob.

The minute she stepped through the doorway she found herself in a fireplace, which thankfully was not lit. Tella brushed ash from her dress as she stepped out into the suite.

Scarlett's room was as cool as tears. At a glance it looked like the inside of a music box—quilted walls of sapphire-blue satin surrounded a circular chamber full of delicate crystal tables with scalloped edges and chairs with stained-glass feet. Even the slender canopy bed looked like an ephemeral thing formed of sparkling quartz and dreams. It was a room for an enchanted princess. But in this particular story Scarlett looked more disenchanted. Her face was pale, framed by limp dark hair. Even her surprise looked dull as she noticed her sister.

The only thing that did not look dim was her dress. Tella had expected her sister to be in a nightgown, but either Scarlett had just come from a secret ball, or she was still wearing Legend's magical gown and the dress was determined to do its part to keep Scarlett and Julian together. Her bodice was strapless red silk that flowed into a crimson skirt so full it covered a quarter of the room.

Tella doubted her sister had attended a ball. The dress must have been Legend's enchanted gown, which left Tella even more perplexed. The last time she'd seen Scarlett, Scarlett had told her she didn't trust Legend or anyone who worked for him, and yet she still wore his dress.

Tella didn't want to be suspicious of her sister, but the sight of her in the gown was enough to make Tella wonder if Scarlett was in on the game. Perhaps to repay Tella for tricking Scarlett the last time around.

Tella's mouth hardened.

Then she saw a tear glide down Scarlett's cheek. Followed by another.

Unlike Tella, Scarlett didn't know how to fake tears, or Tella would have certainly seen her do it before.

Another tear fell. And another, leaving streaks on Scarlett's cheeks.

No. Her sister wasn't acting. Tella was being paranoid. Just as her sister had warned, Tella was no longer clearly able to see what was real and what was merely part of the game.

Frustrated at herself and the game for making her doubt Scarlett, Tella cast about the rounded room for something compassionate to say, since Scarlett appeared genuinely miserable, and Tella had obviously been listening in as Scarlett had argued with the cause of her pain. But all that came out was "Is Julian really Legend's brother?"

Scarlett fell back against the bed in a pile of crumbling red silk.

"Julian told me they were brothers at the end of Caraval, but I'm starting to think he would say anything to keep me."

"At least you know he cares about you."

"But does he really?" More tears streamed down Scarlett's face. "When you truly care about someone, aren't you supposed to be honest, even if it means you might lose that person?"

"I don't think it's usually that simple. I love you more than anyone in the world, but I've lied to you, a lot," Tella said cheerfully, hoping to make her sister smile.

Scarlett's frown wobbled, as if she wanted to laugh but then it fell as if she couldn't remember how. "I can't tell if you really think I should forgive him, or if you're trying to make me feel better."

"Of course I'm trying to make you feel better. As far as whether to forgive him, that depends on whether Legend is actually his brother." Tella said it half joking, but she was also serious, and for a moment she hated herself for taking advantage of her sister. But if Tella didn't win the game and find Legend, if she died again, Scarlett would be beyond inconsolable. Tella was the sister who would destroy the world if anything happened to Scarlett, but Scarlett's world would be destroyed if anything happened to Tella.

"I've already tried asking Julian, but he won't tell me who Legend is." Scarlett slumped against the bedpost. "He's made it seem as if it's physically impossible for him to betray the secret, yet it wasn't difficult for him to give me the impression Legend was his brother." She wiped furiously at her damp eyes with the backs of her hands. "It makes me wonder if it was all a lie. I'm almost more inclined to believe *Julian* is Legend, but he didn't want to tell me so he claimed Legend was his brother." Scarlett sniffled against her pillow, deflating further.

Tella considered what her sister said as she watched the skirt of Scarlett's gown shorten and grow slimmer, turning into more of a nightdress, while its color softened to pale pink. It was a marvel. Tella had been a little envious of the dress during the last Caraval. The gown behaved as if it had thoughts and feelings of its own, shifting fabric, cut, and color of its own caprice. Its magic was exceptional even by Caraval standards, and Legend had given it to Scarlett. Tella had heard performers whisper about it during the last game, wondering why he'd given her such a singular gift. Suddenly it made more sense if Julian was actually Legend, as Scarlett had just suggested.

Tella sat down on the bed beside her sister. "Do you really believe Julian could be Legend?"

"I don't know," Scarlett mumbled. "I think Legend has power over his performers; I don't believe he controls their every action, but I get the impression he can prevent them from revealing certain secrets. So if Julian really were Legend, I doubt he'd have allowed Armando to tell me the truth about the role he'd played in the last Caraval."

"I hate Armando," Tella said.

"He was only doing his job. But I can't say I like him very much either." Scarlett punched the pillow she'd been sniffling in, a bit of her fight returning.

"Do you think he could be Legend?" Tella asked.

"I think anyone could be Legend." Scarlett sucked back the last of her tears. When she looked at Tella, her face was determined. "I think the only way to find out for certain who Legend is, is if we keep using Julian to win the game."

"You want to use him?" Tella nearly toppled off the bed. This was not like her sister at all. "Where did this come from? I thought you didn't even want me to play."

"I don't. But if you win and meet Legend, then we can find out the truth about Julian." Scarlett pulled out a slip of paper as if it were a dagger she'd hidden up her sleeve.

This was definitely a new side of Scarlett.

Tella liked it.

"Julian gave me this," Scarlett said. "It's the next clue. He said he wanted to help you, but I think he was trying to bribe me with it."

Tella took the page, recognizing the script from the first clue card she'd received at the party.

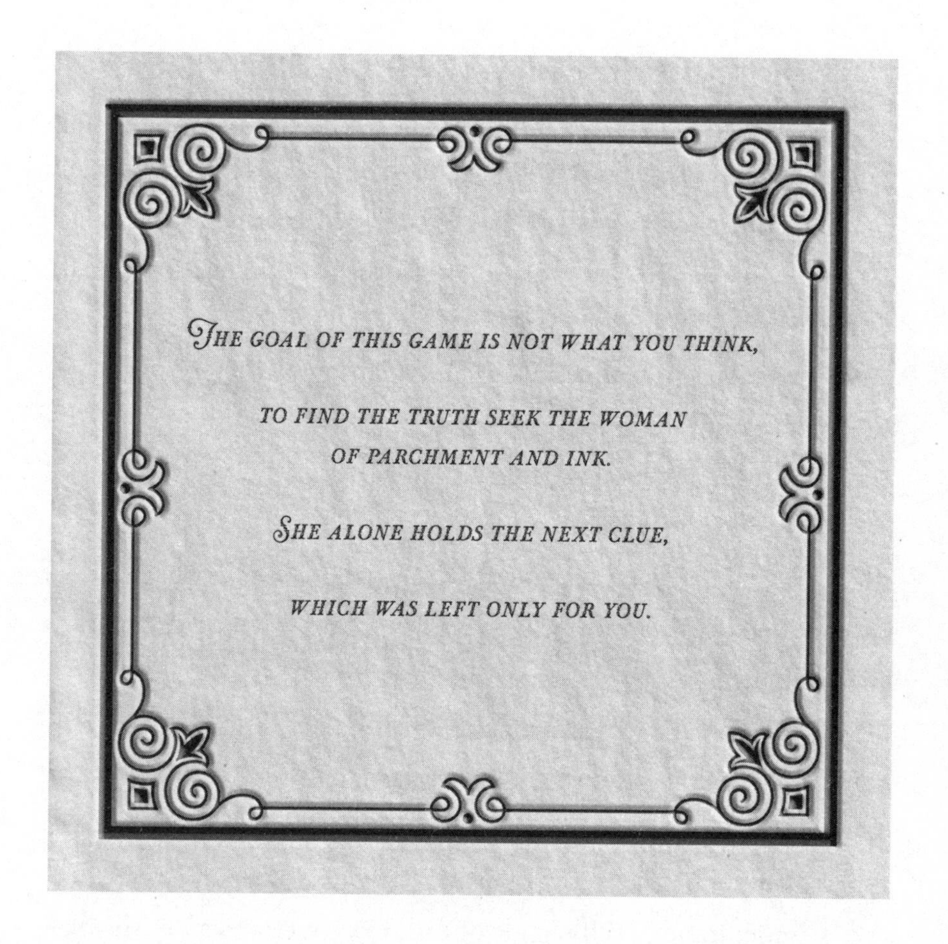
THE GOAL OF THIS GAME IS NOT WHAT YOU THINK,

TO FIND THE TRUTH SEEK THE WOMAN
OF PARCHMENT AND INK.

SHE ALONE HOLDS THE NEXT CLUE,

WHICH WAS LEFT ONLY FOR YOU.

"This sounds like a woman I met at a Wanted shop the other day in the Spice Quarter."

It also sounded as if it truly were meant for Tella alone. She doubted everyone playing the game had paused at the same shop. Elantine's Most Wanted. Tella had hoped to return there, but it seemed like a rather great coincidence that Legend was leading her back to the very place that had first put her in touch with Jacks.

The game was starting to seem too real again.

Tella reminded herself of all the trickery she'd just witnessed from Legend's performers in the Temple District. She would have been intentionally naive to believe that Caraval was more than just a game. Caraval was just one giant deception, but Tella could feel it trying to pull her in.

She held out the clue card Scarlett had just given her. "Come with me tomorrow night to look into this."

Scarlett bit down on her lip.

"What, do you have other plans?"

"Who would I have plans with?" Scarlett asked. But the question came out oddly shrill, and Tella swore her nightgown flinched, quickly flickering from pink to black.

Tella didn't know what her sister was hiding, but again she had the feeling that Scarlett was concealing something.

"I'd just prefer not to go out at night," Scarlett added. "I can't risk getting caught up in the game again."

"I understand," Tella said. She just wasn't certain if she believed her.

NIGHT THREE OF CARAVAL

Tella would have traded a year of her life for another hour of sleep. She didn't even care that she possibly had less than one year to live. She never wanted to leave the blissful blue comfort of her bed with all its soft blankets and downy pillows. Yesterday had been brutally long. But she'd already slept much more than she should have—and if she never got up she would definitely have less than one year to live.

Beat . . . beat.

Nothing.

Nothing.

Beat . . . beat.

Nothing.

Beat . . . beat . . .

Nothing.

Nothing.

Her heart was even slower than it had been the night before. But it was still beating. And Tella would make sure it didn't stop. It did slow her down a bit, but after drinking a pot of strong tea and eating several toffee tarts and berry puffs, she felt a little more like herself.

She managed to finish dressing just before twilight. For that evening she'd chosen to wear a slender-skirted, corset-less dress the dark blue color of tears cried from storm clouds. It was perhaps too thin of a gown to wear at night, but it was easy to move about in. Although Tella was still a little breathless by the time she reached the sapphire wing, where Scarlett was staying.

Only Scarlett wasn't in her room.

Tella knocked for a full minute, nearly bruising her knuckles on the heavy wood door.

Given how adamant Scarlett had been about not leaving the palace at night and becoming accidentally caught up in the game, Tella expected her sister to be safely in her suite. But either Scarlett had lost track of time—which was doubtful—or she really was hiding something from Tella.

Tella hated doubting her sister again, but as wary as Scarlett was, it made no sense for her to be out. Especially on an evening like this, when it seemed all of Valenda was Legend's game board.

Unlike the previous two nights, where Legend's constellations had been specific in their location, on this night they covered every district in shimmering bursts of celestial blue.

Tella found herself unusually grateful to Armando for pressuring her into earning the second clue. Without it, Tella would have had no idea where to begin her search.

As she left the palace in a sky carriage, she saw stars forming all the traditional symbols of Caraval: a dazzling blue top hat; a bouquet of blue roses; a blue hourglass. Though those weren't the only shapes in the sky. Constellations reminiscent of the Fates hovered over Valenda's hills and districts as well. Tella spotted a jeweled eye patch, a dagger crown, a skeleton key, a cage of pearls, lips sewn shut, and a pair of shimmering dark blue wings. The wings were probably meant to represent the Fallen Star, but they were so achingly similar to the wings tattooed on Dante's back that Tella's dying heart managed to speed up at the sight of them, filling her veins with a warm rush of blood.

When her carriage touched down in the Spice Quarter, Tella found herself looking around for Dante, but he didn't appear to be following her that night.

She glanced back up at the star-bright sky, wondering which constellation he was beneath, and if he was there with someone else. She pictured his wide, tattooed hands on another girl's neck, brushing her pulse as he charmed her with the same low words he'd said to Tella the night before. *Even if I wasn't Legend I would want you to win.*

Tella's stomach clenched painfully at the thought. Not that she wanted Dante there with her. She didn't need to be distracted by his cryptic teasing or the low sound of his voice. The narrow streets of the Quarter were enough of a diversion.

Every lane and alley was packed, much fuller than the last time she'd visited. The colorful inhabitants of the Spice Quarter mingled with the holiday merchants, who appeared to be preparing the city for Elantine's Eve by selling overpriced bits of costumes. The merchants stood in front of almost every shop, all of them shouting.

"Five coppers for the Murdered King's crown!"

"Three coppers for the pearly cage worn by the Maiden Death!"

"Four coppers for a Prince of Hearts mask!"

"Two coppers for Chaos's gauntlets!"

"One copper for the Unwed Bride's veil of tears!"

Tella didn't notice any of Legend's performers, at least that she knew of, among them, but she thought she spied other people playing the game. More than once she'd heard someone knock on a brick wall and say, *Legend sent me*, as if it were a code to open some hidden door that would lead to the next clue. She envied their energy and their careless effervescence. Whatever courses these people were on, they seemed very different from hers.

Either Legend was personally toying with Tella, or they weren't all playing the same game.

The second clue she'd received told Tella to seek the woman of parchment and ink, which clearly indicated the older lady who worked at Elantine's Most Wanted. But when Tella arrived, no one was there.

The scent of tall tales, charcoal pencils, and parchment tickled Tella's nose as she stepped farther in. In one corner of the shop, a slim square of the space was set aside for a disorganized yet well-appointed art studio. Everything else was covered in paper—even the ceiling was plastered with yellowing posters that appeared to be older than the shop's absent proprietor.

Tella tried to take in every image as she waited for the old woman to return. These posters were not scraps of paper with hastily drawn faces. These were works of art, with detailed renderings of criminals that Tella had only heard rumors of. There were many she'd not heard of as well. Every square of parchment and canvas seemed to tell a tale as marvelous as it was macabre.

Augustus the Impaler's name apparently said it all.

There was also the Duchess of Dao. Wanted for inland piracy, selling poisons, and seduction.

"I didn't know seduction was a crime," Tella murmured.

"Depends on who you're trying to seduce."

Tella spun around. But instead of finding the ink-stained crone, Tella came face-to-face with a girl in a luminous parchment-white gown, sewn together with thick black stitches that made her look as if she could have been one of the inked portraits escaped from the wall. Aiko, another one of Legend's performers.

She was always difficult for Tella to read. Aiko generally kept to herself, since her job was to observe. She worked as a histographer, immortalizing the history of Caraval by drawing significant events in a magical notebook, which was currently tucked under her arm.

Her appearance clearly meant that Tella was on the correct path. But Tella couldn't honestly say she was happy to see the girl.

Tella liked Aiko well enough outside of the game. But she'd preferred to have avoided her inside the game. Aiko was known for making unforgiving bargains. During the last Caraval she had made a deal with Scarlett that had cost her sister two days of her life; Scarlett's temporary death had not been like Tella's, but it was still not something Tella would ever willingly experience again.

"You're welcome to look as long as you wish," Aiko said, "but choose wisely before asking a question. I'll only answer one for free, and after that each will cost you something irreplaceable."

"Can I just ask for the next clue?"

"You can, but I won't give it to you. The most I can do is guide you toward it, if you manage to ask a better question next time."

Blast it. Tella hadn't meant that to come out like a question.

She kept her mouth shut as her eyes wandered over several more posters, searching for an actual figure from the Deck of Destiny, hoping it might possibly lead to the next clue.

She didn't spy any Fates, but she did see crimes ranging from blood-drinking and cannibalism to necromancy, selling bad spells—

Tella halted. All thoughts of crimes and clues and Fates fled from her thoughts as she reached a poster in the center of the back wall.

She forgot how to exhale. How to speak. How to blink. How to move.

Trimmed in a starry border, this portrait was prettier than the others, though maybe that was also because of the beautiful face beneath the word *Wanted*—a face that bore an uncanny resemblance to Tella and Scarlett's missing mother, Paloma.

23

Paradise the Lost.

Wanted for thievery, kidnapping, and murder.

Tella couldn't pry her eyes from the picture. She wasn't sure if she wanted to believe it.

After so many years of wondering about her mother, finally Tella might've found an answer to one of her unanswerable questions. But it was not the answer she'd hoped for. Her mother was a thief. A kidnapper. A murderer. A criminal.

Tella wanted to believe the poster was wrong. The mother she knew was not any of those things and yet as Jacks had said, *The reason you couldn't find her before is because Paloma was not her real name.*

Her mother's real name was Paradise, and Paradise's resemblance to Paloma was unmistakable. It wasn't just that she had the same oval-shaped face or thick dark hair. It was the way her lips were curved into that enchanting, enigmatic smile that Tella had grown up mimicking. Her large eyes were just the right amount of narrow at the corners, the perfect balance of clever and thoughtful. With a stab of jealousy, Tella realized she looked almost exactly like Scarlett. In the poster she even appeared to be around Scarlett's age.

Did Scarlett know about this? Was this why her sister refused to ever speak of their mother?

"What can you tell me about Paradise the Lost?" Tella asked.

"She was special." Aiko glided toward the portrait and ran an unadorned finger down Paradise's cheek. "I never noticed until now, but she looks quite a bit like your Scarlett. Although Paradise was much bolder than your sister."

"What else can you tell me about her?"

"Your sister or Paradise?"

"I know my sister better than she knows herself. I want to know about Paradise."

Aiko's dark eyes sparked with a familiar gleam. With her enchanted histographer's notebook, the girl was almost magical and tricky enough to be a Fate. Or maybe Aiko was Legend—it would be brilliant if the Great Master Legend turned out to be a girl. "I'll tell you all I know, but I'll need your payment first."

"You can't have a day of my life," Tella said.

"You're not really in an ideal position to bargain if you want to know the truth about Paradise. She vanished nearly eighteen years ago so most people don't remember her. But I come from a long line of storytellers."

Tella shrugged, as if unimpressed. On the inside all she could think was, *Eighteen years, eighteen years, eighteen years . . .*

Her parents married nearly eighteen years ago. Tella knew because after her mother had first disappeared she'd searched for information about where her mother had lived before she'd married her father, but Tella had found nothing. Because Tella had been searching for a women named Paloma, but before she came to Trisda, Paloma had been the criminal Paradise the Lost. Jacks had been telling the truth about her mother's name.

Tella had always felt bitter, as if she'd been robbed, because she'd only known her mother for half of her life. But now she felt as if she'd never really known her mother at all.

"That's all I'll part with for free," Aiko said. "For the rest of her story, I'll need something in return. And don't worry, I won't steal any days of your life."

"What do you want?"

Aiko angled her head, long black hair falling to one side as she appeared to think. "Caraval is a world built of make-believe, and sometimes it's difficult for those of us who always live inside it to feel as if anything is real. Most of us won't admit it, but we all crave the real." She paused as if she were about to add something else, but then she seemed to think better of it. "All I want from you today is something real. A memory."

"You need to be more specific. I'm curious about my mother, but I'm not going to let you take something like the memory of my name."

"I hadn't even considered that." Aiko's dark eyes gleamed. "Excellent idea. But I'll save it for another time. Tonight I'd like the last memory you have of your mother."

Tella recoiled, instinctively taking a sharp step back. "No. I won't give you any memories of her."

"Then I cannot give you any information about Paradise the Lost."

"Can't you pick another memory?"

"You called Paradise your mother. I want to see why."

"I never called her that," Tella argued.

"Yes you did. You said you were curious about her. And since history is my expertise, I can tell you everything you want to know. So, either you can find another expert, or you give me the last memory of your mother. I will allow you one minute to think about it."

Tella could not give up any memories of her mother. There were too few and they were too precious. But, if the game really was about sacrifice as Armando had said, sacrificing a memory would possibly allow Tella to make future memories with her mother.

And perhaps Tella was better off without that final memory. Ever since finding those cards in her mother's room Tella had been haunted by them, unable to stop wondering what would have happened if she'd never flipped over the card with the Prince of Hearts or the Maiden Death. Would her mother still have left if the Maiden Death had not predicted her departure? Would she have already fallen in love with someone if she'd never turned over the Prince of Hearts?

"All right," Tella said. "You can take the last memory I have of my mother."

"Splendid." Aiko glided toward the work desk in the back of the shop, appearing a little too eager, which only intensified Tella's unease as Aiko opened her enchanted notebook to an untouched page of pristine parchment.

"All you must do is place your palm atop the page. Some people actually enjoy the process. Our memories weigh us down more than we realize."

"Don't try to convince me you're doing me a favor." Tella pressed her hand to the dry paper. It heated against her skin, similar to the sensation she experienced whenever she touched the Aracle, except this warmth went beyond her hand. It crawled up her arm to her neck, coating her like melting butter and turning her head comfortably fuzzy.

"The book needs to access the memory before it can collect it," Aiko said. But now her voice sounded distant, like someone calling from the other end of a very long corridor.

Tella's eyes fluttered shut and when they opened again, she was back in her mother's enchanting suite on Trisda. Her mother was sitting on the floor across from her, clearer than she'd ever been in Tella's memories.

She smelled of plumeria. A scent Tella thought she'd forgotten. Her father had not allowed the flowers anywhere on his estate after Tella's mother left, and until this moment Tella had not thought of them for years. She wanted to bury herself in the scent, to wrap her arms around her mother so that she'd never forget it again. But this was only a memory, and Tella could not alter it no matter how much she wished.

Moments ago, before this memory began, her mother had made Tella promise never to touch another Deck of Destiny. That was the memory Tella had expected Aiko to thieve, but this was something different. A recollection buried so deep inside of Tella she'd forgotten it was there. She'd forgotten the way her mother had taken her hands, lifting Tella's tiny fingers to get a better look at the opal ring Tella had just stolen.

"Oh—what's this?" Paloma asked.

"I was going to put it back," Tella promised.

"No, my little love, you should hold on to it for me and keep it safe." She kissed Tella's fingers, as if that officially made the ring hers. Her mother always sealed things with kisses; another fact Tella had misplaced.

"Now," Paloma whispered, "I will tell you a secret about the cards I just put away. The Fates pictured on them once ruled on earth, and when they did they were very unkind and very cruel. They used to trap people in playing cards for sport and entertainment. Only a Fate could free them . . . *unless* . . ."

No. Tella fought to hold on to the memory as it began to fade before her eyes and ears. Her mother's skin shifted from olive to translucent as her lips formed words that Tella could no longer hear. No. No. *No! These* were words she needed to hear. The answer she was searching for. She didn't know what her mother was about to say, but Tella was certain that whatever she'd said next was of vital importance.

Tella clawed at the memory, tried to dig her fingers into it. But the harder Tella fought to keep it, the murkier it became, turning to smoke that couldn't be held on to at all, and then dissipating into nothing.

When she opened her eyes Tella did not feel as if a weight had been lifted. She felt as if something had been lost. As if she'd been cut, but nothing was bleeding. And nothing seemed to be gone, either. The memory she'd expected Aiko to take was still there, and though Tella had been ready to part with it, she felt relieved it wasn't gone.

So then why did Tella sense that Aiko had stolen something even more valuable?

24

Aiko's cursed notebook was now firmly shut, but Tella swore it looked fatter than before. There was even a soft glow about it.

What had she taken?

"Don't look so glum," Aiko said. "You've just earned a fantastic story about one of Valenda's most infamous criminals."

Aiko glided back toward the portraits on the wall. "Before she disappeared, Paradise the Lost was a bit of a legend in this city. People were so enchanted with Paradise, they used to write her letters and ask her to rob them or kidnap them. Paradise the Lost was truly criminal royalty. There were even rumors of princes from other continents sending letters to the lords of the Spice Quarter offering to marry her."

As Aiko spoke, Tella tried to hold on to her anger and frustration at losing one of her memories, but instead she began to picture her mother, as clear as if Aiko were painting the scene in her evil notebook. Tella saw Paloma as a young and spirited thing, leaving trails of glittering tales as she robbed and thieved and stole her way into history until she became a shimmering part of it.

Then she'd married Tella's father. Out of all the people Paloma could have chosen.

"Why didn't Paradise accept any of the princes' offers?" Tella asked.

"I assume she was smart enough to know most princes are cruel, spoiled, selfish beings. And Paradise wanted adventures far more than she desired love. She bragged there was nothing she couldn't steal. So when she was presented with a challenge, to steal an unstealable item of great magic, she accepted the offer. But the item was far more powerful and dangerous than she'd been led to believe. She didn't want to put it back and risk that someone else would take it, so she fled, and no one has seen her since."

But Tella had.

Now it made more sense that she'd ended up on Trisda with Tella's father. No one would have searched for her on a smallish, unremarkable conquered isle.

"What was the object she stole?"

"If you want the answer to that—"

"No," Tella interrupted, steel in her tone. "No more deals. I already earned this answer, it's a part of the story."

Aiko's nostrils flared, her usually placid expression pulsing with frustration; clearly she was used to taking more than giving.

Tella snatched Aiko's enchanted notebook off the table and held it over a burning candle. "Tell me what she stole or this notebook turns to ash."

Aiko gave her a thin smile. "You have more mettle than your sister."

"Scarlett and I each have different strengths. Now tell me what the object was." Tella slowly lowered the notebook closer to the flame until she could smell the heating leather.

"It's a cursed Deck of Destiny," Aiko spat out.

Tella dropped Aiko's book on the desk with a loud thump. All around her posters flapped, as if their paper heartbeats were racing along with Tella's; it was the fastest her heart had beat since Jacks had kissed her. As if this new revelation possessed magic of its own.

Only the portrait of Paradise the Lost remained unmoved, the calm center of a paper storm.

Tella knew pictures did not have feelings, yet she imagined the portrait of Paradise, the woman her mother had once been, was holding its breath, silently hoping and urging Tella to put all the pieces of her story together.

Tella had always known her mother's Deck of Destiny was unlike other ordinary decks. But Aiko made it sound as if there was nothing else in the world like it, and she'd called it *cursed*.

Cursed. Cursed. Cursed.

The word grew louder in Tella's head, warring with the sound of the posters still flapping on the walls. The Fates had also been cursed by a witch, and according to Jacks, this curse had imprisoned them inside a deck of cards.

I can tell you from experience it's torturous, he'd said.

It seemed spectacular to believe that her mother had stolen this same deck, but the more Tella thought about it, the more sense it made.

If her mother's Deck of Destiny had been the one imprisoning the Fates, it explained why her mother had been terrified to find Tella playing with the cards. Tella remembered how they'd been disguised as a foul-smelling sachet until that day. The spell concealing them must have been wearing off when Tella found them.

Tella couldn't believe she'd touched the deck holding all the Fates—the mythic Fates who'd once ruled the world had been in the palm of her hand.

It seemed impossible, and yet she'd witnessed the proof every time the Aracle had shown Tella images of the future. She'd never seen another card like it, and she doubted she ever would. Because it wasn't merely a card. It was a Fate, and Tella had it tucked inside of a little trunk.

She squeaked out a laugh at the thought. Her mother must have been a force, to steal the Fates.

But now her mother was powerless, trapped inside of a card, exactly like the Fates.

Tella did not laugh at this thought. Suddenly she regretted having laughed at all.

Since the miserable day her mother had left, Tella had believed it was partially her fault, that if she hadn't disobeyed her mother and played with her jewelry box, and if she'd never flipped over the card with the Maiden Death, which predicted the loss of a loved one, then her mother would have never vanished. Tella blamed the cards and herself. And she had been right, though not in the way she'd always believed.

Her mother hadn't left merely because Tella had turned over a particular card; she'd fled because Tella had found the cards, and the cards were even more powerful and dangerous than Tella had ever imagined.

The posters on the walls finally stopped flapping. In their wake the shop went suddenly quiet. Yet Tella still felt the stare of her mother's poster, giving Tella the feeling that despite what she'd just learned, she didn't know nearly enough. There was something vital she was leaving out—something she'd forgotten.

"You look as if you have another question," Aiko said.

Tella had briefly forgotten the other girl was there, and why Tella was really there as well. She still needed to find the third clue, or her mother would stay trapped just like the Fates. Tella didn't think this was the something she'd forgotten, but whatever she couldn't remember couldn't have been as important as this.

Tella pulled out the second clue once more.

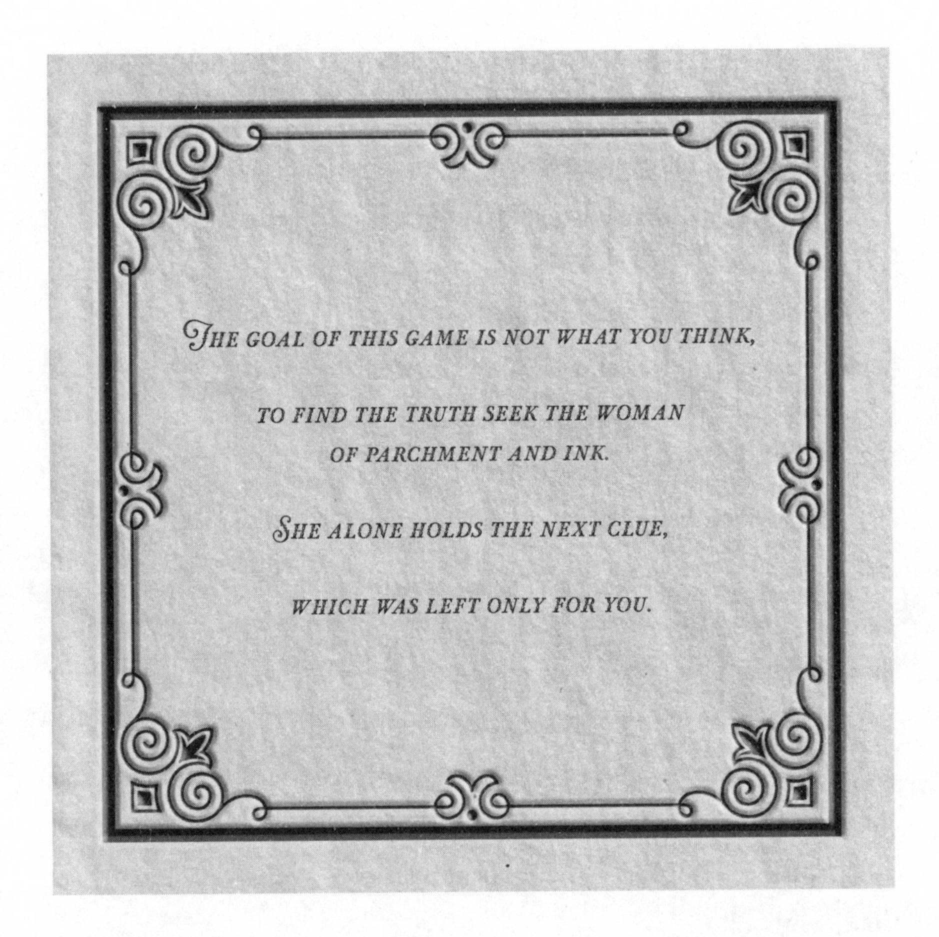
The goal of this game is not what you think,

To find the truth seek the woman
of parchment and ink.

She alone holds the next clue,

which was left only for you.

Tella's eyes went from the clue to her mother's Wanted poster.

What if the clue wasn't referring to the woman who drew the pictures, like Tella had first thought? What if it was referring to a woman on one of them, like Paradise the Lost? Her rendering was made of parchment and ink. And her picture spoke to Tella in a way that it could not have called to anyone else playing the game.

Tella hopped up on her tiptoes and ripped the poster from the wall.

She'd expected a protest from Aiko, but the girl appeared almost as eager as Tella felt when Tella flipped over the parchment and discovered lines of silvery writing on the back.

If you've found this you're on the true track,
but it's still not too late to turn back.
Clues can no longer tell you where to head;
to find the object Legend needs, your heart must lead instead.

The only thing in her heart was her mother, whom Legend must have known about since he'd written the clue on the back of her poster. But what did her mother have to do with Caraval?

Her mother had possessed the deck imprisoning all the Fates, and Legend wanted to destroy all the Fates. Maybe her mother had also stolen the object capable of destroying the Fates? But if she had, why—

No. Tella pushed the thought away. Believing the game was real was the quickest path to madness. And yet maybe Tella was already going mad, because she was no longer certain what she believed anymore.

Tella needed to figure out the truth before she proceeded. She needed to talk to Scarlett. Scarlett would help her sort everything out, especially if Tella's earlier suspicions about her sister were right and Scarlett knew more about the game than she'd been letting on.

Tella started for the door.

"Before you go," Aiko said, "you should hear the rest of Paradise's story."

"I think I know how it ends," Tella said.

"What you know is merely the almost-ending; the true ending has yet to be written."

"Then what's left to say?"

"I kept a part out of the middle of the story. Paradise discovered the deck's true power and danger after using it to read her future. Some said she fled, not to keep the cards safe, but to thwart the future she saw. What she didn't know was that with this particular deck, once a future is foretold, it cannot be undone unless the cards are destroyed."

"Thank you, but I think it might be a little late for that warning."

Aiko's expression went suddenly somber.

Tella felt it then. Wetter than tears dripping down cheeks. It pooled in her ears before trickling down her lobes to her cool neck.

Blood.

Thick and warm and awful.

Her heart choked on a beat, and then skipped over several more, dizzying her head and robbing her of breath. Her hand pressed against the nearest wall to keep herself from falling. The blood she'd lost at Minerva's was a trickle compared to this. It oozed from her ears onto her bodice in thick crimson streams. Another reminder from the Prince of Hearts that she was not playing this game for fun.

. . .

Tella journeyed back to the palace in a blur of damp sounds and hemorrhaging ears. Even after the bleeding stopped she continued to feel weak. Her heart had never beat so slowly.

Beat . . .

Nothing.

Beat . . .

Nothing.

Beat . . .

Nothing.

Soon all that would be left was nothing.

She'd bought a cheap cloak from a vendor on the street. But once she returned to the palace she swore every servant and guard could see her bloodstained bodice through the cloak.

Even after washing and changing into a dress from Minerva's formed of wild layers of elegant topaz-blue fabrics, all Tella felt was the dry blood inside her ears. It must have been cursed just like her, for she'd not been able to completely wash its stains from her neck or hands. She would have soaked her skin until the blood finally left, but she only allowed herself to rest in the tub's scented waters until some of her strength returned. She needed to talk to Scarlett about their mother's criminal past, and Caraval.

Tella put on Dante's gloves to cover up the stains and set out from the tower. She'd lost track of time, but she imagined it was well after midnight by the time she reached the sapphire wing where Scarlett was staying. Inside all the blues appeared gloriously gilded. A lone servant girl flitted about, checking on and refreshing oversize sconces filled with candles as thick as arms. She didn't say a word to Tella, but Tella felt her watching as she made her way to her sister's room.

But Scarlett didn't answer.

Tella knocked louder in case she was asleep.

Silence.

Tella rattled the door handle, hoping to possibly frighten her sister awake, but nothing happened. Either she was lost in a deep dreaming sleep, or Scarlett still wasn't there. But she should have been there. It was the middle of the night and Scarlett wasn't playing the game. Scarlett should have been back from wherever she'd gone by now.

Tella crossed the hall to the young, freckled servant, who was either shamelessly eavesdropping on Tella or relighting a very stubborn candle.

"How can I help you?" said the girl, turning from her task before Tella could so much as clear her throat. Definitely an eavesdropper, and far bolder than most of the mousy servants Tella had encountered.

The servant leaned closer.

Tella flinched back, but the freckled girl wasn't noticing any flecks of dried blood staining Tella's neck.

"If you're searching for the handsome performer with all the tattoos, I can tell you when he comes back. He didn't leave with the others." The servant's eager eyes went bright in a way that Tella was unfortunately familiar with.

"I'm sorry," Tella said, "I don't know who you're talking about."

"Don't worry." The girl gave a high-pitched titter. "I know you're engaged, I won't tell anyone you were looking for him."

Which meant she would probably tell everyone. But Tella had greater concerns at the moment.

"I'm actually searching for my sister." She pointed back toward Scarlett's room. "Her name is Scarlett. She's tallish, with thick brown hair and—"

"I know who she is," the girl cut in. "I haven't seen her since yesterday." Some of the color left the girl's cheeks as she dropped her voice to a whisper. "I heard her ask someone for directions to Idyllwild Castle, but she never came back."

Idyllwild Castle was Jacks's castle. Tella could not think of a single good reason her sister would go there.

"Of course, I'm sure nothing horrible has happened to your sister," the freckled servant added hastily, as if suddenly remembering who she was speaking with. "I don't believe all the stories about the heir. I know how people like to talk."

"And what do people say?" Tella asked.

"Just that he murdered his last fiancée. But they also say he's very handsome," she tacked on, as if that made up for murder. "Lots of the other servants say they'd still marry him."

Tella wanted to say they were fools. She wanted to brush back her hair and scare the girl with the blood still staining her ears and her neck. But Scarlett was missing. Rather than frightening servants, Tella needed to use her waning energy to find her sister.

She tossed the freckled girl a coin, but even that simple act felt weaker than it should have. The coin barely flipped in the air.

When Tella reached the carriage house, bells tolled three in the morning. Time was moving too fast and she was moving too slow. Her floating carriage seemed to be taking longer than necessary as well, gliding sluggishly across the starlit sky.

Legend's blue constellations were still everywhere, except for above Idyllwild Castle, as if warning her not to go there.

On the night of the Fated Ball the castle looked like something stolen from a young girl's fantasy. But after Tella left her carriage and reached the stony stronghold, she wondered if the castle's gleaming white sandstone exterior had been a costume, an illusion put on by Legend. Tonight the stones looked as dark as kept secrets, lit by dim red-orange torches that appeared to be losing their battle against the night.

She halted to catch her breath at the edge of the bridge, grateful she'd brought along Dante's gloves. Not that she saw any threats. In fact, if anything, the castle was too still.

Aside from the wind knotting her hair and ruffling the layers of her wild topaz skirts, everything was steeped in quiet. The sort of silence usually reserved for tombs, cursed ruins, and other places abandoned by the living. Tella suppressed a shudder but it managed to turn into a chill. She wasn't afraid of danger, though she preferred it in the form of swaggering young men. For the second time that night she found herself wishing that Dante had followed her.

Not that she needed him.

But maybe Tella wanted him there just a little. She took a heavy step forward and felt an uncomfortable stab of lackluster victory that he'd finally decided to leave her alone. She'd known he'd only been following her as part of his role, and even if his interest had been real, she had no doubts he'd give up on her eventually. Everyone gave up on her, except for Scarlett—who couldn't seem to stop caring about Tella.

Tella supposed it was another thing the sisters had in common—never knowing when to walk away. Maybe if Tella had a better sense of when to abandon an ill-fated pursuit she'd have turned around just then, or she'd have questioned if the freckled servant really had told the truth when she'd claimed Scarlett never returned from the castle—a castle that now looked emptier than a broken doll's eyes.

The bridge leading to it was even narrower than Tella remembered, taller, too, towering above black waters that weren't quite so still as the first night she'd visited. But Tella remembered what Dante had told her and refused to think about Death this time, unwilling to give him additional power.

Her steps were more unsteady than usual and her breathing was on the labored side, but she was not going to fall, or jump, or do anything else that would land her in the treacherous waters beneath. She was going to reach the end, knock on the door, and retrieve her sister. *If Scarlett was there.*

Tella finished crossing the bridge. For a slow heartbeat she swore she heard phantom footsteps, but there was not a guard or ghoul in sight.

Fisting her hands, she focused her strength and knocked against the heavy iron doors.

"Hello!" she started out cheerfully.

Nothing.

"Is anyone here?" she called a little sharper.

More waves crashed below.

"This is Donatella Dragna, the heir's fiancée!"

Her breath went short as her unanswered knocks turned aggressive.

"Careful, or you might hurt yourself doing that."

Tella slowly turned around, half expecting Jacks to be there, gracefully biting into an apple.

Instead, there were three others.

25

They prowled toward Tella like wraiths, clad in thin, dull silver cloaks that looked as if they'd lost their shine long ago. One was tall. One was curvy. One was fidgety. And they all smelled of too much old perfume, flowering and nauseating.

It was wrong for an unforgiving night like this.

Though impractical, their capes made it difficult for Tella to steal more than a glimpse of their faces, which were either incredibly still or covered in masks.

The trio slithered closer.

Despite the cold, sweat pooled inside of Tella's gloves as her suspicions about the masks were confirmed. The three were disguised as Fates: the Undead Queen and Her Handmaidens.

Tella recognized the Undead Queen's jeweled patch and painted blue lips. Her Handmaidens were equally unmistakable; both had lips sewn shut with crimson thread. In Decks of Destiny their cards represented power and undying loyalty. But in that icy moment Tella saw their combined appearance as three very bad omens. No one wore masks unless they were celebrating something, or committing a crime.

"You're a little early for the costumes," Tella said. "Didn't anyone tell you, Elantine's Eve isn't until the night after tomorrow. Or are you pretending to celebrate early because you're all too ugly to show your faces?"

"By the end of tonight the only unsightly one will be you," said the imposter Undead Queen. "Unless you give us what we want."

Tella turned away and knocked another aggressive rap on the door.

"That won't do you any good," said the Undead Queen. "He isn't here."

As she spoke, all three figures glided closer, replacing the cool night air with their stench. The freckled maid must have sent Tella on a false course, so that these three could rob her, and Tella had been foolish enough to fall for it. She might have been able to run away, despite her failing heart, but they were blocking her from the bridge. Her only clear escape, unless she wished to jump into the waters below.

She swore she heard the voice of Death, urging her to take the leap, but Tella wasn't about to listen. The inky moat looked deep and smooth but upon second glance Tella saw the rocks, poking out like nasty surprises.

She pulled out her coin purse. "If you're here to beg for money because your perfume stinks and your gaudy cloaks are long out of fashion, then here." Tella tossed the purse onto the small patch of land to her left. Since she imagined this was what they were after, she hoped at least one of them might fetch after it like a dog and give her a chance to escape. But dogs were clearly smarter creatures than these three. Instead of chasing for the purse they each took another step toward her.

The scent of their overripe perfume grew, sharpening to the scent of decayed flowers and twisted obsession. Tella gagged. But they didn't even notice.

"We don't want your filthy coins," said the Undead Queen. "We want to return to our full glory. We want the cards your mother stole, the cards you plan to give to Legend so that he can destroy us and take what remains of our once magnificent powers."

"God's teeth." Whoever these women were, they were taking the game too far. "You're all madder than poisoned fish!"

The odd insult seemed to stun them for a moment, but it wasn't long enough for Tella to escape. She still could have made a run for the bridge, but it was more likely she'd fall off one of the sides than make it to the other end before they caught her.

A gust of wind rushed past, but Tella thought it sounded like Death laughing.

"Tell us where the cards are and we will only scar one half of your face."

The Undead Queen flicked both wrists and immediately her maidens removed their hands from the pockets of their cloaks. Their skin was specter-white, glowing against the moonlight as they flashed thick black fingernails, long, tapered, and as barbed as claws. This was not a traditional part of the costume.

Fortunately, Tella had claws as well. She pressed the black pearls on her gloves, and sent a silent thank-you to Dante as ten sharp razorblades shot out.

But Her Handmaidens were undeterred.

The Undead Queen gave another flick of her wrist and Her Handmaidens stalked forward like murderous marionettes, hissing through their sewn lips.

Tella was far from her full strength, but she rallied what she had. She swiped with both hands and kicked out one leg. At first she attempted to scare rather than fight. But a few heartbeats later it became clear the Undead Queen was not lying about maiming Tella's face. Her Handmaidens aimed for Tella's eyes and cheeks, scratching and clawing until everything erupted into painful bursts of chaos.

Tella slashed more wildly with her claws, raking against one Handmaiden's arm with enough force to draw blood.

But there was no blood.

Only smoke poured from the Handmaiden's wound.

Tella staggered backward as the Handmaiden then vanished before her eyes. "Dirty hells!"

A few seconds later, the Handmaiden was back, hazy around the edges, as if she was a little less corporeal than before. But definitely not a ghost. Ghosts weren't supposed to be able to claw and wound.

Now fighting for breath, Tella kept swinging and kicking. "What are you?"

"I'm disappointed you have to ask." The Undead Queen formed a fist.

A second later one Handmaiden punched Tella's stomach with bruising force. Tella's back hit the hard ground, and the air knocked out from her lungs in one aching surge.

Crunch.

A slipper found her wrist and ground down impossibly hard.

Tella screamed. Her bones were shattered. Her heart was sluggish and her head was spinning. But even with her back pressed against the ground she kept swinging with her other hand, harder than before. She scratched and clawed and swiped. Every time she managed to wound a Handmaiden the maiden would magically vanish only to reappear seconds later. Tella wanted to deny it—she'd had enough life-altering realizations for one day—but clearly these were not actors or participants who'd taken the game too far. These were the real Fates.

They didn't bleed because they weren't human.

Tella's knees might have buckled if she wasn't already lying on the ground. How were all these Fates breaking free? Jacks should have warned her there were more running around, with murder on their minds.

Why don't you just give in? Death's voice twisted its way into Tella's thoughts.

"Never!" Tella gritted out.

"What was that?" said the Undead Queen.

"Those cards you want will never be yours," Tella groaned. "Once I give them to Legend, he'll make sure you all vanish for good."

Her Handmaidens hissed again, increasing the ferocity of their attack, but for a moment Tella felt no pain as she realized the truth behind what she'd just said: Her mother's Deck of Destiny wasn't merely the item that had been imprisoning the Fates. According to the Undead Queen, her mother's deck was also the object capable of destroying the Fates.

Tella's world was a blur of pain, but what she needed to do was suddenly clear. To win Caraval, Tella just needed to find her mother's Deck of Destiny. That was the object Legend wanted.

But whatever victory this thought brought was short-lived.

"If you will not help us we will use you to show others what happens to those who defy the Fates," said the Undead Queen.

"No wonder a witch put you inside a card, I'd imprison you just to shut you up," Tella slurred. Her entire body was screaming, she was still on the ground, but until this point her claws had kept the Handmaidens from fully grabbing and subduing her. She just needed to keep fighting long enough for someone else to come.

Why hadn't Dante followed her this time?

Or maybe he had but wasn't there yet. If he appeared, she'd be nicer this time.

Dark whorls swam in her vision. Tella swiped harder, slashing someone's calf. But again it only made the Handmaiden disappear briefly.

"Finish her," said the queen. "We're running out of time."

The slipper ground harder against Tella's shattered wrist, pulverizing her bones to dust and making her want to cry tears of pure pain as both Handmaidens bent toward her, lowering their claws closer to her face. She knew they'd planned to maim her, but now it seemed they wanted her dead.

Tella ceased swinging her uninjured arm for one precious moment and then, crying through the pain, she raised both arms and drove her claws deep into both of their ankles.

The Handmaidens howled and turned to smoke. A ragged heartbeat was all Tella had before they'd reappear again. With her uninjured arm she shoved up from the rocky ground, gasping with every breath, and ran straight off the edge.

It felt like a mistake the minute she hit the water.

She missed the rocks, but it was too cold. Her wrist was too broken. Her heart was too weak. Her dress was too cumbersome. But she fought like a demon trying to break out of hell and into the heavens. She ignored things that sucked at her ankles and anything that slithered against her now-bare feet. Tella didn't escape her father, a trio of Fates, and every other trial in her life to allow herself to be killed by some cold water and a shattered wrist.

Death would have to try harder if he wanted to take her back, and she was not about to let him do that. If she perished there'd also be no one to take care of Scarlett, to make sure her sister had all the proper adventures and kissed more boys than just Julian. Scarlett deserved all the kisses. Maybe Tella wanted more kisses too, ones that wouldn't end in death.

Tella didn't wash along the muddy shore, she raged her way out of the water in a tangle of wet curls and skirts and bruises, chest heaving, blue skin shivering, but she was still standing and breathing and living.

Unfortunately, she wasn't doing any of those things alone.

The Undead Queen and Her Handmaidens of Horror were waiting.

Tella told herself she could outrun them. But she could barely stagger forward as they closed in. Her limbs were liquid, shaking from the pain, the exertion, and the misery of it all. Her lungs could barely swallow the damp air. A lick of wind could have knocked her over.

If she were Scarlett, someone would have come to her rescue by now. Julian would have probably flown in on a hot-air balloon, and then sprouted wings to soar down and carry her away. Unfortunately Tella wasn't the sort of girl people saved—she was the one they left behind.

But she was also the sort they underestimated.

She reminded herself she was the daughter of two dangerous criminals.

She'd once bet her life on her sister's love.

She'd kissed the Prince of Hearts and still lived.

These Fates would not kill her tonight.

Every Fate had a weakness. Jacks's weakness was his one true love; the one who could make his heart beat again. Her Handmaidens were merely puppets of the Undead Queen, who possessed the terrifying ability to control those pledged in service to her. To best Her Handmaidens, Tella needed to best the queen. The queen had mentioned running out of time, and from the way Her Handmaidens turned to smoke whenever Tella wounded one, she wondered if perhaps they were still tethered to her mother's cards. If these Fates weren't as free as Jacks. Maybe if Tella attacked the queen, all three would return to their paper prison.

Thankfully Tella knew the Undead Queen's weakness: *It was said she'd traded her eye for her terrible powers.*

All Tella needed to do was stab the Undead Queen in her jeweled eye patch and Tella would hopefully live to see another night.

"If you're really an all-mighty Fate, come fight me yourself." Tella flashed the remaining razors on her gloves. There were only four left.

The Undead Queen cocked her head to the side, unimpressed.

Another razor fell, leaving only three.

And then Tella was done. She could have possibly kept standing, but she'd been struck enough times in her life to know when to pretend.

She fell to her knees, and then crumpled into the water. A graceless heap of sodden clothes and failure.

Reeking water sloshed against Tella's face as one of them moved closer. Tella's eyes were still closed. She couldn't risk opening them.

Not yet. She could only hope it was the Undead Queen moving closer, finally willing to get her hands dirty. Tella could feel a set of cool hands fumbling for her in the rank water. Long, prodding, invasive. Searching for her pulse.

Slowly, Tella cracked one eye. The outline of her assailant's narrow throat gleamed pale against the dark. It was the Undead Queen. She'd lifted her mask. Tella caught a glimpse of a pretty face marred by a nasty expression.

Tella breathed in as much air as she dared. Her veins were trembling, her fingers shaking. For all her bravado, Tella would have never done something like this before; she'd always been a runner rather than a fighter. The Tella who'd never died might have given up and taken her chances with Death.

But that girl had died, literally.

Tella struck with both eyes open.

The scream that followed was appalling, drowning the echo of her splash as Tella fell back into the shallow water.

"Filthy human!" the Undead Queen groaned, and clutched her ruined eye patch, black blood streaming down her face. "What have you done?"

"I should have warned you—I'm more trouble than I'm worth." Tella once again held up what remained of her claws, right as the Undead Queen and Her Handmaidens turned to smoke and vanished.

This time they did not reappear.

She'd done it. Tears fogged the corner of her eyes. She wasn't sure if she'd already been crying from the pain of her demolished wrist, or from her miserable victory. Tella might have won but she'd rarely felt more broken. She'd never been injured quite this badly before and actually lived through it.

Her muscles were frayed rope, and she had more bruises than skin. Her eyes strained against the night, exhausted tears running down her cheeks. The path to the carriage house was dim and so wretchedly far away. She swore it had moved farther away from her during the fight.

Scarlett had clearly never come to Idyllwild Castle; hopefully she was now back at the palace and would be able to put Tella back together. Tella just needed to get to her.

Tella's legs had other ideas, though. Her knees sunk back down into the water, which wasn't quite so cold as she remembered. And the mud was surprisingly soft. She would only close her eyes for a moment. She'd rest just until she could gather the strength to stand or crawl back to the carriage house. The lapping water was surprisingly soothing, numbing her wounded wrist and washing away all the blood and the dirt and the stench as she sank farther into—

Boot steps. Heavy ones.

"Donatella?" The voice sounded frustratingly familiar, but her head was so murky she couldn't tell if it was Dante, or Jacks. It was sharp like Jacks's, but commanding and resonant like Dante's. She needed to open her eyes, but it required too much movement. If it wasn't Dante, she just wanted to sleep, sleep—

"Donatella!" The voice was closer, more urgent this time, and now paired with two very demanding hands. They dredged her from the water, encasing her with the scent of ink and heartbreak. *Dante.*

Tella could have wept his name. But it all hurt so badly. She might have tried to shove her head back into the water, yet the bastard refused to let her go.

He cradled her sopping head to his chest. "Can you open your eyes for me?"

"Maybe I want to sleep here," Tella mumbled. "I'd wager it's safer than in your arms."

"What's so dangerous about my arms?" he murmured.

"For me, everything." Tella slowly lifted one lid open.

Veins of early-morning fog crowned Dante's dark head like a grim halo. How long had she been lying there?

And why did he look like an avenging angel?

His eyes were black, his jaw nothing but a chain of sharp lines as his mouth tilted into something like a snarl. This was not the same boy whose eyes had sparkled as he'd told her she should always wear flowers. He looked fierce enough to wrestle the rising sun, and yet Tella swore his brutal glaze went glassy as he looked down on her wrist and face.

"Who did this to you?" he asked.

"The Undead Queen and Her Handmaidens. I'm starting to believe . . ." Tella began to slur, "it might not be just a game. . . ."

Her eyes shut again.

"Do *not* fall asleep on me." Dante wrenched her fully from the water.

Drip. Drip. Drip. She sounded like a damp rag and felt even worse.

Dante pulled her closer. Nothing about him was soft. His chest felt like a block of marble and yet she could have closed her eyes, curled up against him, and gone to sleep forever.

"Don't do that," he scolded. "Don't even think about giving up on me. You need to stay conscious until I get you somewhere safe."

"Where is that?" Tella slit her aching eyes, head bouncing against him with every step he took away from the main path. When had he started walking?

They weren't heading back to Idyllwild Castle, but it didn't look as if they were going to the carriage house, either. She wondered deliriously if she was possibly picturing her future because it looked as if they were in some sort of graveyard. All Tella could see were grainy outlines of mossy tombstones topped with crumbling cherubs, or flanked by weeping statues wearing veils. The trees above seemed to be in mourning as well, all raining brittle twigs that crunched underneath Dante's boots.

"Have you decided to bury me early?" she asked.

"You're not going to die. We'll find someone to get you healed." Dante started down a set of aged stone steps edged by a massive sculpture of robed men with wings, all holding a coffin above their heads.

Tella might have snorted a laugh; it seemed everywhere she went death and doom were determined to follow.

"I lied to you in the dress shop," Tella said. "You were right about Jacks. . . ." She forced her eyes open once again. Her head was spinning. The world was spinning. All she wanted was for it to stop. For everything to stop.

"I shouldn't have kissed him," she mumbled. "I don't even know why I kissed him. I didn't really care if he kicked me out of the palace for lying. I think I wanted to make you jealous."

"It worked," Dante said roughly.

Tella might have smiled if everything didn't hurt so much.

Dante held her closer and smoothed back a piece of hair that had fallen across Tella's face. Then his fingers returned, gently tracing the curve of her mouth as he said, "I've never wanted to be someone else until that moment I saw him kiss you on the dance floor."

"You should have asked me to dance first."

"I will, next time." His lips swept a kiss across her forehead. "Don't give up on me, Donatella. If you stay with me long enough to get you somewhere safe and warm, then I promise I won't let go of you like I did that night. Together we'll fix all of this."

The sharpness left his face, and for a moment Dante looked so treacherously young. His dark eyes were more open than usual, rimmed in bits of starlight that made her want to stare into them forever. His hair fell like strands of lost ink in every direction, while his dangerous mouth remained parted, looking vulnerably close to spilling a wicked secret.

"You're the most beautiful liar I've ever seen." She tried to mumble more, but her mouth didn't want to move any longer. Her muscles were so, so tired.

Dante held her hazardously closer as he reached a mausoleum

and opened the gate. Tella told herself she'd only close her eyes for another moment. Dante was murmuring something else, and she wanted to hear it. It sounded as if it might have been important. But it was suddenly so much warmer in here, and hadn't she wanted to know what it would feel like to fall asleep wrapped in his arms?

Tella wanted to fall back asleep the instant she woke up, if this stifling form of consciousness could actually be considered wakefulness. Her eyes would not open. Her lips would not move. But she could feel the pain, searing so sharply. Her entire world was formed of injured bones and sliced skin, punctuated by fragments of sounds and wayward words, as if her hearing couldn't decide whether or not it wanted to work.

There were two voices, male, both echoing. Tella's groggy head conjured images of rocky walls hidden deep underground.

"What did . . ."

"I—"

"Save . . . her . . ."

"I know the risks . . . but Fates . . . She won't heal."

"I thought the Prince . . . was the only Fate free?"

"These Fates . . . stayed hidden for years . . . or the spell imprisoning the Fates is weakening."

The other voice muttered a curse.

Tella felt it then, something that wasn't pain, wet against her lips. Thicker than water and slightly metallic. *Blood.*

"Drink."

Something warm pressed more firmly against Tella's mouth, until she could feel the damp blood dripping onto her tongue. Her first instinct was to spit it out. But it was still impossible to move, and she enjoyed the way it tasted, like power and strength and something fierce enough to make her heart race. With extreme effort she managed to lick and drink down more.

"Good girl." It was one of the voices from before, but now that some of her pain had dulled Tella could add a name. *Julian.*

"That should be enough." The second voice was lower and more commanding. *Dante.*

Tella's heart beat even faster.

An instant later there was no more blood. The pain was still present but it was dulled to an aching.

"Find her sister." Dante again. "Get her into Tella's room at the palace. I don't want her to wake up alone."

A pause followed, extended in a way that made Tella fear her hearing had failed her until Julian's voice broke the quiet. "You really care about her?"

Another pause.

"I care about finding those cards, and she's our best hope for it, brother."

27

It should have felt like the end of existence when Tella came back to consciousness once more. Her everything should have hurt in every possible way. She should have awoken to a world of pain, to a screaming wrist, a swollen face, and battered feet. Instead her body felt whole and rested, and her heart was beating stronger than it had the night before. Wherever she was, this new universe was delightfully cozy and sweet, as if someone had tucked her into the center of a holiday.

Something crackled, a fire that smelled faintly of cinnamon and cloves. There were curling streams of laughter too, uneven and gasping, her sister's laugh when she thought her companion genuinely funny.

If Scarlett was giggling, it couldn't be all bad.

Tella cautiously cracked her eyelids.

And slammed them shut immediately. Or she tried to shut her eyes, but they refused to close, as if they were unable to look away from the vivid sight of her sister, clad in seductive shades of red, and

Jacks, glowing faintly as he leaned lazily across one of the tufted lounges in Tella's tower suite. Her sister and her fake fiancé both laughed and chatted and gazed as if they could not have been more taken with each other.

Tella sat up. It seemed she was atop but not inside her bed. She wasn't sure if she wanted to know who had changed her out of her decimated gown, or how. But somehow she was in a brand-new dress—the same silver sea salt and blue as Jacks's eyes, with sleeves held together by a simple tie, a flowing skirt, and a bodice strung with dark thistle ribbons that made her look like a present someone had halfway unwrapped.

Dante didn't appear to be anywhere and neither did Julian. Tella's gaze took in every corner of the room. The dull peach light streaming through the window gave the impression of a sluggish morning, but there were no hints that Julian or Dante had been there. Just thinking about Dante brought a rush of dizziness that made her want to close her eyes again. Her skin warmed as she recalled the protective way he'd cradled her in his arms. But then it burned when she thought of the last words he'd said to Julian. She wanted to believe everything she'd overhead was only a dream. But then who had healed her? And how had she ended up here?

In front of the dying fire, Jacks and Scarlett were still chatting; neither of them noticed Tella was no longer asleep. Jacks was tossing around a pale blue apple and saying something too low for Tella to hear, but it made her sister's cheeks turn pink.

Tella coughed. Loudly.

"Oh, Tella!" Scarlett jumped up from her seat, and Tella swore her sister's face reddened further. "I'm so glad you're awake. Jacks and I have been so worried."

Tella's head snapped toward the villain in question. "I didn't even think you were allowed in here."

"I love how you forget I'm the heir to the throne," Jacks said smoothly. "This palace is practically mine. But even if it wasn't, no one could keep me from your side, even after such a minor incident."

His eyes hooked on to Tella's as he came to her side of the bed, silently commanding her to go along with whatever he said next. "I know you only fell a few feet, after accidentally leaving the carriage too early and hitting your head. But I still worry what would have happened if I hadn't been there to catch you and carry you back here, my love." He spoke it all affectionately, as if he found everything about her entirely endearing.

Tella swore Scarlett's eyes turned into little hearts.

Tella began to wonder if perhaps this was the actual dream, although it was feeling more akin to a nightmare. Scarlett appeared far too taken with Jacks, who wasn't even supposed to be there. Dante and Julian had saved her—where were *they*?

Jacks picked up Tella's wrist and gently squeezed. If she hadn't known better, she'd have said he looked concerned. "Your pulse feels strong. But you probably need some food." He turned back to Scarlett. "Would you be a treasure and fetch your sister a fresh tray of fruit and tea and biscuits? It will take too long to ring for a servant and I don't think we should risk letting her pass out again."

"Of course," Scarlett said. A few seconds later she was gone, leaving Tella and Jacks alone.

For a moment there was only the crackle of the fire and Jacks's worried gaze, as silver as falling stars; he seemed to be better at mimicking real emotions than when she'd seen him three nights ago.

"What are you doing here?" Tella asked.

Jacks's gaze instantly turned dispassionate.

"I have spies all over the palace," he said. His tone was bored, as if it disappointed him she'd not asked a more original question. "I know everything that happens in here. The moment that actor carried you in through the tunnels I was alerted, and it's a good thing. Your sister rushed in here minutes after I arrived and I had to make up that story about you falling out of a carriage, because she was under the impression you almost died."

"I did almost die! Why didn't you tell me other Fates were free?"

"Who did you encounter?" he asked coolly.

"The Undead Queen and Her Handmaidens."

Jacks took a careless bite of his blue apple, but Tella swore his features sharpened while he chewed, as if he weren't as indifferent as he seemed. "You're lucky they were weak."

"They didn't seem weak to me. Those Handmaidens nearly killed me. How many other Fates are free?"

Jacks gave a bitter laugh. "Just because a few of us are out of those cards doesn't mean we're free. When that witch cursed us, she took half our powers. I'm a shadow of what I once was. You think my only power was having a deadly kiss? I was called the Prince of Hearts because I could control more than just the beat of someone's heart. With one touch I could give or take away feelings and emotions. If I were at my full powers, we wouldn't even be having this conversation. You'd be so uncontrollably in love with me, you'd do whatever I asked without question."

Tella didn't even bother to hold back her laugh. "No power on earth could make me fall in love with you."

"We'll see. Unless you don't live past the week." Jacks tossed his apple into the fire. It sparked celestial blue, briefly covering the room in a shimmer incongruent with their deadly conversation. It reminded Tella of Legend's stars from the night before.

Or were they Dante's stars?

Finally, Tella allowed herself to really consider what she'd overheard between Dante and Julian. Not only had they magically healed her with blood, but Dante had called Julian his brother.

If Julian had been telling Scarlett the truth about Legend being his brother, then Dante was Legend. But if Dante was Legend, why had he brought Tella to Julian for him to heal? Maybe Julian was really Legend.

Tella wished she'd been able to open her eyes and see whose blood she'd been drinking. There was a chance it didn't belong to Julian or Dante; maybe Julian kept stores of magical blood somewhere. That seemed highly unlikely. But it also felt surreal to imagine that one of the brothers was actually Legend, and that he'd fed her blood to keep her alive.

Either way, handing Legend over to Jacks at the end of the game didn't feel quite the same as it had before, not even close.

And yet there was a vicious part of Tella that took pleasure in the idea that Dante was really Legend. After hearing Dante tell Julian he only cared about Tella because she could find the cards, part of her would have gladly given him over to Jacks—even as the rest of her warned that this was a terrible idea.

Tella turned back to Jacks to find him toying with one of her honey-blond curls. It sent a chill over her entire body, making the pieces of her that had been healed feel shattered once again. She tried to shake off the sensation. Instead she found herself imagining what Jacks would be like at full power. When the Fates had ruled before, they were said to be more like gods than humans. She pictured his lips forever stained with blood and a pile of dead maidens at his feet.

"Is this why you want Legend?" Tella asked Jacks. "To get the rest of your powers back?"

"I think you already know the answer to that," Jacks drawled.

"What happens to Legend once this transaction is done?"

Irritation flashed in Jacks's eyes. "Are you worried about the immortal Master Caraval?"

"No, but I am worried about giving monsters like you and the Undead Queen more power."

"Monsters are going to be given power no matter how this story ends," Jacks said pleasantly. "What do you think will happen to Legend if he destroys us and acquires all of our magic? I like power, but no human or immortal should have that much of it. If Legend gets what he wants, he'll be a greater villain than the world has ever seen."

"So you believe the game is real?"

"Maybe not for everyone who's playing, but it is for you and me and Legend. Does that change things for you, pet? Because if you're having second thoughts let me remind you of two things. You fail to hold up your bargain with me, you will die at the end of this week, and so will your mother. There are only two ways to free someone from a card. A human must willingly take their place inside the card, or an immortal with great power must break the curse and free *all* of those imprisoned in cards. Legend would never choose freeing the Fates. If he gets his hands on the cards, he'll destroy them, including your mother."

Jacks leaned close enough to brush Tella's ear with cold lips, as he tucked her hair behind it and whispered, "The card your mother's trapped inside of is linked to the deck of cards imprisoning all the Fates. Unless you want your mother dead, as soon as you win the game you'll contact me with the luckless coin and give me Legend like you promised."

"I hate you," Tella growled.

Jacks chuckled against her earlobe, as if the sentiment gave him a thrill.

"Am I interrupting something?" Scarlett's voice rang out from the doorway.

Tella looked over to see her sister holding a colorful tray of food and still smiling a little too widely at Jacks.

"I was just saying good-bye." Jacks smoothed back an errant hair from Tella's forehead, frowning, as if he hated to leave her.

Scarlett looked as if she might swoon from the sight. And Tella imagined it probably did appear unspeakably elegant, with her lying there all pale atop the cushions, and Jacks looking wild, glowing, and golden, with his gilded hair falling over one uncanny eye.

"I wish I could stay longer. But don't worry, my love, I'll be back to collect you this evening for our dinner with the empress."

Scarlett gasped as she set her tray down next to the bed. "You're having dinner with the empress?"

"Oh, yes," Jacks cut in, before Tella could react to this new piece of information. "Her Majesty is very eager to meet the girl who's stolen my heart. She didn't care for my last fiancée, but I know she'll love Donatella as much as I do."

His tone couldn't have been sweeter if he'd dipped it in honey, and this time Tella could not discern if what he'd just said was for Scarlett's benefit, or Tella's torment. If the empress loved Tella as much as Jacks did, then she would not love her at all.

This dinner suddenly felt like a very bad idea.

In a way the empress had always been as mythical to Tella as the Fates; a powerful ruler she'd heard about but never seen. And, though she was curious, Tella could have done without the honor of meeting Her Majesty. More important, one night with the empress meant one fewer night Tella would have to play the game and find her mother's cards, which Tella was now certain were the key to winning the game.

"I can't have dinner with you tonight," Tella said. "There are only three nights left of Caraval."

"You keep forgetting how important I am," said Jacks. "This means you're significant now, too. I've told the empress how much you've been enjoying the game, and she's cancelled everything they'd planned for tonight so that you don't fall behind."

"But—"

"It's already done," Jacks purred, with a glance at her sister and a hint of mettle in his voice that hadn't been there before, reminding Tella of exactly what she had to lose if this sham of an engagement was exposed.

Tella wanted to ask why it mattered to him so much. When they'd first met he'd claimed exposing the lie would paint him as weak and put his life in jeopardy. As soon as she found out he was a Fate she imagined that was a lie, but perhaps he was vulnerable until he had his full powers.

"Now," he added loudly, "I really must leave." He said a quick good-bye to Scarlett. Thankfully, he made no attempt to kiss her hand or cheek.

Though from the way Scarlett fluttered her lashes as she closed the door behind him, Tella imagined her sister had wanted Jacks to at least brush his lips against her fingers.

"Scar, you need to be careful with him."

"That's funny," Scarlett said, her head turning sharply back toward Tella. "I was about to tell you the same thing."

Scarlett gripped the door's glass handle with five white knuckles while her back pressed against it, as if she were barring it to prevent a particular person's reentry.

"Tella, what are you doing with the heir to the throne?" Scarlett's smile had vanished, and her voice had gone from treacle-sweetness to sour.

"I thought you liked him, from the way you kept grinning."

"His reputation is vicious, and he's royalty—I've seen his pictures all over the palace. How else was I supposed to act?" Scarlett marched back over to the bed and perched on the edge, a brilliant crimson bird about to strike. "Tella, what is going on? When Julian told me to come here earlier he made it sound as if you'd almost died, but then Jacks told me a ridiculous story about you falling from a carriage. Did he hurt you?"

"No, Jacks didn't lay a finger on me."

"Then tell me what happened. Julian refused to explain. He ran off, and this time I didn't even tell him to go."

Tella tugged at the sea-salt blue ribbons hanging off her dress, avoiding her sister's demanding gaze. Scarlett kept looking at Tella as if she'd done something wrong. But Tella wouldn't have been in this situation if Scarlett hadn't been keeping secrets.

"You want to know what happened?" Tella asked. "I was out searching for you. I went by your suite after midnight, but you were gone." Tella finally looked up. "Where were you, Scarlett?"

"I wasn't anywhere," she answered flatly. "I was in my room, sleeping."

Tella's eyes narrowed. "I knocked."

"I must have slept through it."

"I pounded hard enough to bruise my knuckles."

"I was exhausted." Scarlett pressed her hands against her skirt and smoothed a nonexistent wrinkle. "You know how heavy I can sleep."

Tella didn't want to doubt her sister. Scarlett's tone was sincere, but the way her hands continued to fidget with the even folds of her gown gave Tella the impression that even if she was telling the truth, it wasn't the entire story. She just kept smoothing and smoothing and smoothing.

Scarlett seemed to sense her sister's growing doubts. "I'm not playing the game. Where would I have been, Tella?"

"Maybe you're not playing because you're working for Legend," Tella accused.

"You—you think I'm in on the game?" Scarlett sputtered.

"I don't know what to think! After everything that happened last night I'm not even sure I still believe it's just a game," admitted Tella.

To her credit Scarlett didn't say this was exactly what she'd warned her about. Instead she took a deep breath and smoothed her skirt again before calmly saying, "Have you already forgotten what Legend put me through in the last game? Do you really believe I would be a part of doing something like that to you? Don't answer, because it's clear from the look on your face that you do. But I would never hurt you like that, Tella. I swear, I'm not working for Legend and if you believe otherwise, then Legend's tricks are working on you."

Scarlett took one of Tella's hands, her grip warm and firm but a little bit shaky. Tella could have interpreted it to mean her sister was being dishonest, or that Scarlett, who rarely ever lied to Tella, was genuinely hurt.

Tella felt an arrow of guilt.

"I'm sorry," Tella said. "You're right. I shouldn't have jumped to the conclusion you were working with Legend just because you didn't answer your door."

Tella almost laughed when she said the words out loud; she had made a rather large leap. But it seemed too soon to joke about. Scarlett still held on to Tella's hand, and yet the bond between them felt unusually fragile, as if the weight of Tella's many secrets might break it.

She gazed out the window. The light had changed from lazy peach to brilliant apricot, turning everything in the room a little more gilded.

Tella had not been paying attention to the bells, but she imagined it was sometime around or after noon. There were enough hours before nightfall and her dinner with the empress to confess everything to Scarlett. And Tella considered it. But she doubted Scarlett would believe anything that Tella had learned during the game, which scared her almost as much as the idea of Scarlett believing everything.

Tella almost wanted to hear her sister's reassurance that it was all only a game. But if Caraval was all real—as this morning's run-in with the Undead Queen had started to convince Tella—pretending it was just a game would not do Tella any good. However, convincing Scarlett it was real would not do Scarlett any good, either. She would only worry more about Tella.

But maybe there was one secret Tella could reveal that would make things better instead of worse. "I think Dante might be Julian's brother."

"Why would you say that?" Scarlett's tone was pure skepticism. "The two don't even like each other."

"I overheard something last night."

"It was probably just an act for the game."

"It sounded very convincing."

Scarlett slit her eyes. "You really are starting to believe it's not just a game, aren't you?"

"No," Tella lied.

"But you think Julian and Legend are brothers?"

"Yes," Tella said. "I do." Or she did, until her sister had started looking at her as if she'd lost her mind.

Scarlett drew a heavy breath. "I wish I could believe you, but I'm not even playing and it's making me question things." She motioned toward the door. "I still can't figure out why you and the heir are claiming to be engaged. I'm sure it has something to do with the game, but I can't imagine what. All I know is that it scares me, Tella. And if I'm this confused, you must be even more confused." Scarlett's voice cracked and something inside of Tella broke along with it.

Tella didn't want to lie to her sister again, but she also knew that she couldn't tell her the entire truth.

"I'm playing the game on behalf of Jacks," Tella confessed. "If I win and give him the prize," she hedged, "then he'll reunite us with our mother."

Scarlett's expression hardened, but she didn't say a word.

Seconds passed.

Tella almost feared her sister wouldn't respond, that she'd ignore the topic as she always did. But it was almost worse when she spoke.

Scarlett uttered every word as if it were a curse, as if she'd rather have learned their mother was dead. "Why are you still looking for that woman?"

"Because she's not some woman, she's our mother." Tella considered walking over to her little trunk and pulling out the card that Paloma was trapped inside of, but it wasn't indestructible like the Aracle, and she feared Scarlett might do something rash like try to rip it in half.

The color of Scarlett's dress shifted, darkening from sultry crimson to raging burgundy, matching the dark tone of her voice as she said, "I know you want to believe the best about her. For a long time I did too. But she left us, Tella, and she didn't just abandon us, she left us with our father. I know you keep hoping there's a good reason for it. But the truth is, if she'd loved us at all, she'd have stayed, or taken us with her."

Tella considered telling her sister that their mother had left to protect them from a cursed Deck of Destiny containing all the Fates, but when she thought it all at once, it sounded ludicrous. And, if Tella told Scarlett about the cards, she'd also have to confess that their mother was a criminal who had stolen the cards in the first place, and she doubted that would help her case, either.

"I'm sorry we view this so differently," Tella said.

"I just don't want to see you hurt again." Scarlett sagged against the closest bedpost. "Looking at this situation—at the fact that you've teamed up with a violent heir to find her—screams to me that it won't end well."

"I know you don't like this," Tella said, "but if it's Jacks you're worried about, trust me when I tell you that this business between us will end as soon as the game is over."

"Are you sure about that?" Scarlett said. "When he was in here, he didn't look as if he wanted to let you go anytime soon."

"He's a good performer."

"I don't think that's it."

"That's why I'm asking you to trust me." Tella squeezed her sister's hand. "I trusted you when you told me you weren't working for

Legend. I promise, three days from now, neither you nor I will ever have to see Jacks again."

"A lot can change in three days," Scarlett said.

But she didn't argue after that, making Tella wonder if perhaps her sister had a secret of her own after all.

WHAT SHOULD HAVE BEEN NIGHT FOUR OF CARAVAL

Tella could not stop weaving flowers into her hair. She knew there were far too many; her head looked like a garden, full of blue plumerias. And she continued to add more.

After Scarlett had left, a bouquet of plumerias had arrived at her door without a note. Tella imagined they were a gift from Jacks, since they matched the billowing ball gown he'd sent for that evening. Tella had started to toss the flowers out the window, but something about their perfume was familiar in a way that made her ache at the idea of parting with the blue bouquet. She'd put one in her hair, then another, and another, losing herself in their sweet scent and concentrating on the tiny act of weaving them into her curls rather than the fact that she was having dinner with the empress of the Meridian Empire.

Just the thought unbalanced her.

Since her father was a governor, Tella had been taught all the proper manners for banqueting with nobles, but she'd never been very good at following them. And she knew nothing about dining with royalty.

She took another plumeria from the thinned bouquet.

A chuckle floated from the doorway to her bedroom.

Tella spun away from her vanity to spy Jacks, leaning against the frame.

She'd expected that for once he'd make an attempt to look regal. But like the night of the Fated Ball, Jacks didn't even have a coat. He wore a loose shirt the color of spilled brandy, with ripped shoulders that made it look as if he'd torn off some sort of ornamentation, hanging untucked over burnt auburn trousers that were shoved into unpolished leather boots. *Casual* was too fancy of a word to describe him, yet magic still pulsed around him in a glow of burning copper.

In one ungloved hand he held a fresh apple, as white and bright as a virgin's sheets. "Good evening, Donatella."

"You know it's not polite to sneak into a young lady's room."

"I think we left politeness behind a while ago. But"—Jacks shoved away from the doorframe in one lithe movement and offered her his arm—"I promise to be on my best behavior tonight."

"That doesn't say much." Tella smoothed her full skirts as she stood up from her perch. The gown she wore felt heavier than any of the others Jacks had sent. One half of it was unadorned pearl-blue silk, the other was an ornate combination of jeweled swirls, twilight-blue velvet flowers, and glacier-blue lace embellishments, which spilled down her skirt in a haphazard combination that reminded Tella of a knocked-over jewelry box.

"Don't worry," Jacks said. "I'm sure El will adore you."

"Did you just refer to the empress as El?"

"'Elantine' is such a mouthful."

"You call me Donatella."

"I like the way it tastes." Jacks's teeth broke the skin of his apple slowly, revealing deep red flesh as he took a wide bite.

Tella forced herself to accept his arm, knowing that any signs of discomfort and displeasure only seemed to give him delight. But to her surprise he behaved like a gentleman as they traveled up the steps of Elantine's golden tower to meet the empress on the topmost floor.

Jacks held Tella's arm lightly enough that she could have pulled away at any time, more focused on his apple than on her, until after a few flights of stairs. He dropped her arm and turned to face her, abruptly.

His sharp teeth bit into his lips instead of his piece of fruit, while his quicksilver eyes danced over her hair. Tella had lost several flowers on the stairs. It was probably for the best. Yet Jacks began to frown as he took her in.

"What is it?" Tella asked.

"The empress needs to believe we're in love." He paused, as if carefully choosing his next words. "My situation with El is complicated. If I could kill her, I would, but there are protections on her that prevent me. And though she's old, she's not close to dying. She is, however, close to passing on her throne to me. But that won't happen until I've found someone she believes is suitable to share it with me."

"And you think I'm that someone?" A laugh accompanied Tella's words.

But Jacks did not smile. "You convinced Legend to help you, you died and came back to life, and you dared to kiss me. Of course you're that someone." He held her eyes for a moment before his gaze swept past her.

Tella followed the line of his eyes to a mirror hanging on the wall. It reflected both of them. To Tella's astonishment, Jacks appeared different in the mirror; it must have been incapable of capturing his true essence. With his ripped shirt and unpolished boots, he still looked as if he'd just rolled out of bed or fallen from a low window—but he also appeared younger, more boyish, mischievous rather than evil incarnate. His eyes were a bright shade of blue without any cold hints of silver. His skin was still pale, but there was a hint of color in his cheeks and a subtle curve to his mouth that made him look as if he were on the verge of saying something naughty.

"You're staring at the wrong person, darling." Jacks gently pressed a hand to her cheek, shifting her view so that Tella saw her own reflection.

She had sat in front of a mirror pinning flowers into her hair for more than an hour, but she hadn't looked at herself, not really. Sometimes when she gazed in the mirror she swore she saw Death's shadow instead of her own. But as she peered at her reflection now, she did not see Death. Her skin glowed, not just with color from climbing up the stairs, but with life capable of days and weeks and seasons of adventures not yet had. Beside her, Jacks suddenly looked even paler in comparison. His glow meant he would never die of natural causes or mortal wounds, but her radiance meant she would truly live.

"Other people might underestimate you, Donatella, but I don't."

Tella tried not to feel anything at his words. All her life she'd been underestimated, by her father who thought she was useless, her sister who loved her but feared she couldn't stay out of trouble, her nana who thought of her as only a nuisance; Tella even underestimated herself at times. It was almost cruel that the one who seemed to believe in her the most was the same being who was also slowly killing her.

"If I fail, will you kill me early, the same way you murdered your last fiancée?"

Jacks's expression shuttered. "I didn't kill her."

"Then who did?"

"Someone who didn't want me to take the throne."

Jacks dropped his apple, letting it roll down the stairs as he took Tella's arm. He held her a little closer than before, almost protectively, but he stayed silent as they continued climbing, as if her mention of his former fiancée had genuinely upset him. Perhaps if Tella believed him she would have felt guilty. But he was the Prince of Hearts, and everyone knew the prince was not capable of love. The stories said he had one true love, but Tella doubted he'd found her. And given how casually he'd mentioned wishing he could kill the empress, Tella doubted Jacks was affected by the loss of one human life.

"Why does the throne matter to you so much?" Tella asked after a few more steps. "As a Fate I'd think you wouldn't want to be burdened by mortal power."

"Maybe I like the idea of wearing a crown." Jacks tilted his head, letting more golden hair fall into his eyes. "Have you seen the emperor's crown?"

"I can't say I have." But Tella had witnessed how carelessly Jacks dressed, and even if that weren't the case, she couldn't imagine the Prince of Hearts would fight so hard to be the heir simply so he could wear a crown.

She was about to ask what was so special about this crown when they finally stopped their ascent.

Tella hadn't counted the number of flights they'd taken, but she imagined they were near the top of the tower. Two black lacquered doors waited for them, with guards dressed in full armor standing on either side. They must have recognized Jacks. Without a word the guards opened the doors.

Candles fell from every inch of a white ceiling, like waxy, glowing raindrops, filling the domed room with flickering spires of marigold light. Tella only had a moment to take it all in, to glance at the steam rising from the elaborate feast beneath the candles and the intricately carved stage on the other side of the room, before a feminine voice burst through the silence.

"You're finally here!" Empress Elantine rose from a seat at the end of the banquet table.

Tella had expected a pale specter of a woman, thin and bony and colder than her nana Anna, but Elantine was full rosy cheeks, dark olive skin, and a round body that looked as if it would be very soft to hug.

"You, my dear, are lovely." Elantine smiled and it was luminous, as if she'd been saving up grins to meet Tella. The expression lit up Her Majesty's entire face, making the golden diadem atop her head and the jewels lining her royal-blue cloak shine even brighter.

Tella dropped into a curtsy. "It's a pleasure to meet you, Your Majesty. Jacks has told me a great deal about you."

"Has he told you how he plans to kill me?"

Tella choked on a gasp.

"Don't look so frightened. I'm only joking! Jacks is my favorite heir so far." Elantine winked and folded Tella tightly into her arms.

Because of her nana Anna, who'd been slender as a tree branch, Tella had always thought of older people as fragile, breakable things, but Elantine hugged fiercely, warm and careless enough to wrinkle her immaculate garments.

After releasing Tella, Elantine embraced Jacks as well. She even ruffled his head as if he were a little boy. "You'd be so handsome if you put just the tiniest effort into your appearance."

To Tella's astonishment Jacks actually blushed; his skin was more blue than red, but it was definitely there. She didn't know it was possible to fake a blush—there was no way he could have genuinely been embarrassed by her fussing—yet his pale cheeks turned a little blue.

After a heartbeat he added a lopsided grin, no doubt to make the empress believe that even though he was shy, he appreciated her attentions. It was disturbing how good he was at this charade.

The empress beamed, but it quickly faded. "You look too thin, Jacks. I hope you'll eat more than an apple tonight." Elantine turned back to Tella. "You'll have to make sure he eats enough. People are always trying to poison my dear Jacks, so he never munches on a thing at my little banquets. But hopefully he'll enjoy himself tonight. I've ordered a feast fit for—well, me."

Elantine laughed as she directed Jacks and Tella toward the table towering with food. Every dish imaginable, from honeycomb towers with edible flowers to a candied pig with an apple in its mouth, was present. There were miniature fruit trees growing chocolate-dipped plums and brown-sugar-glazed peaches. Wedges of cheese peeking out of miniature treasure chests made of pastry. Upside-down turtle shells filled with soup. Finger sandwiches shaped like actual fingers. Colorful plates of salted pink and red radishes. Water with lavender bubbles, and peach-colored wine with berries at the bottom of the glass.

"You'll notice there are no servants. I wanted this to be an intimate affair to get to know you." Elantine sat at the head of the table. There were only two additional chairs both facing the theatrical stage at the other end of the room. The wooden arch above it was carved with images of unadorned oval masks, frowning and grinning and scowling and laughing and making a variety of other odd faces as they looked down at the closed fairy tale–green curtain below.

"Now, tell me about yourself," said the empress. "Jacks says you're in Valenda searching for your missing mother?"

Tella opened her mouth to reply as she sat but rather than allow it, Elantine continued reciting an impressively long list of the other things Jacks had said about Tella. The empress even knew Tella's birthday was coming up and promised to throw her a little party.

"Jacks also tells me you have a fixation with the Fates. I used to have a special Deck of Destiny myself, a long time ago. It never seemed to predict good things." She laughed again.

The sound surprised Tella almost as much as it had the first time. She'd not expected Her Majesty to be so good-humored. Or to love Jacks so very much. She either nodded or laughed at whatever he said, and piled food on his plate as if he were a child, though Tella noticed Jacks did not touch any of it. He plucked the apple from the pig's mouth, but he didn't eat that, either. He just rolled it around the palm of one hand.

Then his other hand was on Tella's neck, his cold fingers idly playing with her hair. It was for show, but it felt so unpracticed. As if it was the most natural thing for him to reach out and touch her. She swore she felt his gaze as well, as cool as morning frost; it brushed against her mouth as Jacks watched every bite she took.

"You both must try some of these." Elantine pointed to a tray of palm-size cakes decorated to look like presents in every combination of colors. From tangerine and teal to silver and sea frost, the color of Jacks's eyes.

"These are a traditional engagement dish exclusively for royalty. Only the royal baker will make them. It's illegal for anyone else to commission them. There's a different surprise in each one that symbolizes what your future together will hold. Some are filled with sugared cream to represent a sweet life, and others are filled with candied eggs symbolizing great fertility." Elantine winked again and Tella nearly spit out her water.

Jacks, who had not eaten a thing since his apple on the stairs, plucked a jeweled cake covered in blue velvet frosting, the same color of Tella's dress, and brought it to his mouth. When he pulled it away thick raspberry jam oozed out.

Elantine clapped. "It looks as if the two of you will always have passion. Now your turn, dear heart."

Tella was never going to marry Jacks—she'd rather be trapped inside of a card—so it shouldn't have mattered which cake she chose. But she really didn't want to take a cake. There were enough predictions of her future as it was. Both Jacks and the empress were staring at her, though. This wasn't a request; this was a challenge.

"Interesting," Elantine murmured.

Tella looked down to find her fingers had plucked a soulless jet-black cake with a bow made of midnight-blue frosting—the same color as the wings tattooed on Dante's back.

"It reminded me of the moonless night I met Jacks," Tella lied.

"Oh, I wasn't talking about the cake." Elantine fixed her regal gaze upon the starburst-shaped opal ring on Tella's finger. "I haven't seen one of those in a very long time."

"It was an heirloom of my mother's," Tella said.

"And she gave it to you?" Elantine said it just as warmly as everything else that evening, but Tella swore her eyes were now pinched at the corners, as if her smile was no longer genuine. "Did she tell you what it was for?"

"No, it was just one of the few things left behind when she disappeared."

"And you wear it to remember her?" Elantine's expression softened. "You really are a little gem. When Jacks first told me he was engaged again, I was skeptical. I feared—well, it doesn't matter what I feared. I can now see why he would want you. But be careful with that heirloom of yours." Her tone hushed to a whisper. "That looks like one of the keys from the Temple of the Stars, and, if it is, your mother must have paid a very high price for it."

Tella's eyes fell back to her hand. It seemed unbelievable, but the hopelessly hopeful part of her wondered if the ring she'd worn for the past seven years could be a key to unlocking her mother's secrets.

"Pardon the interruption," a raspy voice called out from the stage.

Tella looked up to see Armando dressed like the Murdered King—a Fate that could either represent betrayal or the return of something lost. He smiled at his small audience, the expression as chilling as his costume. A dripping red sword hung from his waist, a thick gash of blood stained his exposed throat, and a wicked crown made of daggers sat atop his head. "What a pleasure it is to be here tonight."

Half the candles dangling from the ceiling blew out, leaving the banquet table in shadows. Only Armando and the stage remained aglow.

"Oh, good!" Elantine clapped. "The entertainment is about to begin."

"Thank you for having us, Your Majesty." Armando bowed low, surprisingly humble. "Since your coronation it has been Legend's greatest wish to bring his Caraval performers to Valenda. We are deeply grateful you accepted his offer. To honor Your Majesty tonight, we have put together a very special performance to show what life was like when rulers were not so wise and gracious. We hope you all enjoy it."

The curtains parted.

The play looked like a parody of a parody.

The stage was set to resemble an ancient throne room, but all of the colors were too bright and lurid—everything was painted in shades of flashy lime, electric violet, flirty fuchsia, cosmic blue, and pulsing yellow—as if a child had colored in the backdrop, the costumes, and the throne, which Armando sat upon. Jovan, dressed as the Undead Queen in a jeweled eye patch and a long, fitted black gown, lounged against his arm.

Tella shuddered, memories from the bridge outside Idyllwild Castle rushing back.

Jovan's lips twisted, uncharacteristically cruel—just like the real Fate—as she surveyed the court assembled onstage.

Tella steered her gaze away. She recognized several of the other actors: some of them were dressed like nobles, but many were costumed to look like more Fates. Tella spied the Pregnant Maid, Her Handmaidens, and the Poisoner mixed among the small crowd.

She did not spy Dante. And she was frustrated with herself for even looking for him.

On the stage, Jovan the Undead Queen sighed dramatically. "I'm so very bored."

"Maybe I can help with that." Caspar sauntered into the scene wearing a red velvet tailcoat that matched the blood dripping from the corner of his mouth and the edge of one eye. Apparently he was playing the role of the Prince of Hearts.

Tella dared a look at Jacks, to see how he would react to finding himself depicted onstage. His expression remained neutral, bordering on disinterest, but Tella felt the arm he'd wrapped around her shoulder turn arctic as Caspar waved a hand, beckoning two young performers onto the stage.

Tella didn't recognize either of them. They were youths, a boy and a girl a little younger than Tella. Something about the way they were costumed was particularly disturbing. All the other performers were clearly dressed as characters. But this boy and girl appeared to be wearing their very best sets of clothing, neatly pressed and ever so slightly out of fashion when compared to the rest of the court, as if neither of them had reason to dress nicely very often, so there was little reason to update their wardrobe. It made both appear more real than the rest, as if Caspar had just plucked them off the street and promised them both bags of sweets if they followed him.

"What's your name?" Caspar asked the girl.

"Agathe."

"What a lovely name, Agathe. And yours?" he asked the boy.

"It's Hugo."

"Another excellent name." Caspar's tone turned from sweet to slippery. "In fact, I like both of your names so much I'm going to write them down to make sure I never forget them."

Agathe and Hugo exchanged bemused glances, as if they sensed something was not as it should be, but then both of them nodded, clearly eager to please a Fate.

Caspar pulled two slips of paper from his pocket, the exact size and shape of cards. "Oh," he moaned, "it seems I don't have any ink. I suppose I'll have to use my immortal blood instead."

He took out a bejeweled dagger and pressed it to the tip of his finger. Blood welled, and Caspar made a show of using the blood to write on the card. As he finished, a puff of theatrical silver smoke appeared, enough to cover half the stage. When it cleared, Agathe was gone. In her place was a card.

Caspar picked it up, and flashed it toward Jovan and Armando.

"You turned her into a card!" Jovan cried. "Do it again! Do it again!"

Hugo started to run, but Caspar's bloody finger was already moving, writing the boy's name on his other blank card.

Another puff of smoke, and then Hugo was gone.

Caspar walked over to where the boy had been and picked up the card from the ground.

Jovan clapped. "How long will they stay this way?"

Caspar glided toward the throne. "You can keep them like this as long as you find them entertaining." Caspar flicked out a long pink tongue and licked one of the cards before passing it on to Jovan. "I'll make you an entire deck, so you can play a real game."

Jacks's arm felt suddenly heavier and icier than before as it clung to Tella's shoulder. "Was it like that?" she whispered. "Is that what you really did? You turned people into cards and played with them?"

Jacks answered against her ear. "I never licked a card like that."

"But the rest . . ." Tella turned so she could see his face, to hunt for any remorse. She knew the Fates were evil—Jacks had cursed her to get what he wanted—but the idea of trapping someone, turning them into a powerless piece of paper, and playing with them for pleasure and entertainment felt like a whole new type of vile.

Jacks gave her a lazy grin and whispered, "What are you trying to find, Donatella? Are you searching for some good in me? You'll never see it, because it doesn't exist."

"I don't need you to tell me that."

"Then why keep looking at me as if you're searching for answers?"

She tilted her head toward the stage. "Is this what you'd planned to do with Legend's true name? Trap him in a card?"

"He wants to destroy me," Jacks said quietly. "I'm merely trying to defend myself."

"So why do you now want more than his name?"

"Because I can have more." The cold arm wrapped around Tella grew even tighter as Jacks said the word *more*.

"How?" Tella asked. "How do you plan to take more from Legend?"

"My answer will only make you more unhappy."

"I'd prefer knowledge to happiness in this situation."

"I'm going to drink his blood, straight from his veins. That is how power is given and stolen. It won't work if it's bottled. I could borrow some of his magic that way, but it would not be mine to keep."

He could do it, too. Tella remembered how he'd stopped the hearts of everyone in the ballroom after their kiss. It had only lasted a minute, but that was all he'd need.

Without another word Jacks turned back toward the stage and smiled as if entertained by the show, but Tella imagined her discomfort was his true source of pleasure.

He enjoyed tormenting her, just like the Prince of Hearts in the play enjoyed toying with the children he'd placed in the cards.

Legend was not walking a fine line with this play, he was crossing it.

She might have been reading too much into it, but Tella imagined the play wasn't truly for Elantine, but for Tella—to convince her just how wicked the Fates were so that she'd help Legend destroy them rather than aid Jacks in regaining his powers.

Another idea occurred to her then. Earlier that day Jacks had told her there were only two ways to free someone from a card. *A human must willingly take their place inside the card, or an immortal with great power must break the curse and free* all *of those imprisoned in cards.*

Jacks said he'd free her mother, but Tella knew he would never take Paloma's place. What if Jacks didn't just want Legend in order to restore his own power? What if Jacks wanted Legend's power so that he could break the curse on the cards and free all of the Fates? Maybe the real reason he wanted the throne was so the Fates could reign once again exactly as they had before.

On the stage the play continued.

A pop told Tella more smoke had exploded. When she looked back at the stage all the nobles who'd been part of the court were gone, and in their place were more cards.

Tella watched in horror as Caspar picked them up and began to shuffle them for Armando the Murdered King and Jovan the Undead Queen.

"If you grow tired of these I can always make more," said Caspar, "or we can easily switch one out by writing the name of another person on the card."

"Could you imagine if we ruled like that?" Elantine began to laugh, a free unbridled sound that quickly turned into a throaty cough as the green curtain swung closed for intermission.

The empress reached for her water goblet, but knocked both her and Jacks's glasses over, along with what remained of their wine.

Tella tried to pass Elantine her goblet, but the empress shook her head as if she didn't trust Tella. "Jacks," she croaked.

Jacks shot out of his chair and left the room to fetch more water.

Elantine coughed, a final crackling sound. Then her expression focused. She looked at Tella with clear, cunning eyes. When she spoke her voice was different as well; she was no longer the cooing empress who doted over Jacks. Her tone was sharp as a lion's tooth.

"Lie to me," Elantine said, "and I'll have you tossed from this room before Jacks returns. Or tell me the truth and find yourself with a powerful ally. Now, answer quickly: What are you doing with that vicious young man who wants my throne?"

Tella's throat went suddenly dry. Her first instinct was to believe this was a test from Jacks, but then her thoughts flashed back to when Elantine had asked how Jacks planned to kill her. She'd claimed to only be joking, but the question had not sounded as if it was merely meant for fun.

"You're running out of time," Elantine snapped.

"He's holding my mother prisoner," Tella confessed. It wasn't that she trusted Elantine, but any woman who could rule an Empire by herself for fifty years had to be shrewder than a fox, which hopefully meant she genuinely saw through Jacks. "Until my mother is free I won't be free of Jacks either."

Elantine flattened her mouth into a sharp line.

Tella's pulse ratcheted up.

But before the empress could respond, Jacks reentered the room and handed her a goblet of water.

"Thank you, my dear boy." Elantine brought the water to her lips, but Tella would have sworn Elantine didn't sip from it. She distracted Jacks by saying, "I was just telling your lovely bride to be that I want her to join us on Elantine's Eve to watch the fireworks from the top of this tower."

Tella didn't remember much of what happened after that. Jacks and Elantine continued conversing, but Tella barely heard a word they said. She couldn't stop thinking about the play, about the Fates she'd met outside Idyllwild Castle, and what she'd be dooming both Legend and the Empire to if she won the game and gave Legend over to Jacks.

Upon returning to her suite, Tella pulled out the Aracle.

The image was unclear until she imagined winning the game and handing over Legend to Jacks as she'd promised. Instantly the image sharpened to a scene with Tella and her sister and their mother, all happy and hugging. A picture too good to be true. Perhaps it was.

For years Tella had trusted the Aracle without question. But if the real Aracle was trapped inside this card, wouldn't it show Tella whatever it needed to so that she would help it escape?

NIGHT FIVE OF CARAVAL

At first it seemed there were no stars. From below, the sky looked like a sparkling mirror of black. But from above, for one brief moment inside of her sky carriage, Tella could see the heavens were not all dark. A thin outline of white stars glittered in the shape of a heart. It encompassed most of Valenda, shining fairy-dust-thin light on the edges of the ancient city, hinting at bewitchment and spells and childhood dreams.

Tella leaned closer to the carriage window. Even with the incandescent starshine, it was too dark to clearly spy the people below. But she pictured those still playing the game rushing through the streets. No one had said anything directly to her, but Tella had overheard a few maids discussing how disgruntled everyone was that Elantine had cancelled night four of Caraval.

With her life dependent on the outcome of the game, Tella hadn't wanted to miss out on a night of play either. But her body had greedily taken the rest. After Elantine's dinner, Tella had slept and slept and slept. She'd half expected to wake covered in blood pouring from her eyes. But either Jacks had given her a reprieve, or the blood Dante and Julian had fed Tella was still working to counteract Jacks's murderous kiss.

Unfortunately, she was not completely uncursed. Her heart once again beat slower than it should have.

Beat . . . beat.

Nothing.

Beat . . . beat.

Nothing.

Beat . . . beat.

Nothing.

Nothing.

Tella clutched at her chest and cursed Jacks. The extra missed beat felt like his way of nipping at her and urging her to hurry.

As her carriage descended on the Temple District, she pulled out the third clue, which she'd copied from the back of her mother's poster, so that it would be easier to carry.

If you've found this you're on the true track, but it's still not too late to turn back.

Clues can no longer tell you where to head; to find the object Legend needs, your heart must lead instead.

Tella was now fairly certain the object she needed to win was her mother's cursed Deck of Destiny. She also believed it was not just a game, and that Legend really wanted this deck. But she imagined he didn't know where it was. So, through the clue, he'd instructed Tella to follow her heart, hoping she would know where her mother had hidden the cards.

A pungent cloud of incense surrounded Tella's coach as it landed in the Temple District. Prayers and hymns still filled the streets, but it was not nearly as busy as it had been a few nights ago. No whispers of Legend reached Tella's ears.

She appeared to be the only player whose heart had guided her here. Though it wasn't so much her heart leading as her mother's fiery opal ring, which Elantine believed was some sort of key connected to the Temple of the Stars.

Tella hoped the empress was right and that if it was a key, it would unlock the secrets Tella needed in order to find her mother's Deck of Destiny. But Tella doubted it would be that simple, and the ring's connection to the temple made her wary.

Religions practiced in Valenda appeared to be shrines of entertainment rather than sanctuaries of faith. But Tella had heard those who worshipped at the Temple of the Stars were true believers, willing to sacrifice youth, beauty, or whatever else the stars asked of them. And though Tella didn't know much about the stars themselves, she'd heard the ancient beings were soulless, even less human than the Fates. It made her suspicious of anyone willing to join their congregation.

She tightened the rope at her waist, which held in place the flimsy sheath she'd asked a palace servant to procure. To gain entrance to the Temple of the Stars, she needed to look like an acolyte, docile and compliant, and dress in a horrid acolyte's sheath.

She shivered at the wind slicing between her legs. Tella had never been modest but she felt as if she were only wearing a split sheet, held together by a knot tied at her shoulder and a braided cord around her waist. The cord dragged on the ground with her every step. Completely unflattering, and difficult to run in.

And everything about the Temple of the Stars made her want to turn and flee in the opposite direction.

Massive wings perched atop the temple's domed roof, glowing as bright as fresh flames, and yet for all their magnificence, no one lingered outside of the temple's great entrance. Perhaps that's why there were so many statues littering its wide moonstone steps, giving the impression of visitors and life. Though anyone who looked at these sculptures up close would never have mistaken them for humans.

Thick and tall as temple columns, the men possessed muscled arms as large as tree trunks, while the women had been given overflowing breasts and eyes made of aquamarines. Tella imagined they were supposed to be the stars. They might have been beautiful, if she hadn't also noticed the other statues. The smaller, thinner ones, on their knees before the stars. Disturbingly real and lifelike. Burning torches cast fireweed-red light on the human statues, on the beads of sweat at their temples and the calluses on their hands. Their feet were all bare, and some hunched in submission while others held out their arms, offering up swaddled babes or toddling children.

Tella choked on something that tasted like disgust as she wondered what her mother might have traded for the opal ring on Tella's finger.

"If you don't like this, you really won't approve of what you find inside." Dante leaned against one of the pillars flanking the temple's massive door, all bronzed flesh and brilliant tattoos—

And, oh glory, he was shirtless.

So very shirtless.

Tella willed herself not to stare, to march past him and ignore him, but she couldn't take her eyes off him or prevent the rush of heat that spread across her chest and up her neck. She had seen young men unclothed before—she was fairly certain she'd even seen *him* without a shirt—but somehow Dante looked different at the top of those steps. Taller and thicker. More consuming. He was dressed like one of the statues, with only a wide white cloth wrapped around his lower half, accentuating the bronzed perfection of his legs and chest.

Tella snapped her mouth shut, but it was too late. He'd seen her jaw drop, and now the vainglorious bastard was smiling. All white teeth and flawless lips as if he were one of the stars worshipped inside the Temple. And Tella had to admit, in that moment he could have convinced her. Just like he'd managed to trick her into believing that he actually cared about her.

This was the first time she'd seen him since he'd carried her broken body away from Idyllwild Castle. She imagined he expected a thank-you for saving her that night. But after what he'd said to Julian, about only caring because she could lead them to the cards, Tella wasn't about to thank Dante for anything. She wanted to say something witty or scathing, but to her horror all that came out was: "You should never wear a shirt."

His grin was devastating. Dante pushed off the pillar then and propped an elbow against one of the statues closer to her. Moonlight danced over the thick black thorns tattooed across his clavicle while his dark eyes did the same to Tella. They slid up one slit of her dress until . . .

He scowled.

Something dipped in Tella's stomach. "Why are you looking at me like that?"

Dante reached down, grabbed the end of the cord holding her scrap of fabric together, and tugged.

Every inch of Tella's skin went hot. "What are you doing?"

"Helping you." He inclined his head toward one of the female statues who wore a garment similar to Tella's, only the rope around her middle started directly below her breasts and then wrapped around several times creating a diamond pattern until it knotted at the waist, leaving only two short tassels hanging near her curving hips.

"You have it all wrong." Dante stole the cord's other end. "We're going to have to remove the rope and retie it."

Tella snatched both ends back and took a wobbly step away. "You can't take apart my dress on these stairs."

"Does that mean I can take it apart somewhere else?" His low voice oozed dark promises.

Tella swatted him with the rope.

"I'm only joking." Dante held up both hands with a surprisingly unguarded grin. "I wasn't planning on undressing you here or anywhere else. But we're going to have to fix your sheet if you want to get inside."

"It's a sheath, not a sheet," Tella argued. "And they won't care how it's tied."

"If you think that, then you clearly don't know enough about this sanctuary. A different world exists on the other side of those marble doors. But if you want to enter like that, go ahead." He flicked one end of the cord in her hands.

Tella glowered. "I think you enjoy tormenting me."

"If you hate it so much, why haven't you walked away?"

"Because you're standing in my way."

It was a poor excuse and they both knew it.

It was so much easier to despise him in her head than it was face-to-face. She just kept seeing the way he'd looked at her as he'd carried her from Idyllwild castle. There'd been a moment when he'd appeared so treacherously young and close too vulnerable. But was it because he'd actually cared about losing her? Or had he only feared because losing her meant losing his chance at finding her mother's Deck of Destiny?

She was tempted to ask, to throw what she'd overheard back in his face and see if he flinched or if he softened.

The words weighed down the tip of Tella's tongue.

But none of them came out.

Tella didn't really want his answer because no matter what he said, there was no good way for their story to end. Tella still wasn't sure whether Dante or Julian was Legend. Her conversation with

Scarlett had sown threads of doubt. But if Dante turned out to be Legend, then Tella needed to make sure any feelings she had for him were turned off.

After watching the play last night and concluding that Jacks intended to free all the Fates, Tella had debated her plans. She didn't want to be responsible for releasing the Fates back into the world so they could reign over the Empire like cruel gods. But she didn't want to die again, and she also couldn't come this close to saving her mother—and finally asking her all the questions that had been building since the day she'd disappeared from Trisda—only to fail.

Tella wasn't going to be a coward and pretend she didn't have choices just because she didn't like them. She did have choices and she'd made hers. At the end of the game Tella would give Legend over to Jacks.

It made her hope Dante wasn't Legend. But even if he wasn't, there was still no future for him and Tella.

Tella wasn't proud of herself for this choice, or for avoiding the unsaid things between them. She knew she was taking the lesser path by not even hinting at how she'd almost died and how Dante had saved her. But he'd not said a word about it either. This was probably what he wanted as well.

"All right." Tella tossed him both ends of the rope. She could let him do this one thing and then she'd send him on his way. "Just be quick about it."

She wrapped her own hands around the upper half of her sheet. She reminded herself she wasn't modest. Yet Tella felt as if she were holding herself together rather than merely keeping her sheet in place. Every inch of her skin turned more sensitive, prickling with awareness as he drew closer. He smelled of ink and other dark, seductive things.

She clutched her flimsy fabric tighter while he found the knot at her waist and slowly began to undo it. He tugged and pulled until Tella stood so close to him that all she could see were the ridges of his tattooed chest. His arms were covered in symbols, but his chest seemed to tell a story. A wrecked ship with ripped sails crashed on his abdomen, while broken stars looked down from above. A forest on fire covered one side of his rib cage. Beneath his collarbone, a black heart matching the one on his arm wept blood so real she thought she heard it beating. When he turned slightly she glimpsed tips of blue-black feathers that belonged to the beautiful wings tattooed across his back.

Tella told herself not to stare. But when she closed her eyes, everything intensified. The brush of Dante's knuckles against the curve of her hip sent her heart racing. The wide thumb gently digging into her waist made her breath catch as he continued to work with the cord until the rope was sliding from her waist into his hands. Leaving her in just the sheet.

Tella's eyes flashed open.

Dante ran his tongue over his lips, like a tiger that had just bested a kitten.

Tella gripped the fabric tighter. "Don't you dare walk away with that cord!"

He hitched an eyebrow. "You honestly think I'd leave you on these steps like this after working so hard to gain your trust?"

"I thought you were working for *Legend*."

He eased closer. "Think whatever you want, but if you honestly believe that's the only reason I'm here right now with my hands all over you, you're not nearly as clever as I thought."

Then the rope was sliding around her.

A fevered rush of blood raced around her heart as Dante's arms wound behind her, and he tugged on the rope, pulling it taut beneath her chest.

"Too tight?"

"No."

"Are you sure? For a moment you stopped breathing. Or do I just have that effect on you?" His lips brushed past her ear, tickling the tender space near the edge of her jaw as he let out a low chuckle.

She would have smacked him if her dress wouldn't have fallen to the ground. "You're enjoying this, aren't you?"

"Would you prefer it if I hated putting my arms around you?" Dante's hands wound around her again, and this time he did a little more than merely skim the fabric of her gown. Tella felt the pressure of his fingers sliding over her rib cage as he wrapped the cord all the way around until it crisscrossed just above her navel.

It shouldn't have made her flush all over. This was where their story ended, not where it became interesting again.

Dante dragged the cord behind her once more, hands now lingering over her waist. "How does that feel?"

"Good."

"I meant the cord."

"That's what I meant too," Tella said. But she was fairly certain her breathless words betrayed that for the lie it was. "Tell me about your tattoos," she said, hoping to distract herself as he finished. "Do they mean anything or are they just pretty pictures?"

"Did you just call them *pretty*?"

"Do you have something against the word?"

"Not if you're using it in reference to me," he answered. But Tella swore he tied the rope at her back a little tighter than necessary as he said, "I play so many roles the tattoos help me remember who I am. Each one tells a true story from my past."

"The black heart weeping blood," Tella said. "Is that for a girl you once loved?"

"That one I don't talk about. But I'll tell you about the ship with ripped sails." His fingers briefly grazed her sides, reminding her of exactly where the ship was inked onto his body. "My father tried to get rid of me when I was young. He sold me to a noble family from another continent. But either destiny was on my side or truly out to destroy me. The nobles' ship was attacked by pirates who kept no prisoners. I might have been a casualty as well, but I told them I was a runaway prince."

"And they believed you?"

"No. But they were entertained enough to keep me alive."

Tella found herself smiling at the thought of young Dante attempting to fool a boat full of pirates. "So, does this mean you know pirate tricks?"

"I know all sorts of tricks." Dante finished knotting the cord. But he left his hands on the indent of her waist, warm against the thin fabric. "If you stop trying to push me away, I'll teach you some."

"Do I look as if I'm pushing you away?"

"No, but you want to." He pressed two fingers beneath her chin and tilted her face toward his. One of his hands remained on the rope at her waist, while the other moved from her chin to slowly stroke her jaw. She'd often thought his eyes bordered on black, but under the torches' brilliant glow, Dante's eyes looked lined in gold and full of something like longing. He gazed at her as if he wanted her to lose herself somewhere in his eyes, so that he could be the one to find her.

But Tella knew this wasn't about finding her. This was about locating a deck of cards. This was about Fates and power and life and death. Tella wanted to know what it would be like to lose herself in someone like Dante and trust that he would find her. But the only person she could trust was herself.

"Thank you for your assistance, but I think I can manage on my own from here." She took a step back, freed her chin from his hand, and swept past him.

When her heart skipped over its next beat, it felt more like sorrow than pressure from Jacks, but she forced herself to keep walking. To not turn around.

The dark air became nectar-sweet, taking on an almost drowsy quality as Tella approached the doors and knocked.

She heard Dante come to her side, but she didn't face him. "Why can't you leave me alone?"

"I can. But I don't want to, and I don't think you want me to either."

Before she could ask him to leave again the pearly door before them opened.

Everything on the other side was as pale as the crushed wings of white doves or as gold as fallen stars. Unlike the Church of Legend, this looked like a true temple. And the young man who'd opened the door looked almost exactly like one of the godlike star statues on the steps.

Tella had half expected to see Caspar or Nigel or another of Legend's players, but this young man was foreign to her. It felt like further confirmation the game had turned very real, or that Tella was on the wrong path. She believed that to win Caraval all she needed to do was find her mother's Deck of Destiny—but believing something didn't make it true.

Doubt nipped at her as she stepped inside the Temple of the Stars.

The man who opened the door really could have been a carving come to life. His arms and legs, and the parts of him that Tella could see peeking out from all the leathers covering his chest and thighs, looked more like stone than muscle. Maybe he didn't tower quite so high as the statues outside the sanctuary, but he was taller than Dante. The sort of tall that made Tella tilt her neck to fully see his face.

She swallowed a gasp as she caught sight of his cheek.

The right half of his face was almost too flawless, from his square jaw to his aquiline nose and the dark kohl around his upswept eyes. But all Tella saw when she looked at the left half was the brand burned into his cheek—a brutal eight-pointed star with a symbol in the center made of intricate knots that Tella didn't recognize.

She tried to avert her eyes, but she was certain he caught her staring. As if to taunt her, he traced the ruthless lines of the star with the tip of one finger.

But though his face was branded, a silver circlet crowned his brow, and a royal-blue cloak draped from his right shoulder held in place by a silver pin that matched the signet ring on the finger he'd used to trace his cheek. He must have been in a position of power, which only made her more nervous. If the temple was as wicked as everyone said, this severe young man must have done unspeakable things to rise to the top of it.

"I'm Theron." With one simple bend of his wrist, as if used to having others follow his commands, he bade Tella and Dante walk deeper into the foyer.

The ceiling arched above them like a series of interconnected wings, all black with pinpricks of gold clustered together like constellations. Below, the octagonal space was primarily filled by a triple-tiered fountain that dripped candlelight. The floors were white soapstone; shiny enough to reflect the glowing gate covering the double doors at the back wall.

It felt like the sort of place a person was meant to whisper. Tella had the sudden urge to take off her slippers, as if they might soil the spotless floors. Though for all its glimmer and shimmer, there was something insidious about the place. More stone statues lined the walls, as lifelike as the ones in the front, only these were all frozen with expressions of shock, horror, and pain.

"Our temple is fueled by ancient magic from the stars," Theron said. "The vaults beneath are more secure than any in the world but occasionally fools think they can break in and steal from them."

"Good thing we're not planning on stealing anything," said Tella.

Theron didn't so much as crack a smile. "What exactly do you want here?"

"I have a question about—"

"If you're here for the game, we do not possess any clues," Theron cut in. "We are also not a tourist attraction like many of the other basilicas. To move beyond this hall and have your questions answered, you'll have to prove your motives aren't tainted and that you truly seek the stars." He led Tella and Dante farther in to a lone ivory pedestal topped off by a hammered copper bowl, old and battered compared to everything else. "For our examination, we require one drop of blood."

Dante side-eyed Tella.

But she didn't need him to remind her how powerful a drop of blood could be. Dante and Julian had used blood to heal her after the Undead Queen and Her Handmaidens had attacked her, but blood could also be used to steal things, like days.

"I only need a prick of one finger." Theron held out his right hand, revealing a black-banded starburst-shaped opal ring, sharp enough to slice skin, and bitingly familiar.

It looked remarkably like her mother's.

Elantine was right.

Tella's eyes shot down to her hand. Both rings' stones were raw and starburst shaped. But the color of Theron's was different. His stone was black, with embers of pulsing blue and threads of green. Tella's was fiery, glowing lavender surrounded by a center of burning cherry with a thin line of gold down the middle that made it look like a spark about to catch flame. But even before it had shifted colors after her mother's disappearance, it had been much lighter than Theron's.

"Your ring," Tella asked, "is it just for pricking fingers, or does it represent something else?"

"You haven't earned the answer to that question."

"What if I have a similar ring?" Tella held out her hand.

Dante's gaze narrowed and landed on Tella's finger.

A crease formed between Theron's kohl-lined eyes. "How did that come into your possession?"

"It was my mother's."

"Is she dead?"

"No."

"She should not have given that to you."

"Why not? What does it mean?"

"It means she owes a debt to us that has not been paid."

Dante tensed beside Tella.

This wasn't good news, but it was better than no information at all.

"The ring on your finger is a key," Theron said. "If it truly belonged to your mother, she must have placed something in our vaults that can only be retrieved with the ring. However, the color of it signifies it's been cursed."

"How do I break the curse?"

"The only way is to fulfill her debt," Theron answered flatly. "Until that payment is made, the key on your finger will not work to open her vault."

"Tella—" Dante's tone hinted at a warning.

But whatever it was, Tella didn't want to hear it. Her mother had not only been here but something of hers was in the vaults. Maybe it was the Deck of Destiny Tella needed to find. Or maybe it was something else that would tell Tella more about who her mother had been.

"What does she owe?" Tella asked. "What did she place in your vaults?"

"I cannot answer those questions," said Theron. "But the ring can. It has a memory, activated by blood. If it truly was your mother's, your blood should bring forth a vision of what she promised us. All you need to do is prick your finger with one of its tips and drop the blood in the bowl."

"Tella—" Dante growled. "I don't think you should—"

But Tella was already pressing the tip of her finger to her mother's old ring. Red pooled, rose-petal bright, before falling into the copper basin and turning white.

Tella held her breath as the milky drop of blood transformed into a fog that reflected the image of a woman standing in front of a bowl exactly like the one before Tella. But it wasn't just any woman. It was Tella's mother, Paloma. She was older than she'd looked in the picture Tella had seen in Elantine's Most Wanted—she appeared to be around the same age as when she'd disappeared from Trisda. But she looked so much harsher than Tella remembered. There were no hints of her enigmatic smile, no sparkle in her dark eyes. This was a callous version of her mother that Tella was unfamiliar with.

In the vision, Paloma wasn't dressed in a sheet like Tella, or if she was, it was concealed by the dark blue cloak she wore. She appeared to be speaking with someone, but whoever she spoke with was merely a shadow.

"Paradise the Lost," said the shadow. Its voice sounded like smoke come life. Thick and heavy and stifling. "I thought you swore to never make another bargain with us."

"Vows are made to broken," Paloma said. "Apparently spells are, too, because the one you placed on my cards to conceal them grew weak."

"That's why we suggested putting them in our temple vaults, with the other items we're holding for you."

"Suggested?" Paloma snorted. "I thought you said I couldn't put them in my vault."

"No, we said you would need to pay an extra price."

Paloma stiffened.

"So you do remember," said the voice. "And since we are generous, the offer still stands."

"For the same price as before?"

"Yes. Be grateful we are not requiring more to protect such a terrible item."

"What more could you ask from a mother than to give up her firstborn child?"

"We could ask for your second-born as well."

"I'd never give them both to you," Paloma said. "But you can have my second-born."

"What use to us is your second child," asked the shadow, "aside from being a pretty ornament?"

"I've seen the future. She'll possess great power. If you don't believe me, I have the cards to prove it. Though I think we're all better off if I never use them again." Paloma lifted her chin stubbornly. "The curse imprisoning the Fates is losing power. It weakens every time the cards are used."

"That's not our concern."

"It should be. More Fates will escape. Let me use your vaults to hide these cards while I search for a way to destroy them. Unless you want this place of worship to become the Temple of the Fallen Star—because I guarantee that if the Fates return, they will only allow people to worship them."

The shadowy figured appeared to darken, turning from smoky gray to almost black.

"Very well," it said at last. "Give us your second-born daughter and we will let you use our vaults to hold your accursed cards."

"Done." Paloma used a knife to slice her palm. "My daughter—"

"No!" Tella knocked the copper bowl from the pedestal, destroying the image before it could show her any more awful things. "My mother had no right to do that!" Tella shook her head, ripping her fingers through her curls as she backed away. "Even if that image is real, I'm not hers to give away."

"And yet," Theron said, "she already has. It's been pledged in blood. Once you—"

Tella started running before Theron could finish. He said *once you*, which made it sound as if Tella had to do something before they could take her, and she didn't plan on allowing that to happen, ever. Tella would never belong to anyone.

Theron didn't follow. Maybe that meant it had been a test and that what she'd seen wasn't real, or maybe he didn't have to follow, because people only chased after things they didn't already possess.

From the sound of it Dante did not pursue her either, though Tella didn't spare so much as a look behind her as she raced down the Temple of the Stars's steps. Her worthless sheet nearly ripped in her haste, but she didn't stop running.

Scarlett had been right. Her mother had been worse than her father. At least he'd waited until Scarlett was of age before selling her off like a goat. Tella's chest had never felt so hollow. She'd sacrificed everything for her mother, risked her freedom and her life, believing her mother still loved her and needed her. But the truth was she'd never cared. Not only had she left Tella, she'd given her away like a used dress.

Tella could have kept running, but her slippers were starting to tear, and the roads had turned unfamiliar.

Uneven grass, made dark by the night, rubbed against her shoes. Rather than incense and oils, the air smelled of thick beers and tart berry ciders. With a quick sweep of her eyes Tella saw temporary stages, and theatrical curtains hanging from trees.

She'd stumbled into a park. But Tella had no idea to what part of the city it belonged.

Not the Spice Quarter. Everything was far too pretty. From the street vendors' deep-fried confections dusted with crushed violets and sugar to the bejeweled dresses worn by the women and the shining weapon-belts ornamenting the men. Only the swords on the belts did not look real, and neither did the women's jewels.

It seemed she'd run right into the middle of a small festival made of park-plays, or some sort of fair to celebrate the empress's upcoming birthday—perhaps for all of the Valendans not participating in Caraval. Curious gazes were moving in her direction. But Tella doubted anyone would mistake her for one of the performers. Unless these particular plays involved a female sacrifice, Tella was dressed entirely wrong. The women here were all covered up by bell-sleeved gowns with flowing skirts, while Tella had naked legs and exposed arms. Suddenly she was freezing. Now that she'd stopped, fatigue hit her like a wave of ice, leaving her shaken and out of breath, without a properly working heart to warm her up.

Spying a vendor selling cloaks, Tella snatched a dark one that looked about her size.

"Thief!" screamed the vendor.

Tella started to sprint.

"Give that back!" A heavy set of arms knocked her into the ground, and a weighty chest pressed her into the rough grass.

"Getoffame!" She tried to wriggle free. "Youcanhaveyourfilthyfabricback!"

The vendor rolled off her, and yanked the cloak from her shoulders. But he left a hand on her neck, and squeezed. Hard and tight. Until Tella felt the cords of her throat rub together. "Dirty thief." He kept her face pinned to the ground. "This will teach you not to—"

"Let go of her!" roared a voice.

The hand was ripped from Tella's neck. Then arms were scooping Tella up, pulling her tight to a pounding chest that smelled of ink and sweat and fury.

"I believe it's against the law to kill someone for borrowing a cloak," Dante snarled at the vendor.

Splotches of angry red colored the man's bearded face. "She wasn't borrowing it. She stole it!"

"That's not what it looked like to me," Dante said. "The cloak's in your hands now. I never saw it in hers. But I did see you trying to kill her."

The vendor sputtered a string of curses.

"Give us the garment and I won't have you arrested," Dante said.

Tella could only see his chest from this angle, but she imagined he looked like a warrior—standing there without a shirt in all his godlike splendor and dressed like a vengeful star just fallen from the heavens.

"Fine," grumbled the man. "I don't want the soiled thing anymore."

"And I'll take one for myself, in black." Dante's voice was merciless, a tone Tella had never heard cross his lips, yet everything he did with her was gentle. He tenderly tucked the cape around her bare shoulders and shaking legs.

"Are you all right?" he asked.

Tella wished she could have nodded or laughed and teased him for being so concerned. But when she tried to laugh it sounded strangled, and when she attempted to nod her head fell pathetically onto his chest.

She didn't want to cry. Neither the filthy vendor nor her mother was worthy of a single tear. But while Tella could easily shake off the feel of the vendor's rough hands, she couldn't do the same with the words her mother had said. Not only had her mother left her, she'd sold Tella off. Not Scarlett; that hadn't even been a consideration. It seemed her mother hadn't been without love. She just hadn't loved Tella.

More tears fell from Tella's eyes.

"I hope she dies!" Tella didn't know if she'd muttered it, or raged it. "For years I prayed to any saint who might be listening to please keep her alive until I was able to find her. I wasted all my prayers on her, and she gave me away like a stained rag. But I take it all back!" Tella did shout then. "I take it all back! You can let her die or rot in her paper prison. I don't care anymore. I don't care anymore. . . ."

Tella didn't know how many times she muttered those last four words.

Dante just kept stroking her hair and her back with strong, comforting fingers as he continued to carry her. Occasionally he'd press something that felt like a kiss to the top of her head. But it wasn't until she fell silent that he finally asked, "Where do you want me to take you?"

"Somewhere to forget."

Tella buried her head back against Dante's warm chest. She was so tired. Tired of games and lies, and broken hearts, and tired of trying to rescue herself and her mother. She wanted to forget about it all. Maybe she closed her eyes and slept, or maybe it only took him a moment to carry her far away from the park. It seemed very little time had passed before she heard his low voice again.

"Are you all right to walk?"

Tella managed a nod and Dante smoothly set her down in front of a narrow set of crumbling steps overrun by moss and laced with forsaken spiderwebs. Ruins so abandoned not even the insects had stayed. But they seemed to be lit by the stars. Tella looked up and saw that they were on the edge of the sparkling white heart Legend had placed in the sky.

"What is this place?" Tella asked.

"Valenda's older myths claim this belonged to a governor who ruled long before the Meridian Empire began, back when the Fates reigned on earth." Dante guided her up the steps into the skeleton of an old estate. Tella's nana Anna always said a person's beauty was determined by their bones. If that were true, the bones of this manor made Tella think it must have been resplendent once.

The crumbling pillars and overgrown courtyards spoke of ancient wealth, while the cracked statues and ghosts of painted ceilings hinted at disappearing art. Only one relic seemed to have avoided the deadly caress of time. A fountain in the central courtyard, shaped in the form of a woman dressed similar to Tella, who held a pitcher that poured an endless stream of currant-red water into the pool surrounding her ankles.

"They say this place is cursed," Dante continued. "During one of the governor's many parties, his wife discovered that he planned to poison her so that he could wed his younger mistress. Rather than drinking the poison, the wife added three drops of her own blood and poured it out as an offering to one of the Fates—the Poisoner. She vowed to live the rest of her life in service as one of his handmaidens, as long as he granted her one request."

"What did she ask for?"

"The wife didn't know who her husband's mistress was, but she knew the woman was at the party. So she wished that her husband would only remember his wife."

"What happened then?"

"The Poisoner granted her wish. After drinking a poisonous glass of wine, her husband forgot every person he'd ever met, except for his wife." Dante shot a wry glace at the statue pouring her bottomless pitcher.

"Is that supposed to be the wife?" Tella asked.

"If you believe the story." Dante sat on the edge of the fountain, letting the red water trickle behind him in soft musical notes as he continued with the tale. "The wife wasn't pleased. The Poisoner had erased everyone from her husband's memory. A governor isn't useful if he only knows one person. Once word of his condition escaped he was stripped of his position, and soon they were to be forced out of their house. So, even though her first bargain had not ended well, the wife spilled more blood and called on the Poisoner again, asking him to restore her husband's memory. He warned her if they did this, her husband would try to kill her once more. So the woman promised to serve the Poisoner in the afterlife as well, and asked for another favor. She requested the power to make her husband forget just one person. The Poisoner agreed, but again he cautioned that there would be consequences. The woman didn't care—as long as she kept her home and her title."

"I think I know where this is going," Tella said.

"Do you want to try finishing the story?" Dante offered.

"No." Tella sat down beside him on the edge of the fountain. "You have a voice for telling stories."

"Of course I do."

"You are so full of yourself." She leaned closer to elbow him in the ribs, but Dante took the opportunity to slide his heavy arm around her waist and tuck her into his side.

He was so warm, a human shield sheltering her from the rest of the world. She allowed herself to press closer to him as he said, "The Poisoner restored her husband's memory. Then the Fate told the wife that if she took a pitcher of water and poured it out into the pool in the center of the courtyard, it would turn to wine that would have the power to make her husband forget the other woman he loved. The wife obeyed, but as she poured out the water and it turned to wine, she also began to transform, shifting into stone while her husband watched from the balcony above. He'd only had his memory back a few short hours, but it had been long enough for him to call on a Fate as well."

"So he had her turned to stone?" Tella asked.

"He wished her dead, but the Poisoner had promised she'd keep her home and her title, and the Fates always keep their bargains."

Both Tella and Dante shifted to watch the frozen woman once more. She didn't look furious, as Tella would have suspected, or as if she were attempting to fight the spell. Instead, she almost appeared to relish it, tipping out her cursed wine the way another person might spill a dare or a challenge.

"It's believed that anyone who drinks from this fountain can forget whatever they choose," Dante said.

"And I thought you were telling me the story to help me forget."

"Did it do that?" he asked.

"For a minute," she admitted. But sadly that moment had already passed. Tella dipped her finger into the fountain, coating it in swirls of bitter burgundy. It would have been so easy to put her finger in her mouth, close her eyes, and erase what her mother had said and done.

But even if she believed Dante's tragic myth, she wasn't sure she really wanted to forget. Tella dropped her hand, smearing the cursed wine against the white of her sheath.

"You know what the saddest part is? I should have known all along. I was warned," Tella said. "When I was a child, I read my fortune. It contained the Prince of Hearts. So for almost my entire life I've known I was destined for unrequited love. I've never let myself become close to anyone, except my sister, for fear they'd break my heart. It never even occurred to me that the one I really needed to protect myself from was my own mother."

Tella coughed on a sound that felt like a sob and sounded like a wounded laugh. "It seems the people who say you can't change your fate are right."

"I don't believe that," Dante said.

"Then what do you believe?"

"Fate is only an idea, but I think by believing in it we turn it into something more. You just said you've avoided love because you've believed it wasn't in your future, and so it hasn't been."

"That wasn't the only card I pulled. I also pulled the Maiden Death, and shortly after, my mother vanished."

"Just a coincidence. From what I've heard of your mother, it sounds as if she would have left whether you pulled the card or not."

"But—" Tella almost told him about the Aracle and all the predictions it had shown her. But had it really revealed the future, or had it been manipulating her along as she'd suspected last night? Had it used glimpses of possible futures not to help her, but to guide her toward Jacks so that he could free the Fates?

Tella had thought herself so bold and daring by attempting to change her mother and her sister's fate. But maybe Scarlett's fiancé was actually a decent person. And maybe the Aracle had lied about her mother, too. It had shown her in prison and dead, but if Tella didn't win Caraval, if she left the cards locked in the stars' vault, her mother wouldn't die or end up bloody in a jail. She'd just remain where she was, trapped in a card.

Like she deserved.

As if reading her thoughts, Dante added, "I don't believe what you saw today proves that your mother didn't love you. What she did looked terrible, but judging her based on a moment like that is the same as reading one page from a book and assuming you know the whole story."

"You think she had a good reason for what she did?"

"Maybe, or maybe I just want to hope she's better than my mother." He said it the same careless way he'd told the story about his tattoos, as if it happened so long ago it didn't really matter. But people didn't tattoo tales they no longer cared about onto their body, and Tella sensed Dante felt the same about his mother. His mother might no longer have been in his life, but he still felt wounded by her.

Tella's hand found Dante's fingers in the dark. Somewhere in the space between the Temple of the Stars and this cursed place something had shifted between them. Before their relationship was much like Caraval. It had felt like a game. But the moment he set her down on the steps of these ruins, it felt as if they'd entered the real. When she asked her next question it wasn't because she was trying to figure out if he was Legend; if anything, she desperately hoped he wasn't. "What did your mother do to you?"

"I guess you could say she left me with the circus."

"Are you talking about Caraval?"

"It wasn't Caraval then, just a talentless group of performers who lived in tents and traveled the continent. People liked to say my mother only did what she believed was best for me, but my father was more honest. He liked to drink, and one night he told me exactly what sort of woman she was."

"Was she a . . ."

"I know what you're thinking, and no. Although I would have respected her more if she was a prostitute. My father said she only slept with him so she could steal something he'd collected in his travels. They'd spent one night together, and when she returned shortly after I was born, to drop me off, she wrote a letter to his wife telling her all about the experience, and ensuring I was never truly welcomed into the family."

Tella imagined a younger Dante, all gangly limbs and dark hair covering the hurt in his eyes.

"Don't feel sorry for me." Dante tightened the hand around Tella's waist and pressed his lips against her head, close to her ear, as he said, "If my mother had been a kinder or better person, I might have turned out good, and everyone knows how boring it is to be good."

"I definitely wouldn't be here with you if you were good." Tella pictured the word *good* withering next to Dante. *Good* was the word people used to describe how they slept at night and bread fresh out of the fire. But Dante was more like the fire. No one called a fire good. Fires were hot, burning things children were warned not play with.

And yet for once, Tella hadn't even thought about pulling away from him. She used to think it was ridiculous, the idea that a girl would give her heart to a boy even though she knew it would also give him the power to destroy her. Tella had exchanged things with other young men, but never hearts, and though she still had no plans to relinquish that part of her to Dante, she was beginning to understand how hearts could be slowly given away, without a person even realizing. How sometimes just a look, or a rare moment of vulnerability like the one Dante had just shared with her, was enough to steal a fraction of a heart.

Tella arched her neck to look up at him. Above his head the sky had changed, filling with ribbons of bruised clouds that made it look as if night had fallen backward. Instead of moving forward the heavens appeared to be shifting toward the sunset, to a time when there weren't any spying stars, leaving them unwatched and alone in the cursed garden.

"So," she said cautiously, "is all this your way of telling me you're the villain?"

His chuckle was dark. "I'm definitely not the hero."

"I already knew that," Tella said. "It's my story, so clearly I'm the hero."

His mouth tipped up at both corners, and his eyes sparked, growing as hot as the finger now reaching out to trace her jaw. "If you're the hero, what does that make me?"

His finger dipped to her collarbone.

Heat spread across her chest. This would have been the moment to pull away; instead, she let a hint of challenge slip into her voice. "I'm still trying to figure that out."

"Would you like my help?" Dante dropped his hand to her hips.

Tella's breathing hitched. "No. I don't want your help. . . . I want you."

Dante's gaze caught on fire and he took her mouth with his.

This was nothing like the drunken kiss they'd shared on the forest floor, a rough combination of lust and desire for temporary entertainment. This kiss felt like a confession, brutal and raw and honest in a way kisses rarely were. Dante wasn't trying to seduce her; he was convincing her just how little goodness mattered, because nothing he was doing with his hands could have been considered good. Yet every brush of his lips was sweet. Where others had demanded, Dante asked, slowly sweeping his mouth across hers until she parted her lips, letting his tongue slip inside as he pulled her onto his lap.

Maybe the fountain's enchantment was at work because Tella imagined by the time she finished kissing Dante, she'd forget every other boy who'd ever touched her mouth.

Dante's lips moved to her jaw, gently nipping and licking as his hands found the rope he'd tied around her waist. Knotting his fingers with it, he pulled her closer, until everything was made of just the two of them. Of their hands and their lips and the places their skin met.

They hadn't even broken apart and Tella was already thinking of kissing him again, and again, tasting not merely his lips but every single one of his tattoos and scars, until the world ended and they were nothing but shadows and smoke, and Tella could no longer remember the sensation of slipping the cloak from his shoulders and running her hands along his back. Or how it tasted when his lips spoke words against her mouth that felt like promises she hoped he'd keep.

And for the first time in her life Tella wanted even *more*. She wanted the night to stretch into forever, and for Dante to tell her more stories about Fates, and his past, and anything else he wanted to say. In that moment, inside of that kiss, she wanted to know everything about him. She wanted him, and it no longer scared her.

He was right. Tella had wanted to blame the Fates for her misfortunes, but she was the one who'd always run from the possibility of love. And deep down she knew it wasn't really about the Fates. It was about her mother and how she'd left without ever looking back.

Tella claimed she didn't want love—she liked to say love trapped and controlled and ripped hearts apart. But the truth was she also knew love healed and held people together, and deep down she wanted it more than anything. She enjoyed the kisses, but a part of her always wished that whenever she walked away from a boy he'd run after her, beg her to stay, and then promise he'd never leave.

She'd accepted the cards she'd been given and turned them into her fate because it felt like the only way to protect herself after her mother left. But maybe if Tella chose to reject what she'd seen in the cards then she could have a new destiny. One where she didn't have to be afraid of love.

When the kiss finally ended, their cloaks were both puddled on the ground, their arms were around each other, and the sky had moved back to where it should be, to the black hour just before sunrise. Only the moon lingered, undoubtedly wishing it had lips after witnessing what Tella and Dante had just done.

Dante spoke against her mouth, this time loud enough for her to hear his words. "I think I'd like you even if you were the villain."

She smiled against his lips. "Maybe I'd like you even if you were a hero."

"But I'm not the hero," he reminded her.

"Then perhaps I'm here to save you." This time she kissed him first. But it wasn't as sweet as before. It tasted acrid. Metallic. Wrong.

Tella broke away, and in that moment she swore the stars returned and shined a little brighter simply to be cruel. Light fell over Dante illuminating the blood dripping out of the corner of his mouth. Slow and red and cursed.

34

Tella shoved up from the fountain and turned away. She didn't even pay attention to where she went as she wiped her lips with her hands. Blood kept pouring out of the corners of her mouth, mercilessly bringing her back to the reality of her situation, and to the game that she and Dante were on different sides of. Her mother might have no longer deserved saving, but Tella still needed it.

Beat . . .

Nothing.

Beat . . .

Nothing.

Beat . . .

Nothing.

It was almost as if Jacks were watching, waiting for Tella's one moment of happiness so that he could rip it away.

In between her dying heartbeats, she heard Dante's heavy footsteps as he rose from the fountain and followed until he stood directly behind her.

"Tella, please, don't run." His voice was as gentle as the hand he placed on her bare upper back. Her entire body had gone suddenly cold except for where his palm rested. Such a contrast to Jacks's forever cold touch and unbeating heart. And yet at the end of it all Jacks would be the one to triumph.

Tella might have been the only person capable of retrieving her mother's Deck of Destiny from the stars' vaults and winning Caraval, but Jacks and the Fates he planned on setting free would be the true victors. Once she gave Legend to Jacks, Tella would no longer be cursed, but she'd be enslaved to the stars for using her mother's ring. The freedom she'd fought so hard for would vanish. And there was a good chance Legend and Caraval would disappear as well.

Tella really was the villain after all.

She still might have felt as if giving Legend to Jacks was the right path to take if she believed her mother was worth saving. But in that moment, Tella preferred the idea of keeping Paloma trapped in a card.

"Tella, please talk to me," Dante said.

"I'm not going to run. But I need a moment."

Without letting Dante see her face, Tella returned to the fountain. She cupped the wine in her hands, careful not to swallow any as she rinsed the blood from her mouth. Once she finished, she spat it out into the bushes and picked up her cloak to wipe her lips before placing it back on her shoulders. She was stalling. Dante had seen her crying, he'd seen her bleeding, seen her on the verge of death. A little blood on her mouth wasn't about to scare him away.

"You still don't trust me, do you?" he asked.

Finally she turned around.

The night had grown darker, but Tella could see Dante's forehead was covered in lines and his hands were stiff at his side, as if holding back from touching her.

"I don't trust myself," she admitted.

Dante took a slow step closer. "Is it because you now believe it's not a game?"

"Does it matter what I say? Would you tell me the truth, if I asked if it was all real?"

"If you have to ask, I'm guessing you wouldn't believe me."

"Try me," Tella said.

"Yes." Dante took another step. "To everything."

"Even us?"

His head dipped a little. "After all that just happened, I would think that was already obvious."

"But maybe I still want to hear it." More important, she needed to hear it. Tella believed the game was real. She wanted to believe whatever was happening between her and Dante was real as well. But she knew that just because she'd finally admitted to herself that she wanted more with him didn't mean he felt the same. The game might have been genuine but that didn't mean everything about their relationship was. "Dante, please, I need to know if you're only here because of Legend, or if this is real."

"What makes something real, Tella?" Dante hooked a finger into the rope around her waist. "Does seeing something make it real?" He tugged on the rope and pulled her closer, until all she could see was his face. "Or does hearing something make it real?" His voice turned a little rough. "What about feeling something, is that enough to make it real?" His free hand slid up and underneath her cloak until it rested over her heart. If Tella's heart had been working properly it might have leaped into his palm from the intensity of his rough voice and his dark, depthless eyes as he lowered his head toward hers.

"I swear to you, this—*us*—we were never a part of Legend's plan. The first time I kissed you I did it because I'd just died and come back to life, but I wasn't feeling alive. I needed something real. But tonight I kissed you because I wanted you. I haven't stopped wanting you since the night of the Fated Ball when you were willing to risk your life because you wanted to make me angry. After that, I couldn't stay away."

His hand slowly slid up from her heart to around the back of her neck, pressing against her tender skin as he leaned in even more. "I kept coming back to you, not because of Legend, or the game. But because you're so real and alive and fearless and daring and beautiful and if what's between us isn't real, then I don't know what is."

Dante's fingers tensed around her neck and he kissed her again, as if it were the only way he knew how to finish what he'd been saying.

It didn't last nearly long enough. But it upended her. It made her wonder if jewels hidden away safely in boxes sometimes longed to be stolen by thieves—because now he was definitely stealing her heart, and she wanted him to take even more.

When he ended the kiss, his hands wrapped gently around her waist, a soft contrast to the barbed tone of his voice as he said, "Now, tell me why you were bleeding."

Tella took an uneven breath.

It was time to confess the truth.

"It happened the night of the ball when Jacks kissed me," she said. She'd meant to keep it short and simple, but the moment she opened her mouth it all started spilling out, as fast and sloppy as water pouring from a shattered jug. The entire history of her relationship with Jacks, why she first made a deal with him, how she'd failed him, how he'd given her a card with her mother trapped inside of it, and everything he'd threatened if Tella failed him again.

For his part, Dante remained still and unreadable as the statue poured an endless stream behind them, except for whenever Tella said Jacks's name; Dante's teeth would grind together then. Otherwise he remained painfully calm.

"Let me make sure I have this right," Dante said. "If you don't win this game and give Legend to Jacks, then you'll die."

Tella nodded.

Dante worked his jaw as if preparing for another round of curses. "Did Jacks say why he wants Legend?"

"Jacks told me he wants his full powers back, but I think it's more than that. I believe Jacks wants to harness Legend's power to free all the Fates from the cards they're trapped in."

Dante's hands tightened around Tella. "This is my fault. I should have admitted it was a mistake you weren't on the list. If I hadn't told that lie about you being engaged—"

"I probably still would have kissed him," Tella finished. She no longer wanted to believe in fate, but that night had felt fated. Even without Dante's lie Jacks would have found her at the ball. She wouldn't have had what he wanted and things would have progressed the same way. "It's not your fault. Jacks is the one who cursed me. He did this."

"I could kill him." Dante's hands fell away from Tella as a splinter of moonlight cut across his face, slicing between the two sides of his torn expression. It was the way someone looked in the middle of a fight when they were debating between what they should say and what they wanted to say.

Then his hands went around her once more, as if he'd come to a sudden decision. "Do you trust me?"

Tella took a ragged breath. When Dante was gone she wanted him there. When he was there she wanted him close. She liked the feel of his hands and the sound of his voice. She liked the things he said, and she wanted to believe them. She wanted to trust him. She just wasn't sure that she did. "Yes," she said, hoping that by saying the words it would make it true. "I do trust you."

A sliver of a smile. "Good. There's a way to fix all of this, but I need your trust. Legend is at his most powerful during Caraval, and his magic comes from the same origin as Jacks's. If you win the game, Legend will heal you. You don't need Jacks."

"But to win, I have to give myself over to the stars, and I don't know that I can do that."

"You aren't going to do that," Dante promised. "I'll find another way for you to get inside their vaults."

"How? You heard Theron. He said only my ring can open the vault, but it's cursed until my mother's debt is paid."

"Then I'll find another way to pay it."

"No!"

Dante's grin widened. "If you're afraid I plan on giving myself to the stars instead, don't be, I'm not that selfless."

"Then what are you going to do?"

"Every curse has a way to be broken, and a loophole. If the stars won't accept another payment to break the curse on your ring, I'll find the loophole."

Tella had never heard it phrased like this, but she supposed it made sense. It aligned with what Jacks had said about there being only two ways to free someone from a card—either break the curse, or take a person's place. The latter must have been the loophole. But the idea of it scared Tella more than the thought of breaking the curse.

"Don't worry." Dante pressed his lips to her forehead, his kiss hot against her skin as he whispered, "Trust me, Tella. I'm not going to let anything happen to you."

But suddenly he was the one she was concerned about. And Tella wasn't used to trusting others with her secrets, let alone her life. She sensed Dante was experiencing conflicting emotions as well.

A cloud covered the vanishing moon, leaving his entire face shadowed in darkness as he pulled away, but Tella thought he still looked as if he were battling something. "Do you think you can make it back to the palace safely?"

"Why?" she asked. "Where are you going?"

"I still have a job to do tonight. But don't worry, I'll meet you on the steps of the Temple of the Stars after the fireworks tomorrow night."

The following night was the last night of Caraval. The fireworks would be at midnight, marking the end of Elantine's Eve and the start of Elantine's Day. It would be cutting it close to when the game ended at dawn.

Tella wanted to argue, but Dante was already walking away. He'd reached the edge of the garden. He was still close enough to call after. But Tella found herself quietly trailing him instead.

She told herself she trusted him; she was only following because she was concerned about what he might do to save her. But the truth was she wanted to trust him more than she actually did. A part of her still had not ruled out the possibility that he was Legend. But if he was Legend and he cared about Tella at all, he would have uncursed her in the garden with his blood rather than pushing her to win the game and retrieve her mother's cards first.

Either Dante really cared about Tella, or he was the master of Caraval and he didn't care at all.

Maybe if she found out where he was always running off to she could figure it out. But Tella was too slow. Or perhaps Dante knew she was following him. By the time she reached the exit of the garden, he was gone.

Tella searched the nearby ruins for a while. She even dared to return to the park where she'd stolen the cloak. But there were no signs of him, and her legs were starting to wobble with fatigue.

It was almost sunrise when Tella's sky carriage neared the palace. Legend's heart-shaped constellation was gone. Torches dotted the grounds with light, but the air still felt frigid after a night of being separated from the sun. Tella wanted to close her eyes and collapse inside her tower room, but her coach halted. Whoever was in the carriage before hers was taking forever to disembark.

Tella opened her window and poked out her head, as if glaring at the box before her might hasten its occupants' pace. To her astonishment, it worked.

The carriage door opened, followed by a flash of familiar cerise fabric. Tella couldn't be positive—other than the dress, all she saw was a curtain of thick dark hair. But from the back, the young woman looked exactly like Scarlett.

Tella continued to watch, but her sister didn't turn around. She scurried forward, flitting out of the carriage house before Tella's coach had even moved. Then the door to the carriage before her opened again. Tella only saw the back of this person as well, but she instantly recognized his careless walk, his wrinkled clothes, and his head of golden hair. *Jacks.*

Tella hoped the sun would rise soon because this bizarre night needed to end. If Tella's world flipped on its head one more time, she would crack.

What had her sister been doing with Jacks?

Of course, Tella still wasn't certain the young woman who'd stepped out of the coach was Scarlett. Tella hadn't gotten a clear look at her face. But Tella knew her sister and she knew Jacks, who was low enough to drag Scarlett into this mess.

Tella leaped out of her coach the moment it touched the ground and nearly twisted her ankle. It didn't stop her from rushing out of the carriage house, but it did delay her long enough to lose her sister.

"Are you running from someone, or chasing after someone?" The Prince of Hearts stepped out from the edge of the stone garden, blocking Tella's path as he tossed a glowing purple apple back and forth between the tips of his nimble fingers. Again, he didn't wear a coat and his shirt was only half ironed, as if he'd grown impatient and taken it from a maid before she could finish her job. His pants were unwrinkled, but when the rising sun hit the buttery leather, Tella thought she saw a spatter that looked like blood.

She took several deep breaths, attempting to calm her racing heart. "What were you doing with my sister?"

"Do I detect some jealousy?"

"You're delusional."

"Am I?" Jacks sauntered between forever frozen servants deeper into the stone garden, forcing Tella to follow.

"This relationship isn't real," Tella groaned. "How could I be jealous?"

"Maybe you're wishing it was real."

"You flatter yourself too much."

"Only because my fiancée doesn't flatter me enough." Jacks's tone was flippant, yet he didn't take his eyes off Tella as he propped one booted foot against the terrified stone statue at her side. Then he pulled out a dagger from his boot and began to peel the skin off his apple, as if he'd suddenly lost interest in their conversation.

"You still haven't told me what you were doing with my sister," Tella demanded. "I want you to stay away from her."

Jacks looked up from his knife. "She's the one who came looking for me."

"Why would she do that?"

"I promised I wouldn't tell."

Tella snorted. "Don't act like you have a conscience."

Jacks sliced off the last bit of skin from his apple and took a deep bite. "Just because my moral code is different from yours doesn't mean I don't have one."

"Maybe you should reevaluate it," Tella said. "By most people's standards, killing someone is worse than breaking a person's confidence."

"Have I killed anyone since you've known me?" Jacks ran his tongue along the tips of his sharp white teeth before sinking them into the apple once more. Glowing juice, as red as blood, dripped from the corner of his mouth. Mocking her as he ate.

He acted careless and lazy but he was the most calculating and confident of them all. He probably viewed her the same way he saw his apple, as something juicy to take a bite out of and then discard.

Another drop of red fell from his lips and Tella launched herself at him. She knocked the apple from his pale hands. Then she went for his throat.

His hands went around her wrists in a flash. "You can't kill me."

"But I can try." She kicked at him.

He easily dodged it.

"You're only going to tire yourself out," he said calmly. "You already look exhausted. Save your strength to win the game tonight."

She continued to kick.

He effortlessly evaded her again. His cruel face appeared bored.

But Tella swore she felt the blood rushing through his veins, heating the hands still encircling her wrists. He might have appeared indifferent, but his heart was beating as fast as hers.

Tella stopped mid-kick. His heart was beating.

She stumbled back and he let her go.

"You have a heartbeat."

"No. My heart hasn't beat in a very long time. You're the one who's delusional now." His voice was colder than she'd ever heard it, yet the chill it brought did not erase the searing memory of his hot hands around her wrists.

"I might be a lot of things, but I know what I felt," Tella said.

Only one person could make it beat again: his one true love. They said his kiss had been fatal to all but her—his only weakness. . . .

"I made your heart beat," Tella crowed. It was wild and absurd, a truly feral idea. But Tella felt the truth in her heartbeat as well, which now sped up rather than slowed. Beat. Beat. Beat. Beat. Beat. Beat. Beat. It had never felt so strong. So free. "I'm your one true love. Your kiss can't kill me."

Jacks's scowl deepened. "You shouldn't believe every story you hear. Do I look as if I'm in love with you?"

"You always look like a monster to me, but that doesn't mean the myth's not true." And Tella imagined she didn't have to love him to be his true love. Given that he was a Fate and pure evil, Tella also imagined love for him was not the same as it would have been for a human. But that part didn't matter. What mattered was that being his true love meant she was immune to his kiss. She no longer needed to win the game to live.

"This changes nothing." Jacks's expression turned so sharp that a fistful of knives would have looked soft in comparison.

But Tella was used to his mercurial looks. They couldn't hurt her, and neither could his poisonous lips.

"No," Tella said. "This changes everything."

"Not for your mother." Jacks crushed the heel of his boot atop the apple Tella had knocked onto the ground, until the fruit was nothing but bleeding flesh and juice. "You still need me if you want to free her."

"Maybe I no longer care about saving her." Tella said it as if she meant it, but the words tasted sour in her mouth. Not quite a lie, but not the truth.

Jacks seemed to sense her lack of conviction. He flashed a dimple as he prowled closer. "You called me a monster and even I think that's cold, Donatella."

His dimple vanished, and for a moment she saw his face hollow out with terror, the same way it had the first time he'd spoken of being trapped inside of a card. "If any part of you ever wants to see your mother alive again, you'll rethink helping me. Legend fears the Fates going free and stealing his power, and he wants our powers more than anything. If he ever gets his hands on the Deck of Destiny with the Fates, he will destroy all of us, along with your mother. The only way to save her is to win the game and help me free them. Unless you're foolish enough to take her place, and based on what you just said, I doubt you're willing to do that."

Jacks chucked her chin with one slender finger before sauntering out of the garden as if their conversation had changed nothing at all.

. . .

When Tella trudged back into the palace just after dawn, the golden tower had been transformed for Elantine's Eve. The banisters were covered with boughs of glistening fabric, reminiscent of the Unwed Bride's veil of tears. And to Tella's discomfort, every maid she saw had painted red stiches on her lips, transforming themselves into Her Handmaidens.

The sapphire wing where Scarlett stayed was the same. Tella had stopped by there first to find out why her sister had been with Jacks. Of course Scarlett had not answered the door.

Tella might have pounded on her sister's door a little harder, or waited a little longer, but her body was begging for sleep, and maybe Jacks had been telling the truth. Maybe Scarlett had come after him to warn him not to hurt her sister. It sounded like something Scarlett would do.

Tella had passed more maids with stitched-up lips on the way to her tower room. They must have been working since before sunup. When Tella had left the night before, each door had been unadorned, but now different masks hung atop every archway and entry, an old tradition meant to honor the Fates in the hope they would bring blessings rather than curses.

The Maiden Death's cage of pearls hung above Tella's door. Tella knew it was merely another Elantine's Eve tradition, yet it felt like a warning, one more reminder of what she had to lose if she decided to give up on the game. She no longer needed to win Caraval to live, but could she leave her mother trapped in a card?

Tella wanted to hate her. She'd meant it when she'd shouted at the sky that her mother could rot in her paper prison. And yet half of Tella wanted to free her even more than before. She wanted to prove to Paloma that she wasn't just a useless ornament to be given away, that she was fearless and clever and brave and worth loving.

Her mother's cursed ring weighed down Tella's finger. Maybe Dante would find this loophole he'd mentioned, to skirt around the curse, but if he didn't, Tella knew she couldn't enslave herself to the stars to rescue a woman who might never love her.

But what if Dante succeeded in finding a way for Tella to use her ring to get into the stars' vaults without having to give herself away?

If Dante was really Legend, could Tella then turn on him and give him over to Jacks, knowing what Jacks planned to do?

Everything was so twisted.

Tella told herself that if Dante was Legend it meant he didn't care about her. But maybe he hadn't offered to heal her earlier that night because he'd believed she was no longer cursed. He could have thought that when he'd given her his blood before, she'd been saved. But if that was true, why had she been bleeding again?

Tella wanted to think the best of Dante, but whether he cared about her was beside the point. If Dante was Legend, he would not hesitate to destroy the Fates.

Tella wasn't usually one to make safe choices. In her experience, the safe choice often felt like not making a choice at all, like politely stepping back and allowing others with more power to do what they saw fit. Legend and Jacks both had more power than Tella. But they each needed her to get the one thing they wanted: her mother's Deck of Destiny. Without Tella, neither of them could touch that cursed deck. Without Tella, Legend couldn't destroy the Fates and Tella's mother, and without Tella, Jacks could not free the Fates or steal Legend's magic, so that he'd once again be at his full power and have the ability to control hearts and feelings and emotions.

It seemed both expected her to win the game for them. But perhaps the only way Tella could really come out victorious was if she chose to no longer play in their games, if she left her mother where she was, and her cursed cards where they were, safe in the stars' vault where neither Jacks nor Legend could touch them.

Something like guilt prickled inside of Tella at the thought of allowing her mother to remain trapped in a card. But Paloma had treated Tella's life as if it were a piece of collateral. Her mother was no better than Jacks or Legend, and Tella would be damned before she allowed any of them to use her like a pawn on a game board again.

Tella shot up in bed with a start. Heart pounding, pulse rushing—two more confirmations she wasn't cursed any longer. It should have made her feel ready to conquer the world. Instead, she couldn't shake the heavy sensation that the world was preparing to conquer her.

Her first instinct was to check the Aracle to see if her future had changed, but she could no longer trust the card, and she was done letting the Fates dictate her choices.

The shadows crawling over the floor and the sleep lines etched into her arms made it clear she'd been out for hours. Even though she no longer planned to finish the game, she hadn't meant to sleep so long.

It was nearly twilight. The light pouring through her window dyed everything inside her suite an eerie red, except for the pearly white letter sitting quietly at the edge of her bed, as if it had been waiting for her.

Tella ripped it open, eyes a little blurry as she began to read. But after the first two lines, her vision sharpened and her mind finished waking up.

My dear Donatella,

Thank you for the gift of your company the other night at my little dinner. It was an unexpected pleasure to meet you. I didn't realize until after you left how much you reminded me of someone special I once knew. You don't particularly look like her, but you have the same indomitable spirit and vibrancy as Paradise the Lost. It made me wonder if she was your missing mother.

I probably shouldn't say this given who she was, but Valenda dimmed the day Paradise disappeared. She was a treasure. If she was your mother and I can be of any help in your search to find her, do let me know.

Until we meet again,

Elantine

Tella felt wide awake when she finished reading. She might have read it more than once. By the time she looked up and out the window again, the sun had nearly set. Any minute Legend would form a new constellation in the sky, showing the city that Caraval was starting up again.

Before reading Elantine's letter, Tella had been content to give up on the game, to leave her disloyal mother and her cursed deck of cards exactly where they were. As long as Tella never opened the vault, the Fates would not go free, and Legend could not destroy her mother. It seemed like a reasonable compromise. But now, after this message from Elantine, that choice felt like giving up. It felt like settling for the almost-ending Armando had talked about.

Tella knew it was foolish to imagine a better version of her mother than the one she'd seen inside the Temple of the Stars. And yet Elantine's letter made Tella hope that there was more to her mother's story, just as Dante had suggested.

"Delivery," called a wispy voice from the other side of her door.

Tella hid Elantine's note in her bed as an overeager servant popped inside the suite.

The intruder carried a massive plum box topped with a purple bow the size of a melon. It must have been Tella's Elantine's Eve costume from Minerva's.

"I assume you'll need help dressing for tonight." The maid lifted the box's lid. "Oh, this is the prettiest one I've seen! You'll be sure to draw every eye."

A sheen of silver sparkles floated over the room as the maid pulled a smoky silver-blue gown from the box. The seamstress might have fought Tella about her choice to go as the Lost Heir, but she'd done a sublime job with the dress, even if it did remind Tella a little too much of Jacks's eyes.

It was backless, covered by only a gossamer cape the color of melted silver. After helping her put the gown on, the maid pinned the thin cape to the delicate beaded straps at Tella's shoulders, which fed into a sheer smoky-blue bodice. It would have been indecent if not for the glittering silver-dipped leaves clinging to her chest and trailing over her torso, as if she'd been tossed in the winds by a magical storm. Her flowing skirt was a combination of midnight blue and liquid metal, shimmering in unearthly waves every time she moved, making it look as if she might disappear with one quick twirl.

"It's magnificent," the girl said. "Are you ready for the—" Her sentence cut off as she lifted the candled crown with its grim black veil from the bottom of the box. "You're going as Elantine's Lost Heir? Are you sure that's wise?"

"I'm sure it's none of your business." Tella snatched the crown.

"I was just trying to be helpful," the girl apologized with a quick curtsy. "Forgive me again, but I've heard rumors about your fiancé, and after what happened earlier, I thought you might like a warning."

Tella tried to refrain from asking more. The last time she'd spoken with a cheeky maid it had not ended well, but this maid seemed genuinely nervous, and Tella might have recognized her voice from her first night in the palace. She sounded like the servant who'd reminded her of a bunny and felt sorry for Tella. "What happened earlier?" Tella asked.

"You really haven't heard? The whole palace is bubbling about it. They're saying the real Lost Heir, Elantine's missing child, has reappeared. Of course, no one has confirmed it." The maid hushed her voice. "The empress fell ill right after the rumors started."

"What's wrong with her?" Tella asked.

"I'm not privy to that sort of information," said the maid. "But it sounds serious."

"It's all probably part of Caraval," Tella said. If the empress actually had a missing child, it seemed like a great coincidence that the child would just happen to appear during Caraval.

But what if the empress was genuinely sick? The thought made Tella more uncomfortable than she would have expected. In her letter Elantine talked about Tella's mother as if she'd known her. She'd called her a treasure. Tella wanted to know why, but she wouldn't if anything happened to the empress.

"Thank you for the assistance," Tella said to the maid. "You're free to leave."

Tella was dressed. All she needed to do was crown herself.

Unfortunately the waxy circle of candles forming the Lost Heir's crown was heavy and clunky, and the thick veil attached to it was impossible to see through.

Before putting it on her head, Tella tugged at the veil's fabric. Only the stubborn thing didn't want to budge.

She yanked it again.

The veil ripped free, but so did the crown's ring of black candles. They fell apart in thick, waxen tears, crumbling until all that remained were five razor-sharp points tipped in black opals.

It looked like an unbroken version of the Shattered Crown. The same crown Tella had seen when Armando read her fortune.

The Shattered Crown predicted an impossible choice between two equally difficult paths. Tella knew the circle in her hands wasn't the same crown. That crown was trapped in a deck of cards, and this crown had yet to break. But she didn't like that her fingers went numb wherever they touched it.

She wanted to shove it into the box. It felt like a bad idea to put this crown on. But she refused to be afraid of it or the ideas it brought to mind.

Tella looked in the mirror as she placed it atop her head. The crown wasn't nearly as heavy as it had been when the candles had been a part of it, but from the moment it touched her curls, Tella felt a stirring, as if wearing the crown was the first step toward an impossible choice she wasn't ready make.

She tried to dismiss the feeling. Just because she was going to speak with the empress about her mother didn't mean Tella was going to sacrifice herself to the stars so that she could win the game to save Paloma. And yet Tella found herself tucking Jacks's luckless coin into the pocket of her costume, along with the Aracle and the card imprisoning her mother.

ELANTINE'S EVE: THE LAST NIGHT OF CARAVAL

The stars were spectacularly fiery that night, lighting all of Valenda with their splendor and shimmer. Legend had wrangled them into the shape of a giant hourglass. It glowed desert-gold and scorching red, dripping crimson stars like grains of sands, no doubt counting down until dawn and the end of Caraval.

The hourglass hung suspended above the palace, where the last night of the game was taking place. Tella had glimpsed it when she'd looked out of her window. The glass courtyard below, which filled the space between the golden tower and the other wings of the palace, was beginning to fill with people costumed to look like the accursed Fates.

Thankfully none of the game players were allowed inside the tower. The ancient structure was almost eerily quiet. Tella could only hear the patter of her footfalls against the rickety wooden stairs as she climbed up, up, up.

During their dinner the other evening, Elantine had mentioned watching the Elantine's Eve fireworks from the highest floor. She'd even told Jacks she hoped Tella would join them for the show. It wasn't an actual invitation, and Jacks had never mentioned it again, but Tella hoped the empress had meant it.

Guards stopped her at the top. There must have been a dozen of them, their armor clanging loud and harsh as they blocked Tella's path.

Her legs burned from climbing, but she managed to stand up straight and speak without gasping. "I'm engaged to the heir, and Her Majesty has invited me to watch the fireworks with her this evening." Tella flashed her letter from Elantine, showing off the royal seal as if it were an invitation. But it wasn't needed.

The guards parted ranks for Tella as if they'd been expecting her. She wondered if it was because the empress's invitation to watch the fireworks had been genuine, or if the empress had known that her letter would draw Tella here. She was done letting fate or the Fates dictate her future, but something about this meeting with Elantine felt inevitable.

The top of the tower was much narrower than the bottom, just one room, not particularly large, and yet later she would remember it as endless. The walls and ceiling were formed of seamless glass, an observatory built for watching and dreaming and wishing. Legend's churning hourglass was so close Tella swore she could hear the stars falling inside of it, hissing and sparking out a dangerous song as Tella ventured farther in.

The suite itself was simple elegance. An ash-white tree grew in the middle, full of silver leaves that looked as if they were on the verge of falling. Surrounding it was a circle of tufted lounges, all looking out toward the pristine glass, silver and white, just like the tree. The only spot of bold color in the room came from the bouquet of red roses in the vase next to Elantine.

The empress lounged on a seat so close to the windows it nearly touched the glass. She didn't appear to be in costume, though there was something ghostly about her and it wasn't merely the white gown she wore.

Two nights ago when Tella had met her, Empress Elantine had been the definition of lively, brimming with smiles and hugs. But perhaps she'd given away too many. Now she slumped against her chair, waxen and sickly, exactly like the overeager maid had said.

Even Elantine's voice sounded feverish when she spoke. "You climbed all this way, my dear, you may as well ask the question burning your tongue."

"What happened to you?" Tella blurted.

Elantine looked up. Her dark eyes were larger than Tella remembered, or perhaps her face had become thinner. Elantine looked as if she'd aged two decades in two days. Tella swore the woman grew even older as she sat there. Fresh wrinkles formed across her pallid cheeks as she said, "It's called dying, my dear. Why do you think I wanted to have such a magnificent seventy-fifth birthday celebration?"

"But—but you looked so well the other night."

"A tonic from Legend." Elantine's eyes cut to the red roses on the table beside her. "He's been helping me hide my failing health from Jacks."

"So you've met Legend?"

A wrinkled smile moved the empress's mouth. "After all his help, even if I knew who Legend was, I would not betray his secret. And I don't think you climbed up all this way to ask about him."

Elantine's gaze dropped to the letter in Tella's hand.

Tella still wanted to question the empress more about Legend, who seemed to be everywhere and nowhere all at once.

But even though Elantine was dying, when she spoke again, her tone was sharp enough to cut out any arguments. "Paradise the Lost is your mother, isn't she?"

"I knew her as Paloma," Tella confessed, "though my father always got upset when I called her that instead of Mother."

Elantine clucked her tongue. "Paradise had such unfortunate taste in men."

Tella would have agreed, but she didn't feel like talking any more about her father.

"How did you know her?" Tella asked as she took a seat. She still didn't know all the proper etiquette as to how to treat an empress, but it felt odd to look down on the woman who ruled all of the Meridian Empire.

Elantine took a deep breath, her body shaking more than it should have at the exertion. "The last time I saw Paradise, she was stealing the Deck of Destiny I mentioned the other night. I warned her the cards would only bring trouble, but I should have chosen a different word. Like misery or agony. Paradise merely said she loved trouble. But I believe what she really loved was life."

Elantine gazed out the window, where Legend's crimson stars continued to shine on the game below. "Paradise could have been so much more than a picture in a Wanted poster shop. She was intelligent and clever, quick to laugh, and to love. Though she tried not to let people know how deeply her feelings went. 'Criminals don't love,' she once told me. But I think Paradise was afraid of love because when she loved, she did it as fiercely as she lived."

Tella imagined this was all supposed to make her feel better, yet somehow it only hurt more to know her mother could love so intensely, and yet she didn't even care about her own daughter.

Tella should have walked away and stopped torturing herself. But there was something almost intimate about the empress's knowledge. Her two sentences alone felt so much deeper than almost everything Aiko had shared. Tella had heard Elantine was wild in her youth, but she would not have been a youth at the same time as Tella's mother.

"How did you meet her?" Tella asked.

The empress slowly turned back to Tella. "That's a story you'll have to ask Paradise."

"I don't think that will be happening." Tella slowly rose from her seat. "This is where my search for her ends."

"Pity," Elantine said, "I didn't think you were the sort who quit so easily."

"She gave up on me first."

"I'm not sure I can believe that." Elantine's voice went soft. Tella might have thought it was from fatigue, but there was nothing weak about it. "The Paradise I knew didn't believe in quitting. And if you really are her daughter, then I'm certain she would not have quit on you. In fact, I imagine that if she was your mother, she loved you very deeply."

Tella snorted.

"I'll pretend I didn't hear that," Elantine said. "I'm sure there's a law that says you cannot mock your empress to her face. But I imagine what you just did has more to do with your mother than with me. And, I'll admit, I suspect my child feels the same way about me as you feel about your mother. I was also a failure as a parent. I made mistakes that meant I was parted from my child for a long time. But that didn't mean I didn't love my child. So many of the choices I made that I believed were for the best only served to tear us apart."

"But I've heard your missing child has returned."

"I forgot how quickly news spreads in this palace." Elantine smiled, but somehow the expression made her eyes look sad instead of happy. As her wrinkled lips tipped up, her eyelids drooped. This was not the expression of a mother who'd just been reunited with her child.

But the empress was not dismissing the rumors. It made Tella wonder if this person who'd come forward was really Elantine's child, or just a way to prevent Jacks from taking the throne now that Elantine was dying.

"For most of my life I put the Meridian Empire above everything, even my child. I now regret so many of those choices, but it's too late to change what I've done. I suppose that's why I was thinking of you this morning." The sorrow in Elantine's eyes intensified. "I don't know what happened to your mother after she left you, but I hope you find her, Donatella. Don't be like me and settle for the ease of an almost-ending, when you could have the true ending."

"I'm not sure I understand what that even means," Tella said.

"Not everyone gets a true ending. There are two types of endings because most people give up at the part of the story where things are the worst, where the situation feels hopeless. But that's when hope is needed most. Only those who persevere can find their true ending."

Elantine smiled, more happy than sad this time, as she peered down at Tella's hand. "Look. I believe even your mother's ring agrees."

Tella jolted backward as the opal on her finger pulsed. The colors inside it were moving. The gold line in the center burst like a flame inside the stone, devouring the violet and cherry around its edges until the entire gemstone blazed luminescent amber.

The tower rocked, shaking Tella's legs. It lasted only a second. But Tella swore that in that moment even the stars outside blinked. The ring had always been pretty, but now it was otherworldly, glowing bright enough to light up her entire hand.

What had Dante done?

White-hot panic moved through Tella's veins. He must have found the loophole around the ring's curse. Why did he have to do that for her? He'd said not to worry, that he wasn't that selfless, but he must have paid a price for the stone to become un-cursed.

Tella trembled and the crown on her head wobbled. She reached up to steady it. But her hand was as shaky as her legs. Instead of righting the crown she knocked it over. It tumbled and hit the ground with a lyrical crash.

"Oh my." Elantine placed a hand over her mouth.

Tella swallowed a curse. Five sharp pieces of obsidian, tipped in gleaming black opals, stared at her from the floor. It was now a mirror image of the Shattered Crown.

Tella's voice shook as she said, "I'm so sorry."

"Don't be, child. I have people who can clean that up for me, and you've done nothing wrong."

But Tella would do something wrong.

Still trembling, she stared at the shattered crown on the floor as her impossible choice became far too clear. Dante had found a way for Tella to get inside her mother's vault that would require no sacrifice on Tella's part. Of course, Tella didn't know if Dante had done it to save her from the stars, or to ensure she'd get the cards. Tella wasn't even sure which one she wanted to be true. If Dante had sacrificed something to save Tella, what kind of person would she be if she then betrayed him to Jacks? But that was assuming Dante was Legend. Tella still didn't know who Legend was.

And she wouldn't know if she didn't win the game.

But maybe it would be better *not* to win the game.

Winning the game will come at a cost you will later regret. Nigel had warned Tella of this, though even if he hadn't, she knew regrets were in her future. If she chose to betray Legend to Jacks so that Jacks could take Legend's power, Jacks would free the Fates and most likely destroy Legend in the process. But, if Tella didn't betray Legend, if she gave him the cards with the Fates, he would destroy them. In doing so, Legend would destroy her mother as well, since all the cards were connected.

Tella's gaze traveled out the window. From so high up the people below were little more than specks of color, lit by the churning stars, the brilliant lanterns, and all the feverish excitement for the last night of Caraval and Elantine's Eve.

In another story Tella might have gone down there and joined them. She might have drunk spiced wine and danced with strangers. Maybe she'd have even kissed someone beneath the stars. It should have been what she wanted. She told herself to want it. To walk away from the separate game she'd been thrust into and the woman who'd walked away from her. To stop pretending her mother cared. But Elantine's words about true endings and almost-endings continued to torment Tella.

She wanted to turn her back on her mother, but it felt more like giving up than letting go, settling for less when she had a chance at so much more. Tella didn't want to let her mother hurt her again. But what if Elantine was right and her mother really had loved her?

Tella's mother had placed the cards in the stars' vaults so that no one could get to them. Maybe her mother had never planned on touching them again either. What if she'd offered Tella to the stars, but she'd never intended to give Tella away? Maybe locking the cards in a vault that could only be opened by a cursed key had been Paloma's way to keep them safe. But then somehow her mother had ended up trapped in a card.

Tella didn't know when she left the tower—but suddenly she was running down the stairs, rushing toward the courtyard where Caraval was taking place, thinking only of her mother.

The air was so thick with magic it fell like confectioner's sugar on Tella's tongue, a sweet welcome to a darkly enchanted world. Fates and symbols of Fates were everywhere.

The palatial courtyard had been transformed into a market that looked as if it were something plucked from a myth. There were tents bearing names like:

Her Majesty's Magical Gowns

Priestess, Priestess's Charm Emporium

Assassin's Knives and Killer Neckwear

Aracle's Magical Glasses

Then there were the signs, giant posters in honor of even more Fates:

Give Mistress Luck a kiss and she'll give you your heart's greatest wish.

For a short-lived but good time, find Jester Mad!

If you see the Pregnant Maid, your future is about to change. . . .

Tella refused to be distracted—she needed to get to the Temple of the Stars, though it was a little harder to move through the courtyard when people started approaching her. A shadowy figure costumed as the Poisoner invited her to taste his poison. A number of Fallen Stars offered her a lick of stardust.

Tella didn't even bother to respond; she hurried through the crush as quickly as possible. The only moment she stumbled was when she thought she saw Scarlett, dressed as the Unwed Bride in a veil of tears that dripped over her face like weeping diamonds. But if Scarlett knew what Tella was about to do, she would certainly try to stop her.

Tella didn't want to be stopped. This was her one chance to save her mother, and if she didn't take it she'd regret it as long as she lived.

During the carriage ride to the Temple District she still felt pangs of guilt at the idea of giving Legend over to Jacks. But Tella imagined it was only because of her infatuation with Dante. Betraying Legend felt like betraying Dante. But maybe they weren't one and the same. And if Dante was really Legend, then he was the one who'd been betraying Tella all this time.

She reached the Temple of the Stars after the clang of ten bells.

She didn't need to knock when she arrived at the sanctuary's forbidding doors. They opened soundlessly, as if the temple were giving her an inaudible hello.

Theron stood on the other side, a tower of a man, made more imposing by the brutal eight-pointed star burned onto his merciless face. He was dressed in the same manner as when she'd met him the night before—thick leathers and a royal-blue cape.

To his credit, Theron didn't mention Tella's rapid departure the night before. Whatever he made of her disappearance and reappearance remained guarded by his stoic demeanor.

The slap of Tella's slippers against the polished floor made the only sound as she followed him inside the shadowed entry. The fiery fountain in the center had not yet been lit, allowing a thick layer of cold to settle.

Tella had lost her cape somewhere in the royal courtyard, leaving her back and arms exposed, so she should have been freezing. Yet her neck dripped sweat as she said, "I'm here to open my mother's vault."

Theron's eyes dropped to Tella's ring. "You are fortunate to have such a good friend."

A prickle of fresh unease joined the sweat dripping down her neck as she thought of Dante. "What did he give you to break the curse on the ring?"

"There's only one way to break the curse. But there is always one way around every curse. In this case, we made an exchange that has temporarily lifted it from your ring. Now do you wish to keep asking questions, or would you like to see your vault?"

"First, tell me what Dante gave you in this exchange."

"He made us a promise. I cannot tell you what it is, but if you care about him, you'll want to make sure he keeps his word."

"What happens if he doesn't?"

Theron traced the star-shaped brand on his face. "If your Dante fails us, he will die."

Tella's mouth went dry.

Without another word, Theron guided Tella to the door at the back of the foyer, the one watched by the agonized stone statues. He used his ring to unlock the gate.

Warm air smelling of buried mysteries and old magic filled the octagonal annex on the other side. Unlike the entry, this area was not all glowing gold and pearly whites. It was wooden and aged, and filled with the same sort of hushed gravity as the first floor of Elantine's golden tower. Primeval light ghosted across the grainy floor, while magic, far older than Legend's or Jacks's, brushed against the backs of Tella's hands, tasting her with unseen tongues.

Theron had told the truth when he'd said this temple was not a tourist attraction.

The vaults were buried deep beneath. From the annex, Theron took Tella through a door that led to a winding case of earthy stairs. She didn't count the number of steps, but it was enough to make her legs sweat beneath her sparkling gown. When they finally reached the bottom, the passages were narrow and dim, lit by a row of candles that looked as if they grew out of the ground. Theron and Tella had to cautiously skirt around them.

Halfway down a corridor so dim Tella could only make out Theron's outline, he finally stopped in front of a stone door without a handle. "This will open only for you. To gain entrance, all you must do is press your ring to the door. But be warned, the bargain your Dante made with us allows you to open this vault only once. If you choose to remove or leave an object inside here, be very certain about your choice. Once you close this door, the only way you may open it again is by paying your mother's debt."

"If I never open it," Tella asked, "will that undo the bargain that was made on my behalf?"

"No. That vow has already been sealed. To leave the vault locked would be a waste of the sacrifice he has made."

Sweat coated Tella's palms. Dante should not have come to her aid. It gave her more hope that he wasn't Legend. Legend was not known for making sacrifices, and as flattering as it would be if he'd changed for her, Tella silently prayed that wasn't the case, because she could not do the same for him. She'd come here to save her mother, no matter the cost.

Tella waited for Theron to leave before opening the door to the vault. Unlike the narrow hallway, the room on the other side of the door was wide and beaming with light, illuminated from some unseen source. The center was unoccupied but the walls were lined with milk-white shelves full of fantastical treasure. Lifelike paintings, golden instruments, elaborate weapons, dancing figurines, ancient relics, jeweled tiaras, heavy books, and unlabeled bottles with churning contents that might have been magical.

This had been Paloma's life before she'd come to Trisda.

Tella gave herself a moment to take every stolen inch of it in. She burned with curiosity—and desire for some of the prettier items—but she didn't want to waste time, or risk touching anything that might be cursed like her mother's cards.

Tella kept her hands clasped in front of her as her eyes continued searching, until she spotted the box. An unnatural breeze ghosted across Tella's shoulders. It was a simple wooden thing, unremarkable save for the halo of darkness throbbing around it, as if the light in the rest of the room could not touch it.

Tella saw nothing else as she crossed over to it and lifted the lid. The cards looked exactly as Tella remembered. Such a dark hue of nightshade they were almost black, with tiny hints of gold flecks that sparkled in the light and swirly strands of deep red-violet embossing, which had once made Tella think of damp flowers, witches' blood, and *magic*.

Tella wondered what the cards would show if she tried to read her future now, but she didn't dare flip any over.

Without so much as grazing a swirl, Tella placed the Aracle atop the deck. Then she retrieved the card imprisoning her mother from where she'd tucked it safely inside her dress.

The halo around the cards pulsed darker, as if adding additional cards had somehow made the deck more powerful.

Tella ignored the ill feeling that came with it. She exhaled, breathing out the heavy press against her chest that warned her to stop. She was almost there. All she needed to do now was pick up the deck and win the game. Then she could have her mother back.

Her hand hovered above the tiny stack, wondering how long it would take Legend to find her. Dante must have told Legend that the cards were in the temple. There was a chance Legend was already waiting on the steps. And Nigel had promised, *If you win Caraval, the first face you see will be Legend's.*

Tella took a deep breath. If this was going to work, she needed to summon Jacks before she officially won the game or stepped out of the stars' temple. She reached into the pocket of her silver gown, fingers fumbling for his luckless coin.

Theron's voice instantly flooded the vault. "Do not use that vile magic here, or I will close this door and you will never get out."

Tella ripped her hand free from her dress. Her fingers trembled.

She should have summoned Jacks before she'd stepped inside. Being unable to call him now felt like another chance to change her mind. But Tella's decision was made. Once she took the cards and stepped out of the vault, there would be no turning back. She'd just have to be quick to grab the luckless coin.

But she was still taking a risk. Once she stepped outside of this temple, every Fate and person trapped inside the cards would either be released by Jacks once he took his full power back from Legend—or all the Fates along with Tella's mother would be destroyed by Legend if Jacks did not arrive quickly enough.

The world was about change. Either all the Fates and Tella's mother would go free, or Legend would destroy them and become the most powerful human in the world.

No wonder the stars had blinked earlier that night. Tella imagined them doing it again as she reached into the wooden box, boldly picked up her mother's cursed Deck of Destiny, and officially won Caraval.

Tella's heart raced as she exited the sanctuary. After everything that night it should have run out of beats, but it managed to pound faster as the cool evening air whipped around her face and rustled the silvery leaves of her dress. Ignoring the chill, her hand dove into her pocket once more for Jacks's luckless coin.

"Tella—" A low, achingly familiar voice, called from the base of the steps, followed by the echo of Dante's heavy footfalls.

She froze.

If you win Caraval, the first face you see will be Legend's.

No. No. No.

Tella quickly shut her eyes before she could see him. Maybe if she didn't open her eyes he'd walk away, she'd see another face, and Dante wouldn't be Legend.

She heard him climb closer. Boots heavy and eager against the stairs.

"I thought you were meeting me after midnight," she called.

"I had a feeling you'd be here early." His voice was a little closer.

"You shouldn't have come."

"Tella, look at me." Another step. Then she felt the heady warmth that always seemed to surround him. It pressed against her shoulders and chest, as if he were standing right in front her. "I can't talk to you like this."

She kept her eyes firmly closed. This wasn't how it was supposed to be. She'd suspected Dante was Legend, but she wasn't supposed to be right.

"I don't want to talk to you," she said. "I want to talk to Legend."

"Then open your eyes and speak to me."

Her legs gave out.

His arms snaked around her, keeping her steady while the world she knew broke into pieces.

Dante was Legend.

Legend was Dante.

And he was still holding on to her. One hand left her waist, moving upward until his fingers gently brushed her cheek before resting beneath her chin and tilting her face toward his. She could feel his words against his lips as he spoke. "Tella, say something."

She opened her mouth to answer, but he was so close all she could feel were his lips touching hers. They were soft and parted and then they were pressing more firmly against her mouth.

She didn't even want to try to resist him. But it was so much more than that.

They kissed as if the world were ending, lips crashing together as if the heavens were breaking and the ground was crumbling, as if a war raged all around them and this kiss was the only thing mighty enough to stop it. As long as they kissed, only she and Dante existed.

Tella never wanted to open her eyes; as soon as she did, the world would shift. Dante would be gone and there would only be Legend.

It was so brutally unfair. She'd only just decided how much she wanted Dante, but even if he made it through the night, Legend was someone she could never have. He was like a moment in time; he could be experienced but never held on to.

His lips pressed harder as one hand threaded through her hair and the other went lower around her hips, digging in and pulling her closer, as if he didn't want the kiss to end, either.

But it had to stop. No matter how good of a distraction it was. The longer it lasted, the more danger she was in.

Tella leaned in toward him for one spectacular heartbeat, tasting his lips a final time. Then she forced herself to let go. She'd never be able to do what she needed if she fell any farther.

Her eyes opened reluctantly.

She wanted him to look different. She wanted his gaze to be cold and distant. She wanted him to look at her as if he'd really been the one to win this game. She wanted his lips to curve cruelly as he tried to steal the deck of cards from her grip. But he didn't even look at them. He only stared at her. One hand was still on her waist. It was hotter than it should have been on such a cold night.

"You won the game," he said. He lifted his other hand, as if reaching for her face.

She caught a glimpse of the black rose inked upon his skin. She might have laughed at how obvious that image had made his identity all along. But then his arm twisted and Tella caught a glimpse of the underside of his wrist, just beneath the scar he'd earned in the last Caraval.

She grabbed it. He winced, but he didn't fight her as she pushed up the cuff of his sleeve.

She gasped so sharply it hurt. "God's blood."

On the underside of his wrist, marring one of his lovely tattoos, was a violent star-shaped brand, exactly like the one on Theron's face.

She told herself he had only done it for the cards, not for her. This was about the Fates's power, she reminded herself. But it still felt wrong that he'd let himself be branded in such a permanent way.

"What did you promise them?" Tella asked.

"It doesn't matter. I did it for you and I'd do it again." Dante rotated his wrist until somehow he was holding her hand. He still hadn't even looked at the cards. He dark eyes stayed fixed on her as if she were his prize.

And, damn her, she believed him.

It was so very wrong.

If he was Legend, he wasn't supposed to care. He wasn't supposed to still gaze at her as if she'd just shattered his world with a kiss. He was supposed to laugh at her for being foolish enough to fall for him.

He wasn't supposed to lean in closer, as if he'd fallen for her, too. He was supposed to rip the cards from her hands and abandon her on the moonstone steps. He was supposed to break her heart.

She wasn't supposed to break his.

Finally Tella's heart stopped racing. She couldn't do this. She couldn't take more away from him than she already had. Jacks would have to find another source of power to free her mother and the Fates.

"You need to leave. Immediately." Tella ripped her hand from his. "I used Jacks's luckless coin right before you arrived. He's on his way here now. When he arrives he's going to steal your powers and free all the Fates."

Dante's eyes finally dropped to the cards clutched in Tella's hands. She still wasn't entirely ready to think of him as Legend. Legends were supposed to be better than the truth. Perfect, idealized dreams and crystalline hopes that were too flawless to exist in reality. And she might have described him that way just then, if the naked expression that crossed his face didn't cut deeper than disappointment. "You want to give the cards to Jacks?"

"I'm sorry," Tella said. She clasped the deck tighter, but Dante made no move to take it, though a muscle jumped in his jaw and his knuckles turned white as if everything in him fought against the urge.

"This is about your mother, isn't it?" he asked.

"I thought I could let her go, but she's my mother. I have so many questions for her, and despite everything she's done, I can't stop loving her." Tella's voice cracked. "I can't allow you to destroy her along with the Fates."

His expression split, as if it had been ripped in half, a two-sided mask formed of regret and determination. "If I could free your mother, I would. But the only way to release someone from a card without breaking the curse is to take their place."

"I'm not asking you to free her," Tella said. "I'm asking you to go before Jacks gets here." She shoved against Dante's chest, but he was indomitable. He wouldn't move. Her panic increased and she shoved him again. But he wouldn't fight back and he wouldn't flee. He wasn't afraid. He was something far worse. He was hopeful that she would choose him. He didn't leave and he didn't take the cards because he wanted her to give them to him.

And maybe he imagined that if Jacks arrived he could beat him in a battle. Either way, Tella still lost her mother or she lost Dante.

Unless she saved them both.

The idea felt fragile at first, but like all thoughts it grew stronger the more consideration she gave to it. All this time, she kept thinking Jacks was the only one who could free her mother. But Tella could take her mother's place. Caspar had mentioned how it was done during the play. All she needed to do was write her name on the card in blood. She still had the blood Dante and Julian had used to heal her pulsing through her veins; if her mortal blood wasn't enough, that blood should do the trick.

It hadn't felt like an option before. Tella feared being trapped more than anything. But perhaps love was an otherworldly entity like Death. And since Tella had now opened herself up to the possibility of Love, it would not stop coming after her, and it felt far more powerful than Death.

She'd underestimated Love in the past. She'd imagined the romantic sort to be a stronger type of lust—but this moment had nothing to do with lust and everything to do with caring more about saving Dante and her mother than saving herself. It made her fearless in a way she'd never been.

Using her mother's sharp opal ring, Tella pierced the tip of her finger hard enough to draw blood.

"Tella, what are you doing?" Dante said.

"You can take the cards, but promise me you'll leave before Jacks arrives." She pressed her bleeding finger against the card imprisoning her mother.

"Tella," Dante repeated. "What are you doing?"

"I'm being the hero."

"No!" Dante roared the word the moment he realized what she meant. "Tella, don't do this. Your mother wouldn't want this."

He reached for her mother's card, but it was too late. Tella's name was written upon it in blood.

"It's already finished," Tella said.

She tried to smile then. She was finally the hero. All it had cost her was everything.

Her lips wobbled, and hot tears fell from her eyes.

"Tella." Dante rasped her name as if he were on the verge of crying too. "I know you don't want to believe me, but I never meant for this to happen to you. When I set up the game, I knew your mother had hidden the cards, but I didn't know she was trapped inside one of them." He pressed the pads of his thumbs to her cheeks. But the more tears he wiped away, the more began to fall. "I'm so sorry, I failed you."

She leaned into his hands. She had not thought Legend would be one to apologize, but it wasn't his fault. This was her choice. She could have made another one if she'd wanted to. She didn't know how long it would be until the spell took effect, but she imagined it would happen soon. And since her story wasn't going to have a happy true ending, at least she could try for one last good moment during her almost-ending.

"I lied to my sister about our kiss," Tella said.

Dante pressed his lips to her forehead. "I know."

"I'm not finished," she scolded. "I wanted you to know why I lied. I wasn't ashamed. I said it so my sister wouldn't worry, because I think I knew even then that I could have—"

The night. The world. The stars watching from above all disappeared.

Then Tella disappeared as well.

Those who had been looking up at the sky, still searching for clues even though the game had just been won, might have noticed the appearance of more stars, stars that had not been seen in centuries. For it had been nearly that long since sacrifices of such magnitude had been made.

Humans were selfish creatures. The stars had witnessed it again, and again, and again.

But tonight, as the stars peered down on the world, they saw what seemed to be truly unselfish acts.

First, from the young woman.

Foolish young woman.

She'd seemed promising. Now she was useless. Paper.

But it was interesting to watch how her young man responded.

The stars leaned closer. He was distracted, allowing them to move more freely than they had the past several nights. It was a delight to see him in pain. This boy, who never seemed to care about anyone but himself, shook with rage. Hopefully he didn't do anything too foolish. He'd made a deal with them that they hungered for him to keep. It would do them no good if he were trapped in a card or dead.

Not that they believed he would sacrifice himself for her. Humans were not that selfless. But, of course, he wasn't fully human.

He picked up the ring that had fallen from the girl's hand when she'd been turned into a card. The ring's stone burned red and violet, cursed once more, but still sharp enough to pierce skin. The boy sliced it across his palm. Blood spilled, as red as heartbreak and terror, and full of power.

The stars watched with grim interest as he covered the deck of cards with the magic from his veins, more magic than a human should possess. Then he spoke the words, ancient, terrible words he should not have known, let alone been willing to utter.

The blood covering the deck turned black, and the world changed once more.

41

Tella should not have possessed the ability to open her eyelids. A moment ago she'd been unable to breathe or move or feel anything other than trapped. She'd been inanimate, powerless.

But now she could feel the midnight breeze playing with her curls and the warm hand against her back, holding her to an even warmer body—Legend's body.

He was Legend now, not Dante. Tella could feel it in the magic pulsing from his heated hands—hands with enough power to rip worlds in half. But they were gentle against her back, holding her up and keeping her recovering body from crumbling to the ground. She didn't know how long she'd been trapped in the card, but the life-stealing effects still lingered. Her heartbeat was fine, but her legs were liquid, her arms were boneless. She could barely move.

She concentrated on blinking, fluttering her eyelids up and down as her vision slowly returned and found focus. They were still on the Temple of the Stars' moonstone steps. The evening was unchanged, as if no time had passed, though perhaps the sky was a little brighter than before. Glittering with additional stars. But Tella didn't want to look at the stars. She wanted to see him.

His expression was so harsh he looked as if he'd stolen a piece of dark from the night. She wanted to reach up and smooth the deep crease between his eyes, to ease the pain from his expression, but she didn't have the strength to move.

"What happened?" she breathed. "Why didn't it work?"

"It did." His grip tightened, pressing her closer to his chest as he rubbed his hands up and down her back as if to make sure she was still corporeal. "I watched you vanish and reappear in your mother's place in the card."

"But then how am I here? And where is my mother?" Tella's gaze drifted around the glowing steps, at the immobile statues that she would have sworn were watching them both intently.

"Don't worry. She's safe," Legend said. His low voice was strained, pained, as if for each word he spoke, there was another word he couldn't bring himself to utter. "I imagine your mother is in the same place she was right before she was turned into a card, otherwise she'd be here with us."

"I still don't understand," Tella said.

The hands against her back stilled. "I know you were willing to sacrifice yourself for her, but I wasn't willing to sacrifice you."

He removed one of his hands from around her and a beam of moonlight fell over his bronze palm, illuminating a jagged cut down the center. "I broke the curse on the cards."

"But—" Tella cut off, unsure which part of all of this to protest. She'd been willing to sacrifice everything, prepared to remain trapped in a card to save her mother and him, and to keep the Fates from going free and ruling over the Empire once more. But a very selfish part of her was so relieved. It seemed her story might someday have a happy true ending after all.

Tella could have sunk into the steps and wept from relief and disbelief. Legend could have destroyed the cards and taken the power of all the Fates. He could have had everything he'd wanted. If he'd destroyed the Fates, his magic wouldn't be limited to peaking during Caraval. He'd have the power of the Fates: the Aracle's ability to see the future; Mistress Luck's good fortune; the Assassin's ability to travel through space and time; the Lady Prisoner's wisdom. And he'd chosen to save Tella instead.

"I can't believe you did this for me." She looked up from Legend's wounded palm to his beautiful face. "I think that means you're the hero after all."

His expression darkened at the word *hero*, as if it was something he'd rather not be called. But she didn't care. He was her hero.

Tella could still barely move her limbs, but she managed to wrap a hand around the back of Legend's neck as the first of many fireworks burst into the sky. She heard them shimmer and pop as she leaned in closer and bought his full mouth down to hers. At first his lips didn't move. Panic tore through her that something was wrong, that perhaps he regretted what he'd done. Her lips moved more tentatively, about to pull away, when he softly kissed the corner of her mouth.

Maybe he'd been afraid of hurting her before.

He was impossibly gentle as he kissed her again; hands barely stroking her waist as his lips slowly traveled along her jaw and then down her neck. So light it was almost painful. It was the delicate sound of music, the distant crash of ocean waves; there but still too far away. Tella wanted to erase the distance. It should have felt like the beginning of something, but somehow it felt like the end. As if every feather-light press of his lips was an unspoken good-bye.

More fireworks exploded above, gold and violet and brighter than before.

She tightened her grip around his neck, trying to hold on to him and this moment, but he was already pulling away as he lowered her toward the steps.

"What's wrong?" Tella asked.

"I need to leave." His gaze shuttered, his lips moved into a severe line, and then he let her go, completely. He set her weak body down, abandoning her atop the cold moonstone steps. "Good-bye, Tella."

Her stomach went hollow. If she'd been standing her legs might have crumbled.

He was striding away. Leaving her.

"Wait—where are you going?"

He continued down the steps.

For a moment she feared he wouldn't turn back around. But it was almost worse that he did. His eyes, which earlier had been so heated, so full of emotion, didn't glitter or shine or spark any longer. They were flat, black, and growing colder with every heartbeat like the fading fireworks above. "There's somewhere else I need to be. And, no matter what this looks like, I'm still not the hero in your story."

Something cracked inside of Tella. It might have been her heart, breaking while he walked away—as if he hadn't just freed the Fates and damned the entire world for her.

42

The steps beneath Tella were cold, but not nearly as icy as the heartless boy who'd left her there. She'd been left by boys before, but it had never hurt this much. She wanted to get up, to walk away with her head high, as if he mattered as little to her as she apparently mattered to him. But Tella's limbs still felt like paper, weak and thin and pathetic.

A dramatic sigh cut through the chorus of fireworks still crackling above. Then Jacks was sauntering up the stairs, shaking his head as he walked. He looked as if he'd dressed up and then gotten into a scuffle. His fitted jacket was covered in swirls of frayed gold embroidery. The cream shirt beneath it might have looked fine if the lace hadn't been ripped from the cuffs and the collar. Two of the buttons near his neck were missing as well. "I told you it was a bad idea to put yourself in a card."

"How do you know that's what happened?" Tella asked.

"I'm a Fate. I know things."

She tried to shove herself into a more dignified position, but her limbs remained firmly planted against the cold stone. "Did you know this would happen all along?"

"It was one possibility." Jacks continued his lazy climb. If he was disappointed that he'd missed Legend, his voice gave no indication. His handsome face appeared unreadable. It looked perfectly indifferent, save for the tiny wrinkle in between his brows. "Pining doesn't look good on you."

"I'm not pining. I'm angry," Tella said. Jacks was the last person she wanted to pour her heart out to, but given that he was the only one there and that her heart was already cracked wide open, it was impossible to hold the words back. "Half the reason I put myself in that card was so you wouldn't take his powers or kill him. And then he just left me here on these steps."

"Did you honestly expect more from Legend?"

Maybe she hadn't expected more from Legend, but she'd wanted more from Dante. How could someone who'd given up everything he'd worked for just abandon her? And why had he bothered to kiss her back? He should have let her go the minute she'd pressed her lips to his.

"You're definitely pining." Jacks's mouth twisted in disgust.

"Stop judging me. It only looks that way because I can't move. If I could, I wouldn't be lying here. I'd be with my mother."

"So you know where she is?" Jacks drawled.

Tella scowled. "Don't you have something better to do? Shouldn't you be off celebrating with all the other Fates that Legend just freed?"

"See how weak you are after being inside a card for a handful of minutes? The other Fates were trapped for centuries. They might be out of the cards, but, at the least, it will take weeks before any of them, or your mother, are strong enough to open their eyes. Once they do wake up, they still won't be at their full powers because of Legend."

"So then why aren't you off plotting how to get the rest of your magic back from him?"

"Who says I'm not?" Jacks's smile was all dimples, the sharp ones she'd seen the first time they'd met. She hated them now as much as she did then. Dimples were supposed to be charming and kind, but his always felt like a form of attack.

Tella's arms and legs still weren't working, but she managed to glare in return. "Leave."

"Fine. But I'm taking you with me." In one agile move Jacks scooped her up, lean arms far stronger than they looked.

"What are you doing?" Tella screeched.

"I'm taking you to your sister. Don't waste your feeble energy fighting."

If only Tella could have fought him. But she didn't have the strength and she was so tired of fighting. Her battle had died on those steps the moment Legend walked away. All she wanted now was for the night to end and for the sun to return, so that when she looked up at the sky she'd no longer see all the bleeding stars and think of

Legend. Her one triumph was that her mother was free, but until Tella saw her in the flesh, it would still feel as if she was missing.

"Are you crying?" Jacks asked.

"Don't you dare criticize me for it."

His hands tensed. A flash of cold kissed Tella, a reminder of Jacks before his heart had started beating again. "If you're crying about Legend, don't. He doesn't deserve it. But if this is about the cards"—Jacks looked down on her, and for a lightning-brief moment all the indolence and carelessness left his expression—"I did the same thing. You wouldn't be human if you didn't cry."

"I thought you weren't human."

"I'm not. But there was a time when I was. Thankfully it didn't last too long," he added, but Tella thought she heard a hint of regret.

She craned her neck to look up at him. He met her gaze and she swore his softened with something akin to concern, his silver-blue eyes tipped down, teardrops about to fall.

"Why are you being so nice?" she asked.

"If you think I'm nice, you really need to spend time with better people."

"No, you're being kind. You're holding me all close and saying personal things. Do you love me now?"

He answered with a mocking laugh. "You're really hung up on that, aren't you?"

Tella gave him a saucy smirk. "I made your heart beat. That practically makes me a Fate."

"No," Jacks answered tightly, all hints of humor vanishing. "You're still very human, and I do not love you."

His hands went so cold she half expected him to drop her and leave her the same way Legend had. But for some reason Jacks kept her close. His arms stayed around her as he carried her into a sky carriage. It had buttery cushions laced with thick royal-blue trim that matched the curtains lining the oval windows. She wondered if it was the coach they'd first met in, the same tiny box he'd threatened to shove her out of just to see what would happen. She went a little stiffer in his arms at the thought. Even though he was being gentle with her, he was far from kind or safe.

"Did you just remember how much you don't like me?" he asked.

"I never forgot. I was thinking of the first time we met. Did you know who I was?"

"No."

"So, you're just that charming to everyone you meet?"

His hand slowly stroked her arm; his fingers weren't as icy as before his heart started beating, but they were still cool to the touch. "When I possessed my full powers, I could do the vilest of things. I could speak words far worse than what I said to you in the carriage, and people would still willingly betray their mother or their lover to please me. Although those powers are gone, being heir to a throne has a similar effect." The eyes that met hers were the color of frost, and as dispassionate as they were unapologetic. "No one likes me, Donatella, but people go along with whatever I say. Sometimes my only form of entertainment is seeing how far I can take things before someone flinches."

"You really have no feelings at all, do you?"

"I feel."

"But not like humans?"

"No. It takes far more for me to feel something, and when I do it's infinitely stronger." Jacks removed his hand from her arm, but for one splintering moment Tella felt his fingers harden like metal.

When the coach landed at the palace the air was thick with celebratory smoke. Jacks didn't even ask if Tella's limbs were working again. He scooped her listless body up once more and carried her from the carriage house as a final brilliant blue firework burst above, raining down sapphire shine over every inch of Elantine's jeweled palace.

Jacks's eyes flashed quicksilver in the light with something a little too inhuman to be called sorrow, and yet that was the only word Tella had for it.

"Why aren't you watching the fireworks with the empress?" she asked.

"Didn't you hear? Her missing child returned, and Elantine has officially recognized him, which means I'm no longer heir."

Tella did not feel sorry for him. Jacks's reign would have been a plague to the entire Meridian Empire. And yet something about the situation stirred up a sense of unease. When Elantine had talked of her lost child earlier that night, it hadn't sounded as if a mother and child had been reunited. It made Tella think that Elantine's new heir was an imposter, a pretender who only existed to keep Jacks from the throne.

It should have impressed Tella that the empress had done what she'd needed to protect the Empire from Jacks. But something about it didn't feel right.

"Don't faint on me," Jacks said. "I'd rather not face the wrath of your sister."

"I'm not faint," Tella lied. "And, speaking of my sister, you still never told me what she was doing with you the other night in the carriage."

"Kissing me passionately."

Tella choked on a breath.

The corner of Jacks's mouth twitched. "Don't die on me now. It was a joke. You told your sister that I found your mother, so she wanted me to help her find someone, too."

This was much better but still disconcerting. "Who was she looking for?"

"Not the boy she's sitting with right now." Jacks pivoted slowly in the direction of the stone garden.

The air was warmer, as if this corner of the palace grounds was untouched by anything ill. Yet the statues appeared more distressed than the last time Tella had seen them. They all flinched and recoiled more than before. It was as if they knew that Legend had just released the Fates back into the world—the same Fates who'd long ago turned this garden full of human servants into unmoving stone because they'd wanted more lifelike decorations.

Tella shivered in Jacks's arms.

Scarlett appeared oblivious to it all. She and Julian sat huddled on a bench in the center of the statues, looking gloriously back in love. Tella swore there were night-blooming butterflies frolicking around their heads.

At least one sister had found happiness that night.

"Did you two finally make up?" Tella mumbled.

Scarlett and Julian straightened abruptly. Then Scarlett was off of the bench, flying toward Jacks and Tella's limp figure.

"What did you do to my sister?" Scarlett's lacy white gloves turned to formidable black leather as she pointed at the Fate.

She might have done more than point if Julian had not wrapped a restraining arm around her waist. He was costumed as Chaos, dressed in heavy armor and a pair of spiked gauntlets that made him look as if he were ready to jump into battle. But Tella saw genuine fear simmering beneath the surface of his rugged features. Unlike Scarlett, he must have known that Jacks was the Prince of Hearts. And if Julian was truly Legend's brother, he must have wondered why the Fate was still alive.

Jacks merely sighed. "Does no one in this family say thank you?"

"Every time I see you, my sister is hurt," Scarlett said.

"Not every time." Jacks flashed his teeth as his eyes quickly cut from Julian back to Scarlett. Tella didn't know what Jacks was silently saying, but whatever it was it made Scarlett's mouth snap shut.

"And this really wasn't my fault," Jacks continued. "Your sister won the game. But it took a lot out of her. She collapsed in the Temple District and Legend, being the gentleman that he's not, just left her there."

"You met Legend?" Scarlett asked, her tone both curious and suspicious. It matched the fractured expression on Julian's face, as if he, too, was both surprised and nervous. Whenever Scarlett was in a room his eyes were always on her, but now he watched Tella, as if he was afraid of what she might say next.

"I—" Tella's tongue grew suddenly thick and Jacks's arms became instantly tense. This must have been why'd he'd been playing at being so concerned; he still wanted Legend's identity to get his full power back, so that he could do more than just kill with a kiss. But even if Tella had been willing to share Legend's secret with him, the weight of her tongue and the press of magic against her throat made her feel as if she wouldn't be able to reveal it no matter how hard she tried.

"I don't remember much of it," Tella hedged. Then she spared a glance for Julian. "As soon as I won the game, Legend walked away."

A flash of relief lit Julian's eyes.

Scarlett's expression turned more wary.

Jacks took a heavy breath, his chest slowly moving up and down against Tella's back. "I think it's time I go. Your mother still needs finding."

"No!" Tella said.

Scarlett went stiff.

Jacks's brows danced up. "After all this, you don't want to see her?"

"Of course I want to see her. I don't want you touching her."

"I'll put some gloves on," Jacks said. Then, more softly in Tella's ear, "People know it's never a good idea to make a bargain with a Fate, but they do it anyway, because we always keep our word. I told you that if you won the game I'd reunite you with your mother, and that's what I'm going to do."

Jacks carefully placed Tella in the cold hold of a statue with outstretched arms.

For a moment she felt a perverted urge to thank him. But he was the last being she would ever thank. "I still hate you," she said.

"It's probably for the best."

His footfalls made no sound as he exited the garden. As soon as he was gone, Scarlett helped Tella down from the statue's stiff embrace.

Tella's legs still felt watery but she could stand as long as Scarlett kept an arm around her. She leaned into her sister's softness. The air in the garden remained warm, but cold was seeping in. Frost was forming on the forlorn statues and the night butterflies were gone.

"Can we go back to the palace?" Tella mumbled.

"Of course," Scarlett said.

"Do you need any help?" Julian asked.

Scarlett gave a quick shake of her head and something unspoken passed between them. Julian pressed a quick kiss to her cheek, and then he turned back to Tella. Something like sympathy filled his amber eyes.

"I'm sorry," he said. He didn't mention his name, but Tella knew he was talking about Legend. "He can make someone the center of his world when they're a part of his game. But when the game ends, he *always* walks away and he never looks back."

Tella sensed Julian was trying to be helpful, but somehow he made it a little worse.

"It doesn't matter," she said. "I'm just glad the game's over."

Julian pulled at the back of his neck. Tella feared he was going to say something else, something that would be harder to dismiss without a show of emotion. But she imagined he was more eager to find his brother than continue a conversation with her. Julian must have known things hadn't gone as planned the moment she'd shown up in Jacks's arms.

Without another word he left the garden and disappeared into the night.

The minute he was gone, Scarlett turned back to Tella with eyes full of her own questions. Tella didn't know if her sister wanted to ask about her mother, or the game, or what Tella had done that had put her in such a weakened state.

All Tella knew was that she didn't want to fight or argue or see any disappointment on her sister's face. Scarlett deserved answers, but Tella wasn't ready to get into the entirety of her story. She just wanted someone to comfort her and take care of her until the dawn.

Scarlett held her fiercely. "I'm ready to listen whenever you want to talk."

"I'd rather forget." Tella sagged against her sister. She didn't mean to say anything, but once she started speaking the rest slipped out. "I made a mistake, Scar. I never wanted to fall for anyone, but I think I've fallen in love with Legend."

ELANTINE'S DAY

43

It was the quietest Elantine's Day the Meridian Empire had ever witnessed. After a week of burning constellations and buildup, all of the empress's birthday celebrations had been cancelled due to Elantine's continued state of failing health. Her people had been informed of her illness that morning, and the entirety of Valenda was in a somber mood. Even the sun didn't shine quite as bright; it seemed content to hide behind clouds. Only one corner of it peeked out, sending a ray of light into the room where Donatella Dragna sat with her sister, Scarlett.

For her part, the younger Dragna sister felt as if she'd entered a world where both her dreams and nightmares had collided.

She'd dreamed of her mother so many times. Usually it was nightmares where her mother had abandoned Tella all over again. But occasionally, Tella had dreams where her mother returned. It always happened the same way. Tella would be asleep in her dream, and then her mother would wake Tella with a tender kiss on the forehead.

Tella's eyes would flutter open, then her arms would fly around her mother's neck, and indescribable joy would take over.

It always felt like the urge to cry mingled with the need to laugh; the kind of happiness that was almost painful. It pressed against Tella's chest, making it hard to breathe and difficult to form words. And it should have been even more potent now that her mother was returned.

She lay atop Scarlett's bed, as peaceful as a doomed damsel in distress, all pale cheeks, dark hair, and unnaturally red lips. Tella tried not to be concerned by the exaggerated colors of her mother's lips and skin, reminding herself that for years she'd been a painting on a card, not a woman.

Her mother was now free, and it was because of Tella. That victory alone should have given Tella wings to soar around the room, out the window, and over the glass courtyard below. But the idea of wings made Tella think of a pair of wings tattooed on a beautiful back. Which then conjured thoughts of the one person she wasn't supposed to be thinking about. *Legend.*

Her veins heated at the thought of his name.

She had no idea where he'd gone after he'd left her on the steps outside of the Temple of the Stars. And she didn't want to wonder about it. She didn't want to replay every encounter she'd had with him, every word he'd said to her, every look he'd given her, or every kiss they'd shared. Each memory hurt, behind her eyes, in her lungs, and in her throat, growing uncomfortably tight whenever she recalled their last moment together.

It felt like weakness to keep thinking of him. Tella knew she'd have had to be completely unfeeling to have banished him from her thoughts after all they'd experienced. And Tella never wanted to be unfeeling. But she didn't want to be consumed with him, either.

The only way to stop her thoughts of him was to keep focusing on her mother, who was there and would eventually wake up.

Tella was still stunned Jacks had kept his promise and returned Paloma to her. Maybe he was in love with Tella after all. She *was* his one true love. Although Tella imagined that being the object of a Fate's affections was a dangerous thing. But she wasn't worrying about the Fates for now. Jacks had made it clear that it would take the Fates longer than it would take her mother to wake up.

Tella wiped Paloma's head with a cool cloth, not that it made any difference. Her mother didn't have a fever. But Tella felt better if she was doing something.

"She doesn't look as if she's aged at all since she left," Scarlett said. "It's not natural."

"I'm fairly certain nothing about being imprisoned in a card is natural," Tella said.

This earned her a deeper frown.

As soon as the sisters had reached the palace the night before, Tella had fallen asleep in her sister's bed. She'd woken up when Jacks had returned with her very unconscious mother. He hadn't mentioned where he'd found her, but he'd let something slip about how she'd been trapped inside of a card and how Tella had made a great sacrifice to save her.

Tella had hoped this would be one of those occasions where her sister would choose to ignore the subject of their mother. But it's rather difficult to ignore someone when they're lying in the room looking cursed. Scarlett had questioned Tella relentlessly, until she'd confessed everything.

Scarlett had not handled most of it well, especially the bit about Tella taking their mother's place inside of a card. After begging Tella never to risk something like that again, Scarlett had turned her anger on their mother; she couldn't look at Paloma without scowling.

Tella couldn't blame her sister. Underneath all the anger, Tella detected that Scarlett harbored a fair amount of guilt for being unaware of so many of the things that went on during Caraval, and that the game was very real this time. Though none of it was Scarlett's fault. And surprisingly, Tella couldn't bring herself to regret anything she'd done. Though she wished she hadn't fallen so far for Legend, which thankfully her sister wasn't mentioning.

Tella was curious to know if Julian had told Scarlett that Dante was Legend, since his identity seemed to be the one thing Tella was physically incapable of talking about. Scarlett had shared with Tella that she was giving Julian another chance. Sensitive to Tella's current feelings about Legend and Caraval, Scarlett had not gone into too many details about it. But Tella imagined her sister wouldn't have completely forgiven Julian unless he gave her more than a few smoldering looks and kisses, which made Tella suspect her sister was more aware of Legend's true identity than she'd let on the night before.

"What if we play a game," Tella suggested. "Do you have a deck of regular cards?" She opened the drawer of the nightstand next to Scarlett's bed.

"Don't!" Scarlett leaped up.

If she hadn't reacted so strongly, Tella might have shut the drawer without looking too hard. But the minute Scarlett shouted, Tella's interest intensified.

There was a book inside the drawer, a fancy red leather thing, with an equally fine-looking letter poking out from beneath it.

"What's this?" Tella plucked the note from under the book. It was addressed to Scarlett. Tella didn't recognize the return address but she was familiar with the name above it: Count Nicolas d'Arcy.

Tella sat there, speechless, because she didn't think shouting was a good idea.

Scarlett's entire face was pink. "I can explain."

"I thought you were giving Julian another chance."

"I am. But I'm giving Nicolas a chance as well."

"Nicolas? You're now on a first-name basis with your former fiancé?" Tella desperately hoped her sister was joking, paying Tella back for all the secrets that she'd kept. Though if this was all true, the strained looks Scarlett and Jacks had shared in the garden now made sense. "Is this the person you asked Jacks to help you find?"

"Jacks told you I asked for his help?" Scarlett sounded surprised, as if she actually trusted the Prince of Hearts.

"I saw you step out of the same carriage as him the other night," Tella said.

Scarlett brought her hands to her cheeks, covering her increasing blush. "I found him after you told me he'd been able to locate our mother. I'd been searching for Nicolas on my own, but I'd had no luck. And going to Jacks for help gave me an excuse to interrogate him about his intentions with you. Not that he was honest about anything."

"I don't think either of us can criticize anyone for being dishonest," Tella snapped.

"I planned to tell you about Nicolas, but I was waiting for the right time." Scarlett shot a look at their mother, a silent reminder that Scarlett was not the only one with secrets. "I wouldn't have kept this from you, but I know you never liked him."

"I still don't. Exchanging letters with him is a mistake."

"Don't worry," Scarlett said. "I'm not planning on marrying him. But I'd appreciate if you didn't mention that to Julian. I think a little rivalry might be good for him."

"So that's what this is about?" Tella was more than a little stunned. "You want a competition between the count and Julian?"

"I wouldn't call it a competition," Scarlett said. "I don't plan on giving either of them tasks to complete. But how can I truly know Julian is right for me if I have no one else to compare him to? I thought you'd be proud of me. You're the one who always wanted me to make my own decisions." Scarlett grinned, as sly as a cat who'd just learned to sneak out of a house and explore the world beyond.

Tella always thought her sister had underestimated her—but maybe she was the one who had underestimated Scarlett.

Tella still didn't like the idea of the count. Even though she no longer trusted what the Aracle had shown her, she had a horrible feeling when it came to Count Nicolas d'Arcy. His letters had always seemed a little too perfect. He was the dictionary definition of a gentleman; no one was that polished in real life. Either he was terribly dull or a fraud. And yet, despite her reservations, Tella was proud of her sister for making such a bold choice. "Scarlett, I—"

Bells. Long and low and sorrowful bells rang across the palace.

Tella shuddered at the tragic sound, instantly forgetting whatever she'd been saying as the bells continued to cry. These were not clocks striking the hour. These were mourning bells, wailing out a song of loss.

In the bed, Tella's mother stirred. She didn't wake from her cursed slumber, but the bells had clearly disturbed her. In between the somber tune Tella heard a flurry of activity in the hall. Rushing footsteps. Chattering voices. More than a few unbridled sobs. And she knew.

Empress Elantine had died.

Tella had only met the empress twice, but she felt a surprising surge of emotion at the thought of her life ending, of her body going slack and her eyes closing forever.

Scarlett must not have been so certain, or she must have had no idea. She rose from her seat and opened the door right as a servant scurried by. "What's all the commotion?"

"Her Majesty passed away," the servant confirmed. "They're saying the new heir—her missing child—is now making his first appearance from the golden tower. Everyone is going into the glass courtyard to see. You can probably view the tower from your window."

The maid darted off and Tella crossed the room to part the curtains of the largest window wider. Light streamed in, honey-thick and bright. The sun had made its way out from behind the clouds at last and seemed to be making up for the lazy job it had done that afternoon. With the mourning bells still ringing, it felt wrong for it to be shining so brightly, beaming over the entire courtyard, which was indeed filling with people.

"I can't believe the empress is dead," Scarlett said.

"You would have liked her," Tella murmured. "She gave hugs the way I'd always wished our nana Anna had."

"Nana actually gave you hugs?"

"Once," Tella said. "Trust me, you weren't missing anything."

Tella had not cried when her nana Anna had died. Although the woman had made a little effort to raise her, Tella never felt any affection toward her. But Tella had liked the empress. Their acquaintance had been brief, but Elantine had shifted Tella's course; if their paths had never crossed, Tella's mother might still be trapped in a card.

Tella craned her neck as she looked past the glass courtyard toward the golden tower. Every window and balcony was open; from them maids and servants tossed black flower petals onto the gathering crowd below. The grim tribute was even sadder than the bells.

Only one balcony failed to rain down any flowers. Instead, this terrace flew royal-blue flags with the Meridian Empire's bold white crest. In the center of it stood one figure.

Every hair on Tella's body stood at attention when she saw him.

Tella could not clearly make out his face, but she could see his top hat. Sharp and black and unmistakably Legend.

That blackguard.

Tella knew Legend was full of secrets, but this was one she'd not even considered. He was posing as Elantine's missing child. This was why he'd left her on the steps right as the fireworks had begun; he'd gone off to watch them with the empress. Although Tella imagined he would have left her anyway.

It was so inappropriate, but Tella couldn't stop the laugh that bubbled up inside her. She'd thought she was the key to his entire game. But, of course, Legend was playing more than one game. He hadn't come to Valenda merely to destroy the Fates and take all their powers for himself. He'd chosen this city as his game board so he could claim the throne.

EPILOGUE

In fairy tales, sixteen was always the age when girls either learned they had magical powers, were truly princesses in disguise, or were cursed and needed a handsome prince to help them break the dark enchantment. Tella didn't know what would await her during her seventeenth year, but whatever it was, it would be more spectacular than any of those things.

With all the sorrow of Elantine's Day, she'd nearly forgotten her birthday. Yet she'd magically woken at midnight, at the very first moment.

Her heart was still a little heavy, but she'd decided carrying it around would only make her stronger.

Two nights before, when she'd taken her mother's place in that card, Tella had feared that was her true ending. But she was too young for endings. Her adventures were only beginning. They would be bigger than promises, and brighter than constellations. By the end of them, Tella would be the legendary one.

Legend would regret leaving her on those steps without so much as a good-bye.

Or perhaps he already did regret it. . . .

Tella quietly sat up in bed. The room was dark, full of night and shadows, and yet Tella saw the gift as clear as if it were daylight. A single red rose with a flawless white stem sat on the table beside her bed. Beneath it a silver envelope managed to shine, because, of course, everything about Legend shone in the dark.

Tella took the card and crept out of the bed toward the window.

She was still furious with him. She was going to make him regret walking away from her. But her heart seemed to have forgotten that. It tripped and skipped and beat out an unwieldy rhythm as she opened the note he'd left for her.

It smelled like him, of ink and secrets and wicked magic. His writing was all thick, dark strokes. As she read she refused to smile, but something like hope began to grow in her heart.

Donatella,

I believe it's your birthday. I also believe we have unfinished business; I still owe you a prize for winning Caraval. Find me whenever you wish to collect.

I'll be waiting.

—Legend

GLOSSARY OF FATES AND TERMS

DECK OF DESTINY: A method of fortune-telling. Decks of Destiny contain thirty-two cards, comprised of a court of sixteen immortals, eight places, and eight objects.

THE FATES: According to the myths, the Fates pictured inside Decks of Destiny were once magical, corporeal beings. They supposedly ruled a quarter of the world centuries ago until they mysteriously vanished.

THE GREATER FATES
The Murdered King
The Undead Queen
The Prince of Hearts
The Maiden Death
The Fallen Star
Mistress Luck

The Assassin
The Poisoner

THE LESSER FATES
Jester Mad
The Lady Prisoner
Priestess, Priestess
Her Handmaidens
The Unwed Bride
Chaos
The Pregnant Maid
The Apothic

THE FATED OBJECTS
The Shattered Crown
Her Majesty's Gown
The Blank Card
The Bleeding Throne
The Aracle
Map of All
The Unbitten Fruit
Reverie Key

FATED PLACES
Tower Lost
Phantasy Orchard

The Menagerie
The Immortal Library
Castle Midnight
The Imaginarium
The Vanished Market
Fire Undying

LUCKLESS COINS: Coins with the magic ability to track a person's whereabouts. When the Fates still reigned on Earth, if one became fixated on a human, they would slip a luckless coin into their purse or pocket so they could follow them wherever they went. The coins were considered to be bad omens.

ALCARA: The ancient city from where the Fates ruled, now known as the Meridian Empire's capital city of Valenda.

ACKNOWLEDGMENTS

I'd been warned that writing a second book was difficult, but writing *Legendary* felt nearly impossible. I could not have done it on my own. I thank God for miracles, answered prayers, and the amazing people who helped me with this story.

I'm so thankful for my family, for my mom and my dad and my brother and my sister and my brother-in-law. When I started writing I didn't realize what a journey it would be for all of us. This book was an especially difficult part of it and I'm not sure how I would have gotten through it without your love, your endless encouragement, and all the times you listened when I cried. I have the best family and I love you all so much.

Sarah Barley, you are truly the fairy godmother of books. Thank you for sprinkling your magic over this story; you have helped make *Legendary* a better book than I could have written on my own. Thank you for your patience as I sent in draft after draft, for your enthusiasm and love for these sisters and this series, and for knowing the heart of Caraval so well. There were times I really veered off course and I'm glad I had you there to help bring me back.

Jenny Bent, you are amazing. I could fill these pages with a list of all the reasons why I'm thankful to have you as my agent. Thank you for never giving up on me, especially during the moments when I'd given up on myself.

Ida Olson, I will never stop being grateful for you and how you swooped in like a superhero to help me save this book.

To the tremendous team at Flatiron Books, I could not ask for a better home for this series. Thank you so much to everyone who worked on this book, with a very special thank-you to Amy Einhorn and Bob Miller—I'm so grateful to have you as my publishers.

To the wonderful team at Macmillan Audio, thank you so much for your endless enthusiasm and for including *Legendary* as a part of your list. Rebecca Soler, my incredible audiobook narrator, I'm so thankful for you and for how you've brought both *Caraval* and *Legendary* to life with your fantastic narration.

Another special thank-you to Patricia Cave. If you ever leave publicity I will cry. Thank you for being the first to love Jacks and for all of your wise words.

Erin Fitzsimmons, you outdid yourself with this cover. Thank you so much for bringing your magic to this book.

Speaking of magic, thank you, Kate Howard and all the delightful people at Hodder and Stoughton, for giving this series a truly fantastic home in the UK. Thank you so much, Molly Ker Hawn, for finding this home and for being a tremendous support.

I feel incredibly blessed for all my amazing foreign publishers; thank you all for putting *Legendary* and *Caraval* in the hands of readers around the world.

A huge thank-you to all of my wonderful friends! Stacey Lee, thank you for sharing your creativity with me when mine had run dry, for endless brainstorming, brilliant ideas, and for being the friend I needed. Amanda Roelofs, thank you for always being my first reader and still being my friend, despite all the messy things I've sent your way; this story is much happier because of you. Thank you, thank you, thank you, Liz Briggs and Abigail Wen, for reading and so generously helping me with early drafts (readers, you might want to thank Liz, too—because of her there are more kisses). Katie Nelson and Roshani Chokshi, thank you for much-needed phone calls and for dropping everything to read early pieces of this when I wasn't sure if I was taking this story in the right direction. Kerri Maniscalco, Julie Dao, and Julie Eshbaugh—thank you for the marathon phone chats, the encouragement, and the treasure that is your friendship. To all the lovely and supportive local authors and writers, Jessica, Shannon, Val, Jenny, Kristin, Adrienne, Rose, and Joanna—I'm so thankful for the dinners and to call you all my friends.

I also want to thank all the amazing readers of this series! My heart is so full from your love and support. Thank you for your enthusiasm, your excitement, your comments, your pictures, and for picking up this book.